A PERFECT KISS

For the first time, Rebecca noticed a shattered glass and the strong smell of liquor. Bourbon, she suspected, although it could have been rum or brandy. "How did you cut yourself?"

"Damn glass," Sloan said. "Had to clean...."

She looked back at the fragments. Some were in a pile, as though he'd tried to gather them after throwing the tumbler. "Oh, Sloan, you fool. You're stinking drunk."

"Not too drunk," he murmured, grasping her by the upper arms while her attention was still on the broken pieces of glass. She could do nothing except squeal before he pulled her onto his lap.

"Sloan, no," she said breathlessly; but then his lips covered hers, enveloping her in the taste of bourbon and the smell that was uniquely his. She thought about struggling, but his lips were warm and heady, slanting across her mouth with the ease of a thousand kisses. Moaning, she opened her lips.

His arms tightened with surprising strength, pressing her tighter against his chest as he deepened the kiss. Just for a moment, she told herself.

In the back of her mind she knew this was pure folly. Sloan didn't even like her, and yet he kissed her as a man possessed. She didn't know his secrets, but she no longer cared. All they had was this moment, this perfect kiss.

VICTORIA CHANCELLOR

BITTERROOT

LOVE SPELL ✦ NEW YORK CITY

To my daughter and best friend,
April L. Huffstutler,
for her constant support and steadfast love.
Thank you.

LOVE SPELL®

April 1996

Published by

Dorchester Publishing Co., Inc.
276 Fifth Avenue
New York, NY 10001

Printed in the United States of America.

Special thanks to Tom Bell of Lander's Pioneer Museum, for his time and insights into early Fremont County, Wyoming.

BITTERROOT

Chapter One

April 1996
Fremont County, Wyoming

Rebecca could not have imagined a more perfect day. She watched wispy clouds float across the bright blue sky like feathers in the breeze. The rolling prairie lay in a half circle, intersected by red ridges of rock, extending from the foothills of the Rockies. All the unspoiled beauty, far removed from the reality of everyday life, gave her a sense of peace she'd never experienced before.

Yes, it was a magical day. And standing in front of her was a man as perfect as this spring afternoon. She thrilled at the spark of awareness in Jordan's clear blue eyes, the subtle flaring of his nostrils as he stepped closer. He smelled faintly of aftershave and mostly of the fresh outdoors.

His eyelids lowered, his face descended, and she welcomed his kiss with an answering awareness, the pounding of the blood in her veins and the rapid beating of her heart. His hands caressed her arms, then settled, warm and strong, on her shoulders, drawing her near.

"You know I'm attracted to you, don't you?" he said softly, with the serious inflection of a man who didn't give his heart lightly.

"Yes, I know." She leaned toward him, resting against the solid wall of his chest, hoping that this man would be the one to make her toes curl.

His kiss seemed softly searching at first; then it grew more bold as he traced her lips with his tongue. She opened her mouth slightly, welcoming him, and he answered her request. Beneath her fingers, his jaw felt firm and clean-shaven. Oh, how she wanted to feel those mythical fireworks go off, to hear bells ringing and orchestras swelling. But there was none of that. His kiss was pleasant, mildly arousing, but not the fabric of dreams.

He pulled back and smiled. "I think we should get to know each other, don't you? We'll practically be neighbors once I build my house."

Rebecca smiled in return. "You're right. What's a few miles between friends?" Her apartment in Riverton was more like twenty-five or thirty miles away, but who was counting? And so what if he didn't reduce her to a shivering mass of sensation with one kiss? He was nice and stable, a former Air Force officer, attractive and well-educated.

Held loosely in his arms, she breathed deeply of the clear, unseasonably warm air, determined not to allow such a mild disappointment to ruin this day. Familiar sounds washed over her like a cleansing stream: larks trilling, the wind whispering through the tall grass, the occasional cry of a hawk, high overhead. Except for paved roads, the land was unchanged from the time her ancestors first settled here over a hundred years ago. Even now, she could almost hear their welcoming voices in the constant wind.

"Your thoughts must be a thousand miles away."

She looked up into Jordan's handsome face. "No, not really. In fact, I feel as though I've truly come home, even though I've never set foot here before. Isn't that odd?"

Jordan scanned the snow-capped mountains in the distance. "No, lucky, I think. I just wish I could feel the same way."

The counselor in her couldn't miss the wistfulness of his tone, but she didn't know him well enough to comment.

They spread a blanket near the trees, on a slight rise that was dry and free from the snow that hid in gullies and near the rocky outcroppings. There would be several more major snows before summer, but today, nature was cooperating. Below them, a stream, swollen with melting snow, cut its way through the hills. Rebecca sank to the ground, spreading her denim skirt around her like a lily pad. The sun was so warm that, with Jordan's help, she removed her denim jacket.

Retrieving a folded square of paper from her pocket, she looked again at the family tree, amazed at the generations represented there, at the fact that Jordan was a very distant cousin. Until this weekend, she'd always thought of family as her mother and father . . . and, years ago, her sister Sara. Oh, how she'd loved her older sister, even when they'd fought over their shared bathroom or which movie to watch. How she missed her, especially when she had something special to share.

Jordan opened the box of fried chicken and put it in the middle of the blanket, then loaded his plate from the various cartons they'd purchased in Lander before driving up here. "I still can't believe Aunt Minnie gave you that heirloom locket that had belonged to Great-great-grandma Radburn."

"Jealous?" Rebecca teased, toying with the engraved oval on the silver necklace. "I don't think it would look very good on you."

Jordan chuckled and rolled his eyes. "That's not what I meant at all. It's just that you look quite a bit like her."

"I suppose." Rebecca folded the family tree and stuffed it in her pocket so she could eat lunch but couldn't resist one last look at the photographs in the locket. Grandpa Radburn's had faded with age, but the one of Leda Houghton Radburn was in fairly good shape to be over a hundred years old. "She looks so sad to me," Rebecca said softly, "almost as though she's resigned to her life."

"Or maybe she just didn't like to have her picture taken. I know I freeze up every time I get in front of a camera."

Rebecca closed the locket and tucked it inside the wide neck of her eyelet blouse. The silver felt warm nestled between her breasts. "Perhaps you're right. I'm not usually so philosophical on an empty stomach."

She filled her plate and ate alongside Jordan, soaking up the welcome warmth of spring. In a few minutes he pushed his plate aside and stretched out on the blanket.

"What a great spot. I'll have to check the survey maps to see if it's part of the land I inherited." He rolled to his side, resting his jaw on his hand.

"What kind of house are you going to build on your land?"

"I'm not sure. Something modern, with wood and glass, maybe. I'm not sure I'll be able to live here year-round. It's pretty isolated."

"That's part of the charm, I think," Rebecca replied, setting her own plate aside and lying on her side, facing Jordan. She noticed that the breeze had stilled, and the grass and even the birds had fallen silent. And she was alone in the rolling foothills with Jordan.

He reached out and caught a strand of her long hair. "You do look perfectly at ease here. I think I've lived in too much military housing to comprehend what a permanent home would be like."

"Give it time," Rebecca said softly, squeezing his hand. "You've only been out of the service for a month. It takes longer than that to go through any major adjustment."

"Yes, Doc," Jordan said with a smile. "I forgot that you probably know what's going on in my head as well as I do."

"I don't think so. I don't diagnose or treat people I know personally, and I only try to make my patients see things clearly; I don't read their minds."

Jordan smiled, as though he didn't believe her modest statement. It was flattering that he thought highly of her abilities. He really was nearly perfect, and she could have spent many more hours with him. However, she needed to get back to her apartment in Riverton before dark, and he needed to go to the Holiday Inn. "I suppose we'd better leave soon."

"Just one more kiss, and I'll help you pack away the food." He cupped her chin in his hand and kissed her a bit more commandingly. Again, no fireworks, but she responded with genuine pleasure.

He drew back, his eyes softly glowing. But then her attention shifted as a gust of wind caught the blanket, knocking over the paper plates and skipping the napkins along the sea of grass like loose white sails. Beneath her, Rebecca felt a faint rumble, almost like the passage of a train or an earthquake. A bank of clouds or a dust storm hovered on the horizon. And the breeze brought traces of an odor that was rare, that she'd smelled only once before but would never forget.

Gunpowder.

"Jordan, what's going on?" she whispered. When she turned to look at him apprehension turned to fear. Gone were the smiles, the easygoing manner she'd found so appealing. "Jordan?"

His brows drew together, his lips drawing back in a snarl. Rage exploded from him like a tangible force, like an animal that had suddenly become rabid. She tried to draw away, but the hands that had held her tenderly now turned to an inescapable vice.

Panic flooded her as his fingers dug into her neck, as the air was trapped inside her lungs. Swamped with fear, she could not breathe, could not swallow. She clawed at his wrists, his forearms, knowing she must be hurting him as her nails raked his skin. But he never let up, never stopped the pressure. As she bucked and twisted, trying to break his hold, she focused on his face, once handsome but now twisted into a mask of anguish and anger. Longing to scream, she could barely moan.

Why me? Why now? I had so much to live for, so much yet to do. Pinpricks of light danced before her eyes, beginning to obscure his face, to dilute the animosity in his eyes. Her head throbbed as a frantic, desperate heartbeat. Then his hands tightened even more as words were ripped from his throat, as raw and anguished as the pain she felt.

"Not again, Leda. By God, not again!"

The pinpricks of light faded, the blackness sucking her into a void of empty, spinning, timeless terror. She screamed in her mind, yet could hear no sound. The pressure on her throat disappeared, vanishing with the light as though it had never existed. Imagining herself tumbling through space, she flailed her arms, screamed and screamed again. But no substance existed, no wind against her skin, or warmth against the cold. Nothing . . . nothing at all.

She awoke to the peacefulness of soothing white, to an insistent light that flirted with her eyelids and dared her to look. No pain forced its way to the surface, no fear or confusion. Only the light beckoned her with endless patience as she seemed to float, no longer in the black void but rather in a weightless state of relaxation.

Rebecca opened her eyes and blinked against the brightness, against the pure whiteness of the light. She seemed to be surrounded by fog so dense that she could see nothing beyond the light, which seemed to come from somewhere up ahead of her. It called to her, much like the wind on the prairie or the imaginary ghosts of the past. She moved toward the light, slowly, watching for a sign that would tell her where she was, where she was going. But the silence was as solid as the whiteness. Even her heartbeat no longer pounded in her ears, and her feet, although moving, could sense nothing beneath her.

Suddenly she felt something, like the anticipated presence of a lost loved one when entering his room: as if he should be there, but wasn't; as though she could feel him, but they existed now only in her mind. She didn't fight the feeling but rather flowed with it, followed where it led and asked no questions. This was a place of spirits, of feelings rather than substance, she felt, and it seemed right to let this benevolent being guide her.

The light parted, formed, and radiated around something up ahead. The brightness intensified, but so did the contrast with something solid, a shape in a world void of shadows. She moved ever closer, urged on, she supposed, by what she could not see, but what she knew was the peace she sought. The shape became human, and the human became a man. She reached out, wanting to touch him, to link hands with him and hold tight. It mattered not that he was a stranger. He needed her, and she needed him.

The spirit enveloped her in peace, and she drew closer to the man. His arms became distinct, his hands outstretched, his fingers curved. Shadows from the bright light behind him kept his features obscure; she barely saw his high cheekbones, his wide brow and strong, straight nose. His mouth, his eyes, seemed sad. His fingers curved in a universal sign for her to come closer, and she did, wanting to ease the loneliness she felt radiating from him, stronger every second.

He opened his mouth to speak, but she heard no sound. Even as she sought to come closer, she felt him pull back, back to the bright light behind him, away from her. She felt a loss so profound that she panicked, reaching out toward his hand, which still beckoned to her in the distance but grew faint as she watched. Then he was gone, swallowed up by the light, obliterated by the brightness that filled the fog, swept over her in waves, and left nothing in its place.

Heat, dry as a blast from an oven, washed over her. Sweat trickled down her neck, tickling as it went. Light beat down, but not the pure whiteness she'd felt before. No, this was the yellow brightness of the sun, the same sun she'd felt before, after falling asleep by the pool, baking herself to a rosy glow. Rebecca propped herself up on one elbow and forced her eyes open again, this time shading them with her hand. Her whole body ached, as though she'd been run over by a car and left for dead in the desert. She tried to swallow and winced against the pain in her throat. Tears formed in her eyes.

Yet she wasn't on some unknown desert, but rather on the rolling prairie. High overhead, a hawk circled, then called out, his cry an echo against the vastness of this land. Far away, she saw the peaks of the Rockies, lightly dusted with snow.

How could that be? In April, the mountains should be white with snow.

The hawk cried again, dipping down, then soaring on some unseen updraft, leaving her. She wanted to call it back, to ask it to stay so that at least she wouldn't be totally alone, but no sound forced itself from her throat.

Then she remembered Jordan's hands around her neck. His pain and hatred. Her fear and terror. The images and feelings rushed over her, leaving her dizzy and confused. She closed her eyes, willing the panic to subside, willing her head to stop spinning and her senses to clear. Her breathing became rapid, her heart pounding until she swore it shook the earth with each beat.

But then she realized the ground-shaking came from hooves, striking the prairie in the even cadence of a horse's canter, coming closer each moment.

She raised up again on one elbow and shaded her eyes against the sun, which hung above the far off mountains as a reminder that daylight would soon fade to night, heat to cold. She was alone, helpless against the elements—or against Jordan, should he decide to return to finish the violence he'd started in the cottonwood grove.

Pushing air into her strained lungs, she tried to call out, to beckon the horse closer. There were no wild mustangs around here, so a horse meant a rider, and a rider, escape from certain death; unless, of course, she was already dead. Could this land be her own heaven or hell, or some strange version of Dante's *Inferno*, existing to make her confront her personal demons, her life story? She almost cried again at the thought, but stubbornly she held to the belief that she was alive, that this was the prairie of Wyoming and she would soon get help.

She heard the horse snort and detected the jangle of his bit or the rider's spur. The pounding never ceased but became stronger, closer. She looked around, to the east, where nothing could be seem except the horizon, to the north and south, where not even a utility pole marred the landscape. Then back to the west, and he was there. With the blazing sun behind him, the horse topped the crest of the hill and halted, rearing back as the rider stopped him on a dime.

Rebecca swallowed the panic that had begun to build when she thought she was dead. This man seemed familiar, yet not someone she knew by name. Almost hysterically, she thought of the old television series "Gunsmoke," of Marshal Dillon coming to her rescue on his big buckskin horse, his face serious and creased with worry. The man swung his leg over the horse and dropped the reins, his hat shading his face, his figure a tall silhouette in the bright sunlight. Then he walked toward her, quick strides that ate up the ground, his hand outstretched, his fingers curled, just as it was in the place of whiteness.

She gave in to the urge to scream for help, to beg for answers, but all she heard was a raw moan that came from her damaged throat. Then the blackness came for her again, swallowing her up even as she felt the man draw closer. This time she didn't fight the darkness. She welcomed it as a trusted friend, as an escape from this unknown reality, from this stranger who seemed so familiar that she dared not hope he was real.

Sloan reined his buckskin gelding to a halt, unsure at first that he was seeing a woman lying alone on the prairie. He blinked and wiped the sweat from his eyes as he resettled his hat, but she was still there, as out of place on these plains as his prize bull would be in his mother's parlor.

The woman was conscious, watching for him, it seemed. She was dressed sort of like a Mexican girl, but this woman wasn't from south of the border. Several of his hands were Mexican or had Mexican wives, and they were a lot darker than this fair, golden-red-haired woman.

He swung down from the saddle and dropped Buck's reins, then walked quickly toward her. He wanted to reach out, to tell her not to be afraid of him; but before he could utter a word she fainted dead away.

He hurried over, driven by the need to know whether she was alive. Kneeling beside her, he grabbed her wrist, then touched her neck when he couldn't find a pulse. He was shocked by the cool smoothness of her skin and relieved by the steady heartbeat he felt below her ear. Bruises stood out as clearly as footprints in new snow, ringing her neck in purple and red. Rage filled him that someone could so mistreat a woman, who should be shielded from such abuse. And he was surprised by the swell of protectiveness that rose within him from just looking at her.

He leaned closer, inhaling her smell, feeling lightheaded from the scent of woman and flowers and something mysterious, soft and seductive. Sloan blinked again, focusing on the bruises, trying to ignore the way she looked and smelled and felt beneath his fingers.

21

It was a losing battle. His pulse pounded in his veins, echoing in his head until all he heard was the rapidly increasing beat of his heart. Slowly, reluctantly, he touched a red-gold strand of hair that curled seductively around his finger. Desire rose, hot and heavy, throbbing with the same pounding as the maddening cadence in his head.

It wasn't this woman, he told himself. It was just that it had been a damned long time since he'd been this close to someone clean and who, despite her dress, almost reeked of innocence. He rarely gave in to the urge to visit a whore; only when demons from the past drove him to the limit did he succumb to temptation and visit one. But even then, the desire wasn't like this. Not this sudden, this overwhelming. Not this powerful. He couldn't remember ever feeling quite this way before, his mind and body focused on only one thing. He wanted to hold her, to blend with her, to feel their hearts beating to a single rhythm.

He removed his finger, the strand of hair holding him until the last minute, when it seemed to let go reluctantly and glide like a whisper to her shoulder. *I have no business thinking of her,* he told himself. *Concentrate on the evidence. Push those feelings aside, hide them, just as you've tried to forget the past.*

Sloan closed his eyes for a moment, thinking of the faces he could never forget, the burned homes, the ravaged land. As he'd done so many times before, he forced his mind to clear, to be swept clean of torment. Only then did visions of the war fade, along with the desire that had flooded him moments before. He opened his eyes, unclenched his fists, and forced his mind back to the present.

She'd been strangled. It was obvious from the placement of the marks that hands had circled her neck, thumbs pressing into her windpipe. Who in the hell would try to kill a woman who looked like this, who smelled this sweet and had the softest skin he'd ever felt? He scanned the area around her for signs of a struggle but found nothing.

Absolutely nothing. No wagons, horses, or footprints appeared in the soft dirt. Not a blade of grass had been disturbed or an inch of land swept over to obliterate the tracks. She could have walked this far from the southern boundary of his land, where the Oregon trail followed the Sweetwater up toward South Pass. But that was a long walk, and some footprints should have been visible in the sandy soil.

It was as though this woman had simply fallen from the sky, landed out here on his property, and waited for him to arrive before fainting. It didn't make sense. He shook his head, then reminded himself to look over the rest of her before he dared pick her up.

Her blouse was white, cut low and off her shoulders with a wide ruffle. It was tucked into a skirt made from the same material as the blue denim pants he now wore daily. There was a wide ruffle on the skirt too, and it was open in the front so her petticoats showed, although he couldn't imagine why, unless she was one loose woman. But then again, maybe the skirt had come unbuttoned in the struggle.

He ran his hands down her legs all the way to her feet, checking for broken bones and discovering only that, just as he'd figured, he wasn't at all immune to this woman. There wasn't one hair on her legs; just smooth white skin with a hint of freckles. He had the urge to run his hand over her again, to see if her skin was really as smooth as it seemed. Swallowing the urge, he rested his hands on his thighs and looked her over with a more critical eye.

She wore the strangest shoes he'd ever seen: white leather low-cut boots with laces and some sort of sole that lapped around and didn't look or feel like leather. Damned strange outfit. Damned strange circumstances.

He didn't like it; not one bit. Gently cradling her jaw, he moved her face so he could see her features better. Her eyes were closed, but the lids were lightly painted in soft colors; unusual, yet not garish, like a dance-hall girl's. Her eyebrows slashed across her forehead, arching down at the ends. Her nose turned up, flared gently, and accented her softly sculpted lips. All in all, she was one beautiful woman.

She also reminded him of someone he'd known very well once; known and loved—and now hated. Leda. Leda Houghton, now married to that ass Radburn, who was intent on seeing him dead or gone. Leda, who'd betrayed him after making him think she loved him.

This woman's hair was near the color of Leda's, an odd shade between blond and red. Soft, like fine silk the color of tall prairie grasses at sunset. He touched it, let the strands caress his fingers until he longed to bury his face in its richness, inhale the scent of flowers that seemed to come so naturally from her, and close his eyes to the mystery surrounding her appearance on his land.

Leda's hair had never been this soft, her skin this smooth. It hurt to compare the two women, to force himself to remember Leda at all.

No, this woman couldn't be related to Leda. He'd known his former fiancée's family well; growing up together in Philadelphia, she'd never mentioned a relative near her own age. It was a coincidence; that was all.

He placed his arms beneath the woman and slowly rose, balancing her weight so she snuggled into his chest. Buck snorted as Sloan walked toward the gelding with his burden, but like the well-trained horse he was, he simply rolled his eyes and stood still. It wasn't easy mounting while holding the woman; although she wasn't that heavy, he didn't want to jostle her too much in case she had other injuries he couldn't see.

"Come on, Buck," he said to the gelding as he nudged him toward home. They set off at a slow, mile-eating canter, the woman still unconscious in his arms, bobbing against his chest with each of Buck's strides. Sloan frowned at her bent, shiny head. He didn't like surprises, and he didn't like mysteries.

One of the reasons he loved the west was because people, for the most part, played straight with you. They didn't hide behind political purposes or dwell on imagined wrongs. Out here things were black or white. If you did something wrong and you got caught, you were punished. That law seemed to apply to everyone except scheming women; but then, if it were up to him, she and Radburn would get what they deserved in the end.

If there was one thing Sloan had learned, it was that you had to live with what you'd done, both good and bad. Sometimes it seemed that you paid more for the bad than you ever got rewarded for the good.

Sloan reined to a halt near the back door of the two-story house he'd built for the bride he'd never married. The woman in his arms slept on, oblivious to the ride.

"Slim! Give me a hand."

The cowboy hurried over from the barn, his bow legs shuffling through the dusty yard.

Reluctantly, Sloan handed over his burden to Slim, then dismounted and held out his arms, again snuggling the woman close to his chest.

"Who is she, boss?"

"I don't know. I found her lying on the prairie about two or three miles from here." He wasn't about to tell Slim of the mysterious lack of telltale signs, his opinion of her odd clothes, or her resemblance to Leda. "See if Claudia can come up to the house."

He looked down at the woman's face, so peaceful and innocent. Could she be pretending to be

26

unconscious, just to get inside his home and possibly gain his affections? He wouldn't put it past Radburn to try something like this. Maybe she looked enough like Leda so that Radburn had come up with the idea that she could spy on the ranch.

If she was working for Radburn, she'd be sorry she ever tried to cross Sloan Travers, he vowed as pushed open the door into the kitchen.

Within minutes he had her lying on a bed in one of several empty rooms upstairs. Claudia, his housekeeper and the wife of his head wrangler, hustled him out of the room when he lingered at the foot of the mattress, staring at the woman's trim white ankles, nicely rounded legs, and strange shoes.

Sloan wandered into the study and automatically poured two fingers' worth of bourbon into a glass, sipping the mellow liquor as he walked slowly to the window. How could there be no tracks, not even her own? He hoped to hell she recovered fast, because he couldn't stand not knowing.

One thing he did know was that those marks on her neck were real. Whoever had done that had meant to harm her—or scare her to death. He had no liking for a man who could hurt an innocent woman or a child.

He finished the bourbon in one gulp, his eyes narrowing as it burned its way down to his stomach. He could understand the kind of rage that might turn a man half mad, especially if the woman was a lying, deceitful bitch. He could un-

27

derstand, because he'd felt just about that violent, that crazy, when he'd found out what Leda had done. If she'd been anywhere near him at the time, he probably would have strangled her.

But Leda was not innocent, and perhaps the woman upstairs wasn't either.

I'm in a western bed-and-breakfast inn, Rebecca thought as she blinked again and surveyed the room. It looked a lot like the one she and her college roommate had stayed in during a trip to Laramie. The only difference was that most B & Bs didn't come equipped with an authentically dressed woman sitting in each room, stitching a quilt.

Rebecca wondered if she'd be in a different place every time she woke up, if her life would now consist of passing out and waking up in strange places. She almost laughed at the ludicrous thought.

There's a reason for this, she thought as she let her eyes wander away from the woman, taking in each detail from the rather gaudy wallpaper to the washstand, complete with a ceramic bowl and pitcher. The window was open, letting in the late afternoon or evening breeze. As the lace panels fluttered in the wind, she saw the rosy-orange glow of the setting sun.

The middle-aged woman set her sewing aside and rose stiffly, as though she'd been sitting there a long time. She lit an oil lamp on the old-fashioned dresser, turning down the wick so that a cozy yellow glow reflected in the beveled mirror

28

and filled the room with soft light.

Rebecca cleared her throat, trying to get the woman's attention, but immediately realized her mistake and shut her eyes against the pain, her hands going automatically to her neck. Memories came flooding back, of the pleasant summer day, the picnic, Jordan's sweetness, and then his anger. What had gone wrong? Tears filled her eyes as she tried not to swallow, to cause herself any more pain.

When she opened her eyes two men stood in the doorway. She gasped involuntarily, her hand going again to her throat as the pain came back. One man was tall, straight, and dark-haired, reminding her of Jordan. The meager light barely reached his features, so she could tell little about him other than receiving an impression of power. The other man was short, bowed, white-haired, and craggy. Rebecca blinked back the tears and continued to stare, even though she knew it was rude. These two men couldn't have been more different, yet somehow they seemed to be perfectly suited to each other, like two pieces of a puzzle that snapped together with ease.

The tall man stepped into the room, going to the lamp and turning up the wick so his features were illuminated. Rebecca almost gasped again, because he began to seem familiar, even though she now saw that he bore only a slight resemblance to Jordan. But she had seen him somewhere.

Before she could discover where, the old man

walked on silent feet and stood beside the bed, looking down at her with all-knowing eyes that she swore could read each secret. He was a Native American, she realized, probably from one of the plains tribes, and perhaps a medicine man. She wished now that she'd taken time to learn more history and culture before reporting to her counseling position, where so many of her clients would be Native Americans. So many of their beliefs and much of their culture was foreign to her, and she'd never felt it so much until this instant.

This man appeared so calm, so controlled, while she felt ready to shatter from confusion and fear. He looked deeply into her eyes, as though he knew her and cared for her. Yet he was a stranger.

She wanted to shrink away from him, to tell him to leave her alone. She didn't want anyone to know her innermost longings and fears. She wanted to hoard them, to proclaim them hers and hers alone. But he apparently wasn't satisfied with staring. He raised a bony hand and she could only watch, fascinated with dread, as he touched her forehead.

Instantly she felt her muscles relax, her breathing slow. She sank lower, bonelessly, into the soft mattress. Familiar sights and sounds of a summer day filled her mind, chasing away the fear that had caused all her attention to be focused on these men. No longer confused, she felt as though she'd come home after a long journey.

Suffused with peace, she watched in wonder

as a slight smile formed on his thin lips, making his lined face appear less foreign. Then the smile faded, though the peace remained, pouring through her until she recognized the feeling. He knew, too. He could tell when she realized that she'd felt this way before.

It was in the time after Jordan strangled her, in the place of bright light and spirits. This old man had been there with her, guiding her, urging her toward the tall man with the pleading eyes.

The Indian stepped away and there was the man, outlined by the lamp, rigid in his stance and appearing not the least bit pleading at the moment. He took a step toward the bed, hesitant, as though he was also uncertain. She knew this man, from the place of light and no shadows, reaching out to her, asking her to come to him, then leaving before she could touch him. And she knew him from the prairie, the man on the big tan horse who reminded her of Marshal Dillon, making her think he'd come to rescue her.

She wanted to cry in frustration, to beat on the bed and demand some answers. For if he had rescued her, it was from the limbo of afterlife, taking her from a place of peace to this one of uncertainty. And if he and the spirit of the Indian were in that place of afterlife, then it meant they were dead, that Jordan had indeed choked her, killed her, on that idyllic spring afternoon.

They were dead, all of them, carrying out some charade of life in this strange place. Nothing made sense; nothing seemed real. The peace she'd felt moments earlier vanished, replaced with an unreal sense of life. Her throat ached, her head hurt; it seemed so bizarre, so ironic, that pain existed beyond death.

The tall man stopped near the bed, staring down at her with a crease between his brows and his lips tight. He opened his mouth to say something, then closed it again, as though he didn't want to speak to her at all. He seemed angry, yet not violent; controlled rather than expressive; tormenting without effort.

She looked back, his face blurring as she blinked away tears. She didn't want to talk; to communicate with these men would be like admitting she was dead, and she wasn't ready to give in to the finality of fate.

But if she were dead, why wasn't she with Sara? Most of the near-death encounters she'd read about stated that the dying person was greeted by their deceased loved ones or friends. Where was Sara? They'd been so close, before the drugs . . . Rebecca wanted to know why she was here with these strangers, especially the tall, intense, dark-haired one.

When he finally spoke his voice was low, grave. "You're safe here," he said slowly, awkwardly, in a tone that one might use to calm a frightened animal. "Whoever tried to hurt you is gone."

Gone, like her life, her hope.

"What's your name?" he asked abruptly, as though he were much more comfortable asking questions than giving solace.

Rebecca turned away, blinking, not wanting to understand this man or be intrigued by him. She just wanted to be alive, safely back in Riverton, ready to start her new job next week. She'd had such grand visions of changing the lives of substance abusers who needed professional help. She'd wanted to do so much, but she'd never even gotten started.

"Can you remember your name?" he asked again, this time a bit more gently.

Lord, why couldn't he leave her alone? *Just vanish, or let me drift off again. I don't want to be here. I don't want to die.*

Yet he stood there, waiting. He wasn't going away, and she didn't feel the least bit faint at the moment.

She tried to wet her lips, but they were dry, as was her throat. The man gestured, and the older woman came forward with a cup, and helped her take a sip. The warm liquid felt heavenly; she wanted to giggle hysterically at the play on words.

"Re . . . Rebecca," she croaked, her voice sounding like ground glass running through a garbage disposal. She swallowed, then tried again. "Rebecca . . . Hartford." The man continued to stare down at her, judging her, she thought. His face was so stern, without one trace of softness. Then he nodded. "Get some more rest, Rebecca Hartford. We'll talk later." And then he turned away, striding out of the room without a parting glance.

The old man placed his hand on her forehead again, but this time the peace didn't come, the confusion didn't ebb. He muttered, "Sleep," in a

33

low but melodious voice, and suddenly she felt bone-weary tired. By the time he shuffled out of the room her eyelids were already beginning to close.

Her last thought before she drifted to sleep was that the tall man, her Marshal Dillon, wasn't an easy man to know. He was intense, driven by something she could sense but couldn't guess. She wished she had asked him his name, but perhaps it didn't matter. Perhaps when she woke again he wouldn't even be here. After all, who knew the rules in heaven . . . or hell.

Chapter Two

The first things Rebecca saw when she awoke the next time were the lace curtains, fluttering in the breeze, bleached white by the bright moonlight. She remembered this room, the men, the woman, and the thoughts that had weighed heavily on her mind. If she were dead, it seemed that her body was still functioning; she had to use the bathroom with urgency.

Cautiously, she sat up, swinging her legs over the side of the bed. She felt fairly well; though she was still sore, she no longer suffered from dizziness or extreme fatigue. Of course, she had been sleeping for who knew how long.

Very little light made its way into the hallway, but she crept along, fingers skimming the wall. The stairs led down, and she stepped carefully in the darkness, her footsteps soundless on the solid boards.

She got to the bottom and saw moonlight shining from the window in a door. It was locked, and she couldn't feel a key as her fingers skimmed the latch and heavy, ornate knob. So she turned left, walking along another hallway, finding an open doorway.

Two windows permitted moonlight to dance across the highly polished wood of a long, dark table, set with two candelabra and a large epergne beneath a sparkling chandelier. Rebecca skirted the table and sideboard, making her way toward a door on the other side of the fireplace. Her foot hit something and she reached out instinctively, catching a large fern in a ceramic or porcelain pot before it crashed to the floor from its perch on top of a stand. Her heart beat wildly for an instant before she took a few calming breaths. *There's no need to worry,* she told herself. *No one will do anything to me for trying to find a bathroom in this labyrinth of a house. Besides, if I'm already dead, what can happen anyway?*

She'd thought perhaps there was a bathroom off the kitchen, behind an interior doorway. She opened the door and looked inside, but only a large tub occupied the space; there was no toilet or other plumbing. Frustrated, she noticed that only one other entrance existed, and from the moonlight coming in the paned window of that door, it led outside. What she needed was a flashlight or even a candle, so she walked carefully toward the built-in cabinets on either side of the large sink.

Instead of faucets, the sink contained a pump on one side. Her eyes scanned the large black stove, and took in the lack of a refrigerator or any other modern appliance. As a matter of fact, everything in the kitchen looked like an authentic nineteenth-century homemaker's delight.

A slight sound alerted her, followed by a prickling of the hair on her neck. She sensed his presence, turned, and found the tall man standing in the doorway. Moonlight from the dining room skimmed his broad, bare shoulders, highlighted his dark, wet hair, and outlined every muscle in his impressive arms. Rebecca was almost scared to look lower but couldn't resist; he at least wore jeans, riding low on his narrow hips.

She swallowed, uncomfortable with his intense scrutiny, feeling the irrational urge to apologize to him for walking into the kitchen. How did she know, she wondered, that this was his house, his kitchen?

"I . . ." Her voice failed and she tried again. "I was looking for the ladies' room."

He walked into the room and struck a match, lighting an oil lamp on the rough, scarred table. "Beg your pardon?"

"The ladies' room." At his blank stare, she continued. "You know, the powder room."

"You're the only 'lady' here. I don't know what you mean." Several lines radiated from the center of his forehead.

Rebecca swallowed, her throat still painful.

"You're kidding, right? Look, I really need to use the bathroom."

"You want a bath at this hour?"

"No!" She winced at the pain her sharp retort caused. "I want to use . . . the facilities."

The lines in his forehead deepened as his eyebrows rose. "Oh, well, I see," he said with suppressed laughter.

"Please don't laugh. You shouldn't make fun of me."

"I assure you, I wasn't. I simply—"

"Please! The facilities."

He grinned, an expression that totally changed his face. He looked younger, more approachable. Gone was the intensity that frightened even as it fascinated. Gone was the severe rescuer and in his place was a compelling, flesh-and-blood man with beard stubble, dimples, and a torso off a hunk-of-the-month calendar.

He pulled a key from a hook beside the other door, unlocked it, and then pushed it open.

"Come on."

Rebecca followed, mostly out of a sense of disbelief. He couldn't mean . . .

But he did. He pointed to a narrow wooden structure about thirty feet away, between two other buildings. "There you go."

"You can't be serious."

He propped a hand on his hip and lost the look of amusement. "Ma'am, I had Claudia put a chamber pot in your room. Now, I don't know what you expect, but I only have one outhouse. If that's not good enough, you can go look for a bush." He turned and went back into the kitchen, as though he didn't care at all whether or not she had a proper place to relieve herself.

Rebecca followed him back inside, grabbed the lamp from the table, and stormed back out, refusing to give him a glance. If she had to go out to the primitive facility, she wasn't going in the dark.

She came through the back door minutes later, brushing a spiderweb off her arm and hoping it wasn't attached to anything with eight legs. The kitchen was empty, so she stepped through the doorway into the dining room, still holding the lamp. Shadows danced eerily across the walls, ceilings, and floors as she walked toward the hallway. Rebecca shuddered at the totally realistic, historical look of the place, down to the lack of electrical outlets or telephones. Peering through a doorway, she found the main hall.

She walked beneath the open, curving stairs at the end of the hall and looked up two floors to where her bedroom was located—somewhere up there. Not wanting to limit her snooping to just a few rooms, she went into a parlor or sitting room of sorts that had a wide opening to another room. Two tall windows highlighted the sleek, dark furniture. A door led outside to a porch, but it was also locked. Walking into the other room, which was a less formal version of the front room, she noticed light coming from beneath another door. Tiptoeing, holding her lamp, she pushed open the door and peered inside.

The man stood near a massive desk, swirling a

glass of liquor and staring out into the night. He was still shirtless, still impressive.

"Did you find anything interesting?"

"I . . . I beg your pardon?" Her voice sounded husky coming from her abused throat.

He turned around and took a sip of his drink. "I saw your light in the parlor. It shares a porch with this room. It's a strange sensation, knowing someone is looking around your house."

"I'm sorry. I didn't mean to pry. It's just that I've never seen such a well-preserved Victorian house before. So many of them have gone to ruin, and even the ones that have been restored contain furnishings that have seen more than their share of wear. You know what I mean; the rugs are threadbare, the lace yellow, or the draperies water-spotted."

"Well, I don't know what you're used to, but everything in this house is new. I had it built a little over two years ago." A note of bitterness had crept into his voice, Rebecca realized, and she saw his fingers tighten on the glass. He took another healthy sip. "Ordered everything new from back east. My mother selected the furniture and," he gestured with one hand, sweeping to encompass the walls and floor, "everything else."

"You mean this is a Victorian reproduction? I would never have guessed. It looks so real."

The man snorted. "I don't know what you call 'real,' but I paid close to ten thousand dollars to have this house built out here. That's plenty real to me."

"Ten thousand?" That wouldn't even cover a lot

in most towns. Even kit houses cost more than that.

"That's right. I wanted a nice place for . . . But hell, it doesn't matter now." He drained the liquor in one swallow.

As he walked over to the sideboard and poured himself another drink, Rebecca began to inch toward the desk. Something was wrong here; something was desperately wrong.

"Can I pour you one?"

"What? Oh, no, thank you." She hoped he didn't get abusive when he drank. He didn't seem to be drunk, but sometimes looks could be deceiving.

She heard the distinctive ping of crystal as he touched the decanter to the glass, but she focused on the desk, on the papers stacked there.

"You sure?"

She looked up, startled, sure that her eyes were wide. Her throat felt raw, but she could tolerate a drink or two. "Well, maybe just a little brandy, if you have it."

He poured her drink and brought it over.

"You never did tell me your name."

"Sloan Travers," he said, staring at her intently.

Rebecca nodded, breaking her gaze and taking a sip of the brandy. "Are you from around here?" she asked, desperate for anything that would ease the tension.

"Philadelphia, originally."

"Oh." *Brilliant conversation, Rebecca,* she chided herself. *Ask him something that will tell you where you are.*

"Your house is lovely."

He shrugged, turning away. "Thanks."

She could see his reflection in the panes of the dark window as he stared into the night. "Do you live here alone?"

"What's that supposed to mean?"

Rebecca felt herself blush, although she knew there was no reason to feel uncomfortable. She didn't mean that as a come-on; besides, she'd seen men wearing far less than the jeans and boots Sloan Travers had on. She'd certainly seen good-looking men before. "It doesn't mean anything. I just wondered if you have . . . family."

He turned back around. "Not blood relatives out here, if that's what you mean. They're all back east. Painted Elk is about as close as family."

"He's the man who was upstairs earlier?"

Sloan nodded.

"He has a certain magic about him, I think," Rebecca said. She could hear the wistfulness in her voice as she spoke.

"It's strange for you to say that, but yes, he does. He's a medicine man. When I first came out here . . . after the war, I met him in the mountains."

The war? He must mean the Persian Gulf War. He was too young to mean Vietnam. Sloan Travers couldn't be over thirty-five.

"So, Rebecca Hartford, where are you from?"

"I was born in Cheyenne, but I've just moved to Riverton. I've taken a job there."

"A job," he scoffed. "I should have known."

42

"Known what?"

His eyes raked over her skirt and blouse, her bare feet, and up again to her tousled hair. "When I first saw you I thought you might be a dance-hall girl, but then I thought maybe you weren't."

Rebecca laughed at his old-fashioned term. "Dance-hall girl? You mean like an exotic dancer? That's funny. I doubt I could bump and grind my way out of a paper sack. Dancing's not my strong point."

He looked confused, startled even, for a moment. "Then what the hell are you doing dressed like that, with your face painted and your skirt halfway up to your knees?"

"What are you talking about?" Rebecca looked down at her modest denim prairie skirt, its wide ruffle and eyelet lace peeking out from beneath the faded blue. She checked her blouse and found it firmly in place, covering her except for her neck and part of her shoulders. Her makeup might be a little smudged, but what could he expect after all she'd been through?

"And you sure didn't object to being around me tonight, even if I'm in no condition to appear in front of a lady," he said, advancing slowly.

"I thought it would be rude to comment on what you're wearing . . . or not wearing," she replied in a haughty tone, retreating around the edge of the desk.

"Rude, hell. That's not all you were thinking."

Rebecca felt the heat in her cheeks increase another ten degrees or so. She *had* been watching him, ogling him, in fact. It was just embarrassing to get caught.

Although her father had always said she'd make a terrible poker player, she tried to bluff her way out of this one. "I don't know what you mean. Besides, you have a right to go around half-dressed in your own house if you want to."

"Damn right," she heard him mumble before he took another sip. "You are one strange female," he said, more as a fact than in conversation.

"I'd like to know how you'd feel if you'd been choked for no reason, went through some sort of mystical hallucination, then tried to make sense of the whole thing. I don't even know where I am!"

His eyes narrowed. "Where do you think you are?"

She hesitated a moment before answering, not daring to tell him what she really feared—that she was dead. "Wyoming . . . somewhere near Riverton."

"I don't know what you mean by 'Riverton.' No neighbors here named 'Riverton.' How did you get out there, on the prairie?"

"I don't know!" Rebecca immediately regretted her outburst as her sore throat spasmed. She coughed, tears stinging her eyes as more pain gripped her.

Sloan was there in an instant, bringing her some water, guiding her into the desk chair. "Take it easy," he said gruffly.

Rebecca breathed deeply, trying to calm her

nerves and her abused throat. But he was too close, too male. He smelled of plain soap and bourbon, an essence of man she'd never known before. Suddenly his presence was overwhelming. She wanted to get away, to find her new apartment and curl up in her big recliner with an afghan, believing all this was a dream instead of a living nightmare . . . or an eternal struggle.

"Can you just call someone to take me home?" she said in a weak voice. "I just want to go home."

"It's too late to go anywhere tonight," he said gently. "Why don't you finish your brandy and go back to bed?"

"I want to go home," she said again, softly, knowing he was right. She couldn't think who to call anyway; her friends lived in Cheyenne and Denver. And what if she was really alive and Jordan was out there looking for her? She probably couldn't go home. Maybe she was safe here, in Sloan Travers's home. She wished she could lean into his body, ask him to hold her and keep her from harm. But she didn't know him, despite the feeling that she'd seen him before in the place of white light. She didn't understand any of it, and the doubts caused a shudder to ripple through her.

"Stay here. I'll be right back." Sloan's long-legged stride carried him out of the room in an instant.

Rebecca braced her forehead on her hands, her elbows on the desk. Her eyes were tired and scratchy, her skin dusty and sweaty, and her thoughts a jumble of images and half-formed fears. She had no business thinking of Sloan Travers as a man, no reason to admire his body or wonder at his moods. She should be thinking of her situation and what she could do next.

She wished she had more of the skills of a private investigator than of a substance abuse counselor.

Her elbows slipped on the slick wood surface, dislodging some papers. Automatically she reached down to straighten the stack, and her eyes were drawn to the bold but artistic handwriting, the style reminiscent of the previous century.

Receipts for seed, lumber, and nails. A bill of sale for a bull. A letter from a banker. All dated in June 1876. All appearing new, crisp, and very real.

The papers in front of her blurred for a moment. She blinked, trying to focus, trying to understand what this meant.

Sloan strode back into the room, carrying a colorful blanket draped over one arm. He'd even donned a shirt, though he hadn't taken the time to button it. It hung open, framing his chest and emphasizing the dark hair that arrowed down his abdomen.

She stared at him as he clumsily placed the blanket around her shoulders.

"What year is this?" she asked, gazing into his cautious blue eyes.

"What kind of question is that?"

"I'm serious," she said, clutching the sleeve of

his shirt. "I need to know."

"It's 1876."

"No," she whispered, afraid to believe what the paper and his matter-of-fact tone told her. "Show me."

"Lady, are you crazy? What year do you think it is?"

She shook her head, not wanting to explain what she knew to be a fact. It was 1996, not 1876. Today was Sunday, April 28. "Do you have a calendar?"

He looked angry, confused, volatile; she didn't care. She needed answers, and right now he was the only source of information available. Shaking his head, he rummaged around the corner of the desk and produced the requested item.

Rebecca took it with trembling hands, noting the year and the month of April. With her finger, she traced the line of Sundays down the page. She looked up at Sloan, feeling suddenly very unsure of herself and this reality.

"The month—it's not April, is it?"

"No, it's June."

Sloan snatched back the calendar and, with an exasperated sigh, pointed to a square. "There: Today's Sunday, June 11." He squinted across the room at the large wall clock, its brass pendulum swinging methodically. "Actually, since it's after midnight, it's Monday already. Now what's all this about?"

Rebecca looked up at him, seeing his sincerity, his honest confusion over her questions. No one was that good of an actor. The impact came

47

crashing down on her, stealing her breath as effectively as Jordan's violent attack, the event that had caused her to be here, somehow, in another century.

"Oh, my God," she said softly, feeling faint again. "I don't know what happened. I don't know why I'm here," she whispered, clutching his solid arms as she felt herself falling.

"Rebecca?" she heard him say from a distance. His face blurred, his scent faded, and she was left with the feel of his arms enveloping her, holding her against his body, anchoring her to the reality into which she'd been thrust.

Chapter Three

Rebecca sat on the bottom step of the front staircase, her chin propped up by one hand, her elbow resting on her knee. No matter which way Sloan went this morning, she would be able to see him. She wasn't sure which bedroom was his and wasn't about to go looking. She had a fairly good idea of the accusation he'd come up with for that social blunder.

She needed to talk to him, to find out more about the time and place into which she'd been thrust. She couldn't piece together any details from her rather uneventful adult life that gave even the faintest hint as to why she was here, even after staying up until dawn thinking. Other than the fact that Sloan looked a little like Jordan and they were in Wyoming, they had nothing in common. As the sun had crept over the horizon, she'd mentally studied her family tree for the slightest mention of the name Travers. There was none.

She yawned, an indication of the little sleep she'd gotten after waking alone in the wee hours of the morning. Memories of last night were vivid; she recalled the moment she realized she was alive in the past. Apparently she'd then fainted, and Sloan had carried her to bed. He'd removed her shoes and covered her with the blanket. If she closed her eyes, she could envision him lowering her to the mattress, standing back, staring at her, his brow furrowed. He would have tucked the cover about her awkwardly, unaccustomed to such tasks. And, she believed, he would have stood there silently for long moments after removing her shoes, wondering why she was so confused about what day and year it was.

Just as she finished her daydream, the sound of advancing footsteps from the room across the foyer jerked her to awareness. The heavy door opened and Sloan walked out, his boots striking the hardwood floor with quick regularity. He held a weathered and creased cowboy hat, rotating it with both hands as he focused his eyes directly in front of him. Rebecca jumped up, ready to talk.

He apparently hadn't seen her before, because he stopped abruptly and stared, looking her up and down, the familiar frown on his face.

"I . . ." she paused, unsure of what to say now that they were face to face. Her eyes swept his lean cheeks, covered with beard stubble. His hair looked slightly damp and had been finger combed. Curly hair peeked out in the *v* of the pale blue shirt. She swallowed, remembering his muscled, bare chest.

He turned away as though she hadn't spoken, walking toward the front door.

"Sloan!"

He stopped but didn't turn around.

"I need to talk to you."

She watched his shoulders bunch beneath the faded chambray shirt, head and neck rigid. "I don't have time now."

"But—"

He opened the door to the vestibule, then tried to close it before she slammed her palm against the dark wood. He kept going, pushing wide the front door and striding out onto the porch.

"I need some answers." Rebecca stood in the doorway, bracing one hand on the frame as she held the knob with a hard grip.

Sloan jammed the hat on his head. Then he paused before going down the steps, looking back, as though turning around would have been too much trouble.

"Lady, I don't have any answers."

"But you must. There has to be a reason I'm here. You're the only one—"

"You think so? Maybe you should consider the other devious redhead around these parts."

"You mean Leda Radburn?"

Sloan snorted, turning finally to give her a hard look. "Who else? You look enough like her to be at least her cousin."

Rebecca felt like stamping her foot and throwing a childish tantrum. "If one more person tells me how much I look like that woman, I think I'll scream!"

He was back up the steps in an instant, his hands large and strong on her arms. "Did she send you? Is that why you showed up out there on my range?"

Rebecca was afraid that he would shake her but wasn't about to back down. "Damn it, Sloan Travers, I don't know how I ended up out there. One minute I was having a picnic, the next I was being strangled. I thought I was dead." She pushed against his chest, trying to wrench away from his powerful grip. "Dead! Until you convinced me I was back in 1876, I thought you, me, and Painted Elk, were all dead! Can't you understand that?"

He let her go so suddenly she stumbled back, hitting her shoulder against the wooden siding.

"I don't understand any of it, especially why you say 'back in 1876' as if that's supposed to mean something. I don't know why you're dressed like that or why you were strangled. But I'll tell you one thing," he said, pointing his finger at her. "If I find out you're in on some scheme with Leda and her husband, you'll be sorry you weren't strangled . . . and killed." With that, he turned and stormed down the steps, jerked the reins of his buckskin gelding off the hitching rail, and mounted the wild-eyed animal. With a kick of his boot heels, he sent the horse into a gallop, raising a trail of dust as he escaped from the ranch.

She watched him, torn between feelings of anger, frustration, and self-pity. He'd never believe that Leda Radburn was her great-great-grandmother. She felt trapped, without a clue or a reason, in the past, with a man who would obviously like to hate her. She pushed away from the wooden slats, wincing at the discomfort. *But he doesn't hate me*, she knew instinctively, as much as he'd like to. He's attracted, and he doesn't know why. Was that an inconsequential piece of the puzzle, or did her entire world now revolve around Sloan Travers?

She turned away from watching the faint cloud of dust drift away in the morning stillness. Sloan Travers was gone, but his house was still here.

She walked out into the front yard, if you could call it that. Tufts of new green grass dotted the sandy red soil. Without large trees or bushes to soften the effect, the pale gray frame house seemed as if it had been erected by some insane architect intent on making the statement that contrast is the key to reality.

The house ruled over a small valley, with jagged red rocks forming a line to the east and rolling hills making the other boundaries. A stream cut through the valley from west to east, and just through an indentation to the west the Rocky Mountains loomed, impressive and snow capped.

Rebecca looked up to the second-story window of the towerlike structure over the front door.

Above the steeply pitched roof, a spire rose in ornate splendor. White gingerbreadtype scrolls and curlicues accented each eave, porch post, and window. It looked like a house that should be safely ensconced between towering oaks on a quiet, city street. Amid the harsh, barren landscape of Wyoming, it seemed as out of place as Rebecca felt.

Walking to her left, she recognized the porch that Sloan's study shared with the parlor, where he'd said that he'd seen the light from her lamp last night. Around the side of the house was yet another porch with a door that she suspected led into the hallway. And finally, around back, were the kitchen, the back stairs, a garden, some other buildings, and the infamous outhouse.

Most of the house was two stories, with only the kitchen being a single floor. She hadn't taken much notice of the other rooms upstairs this morning, but now that Sloan was gone, she decided to look. Perhaps she'd find something to explain the angry, suspicious man.

About thirty minutes later, Rebecca thought she might have a slightly better idea about who Sloan Travers really was. Standing in front of a fireplace in the parlor, her fingers traced the intricate silver designs on a picture frame, which held a brown-toned photograph of two people who must be his parents. His mother sat on a camelback sofa, her hands neatly folded, her back straight. His father stood behind, resting one hand on the carved wood, the other holding his lapel. Both seemed serious and wealthy, with old money and eastern influence.

Their clothes looked rich, opulent, in the style of the period. Victorian, Rebecca knew, yet somehow the term had always inspired images of seductive lingerie in sweet-smelling shops at the mall, or cabbage-rose-decorated, dropped-waist dresses on suburban mothers. It hadn't meant this refined, heavy style of gilt and velvet.

Yes, Sloan Travers loved his parents, but he didn't fit their lifestyle.

Beside the photo of his parents lay a folded sash of silky, dark gold material, fringed on both ends like a scarf, only more narrow. She wasn't sure, but she thought she remembered a movie where the sweetheart gave her beau a sash like this to wear over his uniform, a symbol of pride and possession for an officer. Rebecca reassessed her earlier views about the war Sloan might have served in. As strange as it seemed, he had no doubt been an officer in the Civil War. She could almost envision him in a blue uniform, his saber at his side, ready to defend those values in which he believed.

She turned away from the mantel, strolling around the room, letting her fingers drift over the luxurious cloth covering the top of a dark, carved wood table, feeling the heavy satin brocade of the red drapes. All new, all just waiting for a personal touch to make them part of a home.

Last night he'd said something about building this house for someone, then stopped abruptly. A fiancee, no doubt: a woman he'd loved and lost.

He was touchy about the subject, shying away from personal questions, almost as though he was afraid someone would get too close. She thought perhaps that was why he hadn't made too many personal inquiries of her; if he gave the slightest hint he was interested in her life, she would want to know about his in return. It was a common characteristic of people considered loners but who in reality were simply lonely.

Stop giving him traits, Rebecca chided herself. She hadn't even known him for one full day and already she was analyzing him, trying to find out about his past and anticipate his reactions. Well, that might be her profession, but she didn't need to get involved with the man, except to find out how to return to where she belonged. If there was some lesson to learn or riddle to solve, she just wanted to get on with it. She had a whole population of twentieth-century challenges waiting for her in Riverton.

With a last look around the parlor, she sighed and walked toward the stairs. She couldn't bring herself to invade his study, although she'd looked in briefly. That room, unlike the others in this house, reminded her strongly of him. There were probably clues in there, but she wasn't desperate enough to search . . . yet.

The bright, rich wallpaper of each formal room grated on her nerves, reminding her, strangely, of sixties-style kaleidoscope artwork. The decorating seemed oppressive by modern standards, the fixtures ornate and heavy. She had a feeling Sloan Travers's mind was just as intricate as that silver picture frame, and just as convoluted as the twisted, twining design on the atrocious wallpaper.

She yawned as she slowly climbed the stairs. It was so quiet here, the air so still, the atmosphere so isolated. She wondered how many people lived on Sloan's ranch. This morning she hadn't seen a single soul, although she'd heard someone in the kitchen just after dawn.

In the room where she'd spent so much time, she stretched out on the bed and closed her eyes. Despite a bout of yawning and the absolute lack of distractions, she couldn't go to sleep. Sloan's angry, flashing eyes haunted her. She could still feel his hands, holding her upper arms as he stared at her, asking about Leda. She twisted, punched the pillow, and squirmed like a two-year-old resisting a nap, but still couldn't go to sleep. She wouldn't let that man control her life, she thought. He wasn't happy that she was here, and she should be just as upset that she'd been thrust into his life. She really should.

After tossing and turning for maybe fifteen minutes, Rebecca gave up trying to nap. Too many thoughts kept spinning through her head, too many images of Sloan Travers, harsh yet concerned, kept teasing her consciousness.

The curtains fluttered in a gust of breeze. Outside, a horse neighed and chickens squawked; then silence descended again. Rebecca longed for a television, a radio, anything to fill the lonely void of silence. She'd often turn on a news program or talk show just for company, but stuck here she had no options to fight the loneliness except to seek human companionship.

She found Painted Elk in the garden, sitting beneath the only tree around. Its branches were numerous and spidery, twisting together as new green leaves glistened in the sunlight. The tree reminded her of Painted Elk: lined, stunted by the harsh environment he'd endured, but strong and deep in spite, or perhaps because, of what he'd experienced. She'd seen the same physical manifestations of difficult lives, the same creased brown faces, on some of the Arapaho and Shoshone at the Wind River Reservation, near where she should now be working. She'd often wished she could fully understand them better, but their explanations were fleeting and cryptic, beyond the comprehension of a middle-class white female, even one with a master's degree and a certificate proclaiming her competent to counsel others.

He didn't look up as she approached, merely saying, "You are troubled."

She sat on the ground across from him. "I have no answers."

"Maybe you have not yet asked the right questions."

She fell silent, toying with a blade of grass, sliding it from the stalk and placing it between her teeth. The new green taste reminded her of childhood, of happy times with her sister Sara and other friends. Despite the difference in their ages, she'd always felt close to Sara, always loved her older sister.

"Do you know why I'm here?"

Painted Elk looked up, his gaze searching her face. "Tell me what has happened to you, Rebecca Hartman."

She laughed, a brittle, cynical sound. "Where would you like me to start? I don't know what's important anymore, what might be a clue to this mystery and what isn't. I was alive in 1996; then I thought I was dead, along with you and Sloan. Now I find I'm alive, only it's 1876!"

Painted Elk raised his hand as if to stop her from saying anything else. "You know," he fisted his hand, then tapped his chest, "in here. Tell me of the man who shares the blood of Sloan Travers."

Rebecca cocked her head, confused. She felt her brow draw up, her mouth frown.

"Listen with your heart."

The answer came in the form of intuition, slipping from her lips before she even had time to think about it. "Jordan Davis," she whispered. "He tried to kill me. Maybe he did."

"That future is not yet written."

"It seemed pretty real to me when he had his hands around my throat." She relived the pain, the panic, and involuntarily touched the bruises ringing her neck.

Painted Elk nodded. "Anger is like the rain that falls too fast for the ground. When the water rushes," he said, gesturing in waves of motion, "it sweeps away everything but the strongest tree or rock."

"But I'd done nothing to Jordan! We'd just met."

"You must think beyond yourself, Rebecca Hartman. The anger came from a source you do not yet understand. Open your mind to this."

Rebecca was silent, throwing down the now tasteless blade of grass. "I don't know."

"Find your answers quickly, for the season is short, and with the dying of the flowers the future will be written." He reached inside a small beaded leather pouch tied at his waist.

"I don't understand."

"You must listen to your heart," he said, reaching for her hand. He sprinkled a pinch of tiny black flecks on her palm. They looked like poppy seeds.

"What are these?"

"The seeds of your future."

"What plant are they from?"

"The bitterroot." He held her hand, palm up, near her mouth. "Blow," he ordered.

She blew the tiny specks into the stillness of the day.

"You must make your own choices, make your own wind, sow your own seeds. Only then will you see where the future leads." Rising with surprising agility for one so old, he stood beside her for a moment, then lightly lay his hand on her bent head.

She looked up. "You know more than you'll tell me, don't you?"

"You will know it also, when the time is right."

He turned and walked away, toward a teepee not too distant.

Rebecca sat beneath the tree, watching his slow, steady, bowlegged gait. How did he know these things? Was he guessing, or had he overheard her talking to Sloan?

Somehow she didn't think so. He'd said to think with her heart. Well, right now it was saying that Painted Elk knew it all, from why she'd been thrust back into the past to how all these complications had come together on that picnic yesterday.

And her heart also said that Sloan Travers radiated anger like the brightest shield, sheltering a compassionate soul that had suffered much pain.

Sloan reined Buck to a halt on top of a slight rise, watching his cattle move north toward another grazing range. He'd sent five men along, each heavily armed just in case there was trouble. So far, he'd seen nothing out of the ordinary, nothing to indicate that either Indians or Radburn's hands would cause any problems today.

Buck pawed the ground and snorted, his ears back. Sloan shifted in the saddle, relaxing the reins so the gelding could look around. The sun was already high; it promised to be a hot day, just like the day before. But some things had changed from yesterday with the arrival of Rebecca Hartman into his life.

"Damn fool woman," Sloan mumbled. She wanted to talk, did she? Well, he wasn't ready to listen to her crazy questions. Last night she'd acted strange, getting all upset about the year and day of the week. No sane person, no matter how disoriented, forgot what year it was.

Despite his irritation over her silly questions, the expression on her face had stopped him cold. He didn't think he'd ever forget the look of sudden terror in her eyes right before she'd passed out. That kind of reaction didn't come from being slightly confused. He'd seen terror on the faces of men, women, and children, and they haunted him still.

Of course she'd been through an upsetting experience, what with the strangulation marks on her neck. That would account for some of her confusion, but it didn't explain the indecent clothes, of which she seemed totally oblivious. She didn't mind in the least that he could see her legs and ankles, even without stockings or socks. This morning she'd even had a little of that hungry, predatory female look, and that scared the daylights out of him. She felt too good in his arms, too soft and sweet smelling, for him to give in to that sort of fancy.

If she were working for Leda, that's just exactly the kind of reaction that would be expected. Of course, if she were innocent . . .

"Well, hell." He gathered up Buck's reins and turned the gelding back toward the house. Everything was fine out here on the range, but he wasn't convinced that the woman Rebecca was really well. He could control his response to her, just as he had this morning. He'd just go back and check. After all, he'd forgotten to ask Claudia to look after her.

Sloan rode into the barn, dismounted, and led Buck into a stall. After loosening the saddle girth and removing the bridle, he freshened up in the trough outside. Water ran down his back and chest, wetting his already sweat-damp shirt. If temperatures kept rising, it would be a hellacious, dry summer. That meant he'd need more water for his cattle, which meant more men to guard against Radburn's malicious tricks, like filling in or poisoning a well.

He wiped his sleeve across his face as he walked toward the back steps. Just as he started to open the door, he heard voices from around the side of the house. It sounded like her voice, raised in emotion, then the low, steady reply of Painted Elk.

Sloan eased the door shut and went to the corner, peeking around only enough to see Rebecca and Painted Elk sitting on the ground beneath the scrubby juniper tree.

Eavesdropping had never been a favorite pastime, but in this case he found it really enlightening. Not only was she talking craziness, but Painted Elk seemed perfectly willing to play along.

Anger bubbled up, making him hotter than ever. She had some nerve talking such foolishness to anyone on the ranch, but especially to Painted Elk, who, granted, had some real powers when it came to nature and mysticism. Sloan acknowledged that the medicine man was in touch with powers he couldn't begin to understand. They'd discussed Sloan's need for some sort of retribution, and Painted Elk had said that justice would be done.

But never, never would Sloan believe that a woman could be literally sent back in time.

He watched Painted Elk rise and walk away toward his teepee, the Indian's private dwelling, which he would not give up for the comfort of the house, even in the dead of winter. Sloan waited until Painted Elk entered the teepee, then stepped around the side of the house.

"You wanted to talk." Sloan's gruff voice interrupted her disquieting thoughts, making her jump and look up at the tall, damp cowboy.

"You said you didn't have time."

"That doesn't give you the right to bother Painted Elk with your nonsense."

"Nonsense! It's the truth. Besides, *he* doesn't think I'm lying. And how would you know, anyway? You've been spying on me!"

Sloan grabbed her upper arm just as she started to rise, hauling her to her feet in what was more of a power play than a gentlemanly action. "We'll talk about this inside."

She jumped up and shook off his arm. "I'm not some doll that you can toss around, Sloan Travers. And I'll thank you not to put more bruises on top of those your manhandling gave me this morning!"

He ran a hand over his face, then back through

his damp hair. "Damn," he muttered, more to himself, Rebecca thought, than to her. "I'm sorry if I hurt you. I'm not that kind of man."

"You mean the kind of man who gets his kicks from bossing women around?" she asked sarcastically, putting space between them, rubbing her arm.

"Let's get a few things straight right now. I don't play with dolls. I don't know what you mean by 'get my kicks,' but I don't hurt women or children, and I am the boss here. This is my ranch, my property. You're the one who came here uninvited, so don't get all uppity with me."

"Well, believe me, I'd leave if I had a way to get back. It's not my idea of a good time to be treated like some dimwitted, decorative ornament for some macho cowboy—"

He picked her up so fast she didn't have time to react. One minute she was telling him what he could do with his opinion and the next she was slung over his shoulder like a sack of feed. "Put me down, you—"

"No cussing, either. I told you we'd have this discussion inside, and that's what I meant."

She wanted to hit him, beat on his broad, sweaty back or kick him where it would hurt the most. Something stopped her, probably the uncertainty of what he might do in retaliation. Still, she held her tongue. "*You* told me . . . *you* meant! Did it ever occur to you that I have an opinion too?"

"Yeah, it occurred to me. But I just don't give a damn right now."

"No cussing, remember?"

"For you, not for me."

He took the steps to the kitchen quickly, as though she didn't weigh a thing. "You really are a male chauvinist pig, you know that?"

He leaned down, setting her in the middle of the kitchen. "A what?"

"A male chauvinist pig. It's what women in the twentieth century call men who believe in a double standard."

He pointed a finger at her, narrowing his eyes. "Lady, I'm warning you . . ."

"Yeah, right, all that 'nonsense' I'm supposedly spouting." She put her hands on her hips and glared back at him.

He walked around the table to the sink, pumped some water, and filled a glass, his back to her. After a few moments he turned around. "You can't be from the future."

"Oh, really? Well, let me assure you, I certainly wouldn't have thought I could be sent back into the past if you had asked me yesterday. As I said to Painted Elk, I thought I was dead. At first, when I woke up in the bedroom, I thought we were all dead and this was some sort of purgatory. Last night when I saw those receipts on your desk, when you talked about how much it cost to build this house, I finally realized what had happened."

"What you think happened," Sloan corrected her.

"No," she said carefully, "what really happened." She spread her arms, then let them drop

66

to her sides. "Look, I don't know how it happened. I only know that it did. I'm a substance abuse counselor in Riverton. I live in an apartment on Blue Sky Street and I collect David Winter ceramic cottages. I'm twenty-eight years old and never been married, I drive an American car, and I go to church on all the holidays, and occasionally throughout the year." She took a deep breath, hoping he could see the truth in what she said. "Does that sound like a crazy person?"

Sloan shook his head and gave a bitter laugh. "I don't even know half those words you used. One of us must be crazy."

"Well, I'm not doing very well in the nineteenth century, either. I couldn't even find the rest room." She hoped they had both calmed down enough to talk. Somehow, he managed to get her so angry or confused that she couldn't think straight. She had a feeling he felt pretty much the same way about her.

"You say you're from . . . what year?"

"That's 1996."

"Okay, 1996. I say that you aren't. It seems to me that we're at an impasse."

Rebecca nodded. "I can live with that—for now."

"That still leaves the problem of your clothes."

"There you go again, harping on my clothes. What's so wrong with this outfit?"

"It's indecent. You're not even covered."

Rebecca smiled, amused by his shift from male chauvinist to prude. "Why, Mr. Travers," she said in an affected southern drawl, "I do believe you're embarrassed."

His expression changed from one of cautious combativeness to a cold, hard mask. "That's not amusing." He placed the glass in the sink and walked, stiff and precise, to the doorway. His hands, Rebecca noticed, were tensing into fists, then relaxing.

"What—"

"Don't ever use that tone with me again."

"I was just kidding."

He ignored her explanation with stony indifference. "Come on. I'll show you where there's some sewing things you can use to fix up your skirt."

She followed him, more out of confusion over his sudden mood swing that anything else. In one of the rooms upstairs was a sewing box and several bolts of fabric. Sloan stood beside the small cedar chest, fists at his side, staring at it as though it was a pit of vipers.

This wasn't a man's room, Rebecca knew. He'd purchased these things for a wife, for the woman he must have loved and lost. Because of his anger and bitterness, as opposed to grief, she guessed that this woman had hurt Sloan not by dying, but by refusing to share her life with him. Watching him struggle with all those pent-up emotions, she felt the hurt that rejection had caused him.

But there was something else, something that had started downstairs in the kitchen when she'd tried to joke in a Southern-belle voice. She hadn't a clue as to what had precipitated his change of mood.

"Use whatever you want. The next time I see you I want you to be properly dressed."

She stood just inside the doorway as he turned to leave, his eyes never meeting hers. She touched his arm as he passed.

"Sloan?"

He jerked away as if she'd burned him. "Don't."

"Don't what? Touch you? Be concerned about you?"

He lifted his eyes. She almost flinched at the pain, buried deep inside, that she could see inside his soul.

"Just don't," he said and turned away, his boots making those quick, demanding steps she was beginning to recognize. She listened to him go down the stairs, then heard the back door slam.

Minutes later, as she stood beside the window, her arms hugging her middle, she saw him ride out of the barn, galloping as though the hounds of hell were chasing him.

Perhaps they were.

She wondered, in those quiet moments alone, if she could turn away from his raw need. She'd seen pain and fear in men's eyes before, known horrible stories that had caused her nightmares for weeks afterwards. But never before in her professional life had she seen anyone who needed the kindness of human understanding more than Sloan Travers. And never, in her whole life, had she ever known anyone that she wanted to understand more.

Chapter Four

"Ouch!" Rebecca shook her finger, stuck for about the thousandth time since she'd begun sewing, by hand, a modification to her skirt. She'd never been great at handicrafts of any kind, despite her mother's efforts to turn her into a woman who could "keep house" properly. Well, even if she had learned to sew, she would have done so on a twentieth-century machine with a variety of stitches and powered by electricity, not pricked fingers.

Adding a long ruffle was more work than she'd thought. To make it full enough, she'd had to cut strip after strip of fabric, gathering them with basting stitches before adding them slowly, painfully, to her existing skirt.

Why couldn't she have been carrying an overnight bag, with shampoo, deodorant, makeup, and at least one change of underwear, so she didn't have to do "laundry" each night? Why couldn't she have been wearing a nice pair of jeans or at least a straight skirt, which would have needed much less fabric to modify its length? Of course, if she'd been wearing jeans, they would have been equally indecent to Sloan Travers.

Even if it wasn't his fault, if he was only a product of his environment, she still resented his high-handed attitude toward her. For two days she'd learned the house, lengthened her skirt, and just generally stayed out of his way except to ask a few basic questions. He refused to believe that she was from the future or that she wasn't involved somehow with the Radburns. Since he wouldn't discuss any personal issues with her, she hadn't a clue about why she was back in the past.

Hurrying through the last stitches, she bit off the thread, then shook out the skirt. Now, instead of just the denim and eyelet ruffles, there was a wider hem of calico around the bottom, hiding her lower legs and ankles from the delicate eyes of these nineteenth-century men. Maybe Sloan Travers and his crew should be glad a fairly conservative woman had appeared on his ranch; Rebecca couldn't imagine what his reaction would have been to a punk rocker with a pierced tongue and a black leather mini-skirt. Just the thought of his outrage made her smile.

She pulled on the skirt and buttoned it, shifting her balance from side to side when she noticed that the hem wasn't exactly even. Oh, well, she hadn't pretended to be proficient at the domestic arts. Hopefully she wouldn't be here long enough to need an extensive wardrobe, which she would no doubt be expected to sew herself.

Very little breeze stirred in the hall as she went downstairs, holding up the new longer length of her skirt, the rubber soles of her tennis shoes squeaking on the wood steps. As she reached the bottom, she slowed, listening for the sound of another person in the house. As usual, it was quiet—too quiet. Sloan was no doubt on the range, and Claudia was probably at her own small house between the garden and the bunkhouse.

Then the smell of fresh-baked bread drifted through the dining room, making Rebecca's stomach growl in reaction. She'd found the food plentiful but fairly bland, with beef and beans of various types the standard fare. What she wouldn't give for a nicely equipped spice rack and a few bottles of sauces. Unlike sewing, cooking was something she could understand, just as long as she wasn't expected to do anything really gross, like pluck chickens or prepare internal organs. The thought of what might be in some nineteenth-century dishes made her shudder.

She checked the coffeepot on the wood-burning stove but found it cold. No wonder; it must be midafternoon. Walking to the sink, she primed the pump, as Sloan had impatiently shown her yesterday, and filled a cup of water. She wasn't sure if it was cistern or well water, but whatever the source, she appreciated the clear, cool liquid. The loaves of bread beckoned, sending signals that reminded her she'd missed lunch. She found a sharp, long knife on the sideboard and sliced a piece of the crusty bread. Since there wasn't an ice box—if such an invention even existed in 1876—she had no idea where to find butter. But there was jam on a shelf beside the sink, so she carried everything to the kitchen table and smeared her bread with the condiment.

Heaven! Rebecca closed her eyes and chewed slowly, enjoying the pure taste of the bread and jam. Just tart enough to tease her palate, she loved the sweetness and the soft texture. She really shouldn't go without a meal; she'd already dropped a pound or two since landing in the past. At this rate she'd be much thinner when—if—she ever got back to her time.

She opened her eyes, jolted back to reality by the thought of her strange situation, and quickly swallowed. Standing just inside the back door was Sloan, his hair wet and his dusty shirt water splattered and clinging to his wide chest. Well-worn dungarees molded to his long legs, outlining his thighs.

"How long have you been standing there?"

He stared at her for a long time, it seemed. She lowered the piece of bread and shifted her weight, but still he watched, his eyes narrow. Then he ran a hand through his hair and said, "Too long."

She felt blood rush to her cheeks, although she couldn't imagine why. "I missed lunch."

"You're certainly enjoying Claudia's bread." He walked into the room and hung his hat on a rack near the back door. "Or do you look that way every time you eat?"

"Why don't you have a meal with me and find out?" she replied, angered at his critical tone. He was trying to make her feel guilty for the simple enjoyment of a snack. Well, he wasn't going to succeed. She couldn't help it if Sloan Travers believed everything should be suppressed, from showing a bit of leg to eating a piece of bread. Even if he was from a repressed time, he appeared to take some sort of perverse pleasure in looking at her as though she were the biggest sinner in Wyoming.

If only he would believe her . . .

"I don't have time for fancy meals."

"No one asked to sit down to an elaborate dinner. You go out of your way to avoid me."

"I don't know what you're talking about." He turned away from her and sauntered across the kitchen, all loose-limbed cowboy grace and controlled strength.

"I think you do. I think that for some reason you're afraid to be around me."

He stopped, turning around as his eyes narrowed and his gaze settled on hers. "I already told you not to deceive me. Other than that, you're no threat to me."

"Really? Then why are you treating me like I've got some kind of disease?"

"I'm no lapdog to entertain you all day while you loll around the house."

"Loll around the house! You've got to be kidding. I've sewed for two days to make myself presentable, as you demanded." She marched around the table and grabbed the denim skirt. "See? A nice, decent ruffle."

He looked down, his gaze skimming over her, making her feel hot all over. And then he looked at her skirt, and the tennis shoes that peeked out from beneath the new ruffle. "It's crooked."

"Dammit, I know it's crooked! I've never sewed anything more complicated than a project in Home Ec class! Do you think this is easy for me?"

He looked as angry as she felt. "You're talking crazy again, and if you think I'm going to believe you grew up with so many servants you didn't even learn to sew a straight seam, you must think I'm as daft as you are. Even wealthy girls learn to sew and embroider."

"I'm not daft! I'm from the future. A place, I might add, where clothes are made by machines and union workers and people in Third World countries, not by our own pricked fingers!"

"Machines that make clothes? Lady, you have gone crazy."

"I'm not crazy!" She dropped the handful of denim she was clutching and marched forward so she stood directly in front of him. "If you would just listen to me—"

"I don't have to listen to your ramblings." He broke eye contact with her and moved away, toward the hall.

Rebecca grabbed his arm. It felt damp with sweat or water, hard with tensed muscles. "Oh, no you don't. Every time I try to talk to you, you walk away. Well, I'm tired of it!"

"Lady, I don't care what you're tired of. I didn't invite you here. This is my home and I'll walk away if I please."

She dropped his arm and stepped back, feeling his words as a slap to her pride. A reality check; that's what it was. She *was* an uninvited guest. She just hadn't realized how unwanted until this moment. Unable to face his scorn, she looked away. Somehow, the sun still shone and a warm breeze wafted through the open windows.

"Damn," she heard him mutter. "I didn't mean—"

"Of course you did," she said quietly. He'd mentioned her uninvited status before, when he'd carried her inside the house. The comment just hadn't registered then. "You said exactly what you meant for the first time. I just hadn't thought . . . I didn't realize . . ."

"No, you don't understand."

She turned toward him and gazed into his shadowed eyes. "Then tell me. Why do you hate me so much, even while you've been kind enough to take me in? Why do you look at me at times as though I'm detestable?" She watched and waited, knowing she made him uncomfortable. Breaking though his barriers was too important a matter for her to back down now.

"I don't hate you," he said finally.

"Then what? Have I done something horrible, something disgusting? I'm sorry that my skirt was short and it offended you. I'm sorry I don't

76

know how to do things in your world, but—"

"It's her," he said softly, so tortured she had to strain to hear the words. "I don't hate *you*."

"But why?" The urge to touch him was almost overwhelming. She wanted to feel his strong, firm flesh beneath her fingertips, yet she knew he wouldn't welcome her touch now anymore than he had earlier. The urge to understand rose in her again, pushing her toward a closeness she knew he wouldn't welcome.

"I don't discuss her with anyone. Not now, not ever. What's done is done."

"No! That's no way to approach your problems."

"She's not my problem anymore. She belongs to another man. She's his problem now."

"Sloan, if you don't face this—"

"I won't talk about her. That's final." He walked to the doorway leading to the hall. "You're welcome to stay, eat as much bread as you want, believe whatever you want about where you're from."

"Sloan, please . . ."

He walked away, disappearing around the corner. In seconds, she heard his heavy steps going upstairs to his room. Seconds later, a door slammed.

So much for her counseling technique, she thought.

She walked back to the table, looking at the bread that had tasted so good just minutes before. She'd lost her appetite. Frowning, she tore the slice into tiny pieces for the chickens that pecked around the yard during the day.

Claudia came through the back door, her hands filled with fresh laundry, her eyes narrowed as she spotted Rebecca.

"What happened to my bread?"

Rebecca gathered the scraps, needing to get away from this house and its disturbing owner. "It's a long story," she said as she walked around Claudia and pushed open the door. "If I had my automatic bread machine, I'd bake you another loaf."

"Now what is that supposed to mean, missy?"

Rebecca sighed. "Nothing. I was just being sarcastic." She paused a moment. She couldn't get information from Sloan, but perhaps the nearly silent Claudia would be more cooperative. She let the back door close, then followed the older woman to the table.

Claudia began folding the clean laundry. Rebecca dumped her pile of bread on a dish towel, dusted off her hands, and reached for a large linenlike rectangle, which reminded her of an oversized tea towel more than the fluffy bath sheets she used at home.

"Claudia," she began, looking sideways at the other woman, "have I done something to bother you? Besides cutting your loaf of bread, that is."

"I don't know what you mean," Claudia said, staying focused on the laundry.

"Well, you barely speak to me. I was just wondering . . ."

Claudia folded a sheet into a crisp square and

placed it on the table. "It's not my place to say—"

"But this is your home too! I know it must seem odd to you that I just showed up here." Rebecca clutched the towel in front of her.

"More than odd, if you want to know the truth, missy." Claudia reminded Rebecca of a junior high teacher she'd had, a woman who could make the most innocent action seem suspicious.

"You mean you agree with Sloan. He thinks I'm here for some sinister reason."

"I'm sure Sloan doesn't confide in me."

"Well, believe me," Rebecca said with conviction, "he thinks I'm working with the Radburns. I don't know what I'm supposed to be doing here, but that's what he thinks."

Claudia looked at her for the first time since setting the laundry on the table. "You look like *her*."

Rebecca sighed again. "Leda Radburn. Yes, I know. I've been told before." She finished folding a towel and placed it beside the sheet.

"Seems more than a coincidence to me."

Oh, it is, Rebecca thought. *Believe me, there's a reason we resemble each other. I'm just not sure why I'm back in her time.* "I've never met Leda Radburn in my life. That's the truth."

"And I suppose you're not related to her?" Claudia said with disbelief.

Rebecca remained silent for a moment. Then she reached for another towel, and said softly, "You wouldn't believe anything I said."

Claudia folded another sheet and gave a little

snort of what Rebecca supposed was agreement.

"Do you know her?" Rebecca asked cautiously.

"I know her," Claudia said, her tone as harsh as the frown on her lined face. ·

"How?"

"You'll have to ask Sloan. It's not my place to say."

"Did you work for her?"

Claudia glared at her. "I work for Sloan Travers, not some fickle, loose woman without a brain in her head."

My grandmother? Rebecca thought. But she'd always been depicted as the family matriarch. Her picture made her look like the epitome of virtue and restraint.

"But what relationship does she have to Sloan? Where is she now?"

"I've said enough," Claudia stated, gathering the folded laundry. With that, she marched, stiff-backed, out of the kitchen.

Startled by Claudia's vehement response to Leda, Rebecca walked out of the house and into the sunshine and fresh air. Nothing in this trip to the past made any sense. In fact, the more she learned, the more confused she became. There seemed to be only two people who might know; Sloan wasn't talking and Rebecca had no idea where to find Leda.

In the distance she heard the cowboys talking, laughing, as they settled into the bunkhouse. Horses milled around the corral, occasionally squealing as they challenged for position around the grain trough.

This is my home. Sloan's words came back to haunt her as she threw pieces of bread to the cautious chickens. She had intruded on his not-quite peaceful existence. For what reason? Other than his hatred of Leda Radburn, she still didn't have a clue. Whatever the reason, he felt so strongly about the subject that Rebecca knew Leda had hurt him personally, painfully, in the recent past. The wound seemed too raw to have been inflicted long ago. Could she be the woman for whom he'd built this house, bought the sewing box, decorated each room? Had they been in love before she married Vincent Radburn?

Where was Leda? Claudia probably knew but wouldn't say. Rebecca looked across the plains, turning in a circle until the mountains and horizon blended together like a wide-angle shot in a movie. If only she could find Leda and ask her. But what could she say? Rebecca wondered. *Hello, I'm your great-great-granddaughter and I want to know why Sloan hates you*? No, even if she found Leda Radburn, Rebecca knew she couldn't directly ask the questions that plagued her.

This is my home and I'll walk away if I please. But Rebecca couldn't walk away. She had nowhere to go, no way to earn her keep in this foreign time. If Sloan decided she was too much trouble, she would be on her own, with no money, no skills, nothing to save her from the elements or her fellow man. The best she could do was insist Sloan take her to the nearest town, but even then, what would she do? According to

81

the Radburn family history, Leda and her husband had lived on a ranch outside of Lander. *If I could get to Lander, maybe I could find her,* Rebecca thought. *But I have no way to stay in Lander, no way to earn my keep.*

Rebecca wiped her sweaty palms on the dcnim skirt and tried to calm her racing pulse. It had been years since she'd felt this helpless. She'd never expected to experience such a sense of aloneness. Just beneath the surface, fear lurked like a beast ready to pounce. She had to be strong. She couldn't allow herself to be anything less than competent and confident while facing this problem.

Painted Elk had told her to listen to her heart. She would—but she'd also think with her head. With or without Sloan Travers's help, she'd discover why she'd been sent back to the past. And how to get back to her own time.

Sloan braced his hands on the windowsill and let the breeze cool his heated skin. Damn the woman! She made his blood run hot and his brain freeze solid. He could take one look at her and be as mindless as a stallion around a mare in season.

How in the hell could she make eating a piece of bread look like . . . hell, like she was in the thoes of passion? He'd only seen that expression of pure bliss on a few women's faces, and only after a considerable effort on his part. All Miss Rebecca Hartford needed to achieve the same result was some plain bread and jam!

When he'd walked through the door he'd hoped to slip upstairs without her seeing him—or without seeing her. Just one look at that red-blond hair, those clear, direct eyes, and he felt a combination of anger and lust he'd never experienced before. He wouldn't allow himself to feel anything for her. Just because he didn't choose to deliberately hurt her didn't mean he cared. She was either crazy or working for the Radburns; either way, she wasn't for him.

When he needed a woman there was one in town, and a couple in Fort Washakie, who accommodated him. He'd never thought about getting married, not since Leda played him false. She'd made it damn clear that he wasn't good enough for her, at least not anymore. Maybe at one time, when they were both young, with stars in their eyes and the world stretched before them like a feast. But not after the war, the years, and the miles that had separated them.

Sloan pushed away from the window. It didn't help one bit to think about the past, about all those could-have-beens. Leda had made her bed; let her lie in it. He'd live out his life with the knowledge that she'd betrayed him, that she'd lied and cheated him of the one thing that meant the most. He wasn't about to let another woman work her way into his heart. He'd get Rebecca Hartford out of his house and out of his mind soon.

But not before he figured out who she was and why she was here.

Sloan shrugged out of the dirty shirt and let it

drop to the floor. She wanted him to have a meal with her. Maybe he would, but not tonight. Not when he could still recall the exact way her eyes had closed in ecstasy, the way her mouth had moved and her breasts had risen as she inhaled. Not for him, but for a damn piece of bread.

"Damn woman," he muttered as he unbuttoned his too-tight jeans. He'd better find out soon who she really was, because part of him didn't give a damn whether she was a liar, a cheat, or a crazy woman. Part of him just plain wanted her.

"I need to talk to you."

Rebecca sat down on the built-in bench on the front porch, close enough to Sloan to converse, but not too close. For some reason he seemed to clam up when she looked too directly at him, or invaded his personal space. She supposed he had a good reason; he thought she was crazy.

"What do you need?" he asked cautiously. He raised his eyes to meet her gaze, lowering the bridle he was working on. She could see his muscles bunch up, his spine straighten. He looked even more defensive than ever.

She took a deep breath. "Just some information." She hoped she could reach him this time, that he didn't blow up or storm away before she got some answers. "I know you're not much for talking, but I'm trying to understand why I'm here. I honestly don't know."

"That's kind of hard to believe."

"What about the marks on my neck? Someone tried to kill me."

"Are you saying that caused you to lose your memory?"

"It's possible," she hedged. Maybe it would be better for him to believe she had selective amnesia. The alternative was that she was truly crazy.

"That sounds like another story, lady. I've heard my share of lies in this lifetime."

"I'm not lying!" But she was, in a way. She was misleading him. She knew who had tried to kill her—Jordan Davis, also a great-great-grandson of Leda Radburn. The knowledge that she wasn't being totally honest ate away at her anger. "Okay, maybe I'm not telling you the whole truth. But you get angry when I try."

"When you talk crazy." He looked down at the bridle again, jangling the bit and chin strap as though the sound punctuated his words.

"When I tell the *truth*. I'm not from this time. I don't know why I'm here." She threw up her hands. "I'm trying to communicate. Can't you at least listen to me?"

"I'm listening; I'm just not buying." He continued to examine the metal and leather as though it were the most fascinating item on earth.

"Damn, you're hardheaded," she said in exasperation. "What can I do to prove to you that I'm not from your time?"

"Not one thing," he answered, finally looking up. "And I wish you'd quit cussing. It's not lady-like."

"Being 'ladylike' is not the primary goal of women in my time. We consider ourselves to be the equal of men."

"I've heard of you free-thinking women. I suppose you're one of those who supported the right to vote. I don't know what the legislature was thinking in '69."

"They were trying to attract women to the wilderness! Wyoming was a very progressive territory. And women in the whole nation got the right to vote, in 1920, by constitutional amendment. In all the states. We have fifty now, by the way."

He snorted. "Likely story."

"I don't know why I try to convince you. You're as thick-headed as a Missouri mule."

"What do you know about mules?"

"Not a damn thing! It's an expression."

"Well, express yourself without the cussing, lady. Claudia doesn't like a foul mouth."

"Claudia barely speaks to me."

"She's not a chatty woman."

"That's an understatement," Rebecca murmured beneath her breath. Claudia went about her housekeeping duties with the silence of a monk. When Rebecca had tried to get information from her earlier today Claudia had made it clear she had no respect for Leda and was as suspicious of Rebecca as Sloan was. Getting any more details from that woman would be hard work, if not impossible. Which brought Rebecca back to Sloan.

"Look, Sloan, you said you don't hate me. I'm

trying to understand your side of this, about how I just appeared on your ranch, but please try to understand mine also. I don't know any more than you do. I'll never find out if I don't get some answers."

He took a deep breath. Rebecca could tell he was battling with himself. She supposed he would rather she just sit inside that house all day long and vegetate, but she wasn't about to do that—not when she felt there was a reason she was here, a reason connected to Jordan Davis and his assault on her.

"I don't have any answers. I don't know how you managed to get out there with no footprints, no tracks, but somehow you did."

So he had noticed something suspicious about her appearance, something even she hadn't thought of. "But there is an answer! Surely there's a reason I was placed in your path. Don't you wonder about that?"

"I don't spend time daydreaming about—"

Three roughly dressed men rode in at a slow trot, interrupting Sloan's remarks. Rebecca saw the tension in his face, felt it radiate out like a warning beacon as he watched the trio approach. She looked away from his arresting face and tried to make out details of the men.

"Hello the house," one called out.

Sloan stood, placing a hand on Rebecca's shoulder as she tried to rise also. "None of your crazy talk. These men aren't here for a Sunday visit."

Rebecca started to say something, then decided to take his advice for once. He obviously knew more about what was going on than she did. She edged back against the boards, further into the shadow of the porch.

The men reined their horses to a stop. Even from fifteen feet away, with hardly a breeze blowing, she could smell the sweat of man and animal.

The horses definitely smelled better.

"Came with news of Muley Joe," the man in the middle said, resting his leather-gloved hand on the saddle. His rumpled brown suit coat had seen better days, as had his long, stringy red hair.

"Indians got him, over by the turn of the Little Popo Agie."

"Cheyenne?"

"Arapaho, we figure," the man on the right said, looking around the yard. "You know anything about that?" He rubbed his gray-streaked beard with a gnarled hand.

"I haven't heard a thing," Sloan said. Rebecca watched as his shoulders tensed and one hand clenched.

She'd had no idea that Indians were still a problem. Suddenly, the idea of her own safety hit her. Would they be attacked, perhaps on a day when Sloan was out riding the range, or whatever it was he did all day? How could she defend herself against a group of warriors?

The situation was inconceivable. In her time, there weren't marauding bands of Indians. There were Native Americans, struggling for a place in the mainly white world, or trying to isolate themselves from outsiders, protecting their culture. Some whites thought of them, en masse, as a proud and noble race of maligned people. Others thought they were lazy and drank too much. Hardly anyone had a complete picture of tribal culture, Rebecca knew from her own studies and experience in the area.

She certainly didn't consider herself an expert on modern Native American interactions with whites, much less nineteenth-century conflicts. But she did know enough to be afraid.

"The old medicine man still living here?"

"Painted Elk is here."

"None of his tribe bother you, do they?" the man on the left said, spitting into the dirt. His face sported a few days' growth of stubble, and he was dressed more like a mountain man than a rancher or farmer.

"I do my best to stay safe," Sloan said. Rebecca heard the anger in his voice, the same tone he used with her when he didn't want to hear anymore. She wondered if these men knew enough to back down.

"Having that old man hanging around probably helps," the man on the right said.

"Enough about Painted Elk," Sloan ordered. Rebecca imagined him using the same tone to command troops.

"We came to warn you," the first man said. "We didn't know you had company."

For the first time, Rebecca became the center of attention as three pairs of eyes focused on her. She shifted on the bench, unsure if she was expected to say anything. Social convention paled as her mind snapped back to what she considered a more serious problem—imminent attack. All she could mutter was, "Indians?"

Sloan jumped in, ignoring her question. "She's my new housekeeper."

"Don't recognize her," the man on the right said.

"She's not from around here," Sloan replied, glancing back at her.

Rebecca wondered if he meant geographically or time-wise. She sat up straighter, crossing her ankles and trying to put her fears behind her, at least temporarily, and act as nineteenth century as possible. Should she speak now, or let Sloan continue to talk for her? She didn't know what the standard was, but she remained silent, hoping the men wouldn't think her too forward.

"Didn't see anyone come through," the mountain man said. He reminded Rebecca of a radical survivalist, suspicious of everything and everyone. All he needed was some camouflage gear and an M-16 rifle.

"She got separated from her family," Sloan said, giving her a look that said *Keep quiet.*

"Wagon train?" the man in the middle asked.

"Could be," Sloan replied. "She doesn't talk much."

Rebecca choked on that remark. From what she could tell, Sloan considered any communication too much. The men stared at her as she coughed, swallowing her words like bitter pills.

"Looks a bit frail to me," the mountain man said. "Kind of sickly."

"She does okay," Sloan said, which, she supposed, was high praise.

"Yeah, I'll just bet she does," the middle man said with a leer.

Sloan tensed even more. Again, she felt his anger at the rude, seemingly casual remark. "Don't even think it," he warned in a low, menacing voice.

"Them Indians would like to get ahold of that red hair," the other man said, his grin showing several missing teeth. He appeared oblivious to the sudden tension between Sloan and the man who acted loosely as leader of the three. "Looks like somebody already got ahold of her neck."

Rebecca shivered, hugging herself as she stood. She felt sick at the thought of being in danger from either violent whites or angry, marauding Indians. "Excuse me," she murmured, hurrying across the porch and slipping inside the house.

She didn't want to hear any more, about Indians who might mutilate her or suspicious, gross men who thought she was too sickly to be a housekeeper but perfectly fine for other activities. She leaned back against the door, closing her eyes, wishing she would wake up in her nice, safe apartment.

She didn't belong here. She didn't know how to live here, or to get back to where she belonged.

Without a sound from outside, the door opened and pushed Rebecca across the entry hall.

Chapter Five

Sloan caught her before she stumbled and fell.
The impact spun her around, slamming her into
his chest. Suddenly his arms were filled with over
a hundred pounds of warm, trembling woman.

"Are they gone?" she asked, grasping his upper
arms.

"They're gone." He gazed into her troubled
eyes, not knowing why she was so upset, why she
seemed so shocked. Peters, Carson, and Rooster
were lowlife scum as far as Sloan was concerned,
but they weren't that much different than a lot of
men out here. Surely she'd seen worse.

"I can't believe we're in danger of Indian attack," she said, her eyes wide and her breath
rapid.

He'd heard the same fear in another voice, another woman who wasn't suited for life in Wyo-

ming territory. Maybe females couldn't adapt to the perils of the West. Perhaps the West wasn't ready for women. They should probably all stay in the East, where the most dangerous adversaries they faced were reckless carriage drivers. He sighed. He wasn't able to handle this, didn't know what to say, except to reassure her.

"We're not in danger."

"But Muley Joe—"

"Lived alone with a fine team of mules he used for hauling. It's a wonder a band of Sioux or Cheyenne or Arapaho didn't get him years ago."

"That's so cruel! He shouldn't have to die just because he lived alone."

"That's the way life is out here. You shouldn't have come if you didn't want to face the facts."

"But life's not that way. In my day, the Indians don't attack. Oh, they may protest or lobby for legislation, but—"

"Stop it!"

"It's true! I'm not prepared for this. I'm a substance abuse counselor, not some pioneer woman."

She was getting hysterical, Sloan figured. Damn! He didn't know what to do, what to say. Hell, he didn't even know half the words she used! The danger was there, from Indians, from blizzards or draught. She'd have to deal with it, whether she was prepared or not, whether she knew about the conditions out West before she came.

He didn't believe for a minute that story about how Indians behaved "in her day"—or where she came from. Oh, there were peaceful Indians; the Shoshone didn't war with the settlers. They even joined the army in fighting the tribes or bands who resisted reservation life. There weren't too many attacks now, not like when gold was first discovered in the sixties at South Pass. All the miners swarming into the area had angered the Arapaho, Sioux and Cheyenne. Throughout the early seventies they'd killed in Red Canyon, on the Sweetwater, and near Camp Brown. Men and women had been mutilated across the country-side, and some of their children stolen, when the whites had come to stay.

Dammit, it was a harsh life. Rebecca Hartford should have stayed safe and sound, wherever she came from, if she couldn't face life out here.

"Sloan?"

"What?" He hadn't meant for the word to come out so harsh, but he didn't know how to be gentle anymore.

"I know you don't believe me . . . about where I'm from, but I could really use some under-standing about now. I hate to admit it, but I'm afraid . . . and I feel as though I'm all alone."

He looked into her luminous eyes, damp with unshed tears, and something inside him began to melt. "Damn," he murmured as her hands loosened their grip on his arms, stroking up-ward, across his shoulders and finally twining around his neck. She tilted her head, parted her lips, and he was lost.

"Damn," he whispered again as she pulled him down. He lost himself in her eyes as he felt the first kiss of her breath against his lips. Then he closed his eyes, his arms tightening around her.

It had been so long since he'd kissed a woman with real passion, since he'd enjoyed the mystery of discovery, the thrill of giving and taking pleasure. He couldn't think any longer, of any other women except this one, and how she molded her body to his.

She kissed with equal passion, slanting her mouth across his, teasing his lips. Their tongues mated and she moaned, moving closer, as though she wanted to be inside his skin. There was only one way they could be closer.

His hands wandered lower, pressing her against his arousal, groaning with pleasure and anticipation. She would be his! To hell with her crazy ideas, her past or his future. This kiss went on and on, until he was sure he would die if he didn't have her in his bed, now.

With another moan, she tore her lips from his, pushing against his shoulders. He was so startled that he let her escape, let her lean back and stare at him as though he'd grown another head. "You want me," she said with wonder.

"What did you expect," he said harshly, feeling as though she'd doused him with cold water, "when you threw yourself at me?"

"I wanted some tenderness."

"Then you almost got more than you bargained for," he said, panicking at his strong reaction to her. In another few minutes he would have carried her upstairs and lost himself in her body. Enemy or not, relative of Leda's or not.

He was the crazy one. Before she could say anything else he escaped from the house and the woman he had no business desiring.

Rebecca helped herself to a snifter of Sloan's brandy that night, wandering around the study with a new restlessness. She was an idiot; that was the only excuse she could use to explain why she'd kissed Sloan this afternoon. Still, she couldn't help smiling every now and then, hugging her arms and reliving the passion she'd felt bottled up inside him.

She swirled the amber liquid in the glass, smelling its heady fragrance, yet remembering something entirely different. The smell of sunshine and clean, male sweat on Sloan. The hardness of his biceps, the tension in the muscles of his neck and shoulders. The firmness of his lips, the hard, demanding thrust of his tongue.

She took a swallow of the brandy, but it did nothing to erase the memory of their kiss. She shouldn't have done it! She'd known she was playing with fire, yet she'd asked for a closeness as unreal as this time was to her own. Sloan continually told her he felt no tenderness, yet she'd asked that from him and received both compassion and passion in return. And even as much as he'd desired her, when she'd pulled away he'd let her go. Apparently, all men in the nineteenth century didn't question a woman's ability to say "no."

She stopped near the darkened window, looking at her own reflection. What did he think of her as a woman? Not as an unwanted intrusion into his life, but as a flesh-and-blood woman with emotions and needs not so unlike his own? He'd given her a glimpse this afternoon, a fascinating insight into the attraction he felt toward her. Oh, he might claim that it was purely sexual, but she suspected he'd had more than just a male-female reaction to her. He was lonely, whether he recognized it or not, and he was responding to her own emotional needs, whether he admitted it or not.

But she still shouldn't have kissed him. She had no business complicating an already tense situation by bringing in any type of sexual response. Especially when he'd made it clear he didn't trust her. As a matter of fact, except for his earliest care and for today's passionate response, she would have bet he didn't like her at all.

Oh, but could that man kiss! He'd responded as though he were starved for her lips. If she hadn't broken away, no telling what would have happened. His reaction had been purely male, very physical, very graphic. Her stomach muscles clenched involuntarily as she remembered the feel of his arousal pressed against her.

Whether he liked her or not, whether she knew he was evading issues or not, they both obviously wanted each other. Rebecca shook her head and laughed. How ironic that she had to go back 120 years before she found a man who really knocked her socks off!

She took another sip, looking at her reflection in the dark window. Hardly the picture of desirability. Her straight hair hung limply, not responding well to the harsh soap of the nineteenth century. And her skin, normally pampered with hypoallergenic cleansers, shone with what she could only describe as a "well-scrubbed look." What she wouldn't give for her little travel bag!

"Don't leave home without it," she whispered to herself, smiling with ironic humor.

"Excuse me?"

She whirled, surprised to see Sloan standing just inside the doorway. "I didn't hear you. What happened to the loud clomp of cowboy boots and the jangle of spurs?"

"I don't wear spurs," he said, walking into the room. "What was that about leaving home?"

Rebecca smiled. "Just a little jingle. American Express: Don't leave home without it," she mimicked, as best she could. At Sloan's confused look, she continued, "A saying from where I'm from."

"Oh." He leaned back against his desk, crossing his booted feet at the ankles. "And where is that again?"

"I grew up in Cheyenne."

"That's right."

"Checking up on me?" Rebecca should have been outraged, but she imagined the brandy and her introspective mood kept the anger away. She only felt amused that Sloan was trying to trip her up. Well, it wouldn't work. She was telling the truth.

"I live in Riverton now. Do you know where that is?"

"Not around here."

"It's about twenty or so miles from Lander."

"It is, hmm?"

"That's right. In Fremont County. So where is this ranch?"

"Fremont County," he said slowly, pushing away from the desk and walking toward the decanter. "About fifteen miles from Lander."

Crystal clinked as he poured himself a drink.

"In which direction?"

"Southeast, along Twin Creek."

"I know where that is!" Twin Creek intersected Highway 289, which angled south from Lander. If she could just see more of the land, perhaps she'd recognize something.

"I thought you might." Sloan sounded smug, as though he'd forced a confession from her. Well, he still hadn't ruined her good mood. She now had a geographic location and she'd learned more about him. Not a bad day, really.

"Riverton is east of Lander, mostly along the northern bank of the Wind River. I think, if it weren't all built up, there would be kind of a bluff or at least a plateau there. I'm not sure when it was settled, but maybe it wasn't a town in 1876."

Sloan took a big gulp of his brandy. "I wish you'd stop that."

"What?"

"Talking about the year as though . . . hell, I don't know." He ran a hand through his damp hair. He must have washed off outside or bathed in that big tub this evening. Not that Rebecca knew his normal hygiene routine, but he seemed

99

very clean for a nineteenth-century cowboy-type.

Especially when compared to those three men who had come by this afternoon. She shuddered in distaste and finished her brandy. "Look, I can't help talking that way, because that's the way it is. I really am from the future. Sooner or later you're going to have to accept that as a fact."

"Lady, don't make me lose my temper. I came in here to ask you . . . something."

"What?" Rebecca walked to the small cabinet where the tray and decanter sat, placing her glass on the polished brass. "What were you going to ask me?" She gazed into his blue eyes, trying to gain another clue as to his hidden feelings. She was sure he had many . . . and she really shouldn't be so interested in what, exactly, they were. Perhaps it was the counselor in her.

Perhaps not. Perhaps it was because she was a woman and he was a very desirable man.

He turned away, walking behind his desk as though he could place a barrier between them. *Interesting, very interesting,* Rebecca thought. *He's afraid to be alone with me.*

"I'm heading into town tomorrow to pick up supplies. I just thought you might need some . . . things. If you'll let me know, I'll pick them up for you."

"You're going to town? Oh, Sloan, I'd really like to come with you."

"That's not a good idea."

She leaned her hands on the desk. "But I want to see Lander." She wanted to find Leda, if possible, or at least get a location where she could find her. Maybe she could "borrow" a horse and ride to the Radburn ranch later. The possibilities began to race through her mind as she saw the uncooperative look on Sloan's face.

"There's not much to see. It hasn't grown much since it was Camp Brown. The post moved to Fort Washakie."

She ignored the history lesson. "But I don't know how to tell you what I need. I mean, sizes and such. I don't know how clothes come."

"You've never had store-bought clothes?"

"Of course I have. I wear a size six in women's and a seven in juniors'. Does that mean anything to you?"

"No."

"Well, then, I've got to come. I need some shampoo and lotion too. I promise not to be any trouble."

Sloan finished his drink in one swallow. "Damn," she heard him mutter beneath his breath.

"Please, Sloan. I really need to get away from the ranch for a day. I—"

"Oh, all right." He slammed his glass down on the desktop so hard that Rebecca thought the fragile stem might break. "But you have to promise to do as I say. No wandering off," he said, wagging a finger at her. "No talking to strangers."

"I'll be the epitome of virtue," Rebecca vowed, marking a cross on her chest, over her heart.

"I'm going to regret this," Sloan muttered, carrying his glass to the liquor cabinet.

"No, you won't."

He walked to the open doorway. "We'll leave as soon as it's light. Be ready."

Before he could walk away, she hurried over. "Thank you, Sloan." Reaching up on tiptoe, she brushed a chaste kiss on his cheek, then watched as he blushed a bright pink beneath his tan. "I really appreciate all that you've done for me."

He wouldn't look at her, wouldn't meet her gaze. He ran a hand through his hair again, then turned away. She watched him walk down the hall, his wide shoulders, broad back, and narrow hips moving naturally with each step. She bet his naked back looked as good as that muscular hunk on the Soloflex ads. As he reached the stairs, she barely heard him mutter, "Damn fool woman."

Rebecca smiled as she blew out the lamp and climbed the stairs to bed.

Sloan slapped the reins across the backs of the team, heading away from the sun, which hadn't yet cleared the eastern rim of the valley. Beside him, Rebecca fidgeted on the seat, brushing against him constantly. To fight back, he reached up to adjust his hat, giving her a little nudge with his elbow. Maybe she'd take the hint.

She did—for a moment. Then she reached down and gripped the seat, her hand brushing against his thigh as she held tight to the wood.

After another few minutes of her nearness he wasn't sure whether he would push her off the narrow, wooden seat, just to get her away from him, or throw her down in the wagon bed and have his way with her. He had no idea why he'd consented to let her come along, but he was sure as hell suffering for his decision now.

The only reason he could come up with was that she'd confused him so much last night. After that kiss yesterday afternoon, he'd expected embarrassment or recriminations last night in the study; instead, she'd been almost cheerful. He'd never understood a woman's moods, and this one's seemed stranger than most. When she'd kissed his cheek, like he was some damned favorite uncle, he'd been unable to speak. She tied him in knots, all right, and he didn't like the feeling.

"Look!"

Sloan instinctively reached for his rifle, his gaze darting across the landscape. What had she seen? Indians, a bear, a cougar?

"Aren't they precious?"

Finally locating the source of Rebecca's excitement by following her pointing finger, Sloan relaxed his grip on the rifle. A Pronghorn doe and two fawns stood halfway up the red, rock-strewn hill, poised for flight but staring with interest at the wagon. "Damn, woman, I thought we were under attack."

"Oh, I didn't mean to startle you. I just love antelope."

"They're very tasty," Sloan agreed.

"Tasty? Uck! No, I meant I love to watch them. They crawl through the fences and graze with the cattle. I've seen a lot of them along the highway, just walking around, totally oblivious to the cars."

"Railroad cars?" Sloan couldn't imagine the skittish animals standing too close to a moving train.

"No . . . automobiles. We call them cars. They haven't been invented yet."

"This is more of your crazy talk."

"No, just the truth," she said with a sigh.

Sloan clicked to the horses, giving them a little slap with the reins to get them moving over the slight rise that separated this small valley from the rolling prairie.

"The rocks are so red here," Rebecca said. "It's kind of surprising to see them, all of a sudden, when the rest of the land is brown and beige."

"This valley is a lower part of the Red Canyon area. Twin Creek comes down from the mountains near Red Canyon."

"I've seen Red Canyon from the highway. It's magnificent. But I assumed maybe it was a little too high in elevation or inaccessible for people . . . now."

"Settlers came in maybe ten years ago. It's a good piece of land—good water and shelter—but some of the Indians don't want the settlers there."

"Have there been many attacks?"

"Quite a few. A couple of women living alone, a few years back." Sloan recalled the bloody details that had circulated. No telling how much was exaggeration to get the whites riled, but enough was true to turn the stomach of a strong man.

He felt Rebecca shudder. "I just can't get used to the threat of Indian attack. It seems so . . . foreign."

"I'm sure they feel the same way about us moving onto their land."

"You seem very understanding."

"I've learned that issues are hardly black and white." Or blue and gray, perhaps he should have said. When he'd joined the army, still fresh from the university and full of grand ideals, he'd thought that the preservation of the union was absolutely right. States shouldn't secede, even if they had legitimate concerns. He just hadn't known what war was like. No one could have told him that.

"Has this area been settled long?" Rebecca asked, cutting into the unpleasant memories of his youth.

"Not really. Two years ago the government started paying the Shoshone about five thousand dollars a year in cattle, each year for five years, for the land south of Lander down to South Pass City. The land you're on right now."

"Really? That's so cheap."

"Chief Washakie trusted the negotiator. He should have been more suspicious."

"Yeah, you just can't trust those bureaucrats," Rebecca agreed. "I have trouble getting a new file cabinet."

Sloan had no idea what a "file cabinet" had to do with Indian treaties, but he didn't ask. He didn't want to hear any more wild stories—even if she did manage to make them sound very real. And maybe they were, in her own mind. He'd seen grown men who envisioned everything from their dead companions to hideous monsters, all inside their own heads. He'd seen an enlisted man cry out in feverish delirium, swearing his sweetheart was in the room with him. He'd seen the innocent victims of war, knowing that behind their vacant eyes they could still see the horror and feel the pain.

His own mind still played tricks on him, usually in his dreams, in the dead of night. He had his own demons. Maybe he could imagine why Miss Rebecca Hartford created another world, one where there were no Indian attacks, where machines made clothes and fifty states made up the Union.

Maybe they were both crazy, two of a kind.

She continued to chat occasionally, asking questions about the obvious, expressing delight over the common. They passed several small homesteads, with Rebecca appearing shocked over the small size and rustic construction. Maybe she thought all the houses looked like his. They didn't; he had the only large house in the area—except for the monstrosity Radburn was building for his bride and her son.

They pulled into Lander around midmorning, the sun already heating up the plains. Sloan glanced at Rebecca and decided that she needed a bonnet. The ties would help hide the fading bruises around her neck and the brim would shade her face. Her nose already looked sun-burned. It would be a shame if her soft skin be-came as thick and tough as saddle leather.

Damn, he was doing it again—thinking about her soft skin when he should be turning his team toward the general store. Instead, he'd practi-cally stopped in the middle of the wide dirt street.

He pulled on the reins, his arm brushing against her breast.

"Excuse me," she said, in a startled, slightly hoarse voice.

"My fault," he replied quickly, feeling a little warmer than he had a few seconds ago. His arm tingled and he felt a little breathless.

She turned her head away when he glanced around. Just to check the other rigs and horses, of course.

"Whoa," he called out when he guided the team parallel to the front of the store.

"So this is Lander," Rebecca said, disappoint-ment evident in her voice.

"This is it."

"It's so . . . small. There can't be more than twenty buildings here."

"Sounds about right. It's not Philadelphia or New York, that's for sure."

"No," she said with a sigh. "And I thought it was small in 1996. Around seven thousand peo-ple," she whispered. "This looks more like fifty."

He gave her a glare, wondering where in the world she got her imagination, but she seemed to be oblivious to him as she stared around at the unpainted one-story buildings. Lander wasn't much, but it had most of what they needed.

Quite a few people were in town this early, some bringing produce and others stopping by the farrier, the assayer's office, or the general store. Maybe he had been away from "civilization" for too long, but to his eyes, Lander looked pretty good.

Except when he started to get down from the wagon seat. Walking toward him, dressed in their Sunday best, were the two people he least wanted to see. He froze, unable to think beyond the anger that flooded him.

"Sloan?"

He heard Rebecca's voice, but all he saw was another face, another red-blond head of hair.

She must have followed his gaze, because he heard Rebecca's intake of breath, and then her excited voice. "Oh, God, that's her, isn't it? That's Leda . . . and Vincent Radburn!"

Chapter Six

She hadn't anticipated the emotion that came with seeing her great-great-grandmother, that strong tug of family that came with recognition. They shared the same blood, and so many of the same features. Seeing Leda Radburn was a miracle that couldn't be put into words. Rebecca could only swallow the emotion that threatened to choke her, could only blink eyes suddenly touched by tears.

Leda looked so young! Dressed in a slim, moss green dress and a small straw hat that perched on the back of her upswept hair, and carrying a tiny purse on a chain, she walked silently beside her husband. He appeared to be an arrogant man, someone more proud of what he owned than who he was. Her great-great-grandfather, dressed in a somber gray suit, appeared much less real than Leda, probably because there wasn't the family resemblance.

But Leda appeared proud also, a self-contained woman who held her head high. That is, until she spotted Sloan. Her confident footsteps faltered and, even from twenty feet away, Rebecca could see a flash of pain—and longing—in Leda's wide eyes as she stared.

She's in love with him! The knowledge flashed through Rebecca's mind, stunning her as much as her first reaction to her great-great-grandmother. She felt her breath catch and her stomach plummet, as though she were riding on a roller coaster. It couldn't be! Leda was married to a very successful man. They had four children . . . eventually. The land was still in the family, had been inherited by Jordan Davis . . . who had tried to strangle her.

Suddenly nothing made sense. Sloan hated Leda; and Claudia said Leda was a loose woman with no sense. Had Sloan and Leda had an affair—one that had become a public embarrassment? Leda stood there, looking like the most respectable citizen in Wyoming, staring at Sloan as though she were both afraid of him and drawn to him.

Rebecca's hand reached out automatically, grasping Sloan's forearm. "What's going on here? What's between you two?"

He shook off her hand. "Nothing," he ground out. "Not one damn thing." He jumped down from the wagon with one fluid motion, leaving Rebecca alone and confused on the wooden seat.

She continued to watch Leda and her husband, who had now spotted Sloan and, obviously, his wife's reaction to Sloan. A look of outrage and hatred flushed his face, giving his eyes an evil, slanted look, and making his mouth a sinister, hard line. Rebecca involuntarily drew back from the image; she didn't want to see her great-great-grandfather's anger. She'd often wished she knew more about the family, but not like this. It was too personal. She felt like a voyeur, trapped in some nineteenth-century soap opera where everyone was involved, somehow, with everyone else.

The only problem was that Rebecca hadn't seen any of the past episodes, and no one would share the script.

She glanced at Sloan; he seemed to stare right through the Radburns. Rebecca's heart went out to him, but at the same time she sympathized with Leda, who was also in pain. Strangely, she felt nothing at all for the man who was her great-great-grandfather.

Finally, Vincent Radburn grabbed Leda's arm in what must have been a painful grip and turned her away from Sloan's stare. With their backs straight they crossed the street, never looking back. Rebecca wanted to run toward her distant relative, tell her who she was, and ask why she was here.

But Leda didn't know. She wasn't anyone's grandmother—yet. And she wouldn't understand Rebecca's dilemma or believe her any more than Sloan.

"Sloan?" Rebecca called softly to him, unsure if he would even acknowledge her voice.

But he did. After one last glance at the Radburns' retreating figures he came around the team, reached up, grasped Rebecca around the waist, and swung her down from the seat.

"Are you all right?" she asked, gripping a handful of skirt to keep her fingers from stroking his cheek. She wished she could soothe his hurt in some way; not as a woman but as a friend. Sloan looked as though he needed one right about now.

"I'm fine," he said in a flat voice. He guided her to the overhang of the mercantile store. "I'll have them load my order while we get whatever you need."

She couldn't remember what she needed at the moment. Her heart and her head were still full of the emotions she'd just experienced, from seeing Leda for the first time to feeling the pain that passed between her and Sloan. Glancing again at his stony profile, she thought of the way he hid his inner turmoil. In her counseling career she'd known others, especially strong men, who would not discuss any problems, who saw the slightest admission as a weakness. But somehow she felt Sloan's stoicism went beyond that macho attitude. Something in his past was keeping him from living a full life. He would never be happy until he faced whatever had happened.

In the past she'd had to fight against becoming too involved with her patients. She'd been cautioned by her supervisors to maintain her distance, but her instincts had always drawn her close—maybe too close—to others. She might wonder about Sloan's past, or hope for his future, but she had to stay detached from his problems. She wasn't his counselor, and he obviously wouldn't welcome help, even if she offered. There were no guarantees she could help him if she tried—which she wasn't going to do.

She probably wouldn't even be here long enough for that to be an option, she thought with a sigh as they entered the darkened interior of the mercantile store. The smell of unpainted lumber combined with leather and tobacco. Dusty rays of light came from the two wide front windows, plus a smaller one in the rear. Uneven boards creaked beneath her feet as she walked beside Sloan to the counter.

"Good morning, Mr. Travers."

Rebecca's interest turned immediately from her surroundings to the slight man behind the counter. His crisp English accent seemed as out of place in Wyoming as she was in this century.

"'Morning, Mr. Grant." Sloan handed the man a list. "Did my package come in?"

"Indeed! It was sent north from the railroad at Rawlins with the ox drivers. Came in last week, it did." With a smile he pulled a brown paper-wrapped bundle from beneath the counter. Rebecca barely got a glance at the neatly scripted sender's address on the front: Mrs. Donovan someone, in Philadelphia.

Another woman in Sloan's life? Rebecca thought with irritation. As soon as she realized the implications of her thoughts—her jealous thoughts—she made herself take a deep breath. She had no business wondering about the women in his life, just as she shouldn't try to solve his problems. She wasn't here as a psychologist or a social worker.

But then, why was she here?

"Cory!" Mr. Grant called a teenage boy to the counter. "Fill this order for Mr. Travers, and see that his horses get water." The gangly young man grabbed the list, muttered "Yes, sir," and hurried off.

"And the lady here needs some things." Sloan's voice returned her attention to the present, and to the man waiting for her with a smile.

"Hello, Mr. Grant," she said, remembering the name Sloan had used. "I need some clothing, some shampoo, and some . . ." she searched for a nineteenth-century word, "some toiletries."

"Well, now, I can show you what I have in the way of dresses and the like, but I'm afraid I don't know what this 'shampoo' could be," the small, trim man said with a frown. "As for the toiletries, we have a few items on the shelf here," he said, gesturing behind him.

Rebecca's spirits dropped when she saw the pitiful collection. Apparently skin care wasn't a priority in 1876. Still, there must be something to help her combat the elements.

"I'll just look around, if that's okay with you," Rebecca said.

"Help yourself, then," Mr. Grant replied cheerfully.

While Sloan leaned against the counter, Rebecca wandered through the small store. Mostly Mr. Grant seemed to stock yard goods, but there were two ready-made white blouses with high collars and fairly wide sleeves. A plain brown skirt seemed to be the right size, Rebecca thought as she held it up to her. At least it was long enough to satisfy Sloan's penchant for covered ankles, even if the ensemble would be extremely hot.

Digging through another stack, she looked for underwear. Her cotton briefs wouldn't last forever, but she hoped her only bra would be serviccable for as long as possible. She had no intention of wearing a corset, especially in this summer heat.

She took her small mound of purchases to the counter. "I think this is what I need," she said to Sloan, "but as you probably know, I don't have any money."

He glanced away from the feminine apparel. "I'll take care of it, Mr. Grant." Sloan turned back to Rebecca. "How about those toiletries? Get what you need."

She walked around the counter, finding some mild-looking Castille soap and something akin to facial astringent. "No deodorant, I suppose?" she asked Mr. Grant.

"Sorry, miss, but I don't understand—"

"She uses some odd words," Sloan said curtly. "She's kind of lost her memory, along with her family." His eyes darted to the fading bruises that still ringed her neck, then back to her face, as though he was considering her story again and finding it lacking. But that was nothing new.

Rebecca touched her neck, remembering the way she'd gotten her bruises. The sudden terror, the confusion and fear. Yes, she had lost her family, her home, her career, and even her century. She wondered if she looked and sounded as out-of-place to Mr. Grant as she felt.

And though she knew Sloan was just explaining what he considered eccentricities, his words irritated her. She didn't need anyone making excuses for her, even in the nineteenth century. Still, she was reluctant to say anything, especially in front of others. She told herself she was dependent on Sloan for everything, that she shouldn't antagonize him. The helpless feeling she'd experienced before came back, making her spirits sink.

What she wanted to do was leave the store and Sloan behind, at least temporarily. She wanted to run after Leda and ask her what was going on. But she knew that was impossible. She'd have to bide her time . . . and hold her tongue.

"This is all," she said, knowing her voice sounded flat. Well, that was how she felt: suddenly drained of energy and life. She recognized the symptoms as depression; she knew it was a temporary condition. But that didn't make her feel any more lively or hopeful at this moment in time.

"Will you be staying in town, miss?"

Before she could reply, Sloan said, "She's working at the ranch as my housekeeper."

"Oh, I see." The shopkeeper's eyes widened. No

telling what he was thinking. Probably something similar, but much more civilized, more British, than those three rough-looking men yesterday. "Well, then, if you need anything else, just let me know."

"Throw in a bonnet, Mr. Grant," Sloan said, glancing at her bare head.

While Mr. Grant totaled the bill, Rebecca muttered to Sloan, "I can speak for myself."

"There's no reason to be riled. I'm trying to help," he said quietly.

"I'm used to being independent. Maybe I don't want a bonnet."

"This is not the place," he growled.

She bit her tongue, knowing she had to keep her emotions out of the situation. Since coming to town she'd been exposed to her great-great-grandmother and -grandfather, realized that Leda was or had been in love with Sloan, and reiterated her dependence on him. She'd been through so much, but she had to fight to stay rational.

At the moment all she wanted to do was lash out at someone. Then she wanted to click her ruby slippers together and go home.

Cory returned. "The order's loaded, Mr. Grant." The teenager turned to Sloan. "Your horses have been taken care of."

"Thanks, son," Sloan said as he counted out some bills. then reached in his pocket for a coin, which he tossed to Cory. "There should be another package next month," Sloan mentioned casually to the shopkeeper.

He tossed a calico bonnet on the counter, next to the pile of clothing Rebecca had chosen. "She'll need this on the ride home."

"Yes, sir." Mr. Grant quickly wrapped brown paper and twine around the folded items. Rebecca retrieved her bundle from the counter. The bonnet was remarkably ugly, perched like a garage sale reject, unfit for human wear.

"I'll hold your next package for you. Good day, miss. Good day, Mr. Travers."

Sloan grasped Rebecca's elbow and steered her toward the door. She wanted to pull away from his firm but gentle touch but knew making a scene in Mr. Grant's store wouldn't be the wisest thing to do. The man probably thought the worst of her, based on his wide-eyed reaction to Sloan's comment.

He opened the door for her. The sunlight was almost blinding after the dim interior of the store. "Is there anything else you need in town?" she asked, hoping she'd get to see Leda again, or learn something more about the ranch. "Maybe we could stop for lunch?"

"This does it for me. There's beef jerky and dried apples in the wagon." He replaced his hat on his head, then looked up and down the street. "Besides, as you said, there's not much here to see."

She wondered if he was thinking of the double row of unpainted buildings, or the now-absent Radburns.

Sloan took her purchases and placed them in the back, then helped her onto the wagon seat.

"I wasn't putting your town down," she said.

"What?"

"I didn't mean that there was anything wrong with Lander. It's just so different," she said with a sigh. She couldn't think of one reason to linger here, not when he'd made it clear he was ready to leave.

"Lady, to you everything is 'different.'" Sloan handed her the disputed bonnet. It really was quite ugly and dowdy, with a tan background and tiny yellow flowers. She couldn't imagine if it was meant to complement a Spring, Summer, Fall, or Winter complexion.

"You're being difficult again," she said testily. "You haven't called me 'lady' all day."

"My mistake. I suppose I should be more consistent."

"Meaning you should be in a bad mood all the time. Well, at the moment I don't have the energy to argue with you." She did feel drained. Time lag, perhaps, instead of jet lag, combined with a good dose of depression. With a sigh, she placed the bonnet on her head and tied the sash. Okay, it did provide some shade from the noonday sun.

"Fine. Then we'll have a nice, quiet ride home." Sloan clucked to the horses and slapped their backs with the reins.

"Dammit, Sloan, I—"

"Stop cussing!" Sloan hissed. He turned the horses around in the street and headed back out of town.

Rebecca looked around. Several people had stopped in front of the bare storefronts and were watching them drive by. "What do you suppose they're thinking?" she asked softly. "Do they wonder what I'm doing with you, or, better yet, what you're doing with me?"

"They can wonder all they want. It's none of their damn business."

"You don't care?"

"Not a bit."

"But they're your neighbors. You can't live in a vacuum."

"I live the way I want. If they don't like it . . ."

"But you insist I behave a certain way. Wear certain clothes. Speak without cursing. Why such a double standard?"

"You're a woman."

"I know that! I just don't understand what difference it makes. If they think something is going on between us at your ranch, then so what if my skirt is too short? They're going to think the worst anyway."

"Thinking and proving are too different things. If they don't see you do anything wrong, hear you speak about crazy things, then they're just speculating."

"And that's better?"

"It is. And if you don't understand, then you haven't lived long enough."

"I just haven't lived in your time!"

"Don't start that again." He urged the horses into a slow trot. Rebecca grabbed for the edge of the seat to keep her balance as the wagon lurched forward.

"You don't want to hear the truth, but you're

more than willing to speculate as much as any of your neighbors. I think you're a hypocrite."

"Don't call me names. I saw the way you recognized . . . her."

"Of course I recognized her! I've seen her picture. I know I look like her."

"Where did you see her picture? Not in my house, I know."

"No," she said, reaching inside her blouse for the ornately engraved locket that rested warmly between her breasts. "Here. Stop the wagon."

She felt Sloan's gaze burning her as much as the hot sunlight. The silver seemed to shimmer as the wagon slowed, then stopped. She didn't take her eyes off the heart, and when she was sure she had Sloan's attention she pushed the catch.

She didn't look at Sloan, but she heard his intake of breath. Only then did she glance at him. His eyes were narrowed, riveted on the old photos.

"Where did you get that?" he asked, his voice a fierce whisper.

"It was given to me at the family reunion . . . by a great-aunt. It's been in the family for a hundred years."

He broke his gaze from the locket, then shook his head. "It's a trick. This just proves you're working with the Radburns. They put you up to this."

"No, they didn't," Rebecca said wearily. "I'm from the future. And if you want to know the truth, I'm a descendant of Leda Radburn, not a relative. She's my great-great-grandmother."

Sloan didn't like the turn of his thoughts as they rode silently back to the ranch. For the first time, for just a moment, he'd thought she was telling the truth. But then he'd realized how preposterous her tale really was. She wasn't from the future any more than he was from the moon.

They topped the rise that formed the southern boundary of the Wind River valley. The rolling prairie stretched before them, almost shimmering in the heat. To the west, the mountains appeared cool and distant. Sloan wished he had a few handfuls of snow off the highest peaks right now. It would feel good, rubbed over his body. Instead, he pulled out a canteen, took a drink, and wet his bandanna. A few swipes of relief was all he could afford at the moment.

He passed the canteen to Rebecca, who also took a sip. She didn't say anything else, though. He *wanted* her to be quiet; he welcomed the silence. But it also grated on his nerves as much as the ceaseless groans and creaks of the slowly moving wagon.

Damn, it was hot. Without a good rain soon, he'd have water troubles before the summer really got started. He couldn't run his herd without Twin Creek, Beaver Creek, and the wells that dotted his land, but there was no guarantee that they would be a reliable source of water as July and August approached. His goal of increasing breeding stock would be impossible to reach if draught gripped the land.

Rebecca's head bumped against his shoulder once, then again. She jerked awake and yawned. The wagon reached the bottom of the hill and leveled off. In a few more minutes he felt her nod toward him again, only this time she didn't wake up. He looked down, but all he could see was that damned ugly bonnet. He should have bought her a hat, something with enough of a brim to shade her face. She already had a sprinkling of freckles across her nose and cheeks.

Hell, he should have bought some fashionable clothes for her, if any existed in Grant's Mercantile. From his brief glance at the feminine apparel Sloan gathered that her selections were neither attractive nor stylish. But at the time he'd still been upset from seeing the Radburns—and Rebecca's surprising reaction to them. Of all the times for them to walk down the street in Lander!

With a resigned sigh, Sloan took the reins in one hand. The horses knew the way home. They'd traveled this trail at least fifty times, he imagined, in the last three years. He checked the rifle, making sure it was positioned in the boot so that he could reach it. Then he brought his arm around Rebecca and shifted her a little more comfortably against him.

At least one of them would be comfortable.

She mumbled once and shifted against him but then slept on. Two hours of slow progress went by, the nearly full wagon creaking across the dry, sandy trail. He saw a couple of antelope bucks and would have shot one for dinner if Rebecca hadn't been sleeping so peacefully. Hell, she probably would have been offended if he'd taken down one of her precious animals. She seemed to have a soft heart, something not compatible with life out West. Definitely not compatible with life at his ranch—or with him. He knew that for a fact.

Sweat dampened his shirt where he held her, but she didn't awaken. Only when the wagon turned toward the house, coming up the break between two hills, did she give a little start and raise her head.

Quickly he removed his support. There was no need for her to know he'd kept his arm around her for so long. Hell, he wasn't even sure why he had done it. There was still a good chance she was working for the Radburns, even if she did seem genuinely surprised to see them in town. And if she was crazy, then it wasn't her fault she thought she was from some future time.

Those damned photographs sure did look real . . . and old. Of course, they might have been intentionally exposed to water or sun. Whatever it took to age them. Vincent Radburn would go to any lengths to extract the revenge he thought was his due.

"Oh, we're home," Rebecca said sleepily, stretching.

He felt a ridiculous rush of pleasure at her calling the ranch "home." Sloan gave her one glance. That was all it took to see her breasts rub against that low-cut blouse she wore. Watching her was like seeing his mother's cat wake from a nap on the window seat, all lazy and sleek, arms and legs stretched out, inviting a person to pet her.

Damn! He'd begun to get hard again, in the middle of the day, in the midst of a heat wave, fully dressed and in plain view of God and man. He had no sense anymore, not since he'd picked that woman up off the plains. Not since she'd opened her eyes and stared at him.

"Yes, we're home," he growled, shifting on the seat, needing like hell to adjust himself but knowing he couldn't. Not in front of her.

"Still in a bad mood, I see," she said.

"Not any more than usual," he replied, guiding the team toward the house. The quicker she removed herself from his side—and his sight—the faster he'd be able to control his body.

"I'm sorry to hear that," she said, her voice still breathy from sleep. Her lips smiled in a way that looked seductively innocent. Obviously, she'd awakened in a better mood. "It must not be very pleasant to go through life in a bad mood."

"Actually," he said, pulling the team to a halt near the front porch, "it's very easy." He reached behind him and handed her the package of clothes. "Now, if you'll excuse me, I have some nails to chew before dinner."

She had the temerity to laugh. He'd hoped to be gruff enough to scare her away, and she laughed. "I'll see if Claudia has an old, tough shoe we can prepare for supper. Maybe that will be to your liking. Myself, I think I'll have something tender and nutritious. I think I'm going to need my strength."

She tucked her new clothes underneath one arm, gathered up her mismatched skirt, and jumped down from the wagon before he could put on the brake and help her. Just as well, he thought, scowling as she retreated briskly, her hips swaying slightly as she climbed the steps to the porch. He didn't need to touch her, even long enough to remove her to a safe distance. He had the horrible premonition that the next time he put his hands on her, he wouldn't be pushing her away.

With a shudder at that thought, he yelled, "Giddup," and slapped the reins on the backs of the team.

Old shoe, indeed.

Rebecca closed the front door, leaning against it for just a moment. What had she expected from Sloan? Apologies and roses, for heaven's sake? He didn't see anything wrong with calling her a liar and acting high-handed whenever they had a conversation. Did she suspect that just because he'd put his arm around her and let her sleep on his shoulder, he'd had a change of heart?

"Fat chance," she murmured to herself as she pushed away from the door. Still, his kindness had made her feel . . . cherished, as though her comfort and health were important to him. And maybe they were, just a little. She didn't want to read too much into what might have been a strictly utilitarian action. Perhaps he'd been afraid she would fall off the seat and hurt herself. Then he would have had to stop the wagon and pick her up.

But when she thought back to the other nice things he'd done—rescuing her from certain death on the prairie, caring for her when she was faint, making excuses as to why she was living in his house—she had to believe he cared in some small way. Even though he didn't believe her story about being from the future, he hadn't left her in town or abandoned her to the elements. He hadn't made a pass at her; she'd made one at him. He was one tough man and didn't want to admit any weakness, especially to a woman he didn't trust.

She climbed the stairs, clutching her new clothes to her chest. At least she had a change from the skirt and blouse in which she'd arrived. She hadn't paid much attention to the new clothes, except that they would probably fit and seemed serviceable. Would she look more like a nineteenth-century woman dressed in this new outfit?

What would Sloan think? She wished she had a decent full-length mirror so she could gauge her appearance. Not that it really mattered. She had no business dressing for him, not when he'd made it clear he wasn't interested. Of course, his kiss yesterday had told her something else entirely. She tried not to think of that too often because when she did she longed to experience that magic again. Never before had she felt so swept away by a passion she couldn't explain.

But just because he might care, if only a little, didn't mean that she should confuse her own attraction to him. They were from different times, different cultures. Sloan had his own problems, just as she was in the midst of a major dilemma. If he wouldn't help her, he couldn't stand in her way either. Sooner or later she would find out why she was here, in the past. And then perhaps she would go back to where she belonged, to find that Jordan hadn't really killed her on a picnic blanket that fine summer day.

Sloan handed over the team to Slim, who would also see that the wagon was unloaded. Right now more weighty matters drew his attention.

He approached Painted Elk's teepee, stopping before the open flap. "Painted Elk, may I enter?"

"Come in, my friend."

Sloan ducked into the small opening. The elderly Arapaho sat cross-legged on a buffalo skin, tending a long pipe with a small clay bowl. "You are troubled. We will smoke on it. Then you may talk."

Sloan schooled his face, trying to hide his impatience. He respected Painted Elk's beliefs and customs, but at the moment he wanted answers to questions. Instead, he knew, with Painted Elk he'd get more questions and be expected to provide his own answers. Still, Painted Elk knew much more than any other man about human nature, about nature in general. If anyone could help, the medicine man could.

If he would. If he didn't speak in riddles.

Pungent smoke filled the teepee, swirling in the midday sun filtering through the opening at the top, where the poles came together and provided ventilation. Painted Elk handed him the pipe. Sloan cradled it in his hand, closed his eyes briefly, and willed his muscles to relax. Opening his eyes, he took a long draw on the pipe, holding the smoke in his lungs. The tobacco relaxed him further, giving him a false, brief feeling of euphoria.

How easy it would be to sit here forever, perhaps in time substituting something stronger for the tobacco. He'd never tried opium but had seen it used by the Chinese and some Americans building the railroad south of here, several years ago. Some of the miners in South Pass City had favored the strong drug. They'd been able to forget the cold and loneliness of their lives, but they'd lost the ability to remember other things as well. Love and hate, for example; a drug-addicted man was rarely able to extract revenge.

"You have seen the woman Leda again."

Painted Elk's words jolted him back to reality. "Yes, in town. With Radburn."

"But that is not all."

"No," Sloan replied, passing the pipe to Painted Elk. "Rebecca was with me. She seemed surprised, and even excited, to see . . . her."

"And have you found the reason for her feelings?"

"She said . . . something. On the way back to

129

the ranch she showed me a locket with two photographs inside."

"And did you believe what you saw with your eyes?"

"Those pictures could have been false. I don't know that they're real."

"You know."

"Dammit, you sound just like you did when you talked to her. I don't know a thing."

"You refuse to see what is before you."

"She's not from the future!" Those photos weren't real. Some great aunt might have given the locket to Rebecca, but not with those images inside. She must have gotten them from the Radburns.

"Did you not ask for revenge on the woman who left you? And on her husband, who hates you?" Painted Elk asked, breaking into Sloan's thoughts.

"Yes, dammit, I asked for revenge. I want them both damned for what she did." And what Vincent Radburn continued to do, each day. The knowledge ate away at his gut. "And they'll get what's coming to them, sooner or later."

"When you asked for revenge you thought this man would take your life."

"He still might. He hates me enough for what happened with Leda. If he thought he could get away with shooting me in the back, he would. The only thing that's saved me so far is that everyone around here knows exactly how he feels."

"Your hatred of him is also strong. Such anger is powerful."

"Not powerful enough to make a woman appear from the future."

"You do not know the strength of such power. Have you asked the woman about the marks on her neck?"

"She told me she was strangled."

"Did she tell you of the man who placed his hands on her?"

Sloan shook his head. "No. I . . . didn't ask. She didn't say."

"The woman Rebecca has also suffered. She should not receive more anger from you, my friend."

"She's lying to me."

Painted Elk looked him in the eye. "Are you so sure you can see inside her heart? The woman has much honesty and goodness," he said, touching his chest. "She is a healer."

"You mean like a doctor?" She'd said nothing of the sort, only that she had some sort of job. At the moment he couldn't remember any details of what she'd said almost a week earlier.

"She heals what is inside here," Painted Elk touched his chest again, "and here," gesturing to his head.

"Maybe you're confusing the issue. Maybe she's just crazy."

Painted Elk shook his head and looked away. "Your heart is hard. You will not listen to the voice inside."

"I won't listen to her lies. She's here, now. She's

not from some future time."

Painted Elk slowly pushed himself up from the buffalo robe. "She is your future. Only you can know if that is good or bad."

Sloan sat there for a long time after the old Indian left, taking another drag from the still-smoldering pipe. This time, however, the temporary sense of relief he'd felt didn't come. Instead, Painted Elk's words continued to ring in his ears.

She is your future. He didn't want a future with her. His dreams had died a long time ago, on a march through Tennessee and Georgia, and his future belonged to no one. There was only revenge, and he would have it, even if it killed him.

Chapter Seven

Rebecca couldn't sleep. The nap in the wagon on the way home had thrown off her schedule, and discovering Sloan's arm around her when she first awoke had been a real surprise. On top of that, the hot sun had given her a nagging headache that wouldn't go away. What she wouldn't give for a couple of aspirin . . . Downstairs, she heard the clock strike two.

Kicking off the sheet and swinging her legs over the side of the bed, she stared out the window into the darkness. Thousands of stars twinkled overhead with only a sliver of moon to compete in the night sky. A few wispy clouds floated by. The night was beautiful and cool, with barely a breeze to stir the curtains.

She might as well get up, since she couldn't sleep. Fumbling with the matchbox on the nightstand, she lit the kerosene lamp. A soft glow filled the room. She needed something to do, and as much as she hated to sew, she had to let out the waistband on the new skirt. Apparently it had been designed for women who wore corsets and had twenty-two-inch waists. She wasn't about to strap herself into one of those contraptions.

She pulled the sewing basket onto the bed, searching for dark thread. Her new clothes hung on a line of wooden pegs across the room, and she walked over to retrieve the brown skirt. How did one alter a waistband? She held the garment close to the lamp. The stitches were tiny and tight, and she didn't think she would be able to get the scissors between the fabric to rip out the seams.

With a sigh, she decided to try. Otherwise she'd have to ask Claudia for help tomorrow. She picked up the scissors but almost slashed her hand when she heard a muffled, anguished yell from downstairs.

Her heart pounding, she dropped the skirt, held on to the scissors, and approached the door. She didn't hear another cry. Putting her ear to the door, she listened, her breathing rapid. Was the house under attack? Were there such things as burglars in 1876 Wyoming? Suddenly the night seemed sinister and still, not peaceful.

In just a few seconds she heard the sound of crashing glass. Someone *was* downstairs! She had to make sure Sloan was awake. Edging open her door, she looked into the hall. Nothing stirred. Surely if he'd heard the sounds, he would have been dressed and out of his room by now.

She eased out the door, walking on tiptoe down the hall. She now knew which room was his, although she'd never been inside it. The door stood open, the room's interior dark and quiet.

"Sloan?" she whispered.

Nothing. Taking a deep breath, she crept past the three remaining doors on the second floor and then down the stairs, holding tight to her scissors. She had to find Sloan.

Pausing at the landing and then continuing downstairs, she saw a faint glow of light from the direction of Sloan's study. Perhaps he was being robbed! Or maybe he had surprised the villain and they'd struggled. The image of Sloan lying in a pool of his own blood spurred her on, despite the trembling of her knees. Surely the burglar could hear her rapid breathing and pounding heart.

She approached the study as quietly as possible, scissors poised to strike.

Right hand outstretched and dripping blood, Sloan's motionless body lay slumped in a large chair facing the desk.

"Oh, my God!" Rebecca rushed forward, sinking to the rug. She grasped his hand, expecting his skin to be cool. But his flesh was warm, blood dripping from a cut on the palm near his thumb. "Sloan, can you hear me? What happened? Where else are you hurt?"

He raised dazed eyes to meet her gaze. His head! He must have been hit. Gently, she ran her hand through his thick, shaggy hair, searching gently for bumps or gashes. There was nothing. He closed his eyes. Suddenly he moaned, a low gravelly sound that resonated through her whole body.

"Feels good," he mumbled.

"Sloan, where are you hurt?"

He grasped her wrist, stopping her searching fingers. With surprising agility, he guided her hand away from his head, bringing it lower. She panicked for a moment, because he seemed amazingly strong. But he was injured; he must be. Slowly, steadily, he placed her hand on his lower abdomen, right over his arousal.

"Hurts," he muttered.

She was too shocked to move for a moment. He was hot, both his palm and the bulge in his jeans, and his hand moved over hers, pressing her into his growing need. With a gasp, she pulled her hand away.

"I thought you were injured! I thought someone had broken into the house."

He opened his eyes. "What?" he asked groggily. "Did you scream?"

"Angry," he said, as if that explained everything.

"I heard glass break."

He raised his head and gestured, with some difficulty, across the room. "Threw it."

For the first time Rebecca noticed a shattered glass and the strong smell of liquor. Bourbon, she suspected, although it could have been rum or brandy. "How did you cut yourself?"

"Damn glass," Sloan said. "Had to clean . . ."

She looked back at the fragments. Some were in a pile, as though he'd tried to gather them after throwing the tumbler. "Oh, Sloan, you fool. You're stinking drunk."

"Not too drunk," he murmured, grasping her by the upper arms while her attention was still on the broken pieces of glass. She could do nothing except squeal before he pulled her onto his lap.

"Sloan, no," she said breathlessly, but then his lips covered hers, enveloping her in the taste of bourbon and the smell that was uniquely his. She thought about struggling, but his lips were warm and heady, slanting across her mouth with the ease of a thousand kisses. She'd thought of their last kiss, craved that special intimacy, and couldn't resist the urge to become lost, at least for a moment, in shared passion. Moaning, she opened her lips.

His arms tightened with surprising strength, pressing her tighter against his chest as he deepened the kiss. She slanted her head, instinctively giving him better access. Just for a moment, she told herself. Her head swam with pleasure and excitement. With a moan, he cupped her bottom and settled her more firmly in the wedge of his spread legs, tight against his arousal.

She needed air! She couldn't think. In the back of her mind she knew this was pure folly. Sloan didn't even like her, and yet he kissed her as a man possessed. She didn't know his secrets, but she no longer cared. All they had was this moment, this perfect kiss.

His hand roamed to her breast, molding and shaping her to fit his callused palm. Through only the thin barrier of her nightgown, she felt each ripple of pleasure like nothing else she'd ever experienced. She shifted on his lap, wanting to get closer to the source of heat that pressed urgently against her thigh. What would he do if she straddled his lap, or eased between his legs to lie flush against his hard body?

That vision of boldness was enough to make her break the kiss, to slide her hands more tightly around his neck and twist in his lap until she lay full upon him. He seized her lips again, kissing her as if his very life depended on it. She felt an aching emptiness inside, one that only Sloan, with his guarded eyes and buried passion, could fill.

"Sloan," she whispered, kissing his jaw, nipping his neck lightly.

He grabbed her hair, wrapping his hands in its thickness and bringing it to his face. She moved against him, needing him to understand how much she wanted him, like no other man she'd ever known. Like no other lover, real or imaginary.

With a moan, he shuddered against her, opening his eyes, as if he wanted to memorize her features. A shadow of confusion dimmed his gaze, but Rebecca didn't want him to stop. Not now. She needed this closeness, this affirmation of life in a world gone awry. She tried to kiss him again, but he pulled back, his brows knit together in a look of confusion.

"You . . . not Leda," he whispered.

Rebecca stiffened in his arms, rage filling her. She pushed away from him, horrified at the anger she felt. He thought he was making love to Leda, not to her! All this time he'd wanted the other woman, the woman he couldn't have. The woman who had looked at him today with such emotion.

Stumbling to her feet, she fought the urge to slap his cheek, to sink her fist into his rock-hard belly. She wasn't a violent person, but she wanted to strike out and hurt him the way he'd hurt her. Only this emotional wound felt much deeper, much more long-lasting, than any bruise or cut she'd ever experienced. Instead, she turned and fled up the stairs, her bare feet making no sound at all.

Just before running into her bedroom, she heard the scrape of a chair and then Sloan's heart-rendcring cry, "No, dammit, no!"

She slammed the door, shutting off his anger and his pain. If he couldn't have Leda, he might think he could settle for her. Well, she wasn't about to settle for any man, especially one who consistently confused her with another, giving her the attributes and features of a lover both longed-for and despised. With a burst of strength, Rebecca pushed a chest of drawers in front of the door, since there was no lock. She wasn't going to be a victim of Sloan's anger or his lust.

She was a fool. She would have given herself, body and soul, to him, believing that he cared, that he simply couldn't express his feelings. But he'd been truthful tonight, letting her know exactly who he'd been thinking of: Leda. Rebecca wanted to curse her great-great-grandmother's name, to despise the love she'd shared with Sloan.

She should never have known about her ancestor's lost love! How could fate be so cruel as to reveal the past in this manner? With a cry, she slumped, exhausted, on the bed. She curled into a fetal position, stifling her sobs with a fist. Dear God, she had to get away from here! She didn't belong in the past.

She didn't belong with Sloan. And he would never belong to her.

Morning light pressed against Rebecca's eyelids. She moaned in reaction, burrowing deeper into the bed. Only seconds passed before her groggy brain discovered she wasn't resting on the soft feather pillow, or lying beneath the sundried sheets. Her cheek lay on the rough cotton throw, and her body felt as though she'd gone ten rounds with George Foreman the night before.

She pushed herself to a sitting position, wincing at the brightness. A weak breeze barely stirred the curtains. She could identify with the wind; she felt just as lethargic. Rubbing her temples and yawning, she looked around the room. The chest of drawers still guarded the door.

Apparently Sloan hadn't tried to follow her upstairs last night. Obviously he didn't want *her*. That was just fine, since she didn't want him either. Not anymore. She would never be a stand-in for another woman—especially if that woman was her own great-great-grandmother.

With a sigh, she padded to the washstand. Luckily, the pitcher contained some water, left from yesterday. Rebecca poured it into the bowl, then looked at herself for the first time in the grainy mirror.

A disheveled stranger stared back. Mottled creases bisected her cheek, making her look like a topographical map of Mars. Her eyes appeared puffy and bloodshot, as though *she'd* been the one drinking last night. Her hair was a red-gold tangled mess.

Then she remembered how Sloan had run his fingers through the strands, pulling her close. How he had seemed to luxuriate in the heavy mass.

She didn't want to remember. She picked up the linen square, intent on washing away the temporary effects of last night's insanity. She placed the wet cloth over her puffy eyelids for several moments, then ran it lightly over her face. Opening her eyes, she meant only to watch as she re-wet the cloth; but then she saw the coppery-red stains on the white linen square.

She looked at her face, searching for an injury, but saw nothing. Then she recalled the cut on Sloan's palm, how it had bled. And she re-lived the feel of his hands holding her close, molding her body to his with a strength she hadn't imagined a man in his drunken state could possess. With growing heat, she gazed at the white nightgown, seeing the reddish-brown stains on the pleats and lace of her bodice, where he'd grasped her breast with amazing gentleness and purpose. There were other stains—around her waist, scattered across the gown—as though his hands had been everywhere.

They had been. She could feel them still, even though she longed to forget the crazy, wild passion they'd shared. With a gasp, she imagined the back of the nightgown, where he'd pulled her hips into the wedge of his thighs, and on her back, where he'd pressed her against his hard chest.

She didn't want to remember. She tugged the gown over her head, letting it fall to a heap in the corner. It was probably ruined, just like her feelings for Sloan. If only he hadn't said Leda's name . . .

What was she thinking? She wouldn't want a man who imagined he was in the arms of another woman! She didn't understand the love-hate relationship between Sloan and Leda, but she wanted no part of it. Rebecca narrowed her eyes and picked up the washcloth. She'd scrub away all traces of Sloan Travers, from head to toe. She'd remember his yearnings for Leda, and how he'd tried to explain many times before that he didn't care about Rebecca, that he wasn't someone to tease or analyze. She'd remember and get on with her own business of finding her way home.

Within minutes, she was scrubbed clean. She dressed in her new blouse and old skirt, then tackled the chest of drawers blocking the door. After much shoving and groaning she managed to get it back to where it belonged. Last night the darn thing hadn't seemed to weigh nearly as much.

Stepping into the hallway, she saw no one. The house was as silent as a tomb—its usual state. She walked softly down the hall, noticing that the door to Sloan's bedroom was open. No sound came from inside it, so she glanced into the darkened interior. The bedcovers had been pulled up over the pillows, much as they'd been last night. No clothes were strewn about. It appeared that he hadn't even been upstairs.

Perhaps he'd slept in that ridiculously large chair in his study. But then she recalled the way his palm had bled, staining the rug. Picking up her skirt, she skipped downstairs and walked quickly toward the study. She wasn't really concerned, she told herself. Sloan wouldn't really have sat in his chair and bled to death. The cut wasn't even that deep.

The study was empty; no reclining body, no broken glass. Only the dark drops on the deep red of the patterned rug told her that last night had not been a dream—or a nightmare. That, and the faint smell of bourbon that still tinged the air, as it had his breath. Heady, like his kisses.

Rebecca felt like slapping herself. She wouldn't think of the passion they'd shared, however crazy and brief. The only reason he'd reacted the way he had was because he thought she was Leda. When he'd discovered she wasn't he'd stopped.

143

He hadn't explained, hadn't followed her. Sloan's feelings were as clear as if he'd written them down in black and white. And Rebecca knew she would be ten times the fool if she didn't, finally, heed his warnings: He was off limits to her, as a woman *and* as a counselor.

She spun away from the doorway of the study and walked toward the kitchen. She needed food. She needed to get on with her quest.

Rebecca could tell that Claudia had already been to the house from the pot of warm coffee. She also must have cleaned up the study.

After packing a makeshift lunch of biscuits, ham, and a jar of water, all wrapped in a dishtowel, Rebecca returned to the study. Somewhere in here there must be a map. If she could discover directions to the Radburn ranch, she would go there. She'd been sitting around here for too long. There were answers waiting, somewhere out there on the plains, and she intended to find them, starting today.

Sloan rolled to his side, trying to stop the pounding in his head. Sunlight bore down on his closed eyes, making his head ache even more. His stomach felt as though he'd eaten the south end of a northbound skunk for dinner last night. And the rest of him felt as though he'd washed it down with a gallon of whiskey.

That part was close, he thought. Right now he needed water. And he needed to find out where in the hell he was.

Squinting his eyes open, he checked his surroundings. Cottonwoods rustled overhead, already losing leaves due to the heat. He picked up a handful of dirt: sandy. He must not have gone south from the ranch or he'd be lying on clay. Tiny stars danced in his line of vision when he tried to focus, but eventually he saw a rocky butte, its red and yellow layers shimmering in the sun.

He listened, then heard the faint murmur of water somewhere to his left. Gradually the smell of grass and horse came to him on the breeze, and he realized that his mount—he couldn't remember which one—must be grazing close by.

His hand throbbed. He inspected the cut on his palm, recalling hazy details of collecting shards of glass. He should have wrapped a bandage around the damned thing. He'd probably stained the rug.

With a moan, he heaved himself into a sitting position, and immediately realized his folly. He was as weak as a newborn babe. He put out his arms to keep from collapsing onto the ground. Hell and damnation, why had he gone and drunk himself into a stupor last night?

As soon as the thought entered his head, he knew the answer. He had been angry, about seeing Leda, about Rebecca's assertions that she was from the future, about Painted Elk's enigmatic remarks. He wanted life to be simple again, as it had been long ago, before the war. But that obviously wasn't to be. No matter how hard he tried to reduce life to the basics, people and events just kept getting more demanding, more complicated.

He pushed himself up again, this time focusing on the water. He needed a drink. His mouth felt bone dry. He crawled the few yards to the stream, then sank down on the tall grass and plunged his hands into the current. Cold and swift-moving, he cupped water and tossed it on his face, then leaned closer and took a mouthful. After quenching his thirst he washed the cut on his hand and took a few deep breaths. Within seconds he felt better.

Sloan sat beside the stream, trying to get his bearings. He must have ridden north last night, or early this morning. He remembered that it had been past twelve when he could no longer focus on the clock. He'd heard the chimes at one and one-thirty, and then, at two, he'd hurled his empty glass across the room, thoroughly disgusted with his thoughts.

Shortly after that, the cause of his problems had appeared magically before him, a ghostly apparition in white. She'd said something about his hand, about him being hurt. Her words had made no sense, but she'd smelled of sunshine and sleep, and he'd wanted to capture the very essence of her. He remembered kissing her, and that she had responded like a dream. He had wanted to bury himself inside her willing body, fuse his soul together with hers, and forget all the worries that plagued him.

And then he'd spoken aloud the thought that troubled him, the fear that ate at his insides even while his passion for her had soared. He was terrified that he was only imagining Rebecca in his arms. That somehow he'd confused her with Leda. That the desire he'd felt was just the warped memory of another woman with red-blond hair and green eyes.

But when he'd given voice to the fear she'd broken away. He'd felt the loss like a slap. One moment his arms—and his heart—had been filled with her, and the next he'd been cold and alone, again. So he'd ridden away, from the ranch, from her, from his memories.

She didn't understand! He wasn't a man who expressed himself well. But couldn't she tell by his kisses that he'd wanted *her*, not some other?

Apparently not, he thought as he tried to stand. The world spun around briefly, then righted itself. The horizon leveled off, became one solid line instead of two broken ones. The trees no longer swayed; the brook no longer careened crazily through the stand of cottonwoods. He turned around, searching for the mountains. There they were. He was north of his ranch, and probably not too far east. No telling how long he'd ridden the night before.

He spotted Buck a dozen or so yards away, grazing on the lush grass. Sloan tried to whistle and failed, re-wet his lips and tried again. Buck's head shot up and he broke into a trot. Sloan blessed the day he'd taught the gelding that particular trick.

Despite his pounding head and queasy stomach, he had to laugh at the sight of his horse, trotting forward with a saddle slipped sideways. No wonder he'd ended up in a heap on the ground. He'd probably failed to cinch the damn thing and fallen off as they went down the hill toward the stream. Not that he remembered too much of that particular event. He was lucky he hadn't fallen off at a full gallop and broken his damned neck.

The recollection of falling off his horse wasn't nearly as clear as his memory of making love to Rebecca.

"Whoa, Buck," Sloan said softly as the gelding neared. He checked the bridle, relieved to know that at least he'd put on that piece of equipment properly. He shifted the saddle around, then uncinched it. After using the saddle blanket to give Buck a good rubbing he replaced both and cinched the saddle tight. Before mounting, Sloan checked Buck's hooves and legs, again relieved to know he hadn't ridden his horse to ground in his effort to escape his memories.

Sloan mounted, sitting still for a few moments to let the world right itself again. Then he turned Buck south and said, "Let's go home."

"I don't know about this," Slim said, frowning as Rebecca held the reins of a very placid-looking, small red roan mare. "Sloan didn't say nothing about you hightailin' it out of here."

"I'm just going for a little ride. I'll be back soon." Rebecca wondered if Slim thought she might be leaving for good. Claudia would probably be glad if she did leave, but Rebecca wasn't sure about the rest of Sloan's employees—or "hands," or whatever they were called. Not that she'd had any interaction with them.

She'd tried to confide in Painted Elk, just so someone would know where she'd gone, but he wasn't in his teepee. His fire was cold, so she supposed he'd gone off somewhere alone.

"A body can get lost around here."

"I have the mountains to guide me. I won't go far." Rebecca held one hand behind her back, crossing her fingers to diffuse the lie. She planned on riding as far as necessary to find Leda's house. Based on the map she'd found folded in the back of a drawer in Sloan's desk, that should be about ten miles. How long did it take to ride ten miles? she wondered.

"Oh, all right. But iffen you do get lost, just give the mare her head. She'll head home like an old hound dog."

Rebecca smiled at Slim's acquiescence. If Sloan knew what she was doing, he would be angry, all right. She just hoped he didn't take it out on his hired hand if he found out. And she had every intention of keeping the details from him. "I'll be fine, Slim. See," she said, holding up the towel-wrapped bundle, "I even brought along a little lunch. I'll have a picnic."

"Just follow Twin Crick," Slim said, gesturing southwest, "up a ways through the hills. You'll still be on Sloan's land. There's some trees that aways. Iffen you see any bears, give 'em room."

"Don't worry; I will." The last thing she wanted to tackle today was a wild bear. She'd probably have her hands full with this nice, tame horse.

It had been several years since she'd ridden, and never in a skirt. She led the little mare out of the barn, blinking again at the sunlight. She supposed she should have worn that damned ugly bonnet, but she wasn't about to go back into the house to get it. Besides, if anyone saw her, she'd feel absolutely absurd. Rather like wearing rollers to the supermarket, she thought wryly.

Since the mare wasn't more than fourteen hands, Rebecca was able to mount with the minimum of stretch and strain—and without showing too much leg, she hoped. She was sure to hear about that breach of conduct, if nothing else, when Sloan got back to the ranch. She still had no idea where he was, and neither did Slim. All they knew was that both Sloan and Buck were gone. Of course, Slim didn't know that Sloan had gotten knee-walking, commode-hugging drunk last night, and she wasn't about to say anything negative about "the boss."

Rebecca imagined that he'd gotten up early, although how he could have ridden out of here to work the range, or whatever he did all day, she couldn't imagine. He must have one hellacious hangover. She was surprised that he could even sit a horse, much less in this heat and sun, after drinking himself into near oblivion last night.

He hadn't been too drunk to stop himself before making love to the wrong woman.

Setting her feet into the stirrups and picking up the reins, she reminded herself that Sloan wasn't her worry. If he wanted to ruin his liver or risk alcohol poisoning, that was his business. And if his head felt as though it might explode, then it served him right.

To keep Slim from becoming suspicious, she did follow the creek through the hills that formed the valley where the house was located. As soon as she was out of sight, however, she turned the mare north to intersect the road they'd followed into town yesterday. She'd copied the major points of the map onto the back of the family tree, which she'd found in her skirt pocket. She'd forgotten all about the photocopy that had been handed out at the reunion—six days and 120 years ago.

In the days since she'd been here, the grass seemed considerably drier. Wyoming was notorious for fickle weather, from late spring blizzards to sizzling heat waves. She supposed the climate was no different in 1876 than in 1996. If she stayed here long she might have to contend with a lack of water—in addition to nasty neighbors, no deodorant or shampoo, and Indian attacks. The list just kept getting longer, she thought, urging the mare on with a slight kick of her heels.

They cleared the hill. The ranch buildings were no longer in view. Suddenly Rebecca felt very alone. What if she did get lost? Well, she just couldn't think about that. Sitting around Sloan's big, empty house was making her crazy. She had to do something to find her great-great-grandmother, to see if she could discover why she'd survived Jordan's attack and ended up in the past. Maybe there wasn't a reason, but Rebecca didn't really believe that. In her view, most things happened for a purpose, even if a person didn't see the rationale at the time. Usually the reason became obvious later, when more facts were known, or when events culminated. She hoped that happened in this case—and soon.

Lifting the locket from inside her blouse, she touched the engraving for luck. *Please, let me find you.*

She clucked to the little roan, urging her to trot. Rebecca bounced a bit, then caught the rhythm and lifted herself from the saddle ever so slightly. She hadn't lost the ability to ride, one of her favorite activities when she'd been younger. With a smile, she cleared the hill and spotted the wagon tracks leading to town.

She *would* find Leda today, on what appeared to be a small spread between Sloan's land and Lander. And she didn't care if Leda and Sloan were having a blazing hot affair right under everyone's noses. She would not be jealous. She would not let them stop her. Even if she walked in on them in the throes of passion, she didn't care. She wouldn't let herself care.

Painted Elk had told her to listen to her heart. Right now her heart told her to get back to her own time, far away from Sloan and all his problems. Far away from this stupid attraction that had no future.

About an hour later, slightly sunburned and sore from being in the saddle, Rebecca drew near two people in a wagon. They looked like settlers, dressed in plain, drab clothes, the woman in a bonnet as ugly as Rebecca's. The bearded man seemed stern, a wide-brimmed hat shading his eyes.

"Hello," Rebecca said, reining her mare to a halt. She hoped they were friendlier than they looked.

"Whoa," the man called out, pulling up his team of mules.

"Would you know where I can find the Radburn ranch?"

The couple exchanged glances, the woman's eyebrows arching. The man rubbed his beard. "Well, there's no ranch. Vincent Radburn and his wife live about two miles from here."

No ranch? But the family history said that they did have a ranch. The land that Jordan inherited . . .

"Where? I mean, can you give me directions? I'm afraid I've gotten lost."

"Take this road down a piece, 'til you get to a rock shaped like a big egg. There's a road to the east. The Radburn house is yonder," he gestured, "maybe a mile down that road."

"Thank you so much." Rebecca felt a surge of excitement that overrode the saddle sores and sunburn. Leda was less than two miles away!

She waved to the unsmiling couple, then nudged the mare with her heels. Trotting down the road, Rebecca felt a sense of freedom she hadn't experienced in what seemed like ages. She was going to find the truth.

The egg-shaped boulder was just where the

man had said it would be. Rebecca was surprised she hadn't seen it yesterday, when she and Sloan had driven to town. A faint trail, cut into the earth by wagon wheels and hooves, eased over the hill to the east. No one was around, and no sign announced that she was in the right place. She wondered when street signs and address markers had become popular. She sure could have used some. She was lucky that the couple in the wagon had come along.

Fifteen minutes later, she pulled the tired, sweating roan to a halt, staring at the house, partially under construction, maybe a hundred yards away. What had started out as a modest frame farmhouse was being transformed into a two-story Victorian, much like Sloan's imposing residence. Rebecca immediately wondered if this was a coincidence, or a plan on the part of Vincent Radburn. Was he jealous of Sloan? If Leda had a relationship with Sloan—or even if she had had one in the past—that scenario was entirely probable.

Or maybe she was reading too much into the triangle.

She nudged the little mare forward, skirting the construction and finding a door on the side, near the back. The front door seemed hidden in a web of new framing. The men who were working out front stopped and stared. Rebecca felt exposed and vulnerable, although she didn't know why. Perhaps just because she felt so out of place.

Hidden from the men around the side of the

house, she swung her leg over and dismounted. For a moment she thought her knees would buckle. The unexpected exertion of riding, plus the unusual angle placed on her knees, made her legs feel like limp spaghetti.

In a moment she felt strong enough to walk to the door. Drawing in a deep breath, she knocked three times. She should have cleaned up a bit, she supposed. She imagined her face was pink and her hair unruly, even though she'd pulled it back and tied it with a strip of cloth this morning.

The door was jerked open by a frowning middle-aged woman. "What is it?" the woman asked, reminding Rebecca of the wicked witch in *The Wizard of Oz*.

"I would like to speak to Leda Radburn," Rebecca replied, standing straighter and looking the woman in the eye.

"Don't think I don't know who you are," the woman said, narrowing her eyes. "How dare you come to see Miss Leda!"

"I beg your pardon?" Rebecca couldn't believe what she was hearing. She'd done nothing to deserve this type of greeting.

"You're that woman staying with Sloan Travers. Living in sin, like the evil creature he is."

"How dare you!" Rebecca exclaimed, anger filling her at the older woman's accusatory tone and her attack on Sloan. "We're doing no such thing."

"Everyone knows what's going on out there. There's no need to deny it, not with him marching you into town and showing you off to the decent folks of Lander. He's an evil man, and his fancy woman isn't wanted here!" The woman slammed the door in Rebecca's face for emphasis.

Rebecca stood there for several seconds, trembling in anger. What a sanctimonious old prig! How dare she judge Sloan's life? Rebecca contemplated opening the door, marching in, and demanding to see Leda. She was so close! But on the other side of that closed panel the old woman could be waiting with a shotgun, or she could scream her lungs out and bring down the wrath of the "menfolk." Even if Rebecca stood there and screamed until Leda appeared, that wouldn't do much good. She'd probably just prove to the narrow-minded residents of the house that she was a "loose" woman with no manners or morals.

And Rebecca knew she could be arrested for trespassing. After last night, Sloan probably wouldn't bail her out, or even stand in her defense at her trial. What a great ending to this time journey that would be.

She turned away from the closed door and looked at the little roan mare. The horse's ears flicked forward, as if to ask, *What now?*

"Now we try Plan B," Rebecca murmured, leading the horse to the back of the house, where she noticed a trough. She'd water the mare, then plan something. She just wasn't sure what.

As the mare drank, Rebecca looked around. The modest spread didn't coincide with the family picture at all, nor did it fit with Leda's stylish dress and bearing in town yesterday. In the back of the house a flower garden was just beginning to bloom. A small gazebo graced the center, standing alone and out of place with the other rough outbuildings. A lady's garden, Rebecca thought. Leda's personal place.

She led the mare away from the water trough. There was more than one way to gain access to a person. If the front door failed, try the back, she thought with a smile. Mounting her horse and trotting away from the residence, she looked back and saw the fluttering of a lace curtain in one of the front windows. Good. Let them think she was leaving.

She circled around, glad there were plenty of rolling hills but wishing there were more trees to provide cover. She'd think of something, she vowed. With all her instincts she felt that Leda was inside that house. She had to come out sooner or later.

Rebecca found a dry gully in which to hide her horse, then crab-walked to the top of a small hill overlooking the house. Midafternoon sun beat down on her back as she lay on her stomach, watching for Leda to emerge. Before long, the stern-looking woman who had denied Rebecca entrance came out the door, carrying a load of wash. She watched the woman hang sheet after sheet on the line stretching across the rear of the yard. A few small buildings were located behind the clothesline, probably a smokehouse or something of the like.

Rebecca smiled. If Leda came out, there would be a way to get to her.

Sweat ran down her sides and between her

breasts as Rebecca continued to lie on the sandy ground. Baked on one side and ready for basting, she thought that perhaps she should return to Sloan's ranch. She could come back tomorrow, she thought. And the next and the next, if necessary.

She pushed herself to her hands and knees, then stopped, startled by the sound of a door closing. She flattened to the ground, her heart pounding. Leda Radburn came around the back of the house, holding the hand of a dark-haired toddler. Leda appeared happy and young, not at all the woman Rebecca had seen in town yesterday. Quickly, she backed down the hill, skirting around so she could come up behind the outbuildings.

Leda's laughter and the giggles of the child drifted through the summer air. *Another relative*, Rebecca thought, amazed again that she was seeing her family history unfolding. She just hoped and prayed that there would be no more surprises like the one she'd discovered yesterday.

Darting among the fluttering sheets, she advanced on the gazebo, where Leda sat playing with the child. Rebecca wished she had memorized the family tree, because she couldn't remember from which of Leda's children she was descended. She might very well be staring at her own great-grandfather.

Rebecca edged closer, unsure of her reception. It occurred to her, for the first time, that Leda may not be glad to see her. That she could be as hostile as that old biddy who had answered the door. That Rebecca could still end up in jail or shot by some irate ancestor.

She stopped near the gazebo behind Leda, gazing at the play between mother and child. Leda appeared to glow with maternal pride and joy. The little boy ran around the interior of the whitewashed structure, giggling at a butterfly he couldn't quite catch. Leda grabbed him around the waist, stopping him from running down the step.

"Robert, be careful," Leda admonished.

The boy giggled in reply. Leda twirled a daisy, fascinating the child. Rebecca smiled again at the picture they presented, Leda in a plain blue calico dress and Robert in short pants and a tiny checked shirt. Rebecca hated to disrupt the peaceful scene, but she wasn't sure how much time she would have.

"Mrs. Radburn?" she asked softly.

Leda looked up in alarm. Robert stopped playing and focused on Rebecca. She saw little resemblance between mother and son, but as the little boy ran to his mother, his blue eyes wide, Rebecca knew she'd seen those features before. Deep-set, troubled eyes in a strong face, and a lock of dark hair that defied taming.

Sloan's face. And Robert was his son.

Chapter Eight

Rebecca stared at Robert until the child fidgeted and tried to climb into Leda's lap. Only then did Rebecca look away from his startling features to gaze with equal fascination at her great-great-grandmother.

"He's a very handsome little boy," she said finally, hoping to divert attention away from her rather abrupt, sneaky entry.

Leda hugged him close. "Yes, he is." She shifted Robert to her lap. "But I'm sure that's not why you're here. I must say you have nerve to seek me out."

"I . . . I suppose I do. I know what I'm doing isn't the socially acceptable way to approach my . . . problem, but I just had to see you."

"After seeing who you were with yesterday in town I would suspect that I would be the last person you wanted to meet."

"Sloan hasn't said a word about you." That wasn't exactly true; Sloan had implied that he despised Leda. "As a matter of fact, he refuses to speak of you or your husband."

Leda blinked, looking suddenly shaken. She recovered her composure quickly, however, and said, "I am thankful for that small favor."

"I know you think it odd that I found you, and that I need to speak with you, but something even more . . . strange has happened to me. I won't bore you with the details, just that Sloan found me on the range about a week ago. I had been strangled."

"Strangled? But who did such a thing?"

"I . . . I can't say," Rebecca hedged, knowing that she couldn't reveal everything to Leda. She wouldn't believe in time travel any more than Sloan. "At first I thought I was dead. When I woke up I was at Sloan's ranch, upstairs in a bedroom."

"Sloan always did have a habit of bringing home strays," Leda said, looking away.

She looked very sad, Rebecca thought.

"Not that I was comparing you to an animal," Leda said quickly.

"No insult taken," Rebecca replied gently. "I don't know Sloan very well. He's a very private person."

"He wasn't always so," Leda said, her eyes focused on something Rebecca couldn't see, or even imagine. "Once he was laughing and bright. He was kind, but he loved to play and tease."

161

"You knew him when you were children?"

"Yes," Leda said, setting Robert on the floor of the gazebo and giving him a piece of hard stick candy from her pocket. "We grew up together in Philadelphia."

"Wyoming is a long way from home for both of you."

"Yes, it is. Sometimes I miss it dreadfully."

"Then why did you leave?"

"I wanted to, at the time." Leda obviously tried to school her features, taking a deep breath. "My reasons are not open for discussion."

"But you didn't return to your family?"

Leda shuddered, her face drawn and sad. "No, not after . . . I couldn't go back." She shrugged off her melancholy with what seemed to be practiced ease. "Now I'm married and settled here."

And you had Sloan's child, Rebecca said to herself. "Sloan mentioned something about the Civil War. I suppose he served as an officer for the Union?"

"Yes, he did."

"I saw the sash in his parlor. Did you make it for him?"

Leda stood, pacing the gazebo in a swirl of blue. "I'd rather not talk about those days. And I'm still not sure why you are here, Miss . . . ?"

"Rebecca Hartford." What could she tell Leda about why she was here? What would make sense?

"Well, Miss Hartford?"

"I don't want you to think I'm being rude. And please don't think I'm judging either you or

162

Sloan, but I saw the way you looked at him yesterday, and I know the way he reacts to you. He's angry, but he won't speak of his feelings."

Leda's face flushed. "I hardly think that my . . . that any previous relationship I had with Sloan is your business."

"Under normal circumstances I would totally agree. But you see, I believe that I'm here in Wyoming for a reason. I don't know what that reason might be, and the only way I can find out is by asking questions."

"Are you saying that you have a memory loss?"

"Something like that."

"Then let me assure you, I have never seen you before in my life, which further emphasizes my statement that what happened between myself and Sloan is not your affair."

Rebecca closed her eyes and took a deep breath. How could she explain without revealing the truth? "I know this will sound odd to you, but I think there is a connection between us. Don't you wonder why we look so much alike?"

"There is a resemblance," Leda admitted grudgingly, "but that doesn't prove a thing. It could be a coincidence."

No, it isn't, Rebecca thought, but she couldn't say that to Leda. "Sloan believes that you or your husband hired me to spy on him."

"What? Why, that is preposterous! Why would we do that?"

"I have no idea. But because I look like you, Sloan believes I am working with you somehow. Or perhaps even related to you."

"He's not thinking clearly. He's bitter . . . and confused."

"What is he confused about?" Rebecca asked, frowning at Leda's comment.

"His past. I tried to tell him that he must forget the past and get on with his life, but he never would listen. He can be too stubborn for his own good."

"You think that he dwells on whatever happened because he's stubborn?"

"Of course. If he wasn't, he could put it behind him. He could have had a fine life, but instead he wallows in the past like a priest wearing a hair shirt."

"Leda, I know you've been closer to Sloan than I have, but I really don't think he's hurting because he's stubborn."

"You know nothing about him then," Leda said vehemently. Even Robert stopped his play and gazed at his mother. "I know!" Her face changed suddenly, as though she'd lost the ability to maintain a strong facade. "I know," she whispered.

Rebecca stepped forward, wanting to comfort the other woman, but the thunder of hoofbeats stopped her. Pulling his lathered horse to a stop, Vincent Radburn dismounted, trampling the fragile blooms of Leda's garden under his boots.

"What are you doing here?" he said angrily, approaching Rebecca with hate-filled eyes.

Robert started to cry, and Leda swooped him into her arms.

"I came to visit Leda," Rebecca said, trying to maintain her cool in the face of his anger. She took an involuntary step backward.

"You're not wanted here," he growled. "Get back to that bastard that's keeping you. Crawl back to him, but leave my wife alone."

Rebecca straightened, her fists clenched. "Sloan was kind enough to give me a place to stay when—"

"I'll not listen to your lies, you Jezebel. Get off my property now, or I'll throw you off."

"Vincent, please! You wouldn't harm a lady," Leda said in a consoling, soothing voice.

"She's no lady," he spat. "She's the whore of that bastard. And if I catch her on my property again, she'll be sorry she ever set foot in this part of the territory."

"Believe me, I already am," Rebecca said, looking him dead in the eye. "Good-bye, Mrs. Radburn. I'm sorry to have troubled you."

She turned and walked away, around the flapping sheets, behind the outbuildings. All the while she felt Vincent Radburn's gaze on her back, boring into her with rays hotter than the sun.

She broke into a run as she cleared the hill, then slowed as she reached the little roan mare. Taking several deep breaths, she wasn't surprised to note that her hands were shaking. She retrieved the jar of water, taking several long swallows of the tepid liquid.

After a moment she felt more in control. Even though her mount seemed spooked by Rebecca's nervousness, she swung herself into the saddle and rode away, trying to remember each word of her conversation with Leda. Trying to put Vincent's hateful words from her mind.

She blinked back tears as she urged the mare into a slow canter. She'd told herself that it wouldn't matter, that she could have discovered Sloan in the arms of Leda and still not care. But she did care. Especially now, after knowing that this other woman had grown up with him, had known him through good times and bad, had borne his child. Had loved him.

It mattered.

By the time Sloan rode into the barn he was certain he should have taken a pistol with him and ended his life last night. His head pounded and he'd stopped twice, caught in violent dry heaves. Sweat and dust coated his body. Buck was exhausted and so was he. All he wanted to do was lie down somewhere cool and quiet.

Slim came out of the feed room, his wrinkled face even more sour than usual. "You look like hell," he said without preamble.

"I feel like hell," Sloan said, swinging his leg over the saddle and stepping down. Every inch of his body ached. "Take care of Buck for me, will you? I'm going inside."

"Sure 'nough, boss." Slim led Buck into an empty stall. "By the way, that Rebecca woman rode out of here before lunch."

Sloan stopped, bracing one hand against the doorframe for support, rubbing his scratchy eyes with the other. "What?"

"Took the little roan mare and went for a ride.

Said she was going to have a picnic."

"Hell and damnation," Sloan cursed. If his head didn't already hurt so much, he would have pounded it against the barn door. "She just cut out, all by herself?"

"Well, I told her it weren't a good idea, but she said she wanted to get out. I told her to follow the crick and stay on your land."

"Hell, Slim, she doesn't know where my land ends. She could be anywhere."

"Said she wouldn't go far."

"And you believed her?"

"Weren't no reason not to."

No, Sloan had to admit, there wasn't a reason to distrust Rebecca from Slim's point of view. Only someone who had been inside the study last night would know that she was one mad woman. Sloan still didn't understand why she'd run out, but who could understand women?

Right now all he felt was a sense of panic that Rebecca, who didn't have an ounce of sense when it came to practical matters, was out roaming the range. Her mare could get spooked, go lame, or run off. She could come across mountain men, miners who hadn't seen a white woman in ages, or Indians on the prowl. She could simply get lost and not have the sense to let the mare find her way home.

"Hell and damnation," he said again. "What time is it now?"

Slim walked outside and looked at the sun. "Near on three o'clock, I'd say."

"She should have been back by now."

"Boss, that mare has plenty of sense. Besides, I told yer gal that if she got lost, she should just let the mare find her way home."

"Thank heavens for small favors," Sloan murmured, ignoring the way Slim called Rebecca his "gal." "Get another horse saddled for me. I'm riding out after her."

"I'll go, Boss. You look about as lively as the underbelly of a trout before it hits the fry pan."

"I feel even worse, and I'm going anyway. Now get me a horse and I might forget you didn't use a lick of sense when you let her ride out of here."

"Yes, Boss."

Sloan walked to the trough and stuck his head into the water. When he straightened up, rivulets ran down his shirt, giving him the shivers as his hot skin cooled. He couldn't tell where the sweat ended and the water began, but he didn't want to take time to change clothes. Every minute Rebecca was gone gave her another chance to get into trouble. Besides, his shirt would dry on the trail, chasing after that fool woman.

Slim led a long-legged bay gelding out of the barn. "Like I said, I told her to follow the crick," Slim reiterated, pointing west to the route of Twin Creek through the hills.

Sloan would bet Rebecca wouldn't stay on course. She'd probably taken off at the first chance to see some of her "precious" antelope. Or to pick flowers. Or something. Who knew how a woman's mind worked?

Or she could have been so disgusted by his lusty behavior that she'd run off.

"If I'm not back by sundown, build a fire in the yard. Maybe she'll have enough sense to follow it home."

"What about you, Boss? You probably ought to ride with someone."

Sloan swung into the saddle. "I'll be fine. Just keep an eye out for Rebecca."

He kicked the bay into a gallop, covering the distance to the creek in no time flat. Only then did he pull up and look for any tracks that the mare's small hooves might have made. He found only one, in the soft dirt of the creek bed. He thought Rebecca might have crossed over there. He looked around. Carefully circling, he looked for more indications of the way she'd gone. Unfortunately, the soil was dry and hard nearby, and he didn't find another clear hoof print.

"Damn," he muttered as he turned the gelding toward the foothills. Maybe she'd done just as Slim had suggested. About two miles up ahead was a stand of cottonwoods that would make a fine picnic site. Maybe she'd stopped there. If so, there should be hoof prints. If not, there was no telling where she was.

He kicked the gelding into a canter, following the route of the stream, praying that Rebecca hadn't gotten lost on the prairie . . . again. Only this time, she might get more than a ring of bruises around her neck.

The thought of her lying broken or lifeless made his heart pound and his pulse race. He didn't try to analyze those reactions; he was too busy racing toward the sun.

* * *

Rebecca was almost to the turnoff to Sloan's ranch when she saw a rider galloping toward her. Her tears had dried long ago; in their place a determination grew to fight both the attraction and the sympathy she felt toward Sloan. She was bone tired, emotionally exhausted, and all she wanted was to take a bath and fall into bed.

The rider grew closer. Rebecca squinted. The afternoon sun was full upon the man, washing out his features in the brightness. She wasn't sure, but he looked a lot like Sloan. Galloping off to see his true love, perhaps?

She took a deep breath and told herself not to think such thoughts. Sloan could visit whomever he pleased. His lover, his son . . .

She absolutely could not mention that she'd visited Leda, or learned that Robert was Sloan's son, or that she'd been verbally abused by Vincent and the Radburn housekeeper. No, she definitely couldn't tell Sloan what she'd really been up to this afternoon.

He pulled his lathered horse to a stop facing her, his face flushed. She wondered if it was from the sun or from anger.

"Dammit, woman, are you truly crazy?"

Well, that answered one question. "No, for the thousandth time, I'm not crazy. I'm sorry if you didn't want me to borrow a horse, but you didn't say—"

"You could have gotten lost, or killed, or raped. I thought those three men scared you plenty the other day. What will it take to make you understand that this is no city park?"

She straightened in the saddle, despite being so tired that all she wanted to do was slump over the mare's head and plod into the barn. "I don't think I was in any danger. Mostly I stayed on the road."

"What about your claim to Slim that you were just going on a picnic?" Sloan asked belligerently. "Or does your word mean nothing?"

"I did follow the creek . . . for a ways. Then I decided it would be safer to ride on this road. After all, I know it heads into town."

"And you think nothing could happen to you because you're on a *road*? Lady, that's not how things work out here. This *road* is barely more than a set of ruts in a prairie."

"Well, nothing happened to me or the mare. So if you'll excuse us, we'll be heading to the barn."

"Excuse you? I ought to do what your daddy didn't and turn you over my knee!"

"I won't put up with any violence, not from you or any other man. I'm not some child who can be spanked or put to bed without supper."

"You're damn sure acting like a child. And a spoiled one, at that."

"I'm not going to argue with you. I'm tired and so is this horse." She nudged the mare forward.

Sloan swung his mount around and rode beside her. "I'm not finished with you."

She pulled the mare to a halt and turned toward Sloan. "Yes, you are. You were finished with me last night, when you thought I was another woman. I don't pinch hit for anyone, especially not my . . . her."

Sloan's face showed his confusion, but she wasn't sure why. "You don't *what* for *whom*?"

"My own great-great-grandmother, you dolt!" Rebecca urged the mare into a trot. "I won't be a substitute for her."

Sloan pulled up beside her. "She's nobody's grandmother, and I didn't confuse you with her."

"Oh, yeah? Well, it sure sounded like it to me." She nudged the mare again, breaking into a canter.

Sloan yelled at his own horse, who was blowing hard. "I don't know what you're talking about, but—"

"Of course you don't! You were as drunk as a skunk."

"I wasn't too drunk to know who was kissing me back."

"That's a mistake I won't make again." She slowed her mare to a walk, since it was obvious they were having a full-blown argument right here in front of God and anyone who happened by. At this rate, the horses would expire of exhaustion before she and Sloan finished yelling at each other. "And where were you this morning?"

"Sleeping it off."

"Not in your own bedroom," Rebecca scoffed.

"Not in anyone's bedroom."

"I suppose no one else is good enough for you, isn't that right?"

"What the hell are you talking about?"

"If you can't have Leda, you don't want anyone else. Is that it?"

"Hell, I don't want Leda. She's a liar and a cheat."

"I'm glad you two have such a mutual admiration society going, but I don't want any part of it."

"Quit using those damn-fool words and speak straight."

"Look, Sloan, you made it very clear last night that you wanted Leda, not me. *I* wasn't drunk. *I* remember."

"I remember that part to, and I didn't say any such thing."

"Okay, then, what did you say?" Rebecca pulled her mare to a halt and stared at Sloan. "What sensitive, loving words did you murmur in my ear?"

He turned an even brighter shade of red, glaring at her from bloodshot eyes. "Dammit," he growled, then he kicked his horse into a gallop, heading into the barn without a backward glance.

Rebecca shook her head. She wasn't sure why he always ran away, but he had a definite pattern of behavior. Many men weren't comfortable discussing their feelings, but Sloan had an outright aversion to any emotions. She was sure that if he could become a robot, he'd jump at the chance. All he wanted to do was work, work, work . . . and blame Leda Radburn for some wrong done months or years ago.

Well, let him sulk. Let him stew. She wasn't

going to get involved in his life; not when she had problems of her own.

With a sigh, she nudged the little mare into a walk and headed toward the barn. By the time she arrived, Sloan had dismounted, handed his sweating horse over to Slim, and stalked out of the barn. With only one glare in her direction, he headed into the house.

Rebecca dismounted, her legs rubbery, her spirits low. Who was she trying to fool? She was involved in Sloan's life, whether she wanted to be or not. Somehow, all these details were tied together. Leda's child was Sloan's son. Rebecca knew enough about the past to realize that a son, an heir, was every man's dream. So why was Leda married to Vincent Radburn?

As she struggled to unsaddle the mare, she thought again of the chubby, pink-cheeked little boy with Sloan's hair and eyes. He was a darling, a child any parent would be proud to claim. So why hadn't Sloan claimed him? Why had he let Leda marry another man?

Chapter Nine

The next afternoon, Rebecca approached Sloan's study with a bit of trepidation. She'd spent a lot of time thinking—about him, about her, about Leda and Robert—and she'd finally decided that she and Sloan had to come to terms with each other.

And she'd also realized Sloan wasn't the flexible one in this relationship.

"Sloan?"

He jerked to attention from his seated position, leaning over what appeared to be account books. Apparently he'd been deep in thought. His hair looked as though he'd finger combed it, again and again, until it rested in waves over the tops of his ears and curled against his shirt collar. As she watched, he rubbed his eyes, then focused on her as she stood in the doorway.

"What is it?"

"I was wondering if you'd like to have dinner together tonight." There; she'd made the first move.

He narrowed his eyes, his brows nearly touching. "Why?"

"Well, because we'd talked about eating a meal together, and I thought this would be a good time."

He rubbed the furrows in his forehead. "When a woman starts acting nice I get a little suspicious. What is it you really want?"

"Nothing. I just thought it would be nice to share a meal." She kept her temper carefully under control, not wanting him to see how his distrust hurt her. For some reason she usually lashed out at him—distinctively atypical behavior for her. She'd always considered herself very even-natured. But not around Sloan; faced with his skepticism, she resorted to equally caustic remarks.

She'd analyzed this last night. Now, in the light of day, she had a hard time remembering to "be nice" to her reluctant host.

"I don't mean to be rude, but twenty-four hours ago you were pretty riled at me. It's enough to make a man skittish."

Rebecca took a deep breath and smiled. "I decided that I was wrong to take your horse off on a ride without asking permission first, and—"

"I wasn't angry about the damned horse and you know it."

"All right. Why don't we just forget about that

for now, if you won't accept my apology?"

"I didn't hear an apology."

You would have if you'd just shut up, Rebecca fumed to herself. Instead of lashing out, she said very carefully, "Very well, I'm sorry to have caused you concern."

"And it won't happen again?"

"And I will do my best not to cause you any more problems."

"I still think you're up to something."

Rebecca ignored his rude comment. "Should I tell Claudia we'll be dining together?"

Sloan tore his gaze away from her. "That's fine," he said with a sigh. "But I don't want to cause Claudia any extra work."

"Don't worry; I'll serve the meal myself." She turned away and walked quickly to the dining room.

"Okay, it took some effort," she said to herself as she smoothed a linen tablecloth over the dark, polished wood, "but you did it. You kept your temper."

Now, all she had to do was get through an entire meal without blowing up.

Sloan pushed his plate away from the edge of the table, then dabbed both sides of his mouth with a napkin. "That's all for me." He placed the soiled linen on the table and started to rise.

"Would you like some coffee?"

He stopped, looking at Rebecca as she sat across from him. She needed a new dress, he thought suddenly, something in dark green.

Something beside the plain white blouse and dull brown skirt, or the outfit she'd been wearing when he found her. Damn, why did he have to keep thinking about her? Of course, it was difficult not to when she sat across from him.

Yesterday's outing had colored her skin a deep rose, truly an unflattering color for a lady. But he didn't find the color unappealing on her. Despite her red-blond hair and normally light complexion, he found her slightly sunburned skin and dusting of freckles oddly attractive.

"Sloan? Would you like some coffee?"

He shook himself mentally, tearing his thoughts away from Rebecca's physical appearance. He had to remember who she was—a mysterious stranger who made wild statements and might have a connection to the Radburns.

"Sure, I'll have a cup." He schooled his features, knowing that her odd mood today might be some devious ploy to make him drop his defenses. Still, he was curious about what she really wanted from him. Would she ask for some favor now that she'd apologized for riding off yesterday? She said that wasn't her intention, but he wasn't convinced.

She pushed back her chair and hurried into the kitchen. He should have risen and pulled her chair out for her, but she'd moved so quickly. Besides, he wasn't used to being around ladies anymore. Despite what he thought of Rebecca's past or her present motives, she exhibited a culture and grace that came from a higher-class background. She confused him, because she was both bold and polished, a combination not usually found in ladies.

"I made the coffee myself," she announced, setting down a tray on the table. "I hope it's okay. I've been practicing, but before coming here I'd never made boiled coffee."

"How did you make it?"

She hesitated only a moment. "In something called a drip coffee maker. The hot water drips through the grounds and into a carafe."

"Interesting," he said, taking a cup. It smelled fine and looked like coffee rather than river bottom mud. "I've never heard of such a thing."

"Well, there's a reason for that, but I won't go into detail," she said, adding sugar and cream to her cup.

Probably something to do with her claims that she was from the future, that mystical place she'd created in her mind. He took a sip of coffee. "The coffee's fine."

She looked at him from the corner of her eye. "Thank you so much," she said softly, but he detected a hint of sarcasm in her reply.

Perhaps she was looking for greater praise for mastering coffee-brewing skills. He wasn't that kind of man. She'd come to the wrong place if she needed constant approval. She stood have stayed in a more civilized area, where life wasn't a struggle against man, beast, and nature.

"How was your day?" she asked after they'd sipped their coffee for a minute or more.

"What?"

"I mean, what did you do today? I've never un-

derstood what 'riding the range' really means."
She placed her cup on the saucer and looked at
him with wide, innocent eyes.

He leaned back in his chair, wondering again
what she was up to. This conversation was way
too friendly. What he did was no secret, though.
He did what any cattleman did on a daily basis,
and anyone who knew cattle would know this.
"We check the creeks and wells, make sure no
cows or calves are injured. Make sure predators
aren't making off with calves. Just the usual
things."

"That sounds pretty routine. What would you
do if you discovered a dead cow, for example?"

"Try to find out what killed her," he said with
a shrug.

"What would you look for?"

He leaned forward, resting his elbows on the
table and glaring at her. "What's this all about?"

She looked taken aback. "I'm just making conversation. I'd like to learn more about what you
do."

"Why?"

She shrugged. "Because I'm interested."

"Why?"

"What difference does it make!" she said,
throwing up her hands in a universal expression
of frustration. "I want to know more about you
and about this place where I find myself."

He shook his head. "It sounds to me like you're
trying to spy on my routines to find any weaknesses I might have. Sounds to me like I might

have to watch my back even more than I do now."

"Dam . . . darn it, Sloan, I'm not spying on you! I don't have anything to do with Vincent Radburn. I'm not helping him ruin you, financially or otherwise."

"That's a fine speech, but from where I'm sitting your behavior is suspect. And you shouldn't curse."

She took a deep breath, obviously struggling with her emotions as she rested her clenched fists on the table. Finally, she responded, "I'm sorry I yelled. I promised myself I wouldn't get angry or frustrated. You just seem to bring out the worst in me."

Maybe she brought out the worst in him, too. He knew that ever since she'd shown up, his normal level-headedness had been missing. His own emotions ran riot, along with his body's response to her as a woman. He couldn't be sure any longer if he was thinking with his mind or something a little lower.

"I think maybe we get under each other's skins," he admitted.

She seemed surprised that he'd confessed that much. Perhaps he was, too. He wasn't a talker. He'd been raised in a family that believed in keeping emotions under control, in conforming to a strict set of rules that didn't include dinner table revelations. His mother was the epitome of propriety, his father an example to the community.

Unfortunately, those skills didn't hold much

water in the uncivilized territory of Wyoming.

"I'll try my best to control my responses," she offered, relaxing her hands, palms down on the table.

"And I'll try not to provoke you," he said.

With a smile, she snaked her right hand across the table, coming perilously close to touching him . . . again. He stared at her hand as though it were a serpent ready to strike. For the first time he knew how Adam must have felt in the garden.

"Don't look so appalled. I just thought we could shake on it."

Shake on it? What he wanted to do was grab her, pull her toward him across the table, and kiss her until she was trembling. He might have been drunk two nights ago, but he had no trouble remembering the kiss they'd shared, and his body's response to her.

"You've got to understand one thing," he warned. "I'm a man . . . I'm no monk. If you don't want the townspeople to really have something to talk about, don't tempt me."

"I haven't tempted you any more than you've tempted me," she replied with a bit of belligerence.

Damn, didn't the woman have one bit of sense? She should never have admitted such a thing, especially to a man who'd just confessed to lusting after her. He felt his face flush with a combination of incredulity and embarrassment.

"What I mean is, I kissed you once, then you kissed me, so I think we're even."

"Can we not talk about this?" he said quickly,

rising from his chair. "Let's just agree that it won't happen again."

"Fine with me," she said, pushing back her chair.

He reached back to assist her, as he belatedly realized he should have done earlier, and in doing so, his forearm brushed against her shoulder. He pulled back, feeling as inept as a schoolboy.

"That's okay," she said quickly. "I'm not used to men waiting on me."

"I wasn't—never mind," he replied. "We're in agreement then?"

"Right," she said, taking a deep breath and looking at him in that direct, unwavering way she had. "No arguing, no kissing. We'll try to be polite."

"Good," he said, nodding. "Well, then, thank you for the meal and the coffee."

"I enjoyed it."

He looked at her for a moment, thinking what a proud, feisty woman she was, and what control it must have taken her to hold herself in check. "Look, I really didn't mind that you took out the mare. She's too small for most riders. If you want her, she's yours."

"Mine?"

"Yes. Just take care of her."

Her face softened, and her eyes appeared misty. "Oh, Sloan, thank you. That's so sweet of you. I'll take excellent care of her."

He looked away. She appeared too soft, too vulnerable at the moment, and he was afraid he'd act on his earlier impulse. "I have a little work to do." Before she could say anything to push him over the edge of propriety, he walked out of the dining room, heading for the solitude of his study.

Rebecca smiled as she stacked the plates, flatware, cups, and saucers in a precarious pile. Carrying them into the kitchen, she mumbled, "He gives me a horse, then assumes that I'll do the dishes." How like a man.

She scraped food from the plates into a pail for the couple of hogs Claudia kept, as she'd explained to Rebecca earlier. Then she mixed the heated water she'd put on the stove earlier with the foul-smelling soap and dunked all the dishes into the galvanized sink.

"It's definitely not an automatic dishwasher," she said as she plunged her chafed hands into the lye soap mixture. *Add hand lotion to the list of items I really need,* she added silently.

Before long, however, she had the kitchen cleaned and ready for Claudia to prepare breakfast tomorrow morning. Outside, the sun had set, and a cool breeze blew through the windows on the east and north walls. If she were back in her time, Rebecca thought, she'd take a walk tonight, perhaps the six blocks to the shop that sold frozen yogurt. Yes, a chocolate and vanilla swirl would be great tonight.

But there was no frozen yogurt, or even a sinfully rich scoop of Ben and Jerry's waiting in the freezer. With a sigh she spread the dishtowel over the sink and blew out the oil lamp on the table.

Tonight she'd made some inroads with Sloan. He'd shown that he trusted her enough to give her the mare. She'd call the evening a success. So why wasn't she happy? She took a quick mental inventory as she walked through the silent dining room and into the hallway. She realized that she was lonely. She missed her new neighbors, even though she'd only seen the young couple across from her apartment once and the older man living below her twice.

And she missed being able to call her family and friends on the phone, talking long into the night if she wished. She missed traffic and noise, summer movie releases, and even the evening news, although it was frequently depressing. She missed her own century, and she wanted to go home.

Tonight she would let Sloan work on his books, or whatever he did in his study at night. They'd made progress. Tomorrow, she'd take it one small step further, and each night after that she'd try to ease more into his world. There was no use fighting her existence here; she needed to make him comfortable with her presence.

With a tiny stab of guilt, she realized that she was deceiving him, although not for the Radburns' benefit, but for her own. For her survival in the past, and for her possible return to the future. Instinctively, she knew that she must figure out exactly why Sloan, Leda, and Vincent were involved in her predicament. Something had happened between Sloan and Leda; Rebecca knew that something was going to happen that affected her future. She felt it in the stillness of the days, in the brightness of the sun, in the quiet of each night, just as she could usually feel the approach of a storm.

As she walked into her bedroom and lit the lamp, she remembered the most startling piece of information she'd learned in the last two days. Although Robert was obviously Sloan's son, the cute, chubby infant was not her great-grandfather.

He was Jordan's ancestor. And somehow that piece of the puzzle just didn't seem to fit . . . yet.

For the next two days the truce held. Rebecca began sitting in the study in the evenings, reading from Sloan's limited library of political and social texts. There were also some novels, but most were classics she had read in school. The first time she walked in and sat down, he had practically stared a hole through her. But he didn't say anything, didn't demand she get out. So she sat and read, watching him from time to time as he wrote and figured, sometimes with a great deal of frustration.

She'd curled up in Sloan's big chair and practiced her sewing, which she decided wasn't too difficult as long as she was very careful. Once she'd mended her skirt, sewing the front of the ruffle to the back. Another time she sewed a button on so tight she couldn't get it through the hole. Still, she was learning. And she had to admit to herself that part of the distraction was that she kept remembering her passionate response to Sloan's kisses and caresses, in this very chair.

Today the humidity had risen, and late this afternoon towering cumulus clouds had formed to the west. Rebecca felt the weather change as a lethargic oppression. Tonight, perhaps, there would be rain. She knew it was needed to nourish both the grass and the water supply. Sloan seemed to be particularly worried about the weather, and she knew that was normal for a rancher, whether he lived in 1876 or 1996.

Tonight, she was surprised when she walked into the study and found him unfolding brown paper from what appeared to be a stack of newspapers. She didn't say anything, because she knew that Sloan hated to be quizzed, but as she passed the desk, she noticed the printed name on the wrapping: Mrs. Donovan Travers, Philadelphia, Pennsylvania.

"My mother," Sloan said.

Rebecca's gaze jumped from the parcel to Sloan's face, realizing that he knew she was "spying" on him. Instead of censure, she found him almost smiling. Almost. He seemed amused by her curiosity.

"I . . . I remember you picked up a package at the store the other day."

"My mother sends me the newspaper from home," he said softly, looking at the stack as though it were a rare, illuminated manuscript from the Middle Ages.

"You miss your hometown," Rebecca said with

certainty. *Just like Leda,* she added silently.

Sloan shrugged. "I grew up there. I like to be informed about what is happening. . . ."

"Back in civilization," Rebecca finished for him.

"I don't want to go back," he said, "if that's what you're thinking. My land is here. And I'm staying, no matter what others want."

She had no doubt who those "others" might be. "Of course. You can miss your home without wanting to live there again. I'm sure you have many fond memories." *Like teasing Leda and being a playful child.*

"I left there a long time ago."

"Before the war?" Rebecca asked.

"During the war. And that's another topic not open to discussion." He turned away in obvious dismissal, unfolding a newspaper as though he could hide behind it. His actions reminded her of arrogant male leads in old black-and-white movies who could dismiss their wives or girl-friends with the flick of a crisp sheet of newsprint.

"Okay, I can take a hint." Rebecca picked up the book she was reading and sat in the big chair. Soon, however, she found the text boring and longed for the more concise reporting found in a journalistic approach. Her fingers itched to snatch one of the newspapers, even though the news would be a hundred and twenty years old to her.

She finally couldn't stand it any longer. She pushed herself from the chair and walked to the desk. "Do you mind if I read the one you just finished?"

Sloan looked up as though he might say something, but then he shrugged and said, "Help yourself."

She retrieved an edition marked May 2, 1876. The print was tiny and there weren't too many illustrations, but at least it was a newspaper. She loved to read the Sunday paper at home, cover to cover, while drinking coffee. Yes, that was what they needed tonight.

After dropping the paper on the seat of the chair she walked into the kitchen and measured coffee grounds into the metal pot, adding a dash of salt, as her grandfather had taught her, to cut the bitterness. The stove was still warm from Claudia's dinner preparations, so it didn't take long to kindle new wood and get the water boiling. Before long, she had a fragrant pot of brew that reminded her of those lazy Sunday mornings.

Carrying two mugs back into the study, she placed one on Sloan's desk. He was obviously surprised.

"Thank you," he finally said, looking at her suspiciously, as though she had some ulterior motive for fixing coffee.

"You're welcome," she said cheerfully, curling back up in the chair with her newspaper. Let him be suspicious. Sooner or later he'd begin to trust her, and then she would find some answers.

She read until the words blurred. With a sigh, she leaned her head against the winged back and briefly closed her tired eyes. A cooler breeze blew through the open window; she could smell the rain in the air, along with the scent of horses and the dried grasses of the prairie. In her mind she visualized the dark drapes, stirring ever so slightly. At the desk she heard Sloan continue to turn pages, and she smiled in reply. She'd just keep her eyes closed a little while longer.

"Rebecca," Sloan said, in what he hoped was a controlled, normal voice. She slept like a child, as though she was innocent of the world and all its dangers. Perhaps she was; at times, she didn't seem to have an understanding of the harshness and perils that plagued most people. When faced with reality she seemed surprised, even appalled.

But she was no child. Her breasts rose and fell in an enticing rhythm beneath the white blouse. The redness had faded from her face, leaving a smattering of freckles across her nose, cheeks, and forehead. Her lips were parted just enough for him to remember how sweet her kisses could be. And she rested in the very chair where he'd almost made love to her the other night.

That alone was enough to arouse him to the point of distraction.

He wondered if she had any idea how often his thoughts drifted to her as she sat in the study, sewing or reading. He tried to mask his fascination with her, but he had no idea if she could read the desire that was always just beneath the surface. He wished, at times like this, that he was a man without morals, someone who could kiss her parted lips, caress her breasts, and explore her body, even while she slept. And if she woke and struggled, he wouldn't stop. He wouldn't ask for permission. He'd take what he wanted.

But he wasn't a man like that. His mother and father had raised him to be a gentleman, even though he didn't always act that way when he'd had half a bottle of bourbon. He'd been taught to protect women and children, but soldiers didn't follow those rules in the heat of battle, or in the euphoria of triumph. He'd seen blood lust turn to desire of another kind, and he'd seen the women who had been the recipient of such brutish behavior. He didn't want to remember the dazed look of horror on their faces, but they haunted him still.

Women who had once been cosseted and protected, women with soft, Southern accents, women who tried to maintain the gentility of their lives in the midst of devastation. He'd seen their faces while they watched their homes burn, as their children were pushed into the dirt by soldiers intent on destruction. He'd seen them shoved to the ground when they fought the soldiers who torched their houses and barns, their white petticoats pushed aside by dirty, grasping hands.

Sherman had been praised for his triumphant march across Georgia by the military leaders in Washington, and by the public, who wanted to punish the South for its effrontery. But Sloan had seen the burned homes and fields, the slaughtered animals and shattered lives, and he couldn't see the triumph in such actions. His superior officers had restrained him from interfering in the "normal duties" of the soldiers. They ridiculed him for his softness toward the enemy, threatening a court-martial if he didn't stop his protests.

He was one man against an army, so he had turned away. He'd blocked out the screams of the women, the cries of the children, and performed his duties as a supply officer in silence. He did what he could to control his men, but he couldn't counter the orders of other officers. He could only turn away.

He realized that his fists were clenched tightly, that the blood pounded in his temples. He made a conscious effort to relax his tight muscles and school his features. There was still the small problem of waking Rebecca and getting her upstairs to bed.

"Rebecca," he said, louder this time. He placed a hand on her shoulder and shook her just a bit.

She opened her eyes slowly. He was reminded of the first time he'd seen her, lying so still on the prairie, and the first time he'd looked into her eyes as she lay on the bed upstairs. The same gut-tightening sensation hit him now.

"What is it?" she said sleepily.

"It's late. I'm going up to bed."

"Okay," she murmured, then closed her eyes again.

"Rebecca," he said, touching her shoulder. "Wake up."

She opened her eyes, smiled, and said softly, "Sloan."

He almost took her into his arms and carried her upstairs. Almost. At the last minute he remembered that they had an agreement: No fighting, no kissing. And if he did carry her to her bedroom—or to his—kissing would be involved.

"It's late," he said again, rising to stand before her. "I want to turn off the lamps and close the windows. We're going to get some rain."

"I know. I smelled it earlier." She stretched, pulling the blouse tight against her chest. He watched, fascinated against his will, by the outline of her undergarments beneath the cotton. What was the woman wearing, if not a corset? But then she finished stretching and got up, folding his newspaper as she walked the few steps to the desk.

"I didn't realize it was so late. Did I sleep long?"

"Not very." In fact, he knew she'd slept about forty-five minutes, because he'd watched her over the top of the paper every thirty seconds or so.

She smiled tentatively over her shoulder as she walked into the hall. He knew he was staring, but he couldn't help himself. He also knew she wasn't giving him a come hither look, but just being pleasant. When she wasn't arguing with him— and she hadn't been lately—she smiled a lot.

He turned away from her softness and reached for the desk lamp, turning down the wick until the flame disappeared. He did the same with the lamp on the table across the room. When the room was dark he walked to the window and pulled it down, shutting out the smell of rain and the cool wind. In the distance, probably over the mountains, lightning flashed.

They would get much-needed rain tonight. He just hoped the thunder didn't come too close, or boom too loudly.

Her sleep schedule was off again. Rebecca lay on her bed, listening to the rain pound against the closed window. The storm had started about thirty minutes ago, probably an hour after she'd gone to bed. She'd gotten up and closed the window when the rain started, but now the room seemed stuffy, especially when nature was putting on such a show outside.

She swung her legs over the bed, then walked on bare feet to the window that faced west. Lightning flashed across the sky, briefly illuminating the ground below. Puddles had formed on the dry earth, and already small rivers ran down the slight incline toward Twin Creek. Another lightning bolt crashed overhead, and Rebecca could see the outline of storm clouds overhead. Thunder boomed once, shaking the windows, and then again, making her jump.

She loved a good storm. All the power of nature, the force of wind and water, left her in awe. Of course, she liked to experience a storm from the safety of a sturdy house, and she did feel perfectly safe in Sloan's home.

With a sigh, she turned away from the window. She should probably get some sleep. She didn't want Claudia and Sloan to think she was lazy because she slept late, even if she was up half the night. She wasn't a morning person, but she did manage to get up and function at a reasonable hour. The problem she ran into was that "morning" came earlier in 1876 than in 1996.

Another flash of lightning and crash of thunder came right on top of each other as she slipped into bed. She tucked her feet beneath her and sat on the bed, listening to the reverberations of the boom. Suddenly, she heard another sound—an eerie, half-human cry. It curled around the room, as though it had a life of its own, bouncing off the wall and into her body, filling her with a bone-deep chill.

Sloan. She knew that was his cry, his pain, that she felt as a lance to her soul. With an answering cry, she leaped from the bed, her bare feet pounding across the wooden floor.

Chapter Ten

He pressed his hands over his ears as hard as he could, but he couldn't stop the sound of cannon fire and the flash of rifles in the night sky. He tossed and turned beneath his blankets, wondering how the other officers could sleep through such bombing. Maybe they were like him—cowards. Or perhaps they were exhausted and couldn't fully awaken.

He felt riveted to the floor of the farmhouse they'd commandeered. He couldn't rise, couldn't fight or run. He wasn't sure what he would do if he could get up. Sick of war, he wanted to go back home to Philadelphia, to the safe life he'd lived before being commissioned as a lieutenant in the U. S. Army. He was a weakling and a coward, frozen in fear on the floor in a Georgia farmhouse.

The cannon fire kept coming. He could hear the screams of men and horses. The enemy was right outside, and he couldn't move. He could only toss beneath the blanket, stare into the darkness, and scream with his dying men.

"Sloan, Sloan, wake up!" Rebecca grasped his shoulders with her hands, trying to shake his rigid body. She could only see his face in frequent flashes of lightning, and what she saw frightened her beyond anything she'd yet seen in the past. His normally tan face was pale, bleached white in each bright instant of light by the nightmare that gripped his mind. Rigid muscles bunched beneath cool skin, making her aware of his strength. He was a frightening stranger, and she shivered involuntarily as she realized the danger she faced in trying to wake him.

But she couldn't leave him in the grip of the terror. And she hardly had time to examine her motives.

Another anguished cry broke from his lips, and she sobbed in sympathy. He thrashed suddenly, as though he were fighting bands of steel that held him down. Her heart broke with his pain. She was getting too close, too involved with another person who needed objectivity, but she couldn't help herself. Besides, he wasn't her client.

"Sloan, please, listen to me. This is only a dream." She left one hand on his shoulder but used the other to soothe his forehead. "Only a dream. Please, wake up."

Lightning filled the room, along with the deafening boom of thunder. The storm was upon them, directly overhead, it seemed, as though nature echoed Sloan's subconscious fears. His eyes opened with the fading of the thunder, and he looked directly at her.

"Get out, Private. They're outside! We've got to retreat!"

"Sloan, no," Rebecca said firmly. His gaze bored right through her, although she was certain he didn't see her face in his mind. "It's Rebecca," she said softly. "We're in Wyoming, not in the war. You've got to wake up."

Suddenly the fire of panic faded from his eyes. He blinked. She could tell that his eyes were trying to focus in the darkness. Lightning flashed again. Sloan trembled in unison with the thunderous reverberations. "Rebecca?"

"Yes, yes. I'm here." She ran her fingers over his tense forehead, certain that he could see the concern on her face. She'd lost her objectivity, lost her professionalism somewhere on this rolling landscape of the past. She felt like a woman, not a therapist. A woman whose man was in pain.

"Rebecca," he whispered, "you shouldn't be here. You shouldn't have come." He caught her left hand, pressing it against his cheek, then bringing her fingers to his lips. He brushed his lips over the sensitive pads of her fingertips, then turned his head slightly and pressed a kiss into her palm.

Her heart leaped in response. The tension of the last few minutes changed, turning to desire in the swirl of his tongue on her tender flesh. She pushed her right hand through the thickness of his hair and leaned across his chest. "Sloan, tell me you're awake. Tell me this isn't a dream."

He grasped her shoulders, holding her against him, staring into her eyes. "Rebecca," he whispered again, pulling her across his body, "I don't want to take advantage of you."

"You're not. Not at all. This is where I want to be. This is what I want to do." Even if getting involved with Sloan was the worst possible decision, she wanted to know him as a lover, a friend, a protector in this harsh world.

"You don't know what you're saying."

"Yes, I do. I just want to know that it's *me* you're holding."

"I know you're not a dream, Rebecca. I'm not confusing you with anyone. Not now, not ever."

"Sloan," she whispered. She tried to kiss him, but he eluded her lips. Instead, he nuzzled her neck. She moaned, moving against him, giving him better access. Desire, as bright as the lightning outside, flashed through her body, then centered in a thunderous crash between her thighs.

"No kissing, remember?" He continued to tease the sensitive flesh of her throat, then an especially erotic spot on her shoulder. "Or do you want to release me from that promise?"

Her lips teased him back, tracing the cordons of his neck, nipping his shoulder lightly. His flesh tasted salty and alive, full of passion and pain.

She wanted to experience all of him, absorb every bit of sadness, until he was free of his nightmares.

He groaned, his hands lifting her nightgown and caressing her naked flesh. Calluses rasped against the sensitive skin of her bottom, but the contrast was erotic, not painful. She wanted to know all of him, from the lines around his eyes and mouth to the silky hair on his legs.

"I need you," he said, holding her tight against him. She felt his arousal, hard and pressing against her stomach through the sheet that covered him and her own thin gown. She supposed he half expected her to pull away, or to be frightened by his admission. She wasn't surprised or scared. His honesty only fueled her own passion.

"I want you," she said in reply, "and I release you from the promise." Her lips hovered over his. She could see the flare of desire in his eyes, even without light in the bedroom. "Kiss me."

He seized her mouth with a hungry promise of more, claiming her as no other man ever had. She was lost in the world of Sloan's arms, and she never wanted to find her way home. He worshipped her with his lips and tongue, branded her with each sweep of his hands.

And she knew that Sloan made love to *her*, not to some phantom of his past, not to Leda or any other woman. He needed her, and he would have her. All of her.

She pulled the sheet from between them, discovering that Sloan was naked. With a sigh of longing, she pulled away, straddled his body, and raised her nightgown over her head. Lightning flared outside and was reflected in his eyes as he caressed her with his gaze, which came to rest on her breasts. Her nipples tightened even more.

"Sloan," she whispered as she threw the nightgown across the bed.

He pushed himself to a sitting position, taking her breast hungrily in his mouth. She closed her eyes and moved against him, feeling his heat and strength with each stab of tongue and every pulse of his blood. Her thighs gripped his sides. She wanted him inside her, wanted to be one with him.

"Now, Sloan," she whispered into his thick hair.

He turned her onto her back, her head now near the foot of the bed, her legs locked around him. "Are you sure?" he asked, his voice rough with desire.

"Yes. Yes."

He plunged inside, rocking her back, her head off the side of the mattress. She held tight to his arms as he pounded against her. Staring into the blackness of the night, she felt only him, and the deep satisfaction of loving him, matching each thrust, her nails holding tight to the muscles of his back. Then she convulsed, seeing the bright explosions of color that came from the storm bursting inside her—lightning of another kind. Nature's glorious fury, centered low and deep.

With a cry, Sloan joined her in ecstasy. She

held him tight, drifting to a heaven of warmth and sunshine.

Sloan stared at the ceiling of his bedroom, although he could see nothing in the darkness. Outside, light rain pattered against the windows, no longer part of nature's furious display.

Inside, his emotions had taken up where the storm had left off. His heart had yet to return to a normal beat and his erratic breathing echoed through the room. He wondered if Rebecca even noticed, lying on her stomach, snuggled against his side with one leg wrapped over his own.

He didn't know what to say—or do—at a time like this. He'd only been in a similar situation once, and even that encounter, come to think of it, wasn't so similar. Leda had sacrificed her virginity to him, pale and trembling, like an offering to the gods. All the other times he'd coupled with a woman had been briefer, less emotional encounters, where words weren't as necessary as coin.

Rebecca's passion had equaled his own. She'd given and taken, matched him with an honest desire he'd never expected to find in a woman. The experience was so new, he wasn't sure what to think . . . and he was even less sure what she thought. She wasn't a virgin. She'd known what she was doing, of that he was certain. And yet she had none of the characteristics of a prostitute. No faked moans, no practiced moves.

Perhaps she was a widow. That would explain her lack of virginity. And if she'd been married, she must have enjoyed the marriage bed. She missed making love. Yes, that would explain her reaction to him.

Someone else had taught her passion. Sloan had the irrational urge to find that man and beat him into oblivion.

He must have tightened his arm around her because she murmured something and shifted beside him. Her warm breast nestled firmly against his side, but as he brushed his hand across her back, he noticed that her skin had cooled. He didn't want to disturb her, but neither did he want her to catch a chill.

He eased away. She mumbled something in protest, but seemed intent on sleeping. Searching the bed, he found her discarded nightgown and then the edge of the sheet. Somehow, he and Rebecca had ended up at the foot of the bed, so he flung the sheet over them as best he could. As soon as he lay back down, Rebecca snuggled beside him.

This unexpected intimacy was as foreign as her wild ideas about being from the future. He felt uncomfortable, but at the same time he craved the sense of peace he'd discovered, lying beside her. If he could just close his eyes and join her in sleep . . .

But what would he find in the morning? Would she want to talk about what had happened? Perhaps she would assume he'd marry her now that they'd made love. He had no clue as to her thinking. He didn't understand her any better than he'd ever understood women. He should have thought of the consequences before he made love to her.

He wondered if she would get pregnant from making love this one time. He should have thought of that, too.

Filled with doubts and nervous energy, Sloan eased himself away from Rebecca and rose from the bed. He walked to the window, looking out at a landscape dark and bleak in the aftermath of the storm. Much like his life, he thought. He had no room for softness, no tolerance for deception. If Rebecca had come to his bed to seduce him, and then expected him to confide in her, she was bound to be disappointed. He wouldn't let passion, or any soft emotion, keep him from his goal.

Surely Radburn knew that Sloan planned for his ranch to become the largest, most successful in the area. Surely Radburn realized that he couldn't compete, couldn't acquire enough acreage to rival Sloan's spread. Not that Radburn was really a rancher. More like a politician, he received money from newspapermen and railroad officials to promote their various agendas in the territory. He solicited grants for programs, such as a futile, deceptive effort that encouraged immigrants by claiming Wyoming had an even, temperate climate suitable for farming.

Radburn was a liar. There was no water for farming in this part of the state. And half the settlers would freeze to death in the "temperate" winters.

At some time in the near future, Sloan believed, there would be many cattle ranches in the territory, populated by hardy, knowledgeable men and women, and there would be a greater demand for beef across the country. The rail lines would extend farther, so cattle could be shipped to stockyards and processing plants. An established ranch would have a big advantage, especially if the breeding stock was the finest around.

That ranch would be his. And when he died the son Radburn claimed as his own would suddenly be the heir to the largest ranch in Fremont County. Robert would have his birthright—from his real father—in the reading of Sloan's will. Radburn and Leda would be shocked and publicly embarrassed, a sweet revenge indeed, when the secret of Robert's birth was revealed. Sloan knew he wouldn't be around to enjoy their sputtered explanations, unless he was somehow able to listen from hell.

Painted Elk had once asked Sloan if he wanted revenge on his enemies more than anything else, more than life or health or wealth. He did. He wanted it so much, he burned inside when he thought of Leda taking his son away, of Radburn claiming what was rightfully Sloan's.

He stood at the window and watched the rain strike the glass, then run slowly down the pane. The earth seemed cleansed by tears from the sky. Sometimes the bitter weight of Leda's betrayal, of his own past, seemed too much to bear. He wished tears could cleanse his own life, but too much had happened, too much time had passed.

He was what he was—a man with no future but revenge. And he had no tears to shed.

"Sloan?"

He almost jumped at the soft, sleepy sound of Rebecca's voice. For a moment he'd forgotten she was there, warm and willing, in his bed. He turned slowly, facing her with no defensive shields except his doubts and suspicions.

He felt her eyes caress him at the same time he realized that he was naked. With a sudden burst of energy, he walked away from the window—and her searching eyes—before she could see the effect of her gaze. Draped over the ladder-back chair, he found his pants and stepped into them, quickly fastening each button.

"What's wrong?" she asked, her voice now less sleepy and more curious.

"Nothing," he said quickly, but inside he knew the real answer. *Everything.*

"I think you're having regrets."

He fell silent, looking for his shirt in the darkness. "Aren't you?"

"No. I knew what I was doing."

"Yes, you did." He gave up the futile search and faced the bed. "You knew very well. Tell me, Rebecca, have you been married?"

"No, never."

"But you were no innocent maid. You must have had a lover."

"Not that I think it's any of your business, but yes, I did. Two, in fact. One in college, one since. Nice, stable men who I thought I loved, at the time. And neither relationship is open to discussion."

He could tell she was angry, building up steam for a full-fledged confrontation. He didn't want that, but at the same time he felt a red-hot burst of anger that not one man, one husband, had made love to her, but two men. He focused on that anger and not the longing he felt to take her into his arms again and banish any memories she had of sharing passion with another man.

She rose from the bed, wrapping the sheet around her like an ermine cape just as the clouds parted and moonlight bathed the room in soft, blue-white light. "Look, Sloan, I realize that your standards are different than mine. I'm a product of a different time, where women have more freedom. We no longer have to worry about purity as a test. We have ways to avoid pregnancy and disease. If I choose to make love to a man, then no one thinks I'm ruined."

"The fact is, you're living in this time. I know you think you're from some future where women have all these freedoms, but that's just not the case."

"I am from the future, and we're not discussing that fact."

"We are if you're using it as an excuse for wanton behavior."

"Wanton behavior? You're one to talk. I'm losing track of all the times you've come on to me! Or have you conveniently forgotten the other night in the study? I came in here tonight to comfort you, not to make love with you. And you started it."

"You were lying in my bed. What was I supposed to think?"

"Don't give me that macho bull. You knew why I was here. You remember the nightmare."

He didn't want to remember. He always put the nightmares from his mind immediately. Only the cold, dark fear remained hidden inside. But no matter how deeply he tried to hide the terror, it always returned.

"Sloan? Don't start lying to me now. Not after . . ."

"All right! I knew who you were, what we were doing. But you never asked me to stop. You never—"

"I didn't want you to stop, you dolt! I wanted to make love with you, although at the moment I'm having a hard time remembering why!"

"You want me to believe that you just couldn't resist my charm, is that it?" he asked sarcastically.

He watched her approach, the white sheet resembling furrows of snow drifting across the floor as she took each tentative step. She stopped perhaps a foot away from him and looked into his eyes. "I couldn't resist your pain," she said finally.

He wanted to take her into his arms, to hold her close and never let her go. To make love to her again and again. But he couldn't—he wouldn't. For all the passion they'd shared, she was still a stranger, with wild stories and perhaps even more dangerous agendas. He couldn't find solace in her arms.

So he stood absolutely still, until the longing drained from her eyes and her shoulders slumped in defeat. Only then did he look away, his hands clenched in tight fists, as remnants of the storm still beading rain on the windowpane.

"The hour's late. You'd better get some sleep," he said, trying not to glance back at the hurt look on her face.

But he couldn't resist watching as she walked to the bed and retrieved her nightgown. Her back to him, she dropped the sheet, standing in the moonlight like the pagan princess he'd read about in classic literature. Then, before he could even take a breath, she raised the nightgown and let it drift over her head, down the curve of her back, across the swell of her hips.

Sloan turned away again from the pale perfection of her body. No sound entered the room. Silence stretched into the darkness as a cloud moved across the moon. Then, the faint sound of a sob drifted through the night.

When Sloan turned she was gone, with only the whisper of her bare feet on the wooden floor.

Rebecca was sitting at the kitchen table, nursing a cup of black coffee, when Sloan walked through the room. He didn't see her at first, since the morning was still slightly cloudy and the sun was barely up. Dressed in a faded blue shirt and jeans, he didn't look any better than she felt. She wondered if he'd slept any last night either.

209

"Claudia made coffee," Rebecca offered as he stopped just inside the doorway and stared.

She felt the tension radiating from his body. He was as torn as she but would never admit it. To do so would be a weakness, and Sloan wouldn't give anyone that kind of power over him. He was of the opinion, she was sure, that letting your enemies know your weaknesses ensured defeat. A macho attitude, she'd always thought, but at the moment she only felt the pain of being labeled an enemy.

"No thanks." He continued walking toward the door.

"Sloan?"

He didn't stop, didn't turn around. It was just as it had been when she'd first arrived in the past and he was so suspicious that he wouldn't even speak to her.

She sat at the heavy, scared table for a long time, until her coffee turned cold and she felt the weight of last night's argument press down in a suffocating visc. She'd thought making love would be a turning point, but she hadn't expected the turn to be a bad one. She'd thought they would grow closer, not be torn apart by Sloan's suspicions and doubts. She'd never experienced such spontaneous passion, such profound fulfillment, with another man. But how could she respond to Sloan so thoroughly when there was nothing between them, at least on his part, but distrust? She'd been very selective in the past, opting for relationships only with men with whom she believed there might be a future.

There was no future with Sloan. There was only the past.

Finally she pushed herself away. She couldn't undo what they'd done last night, but perhaps she could get another perspective on her problems.

The ranch was quiet as she stepped off the porch. The sandy soil had drained away the rain from the night before. Rebecca barely left a footprint on the ground or the still-moist grass as she walked toward Painted Elk's teepee. Early this morning she had seen smoke rising from the opening where the poles crossed, so he must have returned.

She paused before the open flap and called, "Painted Elk?"

"Come inside," he said.

She eased through the small opening, then seated herself across from him on a buffalo rug, where he beckoned. "You are troubled again."

"Very," she said candidly. "Sloan and I tried not to fight, and we did fairly well for several days. Then, last night, we . . . Well, let's just say that we reached a turning point in our relationship."

Painted Elk looked very weary. "You have not yet learned the truth about each other."

"Sometimes I think that I know him better; then he does something that makes me believe I don't know him at all."

"You are still thinking here," Painted Elk said, tapping his head, "instead of here." He pointed to his heart.

"I tried thinking with my heart—at least I thought I was—but it was a mistake."

"It was not a mistake."

"You weren't there. Believe me, it was quite a scene."

"And are you afraid of such scenes?"

"Afraid? No, I don't think so," Rebecca replied. "They're not pleasant, but sometimes they're necessary."

"Then why do you not think this was necessary?"

Rebecca threw up her hands in frustration. "Because nothing was accomplished. Now we're not even speaking, just the way we were before. In just a few minutes last night we un-did every gain we'd made in the last ten days."

"You cannot know this, Rebecca Hartford."

She stared at the smoldering fire in the center of the teepee. She couldn't tell Painted Elk that she and Sloan had made love last night. Some things were too private to share, even with a man who seemed wise beyond his years or this world. "I know that Sloan has a son by Leda Radburn. I saw the little boy, Robert."

"Sloan does not know that you saw his son?"

"No. I rode to the Radburn place several days ago. I talked to Leda. I think that at one time she loved Sloan very much. They grew up together."

"Yes, Sloan has spoken of this. I knew of Leda when she lived here."

"She lived with Sloan . . . in that house?" Rebecca asked, gesturing behind her.

Painted Elk nodded. "For two moons, she

stayed with Sloan. Then she left."

"How soon after that did she marry Vincent Radburn?"

"I am not sure. Sloan tried to stop this wedding, but she would not listen."

Painted Elk didn't add, "Just as you will not listen," but Rebecca heard the censure in his voice. "And Vincent is raising Sloan's son."

"Yes. This causes Sloan much pain. Now he wants to hurt the people who hurt him."

"Revenge," Rebecca stated.

Painted Elk nodded.

Rebecca pulled the much folded piece of paper from her skirt pocket. She traced again the lineage of Robert Radburn, all the way to Jordan Davis. Then she raised her eyes to the medicine man. "I'm part of the revenge, aren't I? That's why I'm here."

Painted Elk stared into the fire and began to sing. Rebecca watched his lined, leathery face for a sign of the answer but saw nothing. She gazed into the glowing embers of the fire and looked inside herself for the truth. All she saw, all she felt, was the madness in Jordan's eyes, the burning pain when he'd placed his hands around her neck.

"Then maybe I really am dead," she whispered, folding the paper and placing it inside her pocket.

Chapter Eleven

Sloan watched Rebecca from the doorway as she bent over her bed, folding her meager supply of clothing. When he went to town next time he'd buy her something pretty. And a real hat to replace the ugly bonnet.

She used quick, efficient movements to smooth the wrinkles from each piece. He'd felt those same hands on his flesh, and even now his body tightened in response to those memories.

He'd known who she was, what they were doing, but last night during the storm he had been past caring. She was warm and willing, offering solace and forgetfulness in her arms. And he'd taken all that she offered, with no promises or thoughts of the future.

He didn't have much of a future, but the events

of last night had forced him to think about consequences.

"Rebecca?"

She jumped, placing her hand over her heart as if to still its rapid beating. "You frightened me."

"I didn't mean to." He stuck his hands in the pockets of his jeans because he didn't know what else to do with them. He was very much afraid that he would walk toward her and take her in his arms, even though that was the last thing he should do. "I have something to say."

She stiffened, her hand falling from her chest to hide in the folds of her skirt. "I thought we said everything last night. At least, that's the impression I got this morning."

"I've had some time to think." He paused, trying to read her expression, but she had carefully hidden her feelings. "This is . . . I'm not good at this sort of thing."

"At expressing your feelings?"

"At talking about . . . personal things. But this has to be said." He took a deep breath. "Is there any chance you might be with child?"

He watched her face change from one without expression to one filled with life. Pale pink crept into her cheeks, her eyes sparked with emotion, and her lips parted ever so slightly.

"I honestly don't know. I hadn't considered it . . . before. But I think it's unlikely."

She was looking at him so closely that he felt a wave of feeling wash over him. Her expression changed ever so slightly, until he could swear what he saw was compassion, along with sadness. But she didn't know about Leda, couldn't know about Robert.

She couldn't know how much he wanted his own child.

He stood perfectly still as she walked toward him cautiously, as though he were a skittish colt. He felt like a wild mustang, ready to bolt and run, to hide in the hills and never know the touch of a human hand. But he stood as she reached out, enveloping him in arms that were surprisingly strong. Rigid, he felt her rest her cheek on his chest.

"It's okay, Sloan," she said softly. "It's okay."

He felt a burning in his eyes and a constriction in his throat. He was frightened, of her softness and warmth, of the easy way she could touch him. But this wasn't about sex; he knew that as well as he knew his own name. Slowly, he began to relax. His arms came around her loosely, spreading across her back, just holding her.

Moments passed. The tightness in his throat eased and he blinked away the burning sensation in his eyes. He soaked in the warm feelings that came from Rebecca, feeling at peace for the first time in forever.

She gently pulled away and looked into his eyes. "We both need a friend, don't you think? If you're willing, we can forget about last night. I don't want . . . what happened to ruin any chance of peace between us."

Peace. What a foreign concept. At one time

he'd thought peace was a natural state of mind, the normal state of national affairs. Now it seemed as elusive as the clouds that drifted over the mountains.

"Sloan?"

He stared at her earnest face, completely devoid of artifice or guile. Could he trust her? At the moment he didn't have any choice. His heart told him that she was speaking the truth. "I'm willing to try," he finally said. "I've never been friends with a woman before." He smiled just a bit, enough to make his facial muscles strain with the unusual movement. "And I'll try to forget last night. What we did was a mistake."

He thought he saw a flash of pain in her eyes, but it was soon gone. She smiled in return. "Then we'll be friends. I promise you, I won't betray you to anyone. I won't harm you."

Sloan looked away. A warm afternoon breeze blew through the windows, fluttering the lacy curtains. He wished he could be as carefree as that wind, but he had too much to lose. He refocused on Rebecca, who was looking at him with guarded eyes. "I'll try to believe you. I have to warn you, I'm a cautious man. Trust doesn't come easily to me."

"I understand," she said, dropping her arms and moving back a few inches. "All I ask is that you don't immediately believe I'm guilty of some heinous crime. I don't think I can go on like that."

"I know," he said with a sigh. "Sometimes I feel the same way."

"Then perhaps we have more in common than we thought."

"You may be right."

"I was serious about being friends, though. Being here . . . I feel very alone. I'm not used to that."

"Being alone's not the worst thing that can happen."

"No, I suppose not. But it's difficult for me. I usually talk—really *talk*—to five or six people every day. I feel very isolated here."

Sloan shrugged. "There aren't that many people out here yet. Someday, I think that will change."

"It will, but Wyoming will never be as populated as many states."

"More of your future talk?"

"Yes, I suppose so. Sorry, it just slipped out."

"You can say whatever you like, but don't expect me to believe it all the time."

"Fair enough."

She smiled again. Warmth flowed from her, making him glow inside with a feeling he hadn't experienced in many years. He felt loved, even if it wasn't in a romantic sense. Perhaps it was the kind of love two friends shared. He was certain the feeling was fleeting, that it wouldn't last, but for now he savored the rich sensation.

"I'll see you tonight for dinner," he said, stepping back into the hall.

He walked down the hall, past his bedroom, where they'd made "the mistake" last night. He wouldn't think about that for now. He was going to try to be a friend to Rebecca, not a lover. And if he thought about how good he'd felt, making love with her, he'd make a lousy friend.

Late that night Rebecca lay in her bed and listened to the chirping of insects and the occasional animal sound, far out on the prairie. The last twenty-four hours had been a roller coaster ride for her emotions. She'd felt close to Sloan in those moments as they'd made love, as they took each other to the heights of passion. She hadn't known such an experience was possible, or that Sloan could then be so cruel as to accuse her of "wanton behavior." Her emotions had dipped as she realized he was hiding his pain behind a mask of hypocrisy.

Then she'd learned from Painted Elk why she might be in the past—as an object of revenge—and her heart had plummeted even farther. Sloan didn't trust her or approve of her, but he wouldn't hurt her. Except he didn't think he was hurting *her*. He was just extracting his revenge from some nameless, faceless descendant of Leda and Vincent.

This afternoon, as she sunk to the bottom of the imaginary roller coaster tracks, Sloan had come to her bedroom and bared his soul, as much as he was capable of revealing his emotions. Her heart had gone out to him. She knew explanations weren't easy for him; he kept his own council and thought of himself as self-sufficient. He'd made her soar high again, but when would she fall?

She felt as though she were reaching out for something steady and constant as the cars raced around the track, but never grasping what she really needed, unable to stop the headlong flight. Up and down, she couldn't get off the ride until it was over.

She'd coasted through dinner, which had been pleasant and only a little strained. Even Claudia seemed to be cooperating, fixing a delicious batch of pan-fried trout with the fish that one of the cowboys had caught in a mountain stream. Sloan had shown again that he came from a good family, using excellent manners that were less rusty than the ones he'd used the other night. They had a lot of adjusting to do before they became friends. However, Sloan seemed willing to compromise, and as the old saying went, she wouldn't look a gift horse in the mouth.

She felt a sense of rightness, a ray of hope, that she hadn't felt since waking up in the past. Perhaps Sloan would never believe that she was from the future; perhaps someday he would. That was hardly the issue any longer. She was attracted to the loneliness in his eyes as well as the strength of his body. She wanted to know the man who was plagued by nightmares but had a gentleness inside that he kept well hidden from the world.

She stretched beneath the sheet and light blanket, listening to the night sounds. Sloan no doubt lay in his bed, hearing the same symphony, just down the hall. For the first time in the last two weeks, she looked forward to tomorrow.

* * *

The next morning Rebecca got up early and found Claudia in the kitchen, frying slabs of ham. The smoky, tangy smell filled the big room, making Rebecca's stomach growl in response.

"Can I help?" she asked the stern-faced housekeeper.

"I've been making breakfast for nigh onto thirty years. I expect I can manage just fine."

"I'm sure you can," Rebecca replied, not at all disturbed by Claudia's discouraging remark. "But I'd be glad to help out. What else are you fixing?"

"Eggs. Biscuits are already done."

"Have you ever cooked scrambled eggs?"

"Sloan likes his fried."

"Let me do the eggs this morning, Claudia. I miss cooking. I promise not to get in your way."

Claudia used a large fork to remove the ham slices from the grease in a large cast-iron skillet. She wiped her hands on her apron and said, "Help yourself. I've got enough to do at my own place."

"Thanks."

Claudia looked at her strangely but finished tidying up her dirty dishes before exiting through the back door.

Rebecca smiled, thankful to have the kitchen to herself. She usually came down later, after Sloan had eaten and Claudia had left for the day. This morning she felt carefree and happy. Using a towel, she grabbed the skillet handle and poured the grease into a crockery pot at the rear of the firebox. She couldn't resist the view from the window over the heavy iron stove. Outside, the sky glowed pink, with dark purple streaks radiating across the eastern horizon. No storm clouds today, she thought, humming the theme from *Phantom of the Opera*.

She broke five eggs into a bowl, estimating that Sloan would eat at least three. On the sideboard she found cream, which she beat into the mixture. She didn't even want to think about all the milligrams of cholesterol he consumed daily. Somehow, if she remained in the past very long, she'd have to worry about formulating a healthier diet.

If she stayed in the past . . . Did she really want to leave Sloan now? She wanted to go back to the relative safety of her own time, and she missed modern technology and conveniences, but she'd discovered a special man who needed her. But for how long? Surely they couldn't go on like this forever.

She shook her head. She didn't know the answers. She had to take one day at a time, she reminded herself. Who knew how long she'd remain here, or even if she'd ever go back to her own time? And she and Sloan had agreed to be friends. Just friends.

The eggs sizzled as she poured them into the skillet. With a fork, she continued to stir, making them fluffy, as she hummed. She didn't have a great voice and only occasionally sang in the shower. But she loved music and missed her CDs and stereo. She especially missed watching morning television shows as she ate a bowl of cereal with a banana.

She didn't think there were any bananas in Wyoming territory, any more than there was electricity or television. She was just dishing the eggs onto the heavy, glazed pottery plates when Sloan walked into the kitchen.

"Good morning," he said carefully.

"Good morning," Rebecca replied cheerfully. "I hope you slept well."

He seemed taken aback for a moment. She supposed he wasn't used to polite morning chatter. Well, she wasn't exactly accustomed to making small talk with a man in the mornings, but she felt almost "perky," despite her dislike of that adjective, and despite the things she missed.

"I slept just fine," he answered, pouring himself a cup of coffee. "Where's Claudia?"

"I asked her if I could finish up breakfast. I had a craving for scrambled eggs."

"What?" He pulled out a chair and sat at the table, watching her.

"Don't worry. I think you'll like them." She eased a plate of biscuits, ham, and eggs in front of him, then took her own seat at the table.

He looked skeptically at the yellow glob on his plate.

"Try it."

He did, taking a small bite. Even if he didn't believe her stories of being from the future, he trusted her enough to try her cooking.

He took several more bites before commenting, "These are good."

"Thanks." Rebecca smiled and finished her own meal in silence, glancing at Sloan every so often. He looked handsome this morning, more rested than usual. There was stubble on his strong jaw, but his blue eyes were clear and bright. His hair looked finger combed, as usual, and it was a little long, brushing against his collar in the back.

All in all, he presented a very appealing, masculine package. She might have a difficult time remembering that they should only be friends.

Sloan ate every bite, plus two more biscuits with butter and honey. By the time he was finished, Rebecca had fixed herself a cup of coffee and sat back down at the table.

"Did you have plans for today?" he asked. His tone was light, as though he really didn't care, but to Rebecca's ears it sounded as though the future hinged on her answer.

She smiled. "I think I could squeeze something into my busy schedule."

"Since you wanted to see a little more of the country, I thought you might like to take a ride into the mountains."

"I'd like that very much." Although she still felt a little sore in parts of her anatomy from her long ride last week, she wouldn't pass up this opportunity to spend more time with Sloan. This was the second time he'd reached out to her, only a ride was much more personal that offering to get what she needed from town.

And since they'd agreed to be just friends, she could relax and enjoy his company.

"When should I be ready?"

"I need to saddle the horses. Why don't you put together some food?"

"Okay. I'll be ready in about a half an hour."

Sloan pushed away from the table. "Well, thanks for breakfast." He took his hat off a hook beside the door. Before he opened the back door, he looked back at her over his shoulder.

"What?"

"I . . . nothing. I'll get those horses saddled."

She wondered if she would ever understand his searching looks and barely begun sentences. Maybe he didn't understand them himself, but that didn't mean that she, as a trained professional, shouldn't have a clue.

If he just wanted to be friends, why did he look at her like a lover? Or was that all in her mind?

They rode west along Twin Creek, following the path Rebecca had been advised to take a few days ago by Slim. Passing a beautiful spot with cottonwood trees in a low-lying area near the creek, Rebecca reined in her mare. Sloan stopped also, turning back to look at her.

Her hand went to her neck; she could still feel Jordan's hands, cutting off the air to her lungs.

"What's wrong?"

"Nothing . . . It's just that I remember this place. I've been here before." *One hundred and twenty years from now*, she silently added. She'd sat on a picnic blanket beneath trees just like those with Jordan, talking about his inherited land, his career in the air force, his plans for the future. Jordan, who looked so much like Sloan that she couldn't even separate them in her mind any longer.

"Are you thinking about the man who strangled you?"

Her hand dropped from her neck. "How did you know?"

"You look like you've seen a ghost."

"Nearly," she whispered. She shook her head. Sloan's anger had traveled into the future as a burst of energy, poisoning Jordan's mind in an instant. He'd strangled her because of Sloan's hatred of Leda and Vincent Radburn. So really, Sloan had tried to kill her, not Jordan.

What catalyst had allowed Sloan's anger to overcome the barriers of time? It was probably because she and Jordan were the first descendants to be back together in all those years, the first who had been in the type of situation where revenge was possible.

But Sloan held no hatred for her. He had a streak of inner kindness that rarely showed, but by no means could he be judged as cruel. He wanted revenge, but he wasn't consumed with hate to the point that he'd kill an innocent person.

Perhaps, Rebecca theorized, Sloan grew more bitter with time, until his kindness shriveled and died, until he turned into a cold, unfeeling shell of a man. Would he be angry enough then? Would he seek revenge even more fervently then than he did now? Perhaps her coming back to the past had changed him, so he wouldn't become that bitter old man, but what if it didn't? Jordan had inherited the land, but there was no mention of Sloan on the family tree. Why?

"Who strangled you, Rebecca?" he asked softly.

"A man named Jordan Davis," she answered, looking at the waving grass beneath the cottonwoods.

"I don't know him."

"No, you wouldn't," she said quietly, her eyes losing their focus as she stared at this place where she might die, years from now.

"Rebecca? Why don't we stop for a moment? You look pale."

"No!" she said without thinking, jerking her attention back to Sloan. She didn't want to be alone with him in that same spot. "I mean, I'm fine. Really." She nudged the mare with her heels, moving alongside Sloan's mount. "Let's keep going."

"You're sure?"

He sounded concerned. Not angry, not cruel. But still, she couldn't trust her emotions right now. She might try to explain what had happened, even though she knew he wasn't ready to hear what he considered fantastic tales.

She forced a smile. "Come on. The day's a-wastin'."

They rode on. Saddle leather creaked and horses grabbed a bite of tall grasses occasionally. High rolling meadows gave way to more steeply sloped foothills, then rough outcroppings of mostly red rocks. Scrubby trees grew along the valley that had been carved out by the stream, which seemed to come from high in the mountains. Whether from snow melt or a natural spring, Rebecca wasn't sure. The water was crystal clear and fast moving, reflecting both the wide blue sky overhead and the rocky stream bed below.

Her fears of the incident beside the cottonwood trees dimmed as Sloan led her higher into the mountains. He seemed to visibly relax, moving, as always, with the sway of the horse. One hand rested on his thigh and the other lay across the horn of the saddle, holding the reins while his mount picked its way along the creek. He'd apparently shaved before leaving the ranch, because his tanned jaw looked smooth and strong—just like the rest of him.

She shifted in the saddle, trying not to remember exactly how smooth and strong his back had been beneath her fingers. If they were going to be friends, she had to ignore what had happened after she walked into his bedroom. Sloan wasn't ready for the honest sexuality of a twentieth-century woman, but she wasn't about to apologize for being truthful. She had wanted him.

She was glad that he was enjoying the day; Sloan needed to get away from the pressures of his life. If he lived in her time, she would suggest he develop a hobby. However, she knew from experience that people didn't have time for hobbies when they were struggling for their existence. As a matter of fact, she was surprised and honored that he'd taken the day off to spend with her.

He turned his horse away from the creek and rode to the top of a small outcropping. She followed, stopping her own mare when Sloan dismounted.

"The view is good here," he said, looping the reins over a gnarled sage.

She waited until he walked to the side of her mare, then dismounted. Just like the other day, her legs felt like Jell-O for a moment. Sloan held her arm, giving her support.

"Thanks. I'm not used to riding so far."

"We could have stopped earlier. You should have said something."

"Really, I wasn't tired. And the view up here is spectacular." She turned in a half circle. Behind her, she knew the Rockies rose for several thousand feet, but from this angle they weren't visible. All she saw was blue sky above the upper slopes of the mountain where they stood. To each side, other ridges and valleys fell toward the prairie. Below them, the green and brown rolling hills stretched east into the horizon.

"Wow. This is a Kodak moment," she whispered.

Sloan turned to look at her with a puzzled expression on his face. "A what?"

She smiled. "Nothing. Just a saying. It means that the view is so beautiful, you want to preserve it forever."

Sloan looped the reins of her mare over another bush, then sat on a large boulder. He looked out at the panorama. "I like it here too. I saw it for the first time when I rode away from South Pass City."

"The old mining town?"

"I guess you could call it old. Not too many people live there now. The gold's mined out."

It's a ghost town in my day, a historic site in the middle of nowhere, she wanted to say, but she held her tongue.

She settled on another boulder, where she could watch Sloan and take in the scenic beauty. "What were you doing in South Pass City?"

"Mining. I had a claim."

"Did you? I've never known a real miner before. So what did you do, dig or pan for gold?" She smiled at the image of Sloan, pulling a reluctant burro along a lonely stretch of land, laden with axes and those pans that sifted the sand from stream beds.

"I bought out an existing mine after one of the partners was killed by Indians. Cheyenne, I think." He sighed and looked toward the south. "There's a lot of quartz rock there, running through the hills. The first miners found nuggets in the streams, but by the time I came west, mining the veins into the hills was necessary."

"Did you like it? It sounds like hard work."

"I hated it," he said, gazing across the land. "But I was lucky. I found a vein of gold before I gave up the claim. The work wasn't too bad, but the digging . . . I didn't like that."

Rebecca shuddered, thinking of him in the darkness of an underground hole. No, that wasn't Sloan. He was made for these wide-open spaces, for clean air and a landscape devoid of fences.

"So you came out west and made your fortune. That's the American dream, isn't it?"

"I suppose it is for some. I didn't make a fortune, just enough to buy the land I wanted."

"You knew it on sight?" Knowing that the land had been Sloan's, not the Radburns', made Rebecca view Jordan's inheritance in a different light. However, he'd claimed to feel no ties to the property.

"Before then. My grandfather was with the Lewis and Clark expedition back in 1811, when they surveyed the Wind River valley. He was with the team that went down to South Pass. Hudson, I think the leader's name was. Anyway, my grandfather told me about the land from the time I was in short pants. He loved it out here."

"Did you come west to buy the land?"

He shook his head. "Not really. I didn't have the money, and besides, the land was part of the Shoshone reservation. I couldn't have bought it then if I'd wanted to. I thought about buying other land, so I worked the claim until I had enough. By then, the government had bought the land from the Shoshone. When they opened it up for homesteading I purchased all I could."

"That's a great story. I mean, of all the things that could have gone wrong, you ended up with the land that your grandfather had told you about when you were just a child." *And someday, your great-great-grandson will inherit it.*

He shrugged. "I like to think I made it happen."

She reached across and placed a hand on his forearm. "Of course you did. But you had to buy the claim, find the gold, and be in the right place at the right time to buy the land. Kind of like destiny, don't you think?"

He looked at her hand, resting on his tan, muscled arm. "I'm not sure I believe in destiny. I believe in working to get what you want."

Rebecca drew back her hand. "Well, in my opinion, it was a little of both." She looked at the stream, about twenty yards away. "Is the water okay to drink?"

He looked at her with an odd expression on his face. "Of course."

Of course. There were no contaminants or chemicals in 1876. She pushed off the boulder and made her way down the bank to the creek.

The water was ice cold and clear. She scooped several handfuls into her mouth, then splashed her face. In a minute, Sloan joined her, balancing on the balls of his feet and squatting beside her. He didn't say anything, just drank some water and watched the current.

"I like your place. It's very peaceful," she said softly.

He turned his head to look at her. "I'm glad you rode up here with me. You . . . I've talked to you more in the last few days than I've talked to anyone in a long time."

"Does that bother you?"

"Maybe. I don't understand why I talk so much around you."

She didn't have the heart to tell him that she

didn't really talk that much. "I don't either, except that I'm considered easy to talk to." She paused, wondering how much she should tell him. He always got angry when she mentioned being from the future. Still, she wouldn't feel right keeping a major part of her life from him. "I've had training so that I will be easy to talk to. That's part of my job as a counselor."

"I've never heard of someone having a job as a counselor."

"I don't think . . . that is, you probably haven't." She wondered if this was the right time to mention his past. She didn't want to ruin the mood, yet she knew they needed to speak openly, at some point, about what caused his nightmares. "Counselors are useful to people who are having problems and can't figure them out on their own. For example, your nightmares. Whatever happened during the war is still causing you problems in the form of nightmares."

Sloan pushed himself to his feet. "My nightmares are my concern. Are you hungry? I could use some lunch." He walked to the horses.

Rebecca sighed, acknowledging that he just wasn't ready yet to talk. He didn't trust her; in his mind, he had plenty of reason not to do so. Perhaps, if they really did become friends, he would confide in her about his past.

When Sloan returned she helped him unpack the lunch. A sense of déjà vu swept over her. Picnicking with another handsome man, down the mountain in the cottonwood grove. Feeling good and carefree, enjoying the day. Then, feeling the full strength of his anger and hatred. She swallowed a lump of fear. This wasn't the same situation at all. She knew Sloan much better than she did Jordan, and even if Sloan's anger had somehow caused Jordan's actions, she knew that at this moment Sloan was no threat to her.

They ate in silence, with only the cry of a hawk and the whisper of the wind as background music. Rebecca gazed over the countryside again, at the variety of plants that grew there despite the harsh conditions of the winter and the arid climate during the summer. "What are those?" she asked, pointing to a pink blooming plant nestled among the rocks of the hillside.

"Bitterroot," Sloan answered. He wiped his mouth and placed the napkin on the blanket. "That's what the Indians call it, anyway. They use the root as food, or grind it into flour. I believe the scientific name is Lewisia, discovered by Lewis on the other side of the mountains. They're blooming late this year."

Rebecca got up from the blanket and walked toward the pink flowers. Hardly any foliage peeped through the soil. Only the petals of the flower and an abundance of yet-to-open blooms rested near the soil. She'd never seen bitterroot before. They seemed tenacious, holding fast to the earth and adding beauty in an improbable landscape of rock and grassy tufts.

She thought of Sloan's home and the barren land around the ranch. When she'd first seen the outside of the house she'd thought it needed some shrubs and flowers to break the angles of the Victorian architecture, rising from the soil like an alien structure. The house should have stood on some tree-lined street in Philadelphia, but instead it sat defiantly in a valley in Wyoming.

Just like Sloan, whom, she suspected, no longer fit in Philadelphia. No longer fit into what was "normal" before the war. "Do you mind if I take some of these plants back to the ranch? I'd like to plant them beside the house."

Sloan shrugged. "Suit yourself. I'm not sure they'll grow on the sandy soil we have below."

"Then I'll take some of their own soil with them." *So they'll feel at home. Like the furniture and photos in Sloan's house. Like the newspapers he devours each month, when the bundle from his mother arrives.*

Rebecca used a knife to carefully dig each bitterroot from the earth, packing it in the clay soil of the mountain. She wrapped the plants in a damp towel and placed them in the saddlebags, where their lunch had been.

"Ready to go back?" Sloan asked.

No, not yet. Not until I know how to save myself from your anger. Then she realized that Sloan was asking if she was ready to leave, not to return to her own time. She blinked to clear her head. The bitterroot plants seemed to have a strange effect on her, making her thoughts even more fanciful than usual.

"Yes, I'm ready." She turned to the panoramic view one last time. "Thanks for bringing me up here. It really is beautiful."

Sloan helped her mount, his large hands lingering on her waist. "You're welcome," he said, looking up at her with eyes that silently asked difficult questions. She didn't know the answers; yet somehow, her own questions were tied to his, the answers the same. Perhaps they would find the answers together, if they had time.

But the more urgent question at the moment was, how much time did she have?

Chapter Twelve

Later that night, Rebecca curled up in Sloan's big chair while he sat at the desk. He had some accounting to do, he said, so she'd decided to read some more of his Philadelphia newspapers. She shifted in the chair for about the fiftieth time, trying to get comfortable.

Sloan looked up from his ledger. "What's the problem?"

She hadn't realized he was paying any attention to her. "My bottom is sore. I'm not used to riding all day."

He closed the book and folded his hands on top. "You don't have to convince me how tough you are. You should have said something."

She wiggled a bit more, wincing at the pain. "It didn't hurt too much then."

"You should rub some liniment on. I'll get it for you before bed."

She stared at him, images of his large, capable hands rubbing her bottom and inner thighs dancing in her head. Suddenly she felt hot, but she sat perfectly still, looking at Sloan as the man who had made love with her just two nights ago. His blue eyes widened as he watched her, then narrowed as his nostrils flared. He swallowed as though his throat was suddenly dry.

He broke eye contact, but not before she saw a telltale blush darken his tanned cheeks.

With a flourish, she opened the newspaper, dated April 3, 1876. She heard Sloan open his ledger. Her eyes finally focused on the tiny print and she scanned the stories. She firmly resisted the urge to fan herself.

"Hey, look at this," she said in a moment. "Boston defeats Philadelphia in first National League baseball game."

"Baseball?"

"Yes, it's the national pastime." She frowned, "Well, maybe not yet. But it will be."

"This is a game played with a ball?"

"Yes. You haven't heard about baseball?"

"No. Do you know how to play baseball?"

"Oh, yes. I love the game. It's a lot of fun. I mean, to watch. I personally don't play. Well, actually I've played softball."

He looked at her as though she'd grown two heads.

"You see, there are big stadiums where you watch the game, with the baseball diamond in the middle. And two dugouts for the teams. The fans yell at the top of their lungs, drink beer, eat peanuts and hot dogs . . ."

Sloan looked shocked at her description. Then it hit her; he didn't know any of those words. There were no diamonds or dugouts or hot dogs. Oh, Lord! He probably took that literally. She burst out laughing.

"Rebecca?"

She only laughed harder. Finally, she managed to say, "Not real dogs. They're like sausages, only ground up really fine. You eat them on these long buns. . . ."

He looked confused again. It seemed there was no way to describe the ritual of a baseball game to a nineteenth-century man.

"I'm sorry, Sloan. Do you have a piece of paper? I'll draw it for you."

He shook his head, smiling ever so slightly, as though he found her just a bit amusing. But he pulled out a piece of paper and pushed his pen and inkwell toward her.

She leaned over the desk, her head just inches from his. She dipped the pen and began to sketch.

Within minutes, she'd drawn the basics and explained some of the rules. Sloan smiled along with her, and when she tried to remember the rules of pop flies he laughed.

She stopped explaining, stopped writing. With a smile, she watched his face. Another kind of warmth spread through her. She wanted to kiss him—in a friendly way, of course. When he noticed her intense perusal he stopped laughing and stared at her.

"I'm glad I made you laugh," she said softly.

"It's been a long time."

"You should do it more often."

"Maybe I will."

She straightened, still smiling. "Maybe we could put together our own team. It would be fun."

"Maybe. There's not a lot of extra time on a ranch."

"I know. But the Fourth of July is coming up soon. That would be a great occasion for Wyoming's first baseball game."

"I'll think about it."

"Okay."

She stretched her tired back. "I think I'll go to bed. I can't face that chair another minute."

Sloan pushed himself away from the desk and stood up. "I'll get the liniment for you."

"Really, I don't think—"

"It's no problem. Wait here."

Rebecca folded the newspaper while he was gone and placed it carefully on his stack. He was back in a moment.

"Here it is." He handed her a green bottle that smelled exactly like modern liniment. She remembered it from camp.

"Thanks."

"You're welcome." He looked as though he was going to say something else, but he didn't.

"I had fun today, Sloan. And tonight. Thank you for spending this time with me."

He seemed embarrassed. She'd probably said too much, but dammit, he needed to learn to accept a compliment."

"I had a good time too," he said finally, after looking at her for what seemed to be a long time. "Good night, Rebecca."

"Good night." She turned around, clutching the bottle of liniment. She felt almost giddy and carefree, as if she could run briskly up the stairs. But after two steps her body reminded her she'd spent the day on a horse. So she walked slowly, smiling all the way.

The next morning Rebecca knelt in the dirt beside the house, using a small shovel she'd found in a shed out back to dig holes for the bitterroot plants. She hadn't had time to plant them yesterday after getting back to the ranch late in the afternoon. Besides, she'd needed some time to decide where to place them.

She'd gathered some rocks to build a natural setting. She hoped she had enough clay soil; the ground around her was very sandy and she wanted the small, cheerful pink flowers to flourish. Perhaps they'd come back next year and naturalize around Sloan's house, kind of like daffodils and tulips. That way, if she wasn't here, he'd have something to remember her by. The thought was sobering.

She was just patting the dirt when Painted Elk walked up, his steps so soft she barely noticed his approach. Smiling at his leathy face, she said,

"Sloan told me that these plants are used by Indians as food."

"Yes," he said staring down at the pink flowers. "They are important to all of the people."

"I thought they might grow here. I really like them."

"These plants were not meant to grow in a garden, Rebecca Hartford."

She felt her smile fade. "That doesn't mean they can't grow here. I'll take care of them."

"You may give them water, but they will still die."

"That's an awful thing to say! You don't think I can make them grow."

Painted Elk shook his head. "It is not your care." He bent down and touched the full, pink bloom. "One by one, the flowers will bloom and then wither. The leaves will turn brown and die. The bitterroot does not live through the summer."

"Never?"

He looked up, squinting against the afternoon sun. "When the last bloom of the bitterroot fades you will also fade from this place. You will go back to your own time, Rebecca Hartford."

She knelt in the dirt, staring at the blooms long after Painted Elk walked away. *When the bitterroot fades.* She had an answer, one that left her half filled with dread. If she believed Painted Elk—and she had every reason to trust his insight—she would return to her own time. But would she find life or death at the end of her journey?

With a sigh, she touched the locket that nestled

close to her heart. She had to find a way to understand the past. She didn't want to die, especially not at the hands of Sloan's great-great-grandson.

Sloan dragged himself back to the ranch, bone tired. He'd ridden out with a few of his neighbors at dawn to confront some homesteaders on the Little Popo Agie who had diverted a large part of the water for their own use. With the fear of a dry summer, all the property owners were concerned about the snow melt and levels of well water. Snowfall had been heavy last winter, but the melt had been fast too, causing some flooding in the Wind River valley. No one knew how much water would be available.

He dismounted in the barn, going through the motions of unsaddling Buck, thinking back on the day. They'd ridden to the timber and mud structure, about fifteen miles north-northeast, knowing instantly that the men had put more work into a dam than their house. Two nearly naked children hunkered near the open doorway, looking at the riders with suspicious, old eyes. A woman stood in the doorway, wiping her large hands on a dirty apron. Two men stopped work near the river, which was no longer high with snow melt. Now it trickled gently through the land, appearing sluggish and tired.

The confrontation had been brief. Three men had ridden into the river, looped ropes around the makeshift dam, and pulled it down. Water cascaded, causing the horses to snort and dance away. Within a minute, the private reservoir no longer existed. Daniel Benson, a decent sort, advised the squatters that they'd be run off if they tried to dam the river again. Run off or killed. And then Sloan and the other men had galloped off, having done what they must to ensure water for everyone.

Still, the sight of those children made Sloan hate what they'd had to do. Two children might go thirsty or hungry, but fifty more might have a chance. That was part of the harshness of the West that he'd never quite reconciled himself to. When he was a child he'd never had to worry about water or food. He'd had heat in the winter and a shady spot to play in the summer. His childhood had been ideal, compared to any boy or girl's in the territory.

These children, and hundreds of others like them, had nothing. Their parents had less than nothing, not even owning their own land. All they could hope for was to build a life on these vast plains, or perhaps leave to work on the railroad. If they were lucky, they'd live. If not, they would be killed by Indians, disease or draught.

There was no softness here, and yet this land felt like home to him. He placed his saddle in the tack room, glad that Slim wasn't around to question him. Glad that he could be alone for a few more minutes.

His own son would have more, he vowed. He wouldn't ruin Radburn, because to do so would hurt Robert. He wouldn't kill Leda, although at times he'd wanted to strangle her for what she'd done, because to do so would take Robert's mother away. Every child should have a mother, and even if Leda was a fickle, lying female, everyone said that she was good mother to her son.

He shut the door to the tack room, taking a deep breath. The smell of horse, hay and dust filled his lungs. He was proud of this property. He'd accumulated much over the last seven years, yet he'd always known it wasn't just for him. Before he'd asked Leda to come west, it had been for the idea of children and grandchildren, a family that would build on what he'd started. While Leda was here, he'd hoped, really hoped, that he could live out his life as a normal man, with a loving wife, sons to stand beside him, daughters to make him smile.

Slowly, he'd seen the change in Leda, her desperation to make him be the man—or boy—he'd once been. She'd tried everything, including sacrificing her virginity, to return him to the way he was before the war. The sacrifice had been in vain; he couldn't let go of the past, and she couldn't accept him as he was.

He couldn't go back. The march through Georgia had changed him forever. Now he felt anger building inside him, blocking the sorrow he'd experienced earlier with the squatter's children. Leda had judged him unfit to be the father of his own son. All his hopes for the future had turned to dust at the moment he discovered her deception. If she could do that to him, after all they'd shared throughout their lives, how could he expect another woman to understand him?

With a cry of anguish, he whirled and rammed his fist into the wall of the tack room. Wood splintered. His knuckles burned, then shot shards of pain up his arm. He welcomed the pain; it showed he was still alive, still human. He leaned against the wall, breathing heavily.

Suddenly, the image of Rebecca filled his mind. Kind and caring, she looked at him with sympathy, not pity. She'd come to him because of the nightmare, to comfort, not to condemn. And she had the spirit to stand up to him, even when he wanted nothing more than to walk away from her questions.

Could he expect another woman to understand? Rebecca had said yesterday that she was a counselor, whatever that was. Someone who talked to people about their problems. No one could be more suited for her job, he thought, than a talker like Rebecca. Could she understand?

His family and friends hadn't understood. In Philadelphia, where the trees and buildings pressed in on him, his parents had been alarmed by his nightmares and moods. The doctors had suggested a rest in the country and a brandy before bed. He'd left instead, heading west toward the mythical land his grandfather had described years before. He'd left with little more than the clothes on his back and a roll of bills in his pocket, and now he owned all the land he could see.

Still, he was alone. Perhaps he'd wanted to be alone, at first. But could he have a chance for a future? Not with Leda and Robert, but with Rebecca? If there was a compassionate God up there, perhaps He'd sent her to fill the lonely nights.

Sloan wrapped a bandanna around his scraped and bleeding knuckles. He wanted to walk into the house and find her there. He wanted her to look up at him and smile. He wanted the right to take her into his arms and kiss her warm, willing lips.

Suddenly he realized how ridiculous he'd been to say they would be friends. He wanted more than that, even if she'd suggested they forget about the night they'd made love. She felt too good in his arms, even if she hugged him out of comfort and not desire. And she made him smile, even laugh, with her wild stories of a game called baseball. No one had made him feel that way in many years.

She felt right.

He'd worked for years in that dark mine to get enough money to buy this land and build a house. He was thirty-five years old and had learned to be patient. Rebecca wanted to be friends, but that was at least a start. Over time, she could learn to care for him as a man. They'd already experienced passion; that would be no problem in their relationship. She was young and strong. She could fill his lonely nights, give him sons and daughters, and grow old with him on this land he loved.

They were levelheaded adults. Neither of them needed the illusions of youth. She would see that staying with him was the sensible thing to do, especially since she was so confused about her past and didn't seem to have any plans for the future.

Yes, he would be patient. With a surge of energy he hadn't expected, he washed away the dust and sweat of the day, ready to walk into the house to Rebecca's smile.

Rebecca sat in the darkened interior of Sloan's study, a snifter of brandy in her hand. The drapes were drawn against the late afternoon sun, and the temperature was hot again, after the brief respite they'd experienced after the storm. She had come here to be alone and quiet with her thoughts.

She had only as long as the bitterroot bloomed. It was nearly the end of June, late for the plants. How many weeks did she have left? Two, three? Would she vanish in the middle of the day, or go to sleep one night and wake up back in her own century? She had no idea, of course, but the fact that she had so little time weighed heavily on her mood.

She might not be around long enough to organize a baseball game for the Fourth of July, less than two weeks away.

She took a sip of brandy, knowing that it wouldn't really make her feel better. It might make her relax, though. She felt like an old rubber band, ready to snap at any time. Pulled too tight, too long.

After Painted Elk had walked away this morning she'd worked outside, finding wildflowers and transplanting them to the house. The bitter-roots looked lonely by themselves, huddled between the rocks and against the stone foundation of the house. She'd found other pink flowers with tiny clusters of blossoms, and a variety of yellow wildflowers. She wished she knew their names.

She'd asked permission from Claudia to weed the garden, and the older woman had given it gladly. Apparently, yard work wasn't something she enjoyed. After working outside most of the day, dressed in her denim skirt, peasant blouse, and ugly bonnet, Rebecca had been tired and sweaty. She'd washed herself, her clothes, and changed into the brown skirt and blouse.

Claudia had fixed dinner and left it on the stove. The smell drifted through the house, tantalizing Rebecca with the smell of roasted meat and beans, along with bread and probably gravy. She should get up and set the table, since Sloan was already a bit late. But she didn't want to move from the quiet of the study.

She finished the brandy, settling back in the big chair and closing her eyes. Perhaps she would take a quick nap. Just a little nap.

Sloan walked through the house, his stomach growling in response to the roast warming on the stove. He stopped at the foot of the stairs and called, "Rebecca."

She didn't respond. He walked a few steps to the doorway of his study, looking inside. There she was, curled in his favorite chair, an empty glass dangling from her fingers. One hand was curled beneath her cheek, giving her an almost angelic appearance.

How much brandy had she drunk? He glanced at the decanter, but it was hard to see in the darkness of the interior. He walked to the window and pulled open the heavy drapes, letting in the early evening light. The room filled with sunshine, glistening off the silver tray, sparkling on the facets of the decanter. Hardly any brandy was gone, so she must have had just a glass.

He knelt in front of her chair. "Rebecca?" One of his hands reached up automatically and smoothed a strand of hair behind her ear. He looked closely at her face, seeing the slight redness on her cheeks and nose, along with the freckles that he found so charming. Her forehead was white, so she must have worn her bonnet outside today. He'd seen the results of her labor in the variety of flowers transplanted around the side of the house. Sloan smiled. She was beginning to make this place into a home.

"Rebecca," he said softly again. He quelled the urge to lean forward and kiss her slightly parted lips.

Slowly, her eyelids fluttered open. He looked into the depths of her green eyes, feeling drawn toward something he'd considered impossible just days before. She could give him what he wanted. All he had to do was go slow and keep his deepest, darkest secrets hidden.

"Hello, Sloan," she said in a breathless, throaty voice that made him think of waking beside her every morning. His blood heated and he felt a quick surge of pure lust.

He rose to his feet and walked to the brandy. Perhaps he should have some liquor. Anything to get his mind off making love to her again.

"How was your day?" she asked.

He glanced back over his shoulder. She was stretching, the fabric of the white blouse taut across her breasts. With shaking hands, he poured a bit of brandy into a glass. "I've had better ones."

"You left early this morning, didn't you? Was there trouble?"

"I rode with some other ranchers. There were squatters on the Little Popo Agie who'd dammed up the river."

"That's not allowed, is it?"

"No. It's one of our strictest rules. If one man diverts water, it hurts a hundred people." Immediately, the image of the two dirty children flashed in his mind. He took a swallow of brandy.

"You're probably hungry. I'll get dinner on the table."

"Don't bother if you're tired. I can serve myself in the kitchen."

"I'm fine now. I guess I got too much sun . . . again." She pushed herself up from the chair. "And I was just feeling a little down. I hope you don't mind that I helped myself to your brandy."

He wondered why she was being so quiet, so polite. "Of course I don't mind. Why would you think I did?"

"Oh, I don't know." She shrugged. "Like I said, I'm just feeling down."

"And that means . . . ?"

"You know. Depressed. A little blue. I'm not sure what the current term is."

"Is there a reason you feel this way?" He wondered if he'd done something, or failed to do something, that caused this problem.

She leaned against the doorway, sunshine bathing her face in a revealing light. He saw strain that he hadn't noticed before when she'd first awakened.

"I just wonder how long I'll be here." He heard a little catch in her voice. She looked away from him and blinked. "I mean, you hadn't anticipated picking me up off the prairie. All I've done is eat your food and give you grief. You've bought clothes for me, and—"

"That's nonsense." He sat his glass down on the table. "Last night you made me laugh. I thought we were doing very well together . . . building a friendship. Have I done something to make you believe you're not wanted?"

"No, but—"

"Then you're welcome to stay as long as you want." *As long as it takes*, he wanted to add.

"I just don't know how long I can stay."

Again, he heard that bit of uncertainty in her voice, but he still didn't know what had caused those feelings. "Is someone coming for you? Had you planned to meet someone here?" He walked up to her, stopping a foot away.

"No," she said, looking at the floor.

"Then you'll stay." He tipped her chin up with one finger. "I want you to stay."

"Are you sure?"

He smiled, remembering the other night, when he'd asked that very question in a very different context. "I'm sure."

She smiled slightly. "I guess I'm just being moody."

He wasn't sure what moody meant, but she was no doubt right. "Let's have dinner. There's no reason to talk about leaving."

He took her elbow, guiding her toward the dining room.

She murmured faintly, "No, not yet."

Chapter Thirteen

She had to talk to Leda again. She had to know more about what had happened to Sloan during the war, and also if there was any way to reconcile him with his former fiancée and son. Only when he'd come to terms with his past would his anger be gone. Even though Sloan had changed in the last three days, he was still a man governed by his past. Only when he felt at peace would Rebecca be assured of her survival.

If she returned home before Sloan had come to an acceptance of his life, she could still be strangled. She could die on that picnic blanket, her trip to the past a failure for everyone.

Rebecca sat at his desk to write a note to Leda, which she wasn't sure would ever be delivered. However, she wanted to be prepared in case the opportunity presented itself. But how to begin?

Dear Leda or *Dear Mrs. Radburn?* One sounded too casual, the other too formal. Perhaps she didn't even need a greeting. That would make it less easy to trace, in case the note was intercepted.

She sounded like a spy.

I need to see you to discuss an issue important to both of us. That sounded ambiguous enough. *Please send word through the contact I used and advise when and where we can meet.*

Okay, that got right to the point. Surely Leda would realize who had written the note and why. Rebecca folded the paper, then searched the desk for an envelope. They did have envelopes in 1876, didn't they? She located one, placed her note inside, and sealed it.

Folding the envelope in half, she placed it in her pocket. Perhaps someone would be going to town soon, and she could ask that person to take it to the store. She hoped the Englishman, Mr. Grant, would give it to Leda. The only problem was not letting Sloan know what she was doing. She felt guilty about deceiving him, even if it was for his own good. If he found out, he'd be angry, and that might undo all the trust they'd built up just recently.

But she had to find out about Sloan's past and figure out a way to keep him from becoming more bitter as the years went by. From her professional experience, she knew that old wounds didn't heal. They festered and infected more and more of a person's life, or they stayed so far beneath the surface that one day the person erupted in rage, harming himself or others. Often, people didn't even realize the cause of their anger.

She suspected that Sloan wasn't to the point yet where he could be dangerous, even if prompted into a rage. However, he certainly was in denial about his war trauma. He could become increasingly withdrawn over the years. He could watch Robert grow up and resent Leda more and more, until he became a vengeful old man.

The thought of Sloan living his life that way made her unbearably sad. She wanted him to have a rich, full life. She wanted him to laugh again.

To pass the day, she dusted the downstairs and swept the porch. In the afternoon, she went to the side of the house and checked on the bitterroot plants. They still looked fine, she observed with a sigh of relief, their blossoms spread wide in the sun.

She wandered to the barn, looking for her little roan mare. She liked the calm, undemanding animal, and had spent hours with her this last week.

Slim walked into the barn behind her. "Can I help you, miss?"

"I was just looking for the little' roan. I hope you didn't get into trouble for letting me take her out last week." She hadn't spoken to Slim since the day she'd borrowed the horse, although she'd seen him working with the animals. She hadn't had an opportunity to apologize.

"Well, now, Sloan was mighty riled. He lit

outta here, all horns and rattles, to find ya."

That was bad, she supposed. "I'm sorry. I didn't mean to be gone that long."

"To tell the truth, miss, I don't think he minded how long ya'd been gone. He was jus' plum worried that something coulda happened to ya."

"Really?" Rebecca smiled, feeling warm inside. Sloan was always concerned about her welfare, now that she thought about it. And the last few days, he'd been so even-tempered and sweet that it was almost like seeing another person emerge from inside a rough, thick cocoon.

"Your little roan is in the corral yonder," Slim said, pointing with a crooked finger to the fenced-in area behind the barn.

"Thanks, Slim." Rebecca headed toward the door leading around back.

"She likes sweets."

"I haven't given her a name. What do you call her?"

"I call her Squirt."

Rebecca smiled. "I think you have a soft spot for the horses."

"I like 'em fine. Have a good day, miss." Slim sauntered into the tack room.

Rebecca hurried back to the kitchen. If she wasn't mistaken, there were still some molasses cookies that Claudia had baked a few days ago in the big crockery jar on the sideboard.

Two cookies in hand, Rebecca went around back and leaned against the fence rails. "Hey, Squirt." She held out a cookie in the flattened palm of her hand. "Come here, girl."

The mare lifted her head, her ears up and her eyes bright. After looking around carefully she walked over to the fence.

Rebecca held out her hand, letting the horse sniff the cookie. She wasn't sure she'd take it, though she thought horses liked molasses. After a few seconds of tickling little nips the mare took the cookie, her head bobbing up and down as though she was saying, "Good, very good."

Rebecca laughed. She fed the mare the other cookie, knowing she'd made a friend. After a few minutes she gave Squirt one last pat on her white star and turned around.

Sloan stood right behind her. He was so close, she almost ran into his wide chest. His arms reached out to steady her as she looked into his eyes, shaded by his hat.

"I didn't know you were there."

"You were having a good time."

"I like Squirt."

"Squirt?" Sloan looked over Rebecca's shoulder at the mare.

"That's what Slim calls her."

"Slim's got an odd sense of humor."

"If he had a really odd sense of humor, he'd call her something like Beast or Bruno or Big Red."

Sloan chuckled. "I wouldn't put it past him."

"He is rather a character." *And you almost laughed again.*

They seemed to have run out of words, Rebecca thought, as Sloan watched her intently.

She felt a bit like squirming under his close perusal.

"So," she said, breaking eye contact and looking around the ranch building, "What did you do today?"

"Just the usual."

"Now you're supposed to ask me the same thing." Rebecca began to walk slowly back to the house.

Sloan smiled as he fell in beside her. "And what did you do today?"

"I dusted and did some other housework. I had a very domestic day."

Sloan placed a hand on her arm and stopped. "You know you don't have to clean my house."

Rebecca shrugged. "I don't mind. It gives me something to do. Believe me, I get plenty bored without television or even radio." She watched the confused look on Sloan's face. "Never mind. You wouldn't believe me anyway."

"Is this anything like baseball?"

"Kind of. As a matter of fact, baseball games are often broadcast on TV and radio."

"I have no idea what you're talking about," he said without the slightest bit of anger.

"I know." She sighed, knowing there was no way to explain twentieth-century marvels to a man who didn't believe she was from the future. But it really didn't matter. At least he no longer complained about her "crazy" remarks. She continued walking toward the house.

"Would you like to go to town tomorrow?" he asked.

She stopped and whirled to face him. "Yes! I'd love to go."

"I wasn't sure . . . since there's not much to see."

But there is, she wanted to shout. *There's Mr. Grant, who just might give my message to Leda.* "But I'd like to get out of the house. Like I said, there's not that much to do. I'm used to being busy."

"We'll leave after breakfast then." Sloan waited as Rebecca walked up the steps to the back door.

"I'll be ready." She felt very happy. She pushed aside all her doubts about whether contacting Leda was the right thing to do. Fate—that's what it was. She'd needed a way to get a message to town, and Sloan had just walked up and asked her. And how could she argue with fate?

The ride to town was beginning to seem familiar, since she'd traveled this way once with Sloan on the wagon and ridden it once herself. The temperature was very comfortable today, unlike the other times. And Sloan was even more familiar to her than the landscape.

He seemed more relaxed, his expression open when he glanced at her. She felt no need to talk all the time; sitting beside him on the wagon seat was enough for the moment.

"Do you have a list of things you need?" he asked after a while.

Had he seen her envelope? Did he know she'd written a note the other day? Again, guilt insinuated itself into her thoughts. She didn't want to keep things from Sloan, but did she have any choice? "No, I don't have a list. It's been less than two weeks." Besides, there hadn't been much at the store, at least from her standpoint.

"There's a number of things I need."

"Okay."

"I thought you might like a suitable hat."

"Oh, I don't know if I could part with this bonnet. It's so lovely, after all."

His eyes widened, and he looked at her like she was crazy again. But then she smiled and he apparently saw that she was kidding. His grin was spontaneous, warming her heart.

Sloan urged the horses into a trot. Rebecca settled beside him, leaning against him occasionally when the wagon slipped into a rut or onto an uneven section of road. She watched as the turnoff to the Radburn house came into view, her face expressionless. Sloan didn't give it a second glance.

He seemed to be in a relaxed, receptive mood. And he was a captive audience. Perhaps this would be the best time to talk to him about what she suspected was a serious problem.

"Sloan, you remember I told you about being a counselor?"

"Yes."

"One of the problems we encounter are people who have lived through something very traumatic and can't quit thinking about it. This happened often in the Vietnam War. Soldiers, and some nurses, lived through horrible experiences, and years later they were still haunted by their memories."

"Why are you telling me this?"

"Because I think the same thing happened to you. I think you probably saw things, or maybe even had to do things, that you simply couldn't accept. When that occurs you get what are sometimes called emotional scars. You can't see them on the outside, but in your mind they're very real."

"I don't want to talk about this."

She looped her arm through his and held tight. "I know you don't. And I know you've probably never told another soul what you went through. You probably don't think they'd understand, or that they'd think less of you as a person for admitting your feelings. But that's not always true."

"You don't know—"

"Yes, I do. I have my own demons from the past. I know what it's like to have nightmares, and think that if only I'd done this or that—something—I could have made a difference."

He looked at her with curious, guarded eyes.

"I don't know what you experienced, but I do know that it's eating you up inside. If you want to talk about it, I'm a good listener."

"I don't want to talk about it," he repeated.

"Okay, then. If you feel that you need to talk, I just want you to know that I'm available. Sometimes it helps to share your feelings. Sometimes another person has a different perspective. Whatever, I just wanted to tell you that

I know you're suffering . . . and that I want to help."

He looked at her for another minute, a myriad of emotions flashing through his eyes. Anger, curiosity, disbelief, hope—they warred within him. When the wagon hit a particularly jarring bump he looked away.

She continued to hold his arm. He sat beside her, tense and unwilling to relax his guard after what she'd said. But he didn't pull away, or yell, or get down from the wagon and walk. She considered that a major breakthrough.

The day warmed. The horses slowed to a walk as they came to an incline, one that she thought she remembered from the last trip as being right before town. She got a little sleepy with the slow sway of the wagon, but the knowledge that there would soon be other eyes on them jerked her awake. She was obviously the subject of much vicious gossip, and although the speculations of small minds didn't usually bother her, she didn't want her actions to cause problems for Sloan . . . especially after she was gone.

She wouldn't be here long enough to care about her own reputation.

They came off the hill and approached the town. Several horses and other wagons lined the street. Sloan pulled the wagon to a halt in front of the store, just like before. The teenager—Cory, she believed his name was—rushed out to tie off the horses.

"Mr. Travers," the young man greeted him with one shy glance.

Sloan jumped down from the seat and reached for Rebecca. With a swinging motion that made her feel like she was on a ride at Walt Disney World, he deposited her on the wooden planks in front of the store.

Two women who were walking toward them suddenly gasped and hurried out of the way. Cory looked up from tying off the team and blushed, and Rebecca noticed that he wouldn't meet her eyes. On the other hand, the two women, now making a wide circle around them, seeming intent on staring and whispering.

"Rude old biddies," Rebecca muttered.

Sloan stiffened beside her when he noticed the behavior of the women. Apparently, he wasn't too happy that she'd been judged and found guilty by the residents.

"All your worries about my cussing getting me in trouble seemed to be in vain. They obviously don't like me because I'm staying at the ranch unchaperoned. Tell me, did you have this problem before?" Rebecca knew she was lashing out, that it wasn't Sloan's fault that she'd become a social pariah, but at the moment she was just mad—damn mad!

"What do you mean by that?"

"When Leda lived with you. Did she get the same kind of grief?"

He grabbed her elbow and steered her inside the store. "You know I won't discuss her," he said in a harsh whisper.

"Sorry," she said with false sweetness. "I guess

I just forgot. I didn't mean to compare myself to her."

"Then don't! You're nothing like her."

"Obviously not. She's a well-respected member of the community, while I'm nothing more than Sloan's wh—"

"Don't say it!"

Rebecca turned away from Sloan's angry eyes and took a deep breath. She was behaving like an emotional, irrational, nineteenth-century woman. What difference did it make to her what these people thought? She wouldn't be here by the end of the summer. She'd vanish, and be nothing more than an interesting anecdote by Christmas.

Except for Sloan. Somehow, she knew he'd remember her. And he'd have to deal with these people, who obviously thought he was being taken in by a scheming stranger. She supposed that if she'd been raised to be narrow-minded and critical, she'd act the same way.

The fight went out of her. She wasn't even sure why she'd been so outraged. "I'm sorry," she said, turning back to face Sloan. "I don't know why I reacted like that."

"They upset you."

"Yes, but you didn't." She placed a hand on his arm. "I shouldn't have lashed out at you."

He seemed surprised at her apology. Maybe he'd expected her to be angry longer, or to blame him somehow for the situation in which she found herself. Well, she didn't blame him. He needed professional help and emotional support, not angry tirades.

"Er, Mr. Travers?"

The sound of Mr. Grant's British accent caused both of them to turn and face the storekeeper.

"We'll be right with you," Sloan said, then turned his attention back to her. "You're sure you're not upset?"

Rebecca smiled at him. "I'm fine. Why don't we get what you need? I'll just wait over there," she said, gesturing to the wooden barrels that sat beside the counter.

Sloan smiled in return. "I may need some help from you."

"Really?" She couldn't imagine for what, unless he wanted a woman's advice on new curtains or such.

He touched her elbow and led her to the small section of apparel.

"You need to purchase some ladies' clothing?"

"No, you do." He motioned toward the few dresses, blouses, and skirts.

Rebecca was surprised. She hadn't mentioned needing more clothes, although she had to admit she was awfully tired of her two changes of clothing.

"And a hat," he added, flipping the brim of her bonnet—the very same bonnet he'd insisted she buy on their last trip to town.

"Can I have a cowboy hat?" she asked, suddenly feeling impish.

"A man's hat? I don't think so."

"Party pooper."

"What?"

She laughed. "It's an expression. It means you won't let me have the fun I wanted to have."

"We're talking about clothes and hats, not parties," Sloan replied, acting much like a stern father. Last week Rebecca would have been offended or exasperated; now she understood Sloan much better. He had a sense of humor, but it was neglected and hidden under years and responsibilities.

A week ago, he wouldn't have laughed at her explanation of baseball.

"Okay. If you're tired of seeing me in the same old duds, I'm ready. Just don't expect too much. This isn't the Galleria."

"The what?"

Rebecca laughed. "Never mind."

She again searched Mr. Grant's limited stock. One new item caught her eye: a dress with a green bodice and a plaid skirt. She held it up and looked to Sloan for his reaction. "What do you think?"

"Very nice."

Mr. Grant hurried over. "That just came in on Saturday. The latest fashion, I'm told."

"Will it fit?" Sloan asked her.

"I believe so."

"Get whatever else you need."

Rebecca looked through the skirts, selecting a blue calico that caught her eye.

Mr. Grant smiled, no doubt mentally adding figures.

Suddenly it occurred to her that she didn't

need many clothes. She wouldn't be here that long. There was no need to waste Sloan's money. She dropped the calico back into the pile. "I . . . I really don't need that."

"Of course you do," Sloan said. He picked up the skirt, then handed it and the dress to Mr. Grant.

Rebecca stood where she was, feeling tired and dispirited. Sloan picked up a narrow brimmed straw hat and critically assessed the silk flowers around the crown. "What about this one?"

She tried to summon a bit of enthusiasm. "It's very . . . cute."

"Is that good or bad?"

"It's not very functional."

"Good." He untied the ugly bonnet and pulled it off. Placing the straw hat on the back of her head, he looked at her with a discerning eye.

"If I may?" Mr. Grant asked. He perched the hat forward, until it dipped low on Rebecca's forehead. "Yes, that's much more like it."

"Really, Sloan, I have no need of a hat."

"Of course you do."

He wouldn't listen . . . and she couldn't tell him that she'd be leaving soon. Not when he didn't even believe she was from the future.

He bought her a new blouse, the calico skirt, the plaid dress, and the cute little hat. In addition, he found a wide-brimmed, much more practical straw hat that would be perfect for working in the yard or riding in the wagon.

If she just had some SPF 30 sunblock, none of this would be necessary.

Rebecca was so involved in her own thoughts that she hadn't realized Sloan was still making purchases. Intrigued, she walked to the counter. Small shirts and pants, two pairs of shoes, and some carved wooden toys rested next to her new clothes.

He paid his bill. Mr. Grant wrapped Rebecca's selections and the children's clothes separately; then Sloan picked up both packages and carried them out of the store.

"Are those for some children at the ranch?"

"No . . . some other children."

She would have asked who, but his lips had thinned and his expression closed. Suddenly she remembered the reason she needed to come to town. In the surprise of getting new clothes—clothes she didn't really need—she'd nearly forgotten.

He dropped the packages in the back of the wagon.

Rebecca's hand eased into her pocket. The note to Leda was there. With a sigh, she turned to face Sloan. "I need to run back inside for a moment. I forgot that old bonnet."

"Leave it. Neither one of us liked it."

"Oh, but I can wear it when I work outside. It *is* practical."

Sloan untied the lead reins of the team. "Whatever you'd like."

She hurried inside the store, closing the door behind her. With quick steps, she walked to the counter. "Mr. Grant? I was wondering if you could see that Mrs. Radburn gets this note. It's rather personal, and I didn't know any other way to deliver it to her. Please . . ."

"I'm not the postal service, miss," he said, his voice less friendly now than when he talked to Sloan.

"I know that, and under normal circumstances I would never impose on you. But you see, I have a distant relationship to Mrs. Radburn, one that neither Sloan nor her husband wishes to acknowledge." Well, that was basically the truth. "I really just need to get this note to her. I promise you, it's nothing that will compromise you."

"Very well." He took the note and turned it over in his hand, as though looking for hidden markings.

The door opened. "Rebecca?"

"Coming!" She grabbed the bonnet from the shelf where Sloan had set it, then rushed back to the door. "Thank you, Mr. Grant," she said as she hurried to the wagon.

Sloan walked outside late that night, sipping a leftover cup of coffee he'd reheated. The night was clear, and the temperature pleasantly cool. The moon bathed his house in a weak, blue-white light that cast long shadows. All around him the night sounds echoed: the chirp of an insect, the call of a bird, and the rustling of grass as something small hurried back to its nest.

He'd been called by the night to come outside, to see the house and the stars and the land around him. Maybe even to see his own life. So many times he'd cursed the setting of the sun, dreaded the nightmares that might come. At night the world often seemed to press in on him. During the day, beneath the wide-open skies and endless prairie, he felt free of the demons from his past. But at night he never knew when they would visit.

Rebecca's words echoed in his head. *I think you probably saw things, or maybe even had to do things, that you simply couldn't accept.* How did she know? Had he talked in his sleep during the storm, when the nightmare was upon him? He couldn't recall. He'd waked to her tender touch, and all the visions had faded instantly.

Was she right about many people suffering from the same affliction? He had no idea what war she spoke of, but her words had haunted him all day. Would talking to someone help? There'd been no one in Philadelphia outside his family. Many of his friends from school hadn't served. They saw the war in terms of ideals, just as he had before he'd been commissioned. Other men who'd fought simply wanted to forget, to never discuss what had happened. They'd gotten on with their lives, but he hadn't been able to put his memories to rest.

A gust of wind interrupted his thoughts, ruffling his hair and skittering small, dry leaves across the ground. They sounded so much like the clanking swords of a tiny army that he looked down, just to see the usual tufts of grass and sand and rock. Nothing magical.

When he raised his eyes Painted Elk stood

nearby. Sloan jerked involuntarily. "You startled me."

"You were deep in thought to let an old man walk up on you."

Sloan finished the coffee, then threw the dregs on the ground. "You're right."

"The woman Rebecca is much on your mind."

"Yes," Sloan said, looking at the house—at the window of her bedroom upstairs. "She's not like any other woman I've ever known."

"Yet you still do not believe she is not from your time."

"You know, it's funny, but I haven't really thought about her being from the future, as she claims, in days. We've talked, and she's said things, but . . . I don't know."

"This woman was sent to you for a reason, Sloan Travers."

"You know I respect your beliefs, your abilities, but I can't believe . . ."

"I tell you the same thing I told to her: You must think with your heart. Inside, you know the truth."

"I'm trying, Painted Elk. Perhaps in time—"

"You do not have the time!" the old man said vehemently. "Her days in this world are not counted like grains of sand, but like the petals of a flower."

"She's leaving?"

"When her time comes she will leave. It is not her decision, but the will of the Great Spirit."

"I'll fight heaven and hell, if I have to, to make her stay."

Painted Elk shook his head. "You will fight both, but she must go back to her own time."

He walked away, his moccasins making no sound on the sandy soil. For long moments Sloan stayed in the same spot, staring at the window, wondering if what Painted Elk said was true. He didn't want her to leave. He wanted her to stay and build a future with him. Unable to put a name to his feelings, he only knew that for the first time he felt there was a chance for happiness, for his own future. Without Rebecca, there would be nothing . . . again.

Chapter Fourteen

Sloan stood at the foot of Rebecca's bed, watching the moonlight illuminate her peaceful features. Her red-gold hair was spread across the pillow as she lay on her back, one hand tucked beneath the pillow and one resting on top of the blanket. The thought that she might not be with him forever was like a branding iron in his gut.

Please, God. I haven't done a lot in my life, but I haven't asked for much either. I need her. Please don't take her away.

He walked softly to the side of the bed and sat gently on the mattress. Rebecca stirred, turned her head away from him, and slept on.

He reached out and took her hand. "Rebecca."

She turned toward him and opened her eyes. She jerked, then relaxed. "Sloan. You frightened me." She blinked, then pushed herself into a sitting position. "What's wrong?"

"I've been thinking about what you said today
. . . about what happened during the war."

She squeezed his hand. "Yes?"

"I'm not sure if I want to talk about it. If I knew
that talking would help, maybe I could. But talking won't change the facts."

"Have you ever thought that they might not be
facts at all, but your perception of the truth?"

"I know what happened." He could vividly recall each agonizing month of the war they'd
fought through the South.

"Let me give you an example. In my time, fifty
years after the end of World War II, there is still
a huge controversy over dropping two very powerful bombs on two cities in Japan. These weap-
ons were so powerful that you can't even imagine
their ability to devastate a city. One bomb killed
over seventy-thousand people and leveled the
city. Just one bomb. We were at war with Japan,
but we'd never admitted to intentionally killing
women and children."

"Rebecca, I can't believe—"

"Just let me finish, okay?" she asked softly.
"Many people say that we should never have used
the bombs, that Japan would have surrendered
soon. Others say that Japan had stated they
would never surrender. The military option was
to invade Japan. Hundreds of thousands of soldiers would have died. The people who advo-
cated using the bomb said that the Japanese
people would have fought to the death—all of
them—men, women, and children. So, in the

end, no one can know what would have happened; we dropped the bombs and Japan surrendered."

"I don't see what this story has to do with our Civil War."

"I'm not sure what you did in the war, but whatever it was, you can't be sure how many lives were saved or destroyed by your actions. You can go back and second guess for the rest of your life, or you can say that you were put in a situation way beyond your control and did your best to perform your duty. Just like the men who dropped the bombs; they didn't want to kill all those innocent civilians, but by doing so they may have saved the lives of their fellow soldiers. Who can say which lives are more important?"

"But the women . . . and the children. You can't know."

"I know that terrible things happen during war. I've heard stories that make me cry and have bad dreams, and vow that no one should ever go to war again. But Sloan, if my country was threatened, or my family in jeopardy, I'd fight alongside anyone who was defending them. And I'd probably do horrible things myself, if I had to, to save what I love."

"Oh, Rebecca, I want to believe," he whispered, reaching for her.

She melted into his arms as though she belonged there always. Soft and warm from sleep, she smelled of woman and forgiveness. He angled his head and took her lips, kissing her with all the longing in his soul.

When they'd made love before they were both swept away by passion. He'd wanted her so badly that he couldn't have waited, even if she'd been less aggressive. But she'd wanted him too, and that need had fueled his own.

This time he wanted to go slow, to savor each touch, to revel in each sigh. He broke free of the kiss, trailing his lips down her neck to find the sensitive skin of her shoulder. The opening of her nightgown gaped, inviting further exploration. He held her with one arm and brought the other hand to her breast, cradling it gently. She was perfect, fitting his hand as though she'd been made just for him. The nipple beaded immediately, making his heart race faster.

But even though his body was pushing him toward completion, he resisted. He pushed Rebecca back against the pillows, his lips following and dipping inside the neckline of her nightgown. Her pulse pounded frantically, driving him on. With a groan, he sealed his lips over that tight, beaded nipple and sucked.

She bolted from the bed, gasping his name and holding tight to his hair. He ignored the twinge of pain, giving the same attention to her other breast. She twisted and moaned.

"Sloan, please!"

"Not yet, love. Not this time."

Slowly, he inched the nightgown up her thighs to her waist, to her breasts, and then over her head. In the gentle moonlight her skin glowed in blue-white magic. He molded his hands over her, memorizing each inch of pale flesh. If he had a lifetime with her, he would never grow tired of making love to this woman. If he had only a short time, he would make each moment as special as possible.

Her lips beckoned and he kissed her again. She met his tongue, thrust for thrust, fueling his desire. When she pulled at his shirt he grabbed her hands, pushing them over her head. He began another assault on her senses as she moaned and thrashed. He trailed kisses down the other side of her neck, across her breasts and stomach.

"No . . . please. I need you now."

"Not yet," he murmured, nipping the side of her hip, then traveling to the sensitive flesh behind her knee. When he moved to the inside of her thighs she gasped and stiffened her legs.

"Easy, love. I won't do anything you don't want."

"I want you. Now; inside me," she demanded breathlessly.

"And I want you." Now and forever, he added silently.

He knelt on the bed, jerking off his shirt, and fumbing with the buttons over his bulging fly.

Rebecca couldn't stand the wait any longer. Never before had she been so impatient, so thoroughly aroused. Sloan dominated her with his touch, incited her to madness with his kisses, until all she could think of was the shattering release she knew awaited her in his arms. Making love had never been like this.

She wanted him so much that tears of frustration burned in her eyes and she had to fight back a sob. She pushed herself up from the bed, kneeling in front of Sloan. With a sigh, she kissed his chest, and then one of his flat male nipples. He jerked, his hands going from the buttons on his jeans to her arms.

"Turn-about is fair play," she whispered against his skin. "You made me burn; now it's my turn."

"I'm already on fire."

"I like to play with fire." She reached to his half-opened fly and quickly undid the last three buttons. He surged into her hand, hot and heavy.

"You *are* on fire," she whispered, tracing the length of him with her fingers.

"Rebecca, please," he gasped.

"What's this? You can't stand it any more than I can?"

He pulled her tight against him, her hand trapped between them. Her nipples tingled as they rested against the hair on his chest, and she moved as much as possible, loving each delicious sensation.

"I want this to last. . . ."

His words trailed off as he kissed her again. She felt a surge of emotion so strong, tears came to her eyes again. Only this time it wasn't just passion. She sank into his arms, admitting for the first time what she felt: love. Not just passion, not just compassion or understanding.

Love.

She moaned into his mouth, kissing him back with all the emotion she'd stored for a lifetime. They broke apart, panting and breathless.

Without another word they sank to the mattress. Rebecca pushed Sloan until he lay on his back, then crawled down his body until she could grasp his pants and pull them down. They hung on his boots, so she tackled them next, struggling to remove both of them. Finally, he was naked, stretched out on her bed in the moonlight like a gift from the gods. Magnificently aroused, he reached out to her.

She eased against the hard length of his body, molding herself to him, then kissed his lips. She felt love flow between them but wondered if he even realized the emotion. Probably not. He had much to learn of love and forgiveness, but she would give him all she had to offer . . . all the time she had.

With a cry, she straddled his slim hips and took him inside her, banishing all thoughts of tomorrow. They had now. It would be enough. It had to be enough. She said that to herself, over and over, as she set a relentless rhythm.

"Slow down, love," Sloan whispered.

His voice sounded hoarse and strained, but she couldn't tell for sure over the pounding of blood inside her head.

When she didn't respond he reached out and grabbed her hips, his thumbs near her pelvis, his fingers holding fast to her bottom. "Slow down," he demanded hoarsely.

She did, giving in to the tempo he set. Sensation took over, blocking out all thoughts. In her universe there was only Sloan, filling her, rocking her gently, letting her soar. The passion built until she cried out, feeling nothing but the explosion building where she and Sloan were one.

With an upward thrust and his own cry of completion, he pushed her over the edge. Convulsing, she saw stars burst into the room, blinding her. She collapsed against him, gasping, panting, unable to form a coherent thought or word. She wanted to tell him how much she loved him, how much he meant to her. But the stars were gone, and the darkness of night beckoned. She melted into his warmth, into arms that held her tight.

Sloan eased away from Rebecca as dawn streaked the pink sky with fingers of purple and lavender. She mumbled something, then rolled to her side and hugged his pillow. He smiled, remembering the first time they'd made love, and how she'd slept so soundly afterwards.

This time he was glad to let her sleep. She needed her rest, since he'd kept her busy the night before. Surprisingly, after making love again, just hours ago, he felt relaxed and . . . happy. That was the emotion welling inside him, one he hadn't felt often in many years.

He had something important to do, and this was a good time. With a gentleness he thought he'd lost long ago, he kissed her cheek. "I'll be back this afternoon," he whispered. "I have something that needs to be done."

"What?" she murmured sleepily, snuggling into the blankets and pillow. She never even opened her eyes.

"I'll be back later. Get some sleep. You'll need your strength . . . later."

Rebecca smiled. Sloan picked up his discarded clothes and boots and, catching one last glimpse of her peaceful face, closed the door behind him.

In his room, he dressed quickly, not bothering to shave. He'd clean up later. That way he'd be fresh for Rebecca. Downstairs, he retrieved the package from Grant's store and strode to the barn.

After saddling a paint that was faster than Buck, he rode out into the dawn. This morning was beautiful, with the most gorgeous sunrise he'd ever seen. The unaccustomed smile that he couldn't suppress seemed at first alien; then it settled onto his face like an old friend.

He had Rebecca to thank for that. He had Rebecca, and he'd never let her go. Surely fate wouldn't be so kind as to grant him such a boon, only to snatch it away.

No, she was his, now and always. From this day forward he had a future. He touched the paint's sides with his heels, galloping north toward the Little Popo Agie.

Rebecca felt both a profound happiness and a devastating sense of panic as she washed and dressed late in the morning. She'd traveled over a century to find the man she loved, only to be told she couldn't stay with him forever. It wasn't fair! Last night had been magical, from Sloan's quiet declaration that he wanted to put the past to rest, to the joy of making love, to the peace of sleeping in his arms throughout the night.

She vaguely recalled him saying very early that he'd be back this afternoon. Or had she dreamed that? No, if she were going to dream about Sloan, it would be that he'd slipped back into bed and made love to her one more time, not that he'd left her side for even a minute.

She pulled her hair back, wishing she had some twentieth-century products to tame the thick mass. At her apartment she had colorful bows and scrunchy silk fasteners to hold it in place. But she'd trade everything she owned to stay with Sloan in his time, if that could be her destiny. She was totally, unequivocally in love for the first time in her life.

In the kitchen she found a pot of pinto beans simmering with a meaty ham bone nestled in the middle. She really would have to do something about cholesterol, though, if she stayed. She wanted Sloan to live a happy and long life.

She made a sandwich of sliced ham she found in a dampened crockery dish, used to keep it cool, and some biscuits left from breakfast. The day would be hot, she could tell, but that didn't matter. She was in love, and that was all that seemed important at the moment.

During the day she stripped the sheets from her bed, then gathered the rest of her laundry and proceeded to the wash house. The small structure had a large galvanized tub and a cast-iron pot in which water could be heated. Life would be a lot easier if she had a washer and dryer, but she welcomed the hard work to keep herself busy until Sloan came home.

She paused, harsh lye soap stinging her hands, and looked out the single window toward the Victorian structure. Sloan's house felt like home. She loved each wooden board, each curlicue and brick. She'd never felt that way about a place before—just as she'd never felt that way about a man. They'd been living together for over two weeks now, in many ways, like a married couple. Last night had been like a honeymoon.

She'd find a way to make this work. If she had to ride across Wyoming to find bitterroot plants that still bloomed and bring every one of them back to the ranch, she'd show Painted Elk that he was wrong. She wouldn't go back. Sloan was her destiny, and only now, after experiencing love, did she realize that contentment was no longer enough. She wanted more—she wanted it all. And that meant staying with Sloan.

She hummed as she hung the clean sheets on the clothesline. She felt confident and resolute now that she'd faced her feelings for Sloan and her anxiety about the future. Nothing would keep them apart—not the memory of Leda or the nightmares from his past. Together they would conquer whatever obstacles life threw at them.

Sloan heard the hoofbeats of several horses galloping toward him as he neared the summit of a hill. Had Daniel Benson and the others returned to see that the squatters were no longer damming the river?

Sloan slowed the paint, then stopped him as

the riders crested the hill. Squinting against the glare of the noonday sun, he immediately realized that these were not his amicable, civic-minded neighbors.

Four riders drew abreast, spreading their horses in a semicircle around him so that he could either stand and face them, or wheel, like a coward, and make a run for it. He wouldn't run, and Vincent Radburn knew it.

"Travers, you've gone too far this time," Radburn said, hate dripping from every word.

"What are you talking about?" He hadn't said, or done, anything to Radburn in ages. The other men shifted in their saddles, as though they were waiting for something. Apparently, everyone but him knew what was going on.

"Getting your whore to contact my wife. *My wife*," he roared. "You'll never lay a hand on her again, do you hear me?"

The only warning Sloan had was a whoosh of sound as the rope landed around his shoulders. Before he could bring his arms up to lift it off, the lariat tightened, cutting into his arms and chest. With a jerk, the man tried to unseat him. Sloan held tight to the paint with his legs, resisting the pressure, knowing that his only chance now was to run.

Then another rope settled around him, and two men tugged. The paint shied, half reared at the pressure, and bolted. Sloan felt nothing but air for one brief moment; then he hit the ground hard, with no way to break his fall. His hat tumbled off as his head hit the hard-packed prairie.

His teeth rattled. He heard the sound of hoof-beats. More men? No, just the paint, running off. Then Radburn rode up, his face a hate-filled mask. Sloan squinted into the sun as Radburn dismounted and stood over him.

"You weren't good enough for her before, and you're sure as hell not good enough for her now." Without warning, he kicked out, catching Sloan just below the waist on his side.

Pain exploded through him. With a twist, he tried to catch Radburn's legs with his own, to trip up the man and throw him to the ground. But Radburn stepped away, and Sloan heard the two men who held the ropes yell to their horses.

He was being dragged! Rocks and sagebrush bit into his back as he bounced behind the horse. Soon the kick in his side paled to the agony of being pulled like a sack of feed behind two galloping horses. His shoulders felt like raw meat long before the men turned and galloped back to Radburn.

Was it over, or would Radburn put a bullet through him now? Or maybe they'd drag him to a cottonwood and let him swing. God, no! Not now, not when he'd just found Rebecca. Pain exploded in his heart as well as through his body. He struggled against the ropes, but they were tighter than before, cutting into his arms until he was sure they bled.

All the men dismounted. With a nod from Radburn, they walked toward him, one at a time. Sloan braced himself; he had to survive this. He had to get back to Rebecca. He had to ask her what Radburn had meant when he'd said—

The first man hit him, hard, in the jaw. Sloan's head hit the ground and stars filled his vision. The man grabbed his chin, turned his face to the side, and hit him again. He couldn't tell where the men were anymore. Then someone kicked him in the other side, near his waist. A stomp to his ribs made him groan in pain; he prayed they weren't broken.

Through a haze of pain, he heard Radburn as the man leaned over him. "I'm giving back the note from your whore. If either of you try to see my wife or my son again, I'll kill you."

Sloan heard the crinkle of paper as it was roughly pushed into his shirt pocket

He could tell Radburn had moved because no shadow fell over him. *It's over,* he thought. *They're going to leave me here. They're not going to kill me.*

He had no warning when the last blow came, just Radburn's grunt of satisfaction as his boot connected with Sloan's ribs.

With his last strength, Sloan rolled to his side and retched.

"Take the ropes off him, boys. He's not worth the price of hemp."

Faintly, as if they were far away, he heard the men laugh. Then blackness descended, and he fell into the darkness.

Rebecca walked to the back door, hugging her arms close. The sun was close to setting and still there was no sign of Sloan. What kind of errand had he run? She wished she'd been more awake this morning. She wished he'd told someone where he was going. Slim didn't know anything, and Sloan had left before Claudia arrived to fix breakfast.

The smell of overcooked beans and ham filled the kitchen. Rebecca's appetite had deserted her, and she couldn't eat a thing right now. She'd had an uneasy feeling all afternoon, maybe because last night had been so wonderful.

Unable to stand by quietly in the house, she opened the back door. Claudia's chickens pecked on the ground for the last bit of grain, and horses milled around the corral. She walked past the wash house and the smokehouse, and toward the barn. Maybe Slim had remembered something he'd seen. Maybe he could recall Sloan's habits in more detail now that he'd had time to think.

Her feeling of unease increased as she looked at the sky. The sun had dipped very low to the horizon. It would be twilight soon, then dark. Where was Sloan?

She paused at Buck's stall and rubbed the spot of white on his forehead. He butted against her hand, asking for more. "Where do you think he is, Buck?" she asked the horse. "Too bad you're not Lassie. I could just say, 'Lassie, find Sloan,' and you'd run off and locate him, before he got into trouble."

Was he in trouble? She'd flirted with the idea all afternoon. Never before had she felt such a sense of disquiet.

Slim walked up, bracing his arms on Buck's stall.

"Have you thought of anything, Slim? Anything at all?"

"Oh, shoot, he probably just found a cow in trouble. Or maybe his horse went lame."

"But he left so early. Surely he should be back by now. It will be dark soon."

Slim gave a humorless chuckle. "Sloan's no baby to be afraid of the dark. He knows how to take care of himself."

But I need him here with me. I don't have much time. I have to know he's safe. She felt like admitting that to someone, but there was no one there.

For the thousandth time she wished for Sara. How wonderful it would be to have someone to confide in, someone who would understand. But her sister wasn't here—wasn't even alive in 1996. After two years of experimenting with drugs, after becoming addicted to cocaine, Sara had simply given up. She'd taken their father's pistol from his closet, loaded it, and locked herself in her room.

Rebecca had been outside playing when she heard the shot. She'd rushed inside, pounded against the locked door, and then called 911. At age ten, she at least knew that much.

As the paramedics crashed through the door, she'd stood frozen for a moment, not believing this was real. Then she'd taken a deep breath, forcing herself to move, to think. The smell of gunpowder, along with the blood soaking through Sara's pale blue bedspread, filled her senses.

Sobbing and hysterical, she'd watched her sister's lifeless body as the paramedics worked over her. There had been no way to save her.

In truth, Sara had been lost to all of them for a long time, although no one had realized the extent of her problems. They hadn't understood the warning signs, nor had they taken her symptoms seriously. "Just the pains of growing up," their mother had said, while their father had shaken his head and grounded Sara one more time. But she'd needed help, Rebecca realized later. And no one had been there for her. Especially not her younger sister, who couldn't fathom the kind of addiction Sara had experienced for the drugs that she'd begged, borrowed, and stolen, to obtain.

Rebecca knew that her sister was the reason that she'd gone into counseling as a career. If she could help just one other person, perhaps Sara wouldn't have died in vain. And if she got too close . . . well, that was because she hadn't been close enough once.

Rebecca pushed away from the stall. "I have to do something. I can't stand around and wait. I'll take Squirt out and look myself if I have to."

"Ah, now, Miss Rebecca, you don't need to go galavantin' around the countryside. Iffen you want, I'll take one of the boys with me and look around."

She got the impression that Slim would just go through the motions to appease her. He didn't think Sloan was in any trouble. He'd probably stop just over the hill and smoke a cigarette. "No. This is something I need to do. Will you saddle Squirt for me, please?"

He shook his head but went to the tack room for a saddle. He'd only taken a few steps toward the roan mare's stall when Rebecca heard hoofbeats outside.

"Sloan!" She ran toward the open barn door. Slim was right behind her.

A pinto stood just beyond the opening. One rein was broken; the other dangled on the ground. The horse hung his head, obviously tired, although it wasn't lathered or heated.

Panic increasing, Rebecca turned to Slim. "Whose horse is that?"

Slim took a deep breath, his face suddenly serious and tired. "When he don't ride Buck he sometimes rides that paint. Now, I ain't sure, but—"

Rebecca grabbed Slim's shirt. "Saddle Squirt for me, Slim. And Buck. If Sloan's on foot . . ."

Slim hurried off, all business now.

With shaking hands, Rebecca gathered up the reins of the paint, leading it inside. "Horse, I wish you could talk. I wish you could tell me what happened."

Chapter Fifteen

Painted Elk rode with them, although Rebecca had serious doubts about whether he could keep up. However, he was the one who knew the signs the horse had made on its way home. He leaned low over the neck of his mount, refusing to be rushed, even as the sun dipped low and coral streaked the sky.

Two other groups of men had fanned out in other directions, just in case. Rebecca wasn't taking any chances. She wasn't sure if she'd "elected" herself leader or if she'd just been accepted by Slim and the others. If they'd taken time to think about her take-charge attitude, she might have been following Slim. Then again, she might have ridden off on her own; she was that panicked and determined.

They'd been riding for almost an hour. A sob

caught in her throat. If they didn't find Sloan soon, there might not be another chance until morning. The moon wasn't full, although it should be about half. Would they have enough light to keep on tracking?

Oh, Sloan, where are you? She wiped at her eyes, knowing it would do no good to cry now. He could be right over the next hill.

"Miss Rebecca! Look!"

Slim's voice cut into her sorrow, jerking her to attention. Her eyes scanned the horizon, then dipped lower, following Slim's pointing finger.

"There!" he shouted. He spurred his horse into a gallop, pulling Buck along behind him.

A dark shape huddled on the ground. Oh, God, no! Rebecca kicked Squirt into a dead run, rushing past Slim.

She pulled sharply on the reins. The mare squealed and stopped so fast, she almost sat on her haunches. Rebecca jumped from the saddle even before the horse came to a complete halt.

"Sloan! Sloan, can you hear me?" She knelt beside him. He lay on his stomach, his head to one side. His shirt was in shreds. Had he been beaten? Had his horse dragged him? "Sloan, please." She touched his face and felt the bruising, the hot, dry skin.

He moaned, the weak sound sending a knife of pain through Rebecca. He could have broken bones, internal injuries, a dozen problems. She didn't have the medical knowledge to treat him. She needed a cellular phone to call 911. And a care-flight helicopter.

Slim ran up with a canteen of water. He shrugged out of his jacket and handed it to Rebecca.

She folded the jacket and placed it under Sloan's head. "Sloan, I'm going to give you a drink of water. Don't gulp it, okay?"

Gently, she raised his head an inch or two, then put the open canteen to his lips. He swallowed, his lips lax against the metal mouth.

"That's enough for now." She lay him gently back on the makeshift pillow. "Can you tell us what happened? Do you know where you're hurt?"

"Radburn," he rasped. "And his men."

"They attacked you?"

"Yeah. About noon." He swallowed as though his throat was parched. "More water."

Rebecca complied, giving him small sips when it seemed he wouldn't choke. "Is anything broken?"

"Don't think so. Just hurts . . . like hell. Tried to walk back. Passed out."

"Oh, Sloan." She bent close, her hair a curtain around his face as she kissed his forehead. That seemed to be the only spot not bruised or bleeding.

She turned to Slim. "How are we going to get him back to the ranch?"

"If we had some poles, we could rig a stretcher. But there ain't nothing out here." Slim shook his head. "He'll have to ride, or we can throw him over the saddle."

"No! He could have broken ribs. That could

cause internal bleeding."

Sloan touched her hand. "I can ride," he rasped.

"You can't even stand. You need a doctor. You need to go to a hospital."

"Ma'am, there ain't no doctor around these parts," Slim volunteered.

"But who takes care—"

"We jus' do the best we can," Slim answered.

"But—"

"Move outta the way, Miss Rebecca, and we'll get him on his horse."

Her mind raced frantically. They could kill him! His lungs could rupture, or he could bleed to death. "Wait! First, let me look him over. Then, if nothing's broken, you can try to get him up."

She leaned over Sloan. "I'm going to roll you onto your back. I know that will hurt, but I have to check your ribs and see if there's internal bleeding."

As gently as possible, she rolled him over. He gasped in pain, his body going rigid for a moment. *Oh, God, I've killed him. I don't know what I'm doing, not really. Please don't let him die.*

With trembling hands, she checked his shoulders, his collarbone, his arms, and then his chest. Touching each rib, she eventually guessed that they were bruised, not broken. They might be cracked, but she didn't think that could puncture a lung.

Why didn't I pay more attention to first aid? Why didn't I ever take an advanced course in life-saving techniques? Because there was always an emergency room around, or a doctor. Because you never expected to end up in nineteenth-century Wyoming, she answered herself. She felt so helpless. She didn't even have bandages or an antibiotic creme.

His sides were tender. He winced, and she could tell he tried not to gasp as she probed the injury. From the bruising, it looked as though he'd been beaten or kicked there, hard.

"Does anything else hurt?"

"Everything hurts," he whispered.

"Can you sit on your horse? We brought Buck."

"Don't know. Have to try."

"Okay." Rebecca sat back on her heels. "Slim, Painted Elk, do you think we can get him up?"

"Sure 'nough," Slim said. He grabbed Sloan's arm and placed his other hand under Sloan's shoulder. Painted Elk did the same, although to Rebecca, these two slightly built men seemed the worst possible choices to get a large man like Sloan on his feet.

With a big heave and some help from Sloan, they got him standing. Rebecca rushed forward, helping him as best she could. She didn't want him to topple over and injure another part of his body.

There weren't that many undamaged areas.

Slowly, they shuffled to the gelding. Buck rolled his eyes but didn't shy away as Sloan rested against him. One hand on the saddlehorn, he lifted his leg into the stirrup.

"Slim, get behind him. Make sure he doesn't fall."

Rebecca knew she was being bossy, but these men didn't love Sloan the way she did. They couldn't know how deeply she hurt for him, or the anger she felt at Vincent Radburn, her own great-great-grandfather, for doing such a thing.

She hovered beside Buck, ready to catch Sloan if he fell, although she knew she didn't have the strength. At best, she could break his fall to the ground.

He landed in the saddle with a whoosh. Sloan groaned. Buck shied sideways, then stood still. Everyone seemed to breathe a sigh of relief.

"How do you feel?" Rebecca asked, placing a hand on his thigh. For the first time she noticed the deep, red furrows around his arm, as though he'd been bound.

"Like I've been beaten and dragged and left to die," he said faintly. "A little more water, please."

Rebecca retrieved the canteen from the ground and handed it to him. He managed to drink by himself—a good sign.

"I'm sorry you have to ride," she said, hearing the pain in her own voice. "It's important we get you back as soon as possible."

Sloan handed back the canteen. "Best to go now. How far are we?"

"Slim?" Rebecca asked.

"'Bout an hour," he answered. "It'll be dark soon."

Sloan braced his hands on the saddlehorn and leaned forward. Rebecca mounted her own mare and pulled along beside him. "I'll be right here."

Sloan didn't reply. Painted Elk mounted his

horse and positioned him on the other side of Sloan. With Slim leading the way, they rode slowly toward the ranch.

Rebecca rested her head on the mattress, exhausted by the events of the last four hours. Sloan slept fitfully, but at least he wasn't in too much pain at the moment. The only "anesthetic" they'd had was bourbon, so whether he was drunk or just debilitated, she couldn't tell.

His beautiful, muscled body was covered in scratches, bruises, and scrapes. Only his legs seemed to have escaped the beating. She'd cleaned each abrasion, using witch hazel to disinfect the worst ones, and bound his ribs, in case they were cracked. Now he lay on his stomach, covered by a sheet.

She stroked his forehead, slightly sunburned because he usually wore his hat. There was nothing more she could do; now he needed rest and fluids.

She pushed away from the bed and picked up his tattered, discarded clothing. The shirt was a dirty mess. It stank of sweat and the metallic odor of blood. She'd throw it away before Sloan had a chance to see it. Besides, it was too far gone even for the rag bin. She wadded it into a ball, unable to look any longer at the tears in the fabric, but a crinkling sound caught her attention.

Carefully, she pulled a folded piece of paper from the pocket. It looked as though it had been crammed thoughtlessly inside, perhaps in a hurry. She didn't want to intrude on Sloan's privacy, but no one knew where he'd been all day, and this might be a clue.

She unfolded the paper, then gazed in shock at her own handwriting. Her note to Leda. How had . . . Mr. Grant must have given it to Vincent Radburn, not Leda. And Vincent was just the kind of manipulative, overbearing husband who would read his wife's mail. Didn't Mr. Grant have any sense at all? How could he have given the note to Vincent—but of course: because he was a man. And in this century it was common practice to deny a woman any rights of her own.

Rebecca fumed in anger, clenching the note in her fist, cursing the store owner and her great-great-grandfather.

But why was the note in Sloan's pocket? If Mr. Grant had given it to Vincent Radburn, then Vincent must have given it to Sloan. Which meant that Sloan knew she'd tried to contact Leda. Wouldn't he have been angry with her? He hadn't seemed angry.

But surely Vincent would have told Sloan about the note. He would have been livid that she'd tried to contact Leda. He would have—He would have been mad enough to try to kill Sloan, to beat him and leave him to die on the prairie.

This was all her fault! All the pain he'd suffered, because of her need to know about his past.

With a sob, she ran to the bed. Perching on the chair she'd placed there earlier for her vigil, she leaned close. Sloan slept, his face drawn and tired. What if his horse hadn't come back to the ranch when it had? What if Painted Elk hadn't been there to follow the tracks back to Sloan? What if she'd never tried to pass that note to Leda?

Early this morning, she would have put a different slant on "what ifs." She'd been full of hope for the future. She'd been so confident that they'd find a way to stay together. Yet her own action, not some oddity of time, might tear them apart.

"I'm so sorry. Please forgive me. I never meant to harm you. I never meant . . ."

She couldn't finish. She lay her head on the mattress, sobbing quietly for the pain Sloan had suffered. He could have been killed. And this was all her fault.

Sloan woke slowly, his brain as fuzzy and coated as his tongue. Sunlight streamed through his window. Why was he in bed so late? He should be up and working. When he tried to roll over his body was hit with pain from a hundred different points.

"Sloan!"

Rebecca's startled voice came from nearby, on the other side of the bed. Carefully, he turned his head.

Immediately he felt her soft hand on his forehead. What had happened? He remembered going to her bedroom, talking to her, making love, but then what? It was morning, and he was back in his own room, with a body that felt as though he'd been caught in a stampede.

She eased an arm under his head and lifted a

glass to his lips. He drank, swallowing the water greedily. He didn't think he'd ever been this thirsty.

"How do you feel?"

"Like I've been run over by my herd," he said. Despite the water, his voice sounded hoarse and unused.

"I'm so sorry," she said faintly, lowering him to the pillow.

"Why do you say that?" His brain still felt as if it was filled with fog. As he rolled to lay on his side, every muscle screamed in protest. The skin on his back felt as though it was on fire.

"I . . . I'm so sorry you suffered like this."

He touched his eyes; the skin was puffy and tender. His jaw ached; his teeth felt a bit loose. "I left here early. Was that yesterday?"

"Yes. You've slept through the night."

"I rode to the squatters' cabin."

"Was that the reason you bought the children's clothing at the store?"

"Yes." He remembered riding across the plains to the tiny, rough cabin. "They didn't have proper clothes or shoes, or even enough to eat, probably. I couldn't stand to see them with so little, when I have so much."

"Did you deliver the children's gifts?"

"Yes." He frowned, remembering the suspicious looks on the faces of the adults, the cautious curiosity in the eyes of the urchins. He imagined that they'd torn into the package as soon as he rode out of sight.

And then he'd seen the riders come toward him over the hill.

"Radburn," he rasped.

"Yes, you said he and his men beat you, dragged you with ropes. You were kicked," she said, her voice breaking, "in the sides—"

"I remember the kicks," he said, wondering just how badly he was bruised. He was almost afraid to raise the sheet and look.

"What else do you remember?" she asked softly, almost tentatively.

He closed his eyes for a moment, remembering Vincent Radburn's hate-filled face as he leaned over him. "Getting your whore to contact my wife," he'd said, although Sloan had no idea what he was talking about. Then, later, he'd given him a note. Had Rebecca written a note to Leda?

He needed to know, yet he didn't want to ask. If Rebecca had gone behind his back to write to Leda, that meant she'd betrayed him. She knew how he felt about the Radburns. There was no reason for her to pry into his past, not when he'd been thinking about their future.

"Sloan, I'm so sorry. I want to explain everything that I know, but you're weak. You need to rest. I think perhaps you're still suffering from heat exposure, in addition to your injuries. I'm going to get you some broth; then you can rest. When you feel better we can talk."

Sloan reached out and caught her wrist. "Just answer one question: Did you write a note to Leda?"

Rebecca looked him in the eyes, her own glistening with unshed tears. "Yes, I did. I'm so sorry, but I did."

He let his hand fall to the mattress and closed his eyes against the pain in his heart. In a moment he heard her footsteps as she walked across the floor and out the door. The sounds of the day rose around him: Slim shouting to someone outside to close the gate; Claudia calling to her chickens; Rebecca clanging shut the iron door on the stove.

At least he knew for sure now that she wasn't working with the Radburns. But he also knew he couldn't trust her. Before he'd made love to her she'd tried to pass a note to Leda. When? In town, perhaps, when he'd bought her the new clothes?

She'd made love with him, showed him with words and actions that she cared, after she'd gone behind his back to contact his worst enemies.

She had an odd way of showing that she cared. If she couldn't respect his wishes, something that he'd been absolutely clear about, then they had no future. As soon as he could, he'd tell her that she'd better find another place to live. He had no room in his life for another scheming, deceiving woman.

Chapter Sixteen

Sloan slept most of the day. Rebecca came in to check on him occasionally, giving him liquids when he was awake, but she couldn't stand the censure in his eyes when he looked at her. She silently spooned the broth into his battered mouth until he finished and she could escape the room.

He didn't understand her reasons, of course, but even if he did, would he care? He was so convinced that ignoring the past was the best approach, at least when it came to Leda. He'd listened to Rebecca talk about post traumatic stress syndrome, and perhaps in time he would talk about his experiences in the war, but he'd firmly refused to talk about Leda.

Rebecca hadn't even told him she knew about his son, Robert. She wondered how Sloan would react when she confessed that she'd seen the boy, and that she and Leda had talked about Sloan. He'd probably kick her out of his house and his life. She'd end up with nowhere to go, waiting to be sent back to her own time, where she'd be dead.

Not a lot of options.

She had to make Sloan understand that she'd contacted Leda to save them both. Not just because she was afraid to die, but because if he wouldn't listen and change, then he condemned himself to a lifetime of pain, and her to death by strangulation. How would he handle the guilt? Sloan was a fine, decent man. Even if he was angry with her, he wouldn't want to be responsible for her death.

Perhaps he would listen to her claims that she was from the future if she showed him some proof.

She fingered the locket. She'd already shown him the photos, but he'd suggested that all they'd proven was that she might be working with the Radburns. But if Sloan knew that Vincent had had him beaten because of the note, he wouldn't think she was conspiring with them.

The family tree might be more proof. Of course, he could also see that as a carefully engineered fraud to make him believe something that wasn't true. She had to convince him of one thing; there was no reason for her to lie. She wasn't crazy, she wasn't working with the Radburns, and she knew too much about psychology to be ignored.

To fill her day she washed Sloan's dirty, slightly torn jeans, and hung them on the line to dry. Claudia came to fix dinner, and to check on Sloan. Apparently, no one else was too worried; they definitely weren't as concerned as Rebecca, who knew that serious infection could result from injuries such as the ones Sloan had sustained. Maybe because they couldn't do anything to affect the outcome, they didn't fuss over a patient.

Clouds built up in the northwest toward late afternoon. Rebecca checked the bitterroot plants, which were still blooming, then retrieved Sloan's jeans from the clothesline. She had another mending project, she thought, smoothing the worn denim. She hoped she'd be there long enough to finish the sewing.

As twilight deepened, she entered Sloan's room and lit a lamp beside the bed. A soft yellow glow filled the room. She wished she had a CD player; some soothing music might be helpful. Sitting in the chair beside the bed, she pulled Sloan's jeans from her sewing box. After threading a needle she began to darn the torn pockets and "L" shaped tear in the seat of the pants.

Sloan woke when she was half done with the mending. She looked up when he opened his eyes, startled again by the bruises on his face. He no longer looked like the handsome, stern-faced man who'd rescued her on the prairie, nor did he resemble the tender lover she'd discovered two nights ago. She remembered him laughing at baseball, and wondered if she'd ever see him smile again.

She carefully placed the jeans on the floor. Facing Sloan, she took a deep breath. "How are you feeling?"

"Better, I think." He moved his body cautiously, grimacing as his back touched the mattress.

"I don't think you'll have many scars," Rebecca said, standing up to fluff his pillow. "You're lucky that the ground wasn't more rocky or rougher."

"Yeah, I'm real lucky," Sloan said sarcastically.

"I didn't say—"

"Forget it," he cut in.

"Sloan, I understand that you're angry with me."

"That's the least of what I'm feeling."

"Why don't I get you some solid food. You must be hungry."

He nodded, turning his head as though the sight of her caused him pain.

Rebecca almost ran from the room, glad to be out of Sloan's sight so he wouldn't see how upset she was. She had to keep her emotions under control so she could speak to him rationally. But the knowledge that he clearly despised her, was only tolerating her presence because he was injured, ate away at her composure.

In the kitchen she dished up some of the chicken stew Claudia had prepared earlier. There was also some custard, baked to a golden brown. "Invalid food," the housekeeper had called the dish.

She found a tray in the dining room, loaded it up, and carried the meal upstairs. Sloan would probably want coffee, but the caffeine wouldn't be good for him.

She should have poured herself a shot of brandy, she thought, just before she walked into his room. She'd probably need it before the evening was over. *You're sounding like one of your patients*, she warned herself.

"Here's your dinner," she said as cheerfully as possible as she set the tray on the table beside his bed.

"I'll sit up," he said.

"Are you sure? I could—"

"Don't baby me! I'm just sore and mad. Nothing's broken."

"Okay. Fine. I'll just sit over here in case you need anything else." She moved her chair away from the bed and sat down.

Sloan pushed himself into a sitting position. His vision swam for a moment, and tiny stars exploded around him. Maybe he'd taken a crack on the head. When the room righted itself again he inched toward the edge of the mattress. Everything hurt, from his ribs to his back to his scalp. With care, he lifted his legs over the side of the bed and sat up.

Breathing heavily, he glanced at Rebecca through narrowed eyes. Perched on the edge of her chair in her new blue calico skirt and a white blouse, she looked as though she wanted to jump up, run over to the bed, and "help" him. He didn't want—or need—her help. Twice now he'd made serious errors in judgment when it came to women. His feelings for Rebecca were still a jumble, from anger to something else he didn't want to address. Just the thought that she had to leave, that there was no place for such a woman in his life, caused him more pain than his bruised ribs.

He tore his eyes away from Rebecca and focused on the meal she'd brought him. The smell of chicken in a rich broth with vegetables caused his stomach to rumble. How long had it been since he'd eaten? Two days? He spooned the stew into his mouth, chewed, and swallowed.

"Is there coffee?" he asked.

"No, it's not good for you. Too much caffeine—"

"What?"

"It's a . . . component of coffee. It keeps you awake, gives you energy, but also acts as a diuretic."

He scowled at Rebecca. She was using words that didn't make sense to him but seemed perfectly normal to her.

"A diuretic takes fluid—water—out of your cells. That's not good when your body is trying to recover."

He shook his head. "You sound like a damned doctor."

She shrugged. "I know enough about basic physiology to do my job."

He ignored her comment. He supposed counselors needed to know such things, if Rebecca could be believed.

"Can I get you something else to drink?"

"Not if you're going to say liquor is bad for me too."

"It is."

"Then don't bother."

He took several more bites. Although he'd been very hungry, he was finding it difficult to stay seated on the edge of the bed. He felt tired, and even though he'd told Rebecca not to baby him, that's exactly how weak he was at the moment. Grabbing his spoon and the custard, he eased back on the bed and leaned against the headboard. His back screamed in protest.

He must have winced, because Rebecca rushed to the bed. "You've got to be careful," she admonished. Fetching a pillow, she placed it behind his tortured back.

Although the injuries still hurt, he felt slightly better. He took a bite of the custard. As usual, Claudia's cooking was excellent. He hadn't had custard since his mother had fixed it for him when he'd had the croup, many years ago.

"There's no shame in going easy on yourself."

"I didn't say there was."

She stood beside the bed and folded her arms over her chest. "There's something I need to get from my room. I'll be right back."

Within a minute, she was back, her fist closed around an object, a piece of paper in her other hand. "If you feel up to it, I'd like to show you some proof of who I am."

He sat the empty bowl on the table. "Go ahead. I'm probably not going anywhere."

Annoyance at his glib remark flashed across

her face. Then she schooled her features into a calm mask. After sitting on the edge of the mattress she unfolded her fingers to reveal the object in her hand.

"This is the locket I showed you the afternoon we went into Lander for the first time."

"And you never did tell me the truth about where you got it."

"I told you: at my family reunion. My great-aunt gave it to me because I look so much like Leda. Everyone remarked on it. That reunion was also the place where I met my distant cousin Jordan—the man who later strangled me."

"I got the impression you didn't know how you got strangled and ended up on the prairie."

"I didn't tell you everything then because I knew you wouldn't believe me. I'm not sure that you'll believe me now, but I have to try to make you understand why I did what I did."

"So now you're admitting that you deceived me, as well as going behind my back to contact *her*."

She frowned and looked away. "I didn't mean to deceive you. I might have omitted some details, but that was because you made it clear you didn't believe me."

"What makes you think I believe you now?"

Her gaze collided with his; she looked distraught, almost panicky. "I have to make you believe me. My life depends on it."

"You think this cousin is going to find you again and finish the job?"

"No," she said in a small voice. "I think that

somehow your anger came forward in time and overcame Jordan. I think you hated Leda enough to want to make her descendants suffer. I think that, in a way, it was you who strangled me."

He blinked, staring at her, wondering if he'd heard her correctly. She was crazy; there was no other explanation.

But even as the denial sprang to his lips, he remembered Painted Elk's affirmation that Sloan would seek revenge against his enemies, even after death. He'd seen evidence that Painted Elk knew things outside the realm of his experience. When they'd first met the Arapaho had known about the horrors of war that Sloan couldn't put to rest. He'd predicted Vincent Radburn's arrival in the county, and that he'd be a dangerous adversary.

Could Painted Elk have done something mystical that caused a descendant of Leda to be strangled? He'd said Rebecca would go back to her own time. It was too farfetched to be believed, and yet . . .

"Sloan, I believe this: I only have a few more days or weeks here. Painted Elk says I'll go back to my own time when the bitterroot dies. If you're still angry and seek vengeance on Leda, then your anger will travel over time. And when I go back I'll be dead."

He watched her face for any signs of deceit or melodrama. There was nothing there except her honest belief that she was telling the truth.

"The day I went for a ride, I found Leda's house. I waited around back and talked to her."

"You what?" he roared.

"I had to do it. My life depends on finding the truth."

He didn't believe that for a minute. She'd been curious, and had taken action to find Leda, despite his warnings that she leave it alone.

"Sloan, I know Robert is your son."

He felt as if she'd punched him in the gut; the breath seemed to go out of him. *Robert.* How often he'd longed to see his own son, and not at a distance, hustled away as though he might catch some horrible disease from his natural father.

"How?" he managed to say.

"He looks just like you. He's such a bright, active little boy. I'm so sorry for what Leda did, taking him away from you."

"I don't want to discuss him any more than I do Leda." Even as he said the words, he soaked up her impressions of Robert like a sponge. Would he ever know the boy?

She took a deep breath. "There's something else you need to see." Rebecca handed him a sheet of paper. At the top was the heading "Radburn Family Tree." Below that, small squares were connected by lines to form the family relationships.

Rebecca scooted closer. "This is me," she said, pointing to a square. "I was born in 1968. And this is . . . was my sister Sara. She died in 1979."

He peered at the small print, reading the names.

"And these are my parents, Chloe and Michael Hartford. My mother's father was Vincent

Burton, who was named after Vincent Radburn."

He traced the lines back. Sure enough, he saw the names of the people Rebecca claimed were her grandparents, who had married in 1930.

"Vincent Burton was the only child of Daphne Radburn and Charles Burton, who married in 1899."

Sloan looked at the two blocks for the children of Leda Houghton and Vincent Radburn. A knife of pain stabbed through his heart when Robert's name was listed as their son. He was *his* son!

Rebecca must have sensed his growing anger, Sloan realized. She drew back, a wary look on her face.

"I'm not going to hit you, dammit."

Her gaze darted to the paper and back to his face. "Okay. Just look at this, please." She pointed to the square for the other child. "Daphne Radburn was born in December 1876. That means that Leda is pregnant with her now."

"You don't know that—"

"Yes, I do! Dammit, Sloan, this family tree is *real.* I didn't make this up. It came with me from the future, in the pocket of my denim skirt." She grabbed the paper from his hand, waving it in front of his face. "This is *real.*"

He was quiet for a long time, staring at the paper, talking in Rebecca's angry expression. "You're asking me to believe someone who hasn't been totally honest with me before. You're asking me to have faith in something that defies logic."

She looked deeply into his eyes. He felt her pain and confusion all the way to his soul. Another image of her flashed through his mind: the way she looked when she was filled with passion and love. He pushed that vision aside. He refused to think with his emotions. He knew what was real, dammit, and traveling through time wasn't it.

"After what we shared," she said softly, "I'm asking you to have faith in *me*."

He said nothing, just stared at her. She let the paper flutter to the mattress as she backed away from the bed. Without another word, she pivoted and fled the room.

Rebecca paused before the door to Claudia's cottage, taking a deep breath. Leaving wouldn't be easy, but it was her only option. She couldn't stay under Sloan's roof, knowing how he felt about her. Knowing he didn't trust her. Knowing there was no chance he would love her.

She knocked, then waited as she heard the housekeeper's footsteps walking toward her. The door swung open, and Rebecca faced the woman who had never approved of her presence in the house, or in Sloan's life.

"I'm leaving very early in the morning. I wanted to let you know because Sloan will need . . ." Her voice broke, and tears welled in her eyes. She blinked them away, unwilling to break down completely in front of another person who didn't want her there. "Sloan will need someone to look in on him tonight and tomorrow. He probably thinks he's okay, but he's not. He's still . . ." She paused again, taking another deep breath. "I just wanted to let you know."

She turned away from Claudia's stern-faced demeanor. Rebecca knew she had much to do. She didn't even know where she could go.

"So you're leaving him, just like Leda."

Rebecca whirled back around. "No! Not like her. She couldn't face who he was. I can. But he can't face who *I* am." She laughed, but there was no humor in it. "Kind of ironic, isn't it, Claudia? I wanted him to be happy. I wanted . . ."

With a sob she couldn't control, Rebecca turned away from the cottage and ran toward Painted Elk's teepee. Before she approached the closed flap she took a moment to compose herself. He would know, of course, how upset she was. He, of all the people she'd met, knew how urgently she needed to help Sloan overcome his past. Painted Elk was the only person who'd believed her, guiding her through this trip into the past.

She dabbed her eyes, smoothing the moisture from her cheeks, and called out, "Painted Elk?"

"Come inside," he said. She could hear him moving around.

She pushed aside the animal hide and almost crawled in. The air was thick with smoke and steam, but the smell wasn't offensive. The smoky tang provided an excuse for her teary eyes.

"You are leaving him," the old man said.

"I can't stay," she said simply.

"He is a man in much pain."

"I know." Rebecca looked down at her clasped hands. "He won't believe me. He won't talk to me.

And worst of all, he thinks I deceived him."

"He does not trust easily."

"He doesn't trust me at all."

"If you leave here, there is much danger."

"I know. But what can I do? I can't stay in his house, knowing how he feels about me. I've got to go away."

"He may change."

"But not in time," Rebecca said, her voice breaking. "You said I only have until the bitterroot dies. That should be in less than two weeks. Then I'll go back to Jordan, and he'll kill me, and . . ."

She couldn't finish. She hid her face in her hands, sobbing quietly for the loss she felt. Not because she would die, but because Sloan wouldn't try to live. He'd condemned them both.

Painted Elk pressed a cup into her hands. She accepted the unknown liquid, sipping the warm broth while she thought of Sloan. If only he could believe . . . Just two days ago, she'd been so full of hope that they'd find a way to stay together forever. If she could, she'd stay here in the past. If Sloan would only love her, she would stay with him forever.

The air grew still. Vaguely, she heard Painted Elk chanting, but she didn't pay any attention to the peaceful sound. In her mind she saw Sloan as she wanted him to be, his eyes full of love, his heart open. He smiled, and the sun shone brighter. He laughed, and the whole world rejoiced. This was the Sloan who should have been, before war and deceit deprived him of his dreams.

The sky stretched out, blue and bright above them, and below, the bitterroot bloomed in profusion. Gentle breezes blew the long grass and rustled the leaves of nearby trees. The day was perfect.

She saw herself, almost as though she were another person, smiling back. She felt the rush of love and hope that flowed through her veins. When she reached out to Sloan he took her hand, took her love, and gave his in return.

The sizzle of water on hot stones broke into her vision. She jumped, dropping the cup, dissipating the images into the wispy steam that filled the teepee.

"What did you give me?" she asked accusingly.

"Only a soothing drink. Nothing to harm you, Rebecca Hartford."

She struggled to her feet. Her thoughts seemed as disoriented as the thick atmosphere surrounding her. "I've got to get out of here. I've got to leave."

"I will take you in the morning," Painted Elk said. "Come here when the sun rises, and we will go to a safe place."

"Is there any such place?" she asked quietly.

Painted Elk remained silent, staring into the glowing embers of the fire. Rebecca slipped outside. A gust of cool wind cleared her head and raised goose bumps along her arm.

What she'd just experienced inside the steamy teepee was nothing more than the images of her hopes. Tomorrow she would leave Sloan's ranch, and in a week or two she would leave his time. There would be no future for her with Sloan, and probably no future for herself at all, unless she could find another way to change the course of his anger. Or maybe she'd done enough, just by making him aware of the danger. Maybe she had saved her life, but she hadn't changed her love.

Or maybe she'd made him even more angry by trying to send the note to Leda.

She hugged herself as she hurried toward the house.

Chapter Seventeen

Rebecca stopped stirring the thick antelope stew and pushed a strand of hair back from her face. She supposed she was lucky to have a "job" at all, but cooking for a rough group of trappers and traders didn't seem like such a great career. The weather was hot again, the cook shed was poorly ventilated, and her spirits were low.

Three days ago Painted Elk had brought her here. The men were decent, he'd assured her, and no harm would come to her. He'd stayed two nights, to make sure she was settled in, before leaving early this morning. She wasn't sure where he was going. He might join his tribe, somewhere to the north and east, or he might go back to the ranch.

With his leaving, her last contact with Sloan was gone. She was truly alone, unsure of how long she would stay in the past. Perhaps she would simply go to sleep one night and wake up—or not—in her own time. Perhaps she'd just disappear while performing some of her duties.

At least she had some idea where she was. In her day there was a store of some sort on this site, with a historical marker nearby, just outside of a small town called Hudson, off the two-lane state highway between Riverton and Lander. She'd noticed it as she and Jordan drove from Riverton to the picnic site. That seemed a lifetime ago.

She wasn't too far away from either Sloan or Leda. If she could come up with a plan, perhaps she could find her way back to the ranch. Or she could get to Lander, which was only about ten miles away. She still had Squirt, hobbled out back, underneath the cottonwood trees.

She continued stirring the stew. She had enough to eat and a safe place to stay, according to Painted Elk. The trappers seemed to think her reaction to fresh kill was humorous and pitiful, but they hadn't insisted she skin and butcher the meat. For that she could be grateful. She hated the fact that she was preparing meat from the beautiful and free animals that grazed along the highways and in the fenced pastures of Wyoming.

After dinner this evening, she would go to her small room in the back of the trading post, curl up on her cot, and try to think of a way to reach Sloan. She knew she'd second guess herself about her decisions to keep information from

Sloan until the dead she died. Was there any way she could have convinced him that she was from the future? She hadn't thought so at the time, but now she wondered.

Was Sloan recovering? Had her departure caused him to become more bitter because of her "betrayal," or was he relieved that she'd left? She wished she could see him once more. Perhaps she would ride back to the ranch in a few days, just to see if he was well.

"How's dinner comin', gal?" Harvey, the good-natured, overweight trading post owner, asked. He reminded her a little of Jerry Garcia, the deceased leader of The Grateful Dead, except this man slicked back his frizzy gray hair and wore greasy homespun instead of T-shirts and jeans.

She hadn't even heard him approach. "Let me check." She peeked at the corn bread, browning inside the wood-burning stove. "It should be ready in about ten minutes."

"Fine, that's fine, gal."

Rebecca fantasized that when he called her "gal" the next time, she'd pour a whole cup of pepper in his stew. Instead she smiled at him weakly before he turned and lumbered away. He wasn't a bad guy, but in her day he'd definitely be considered a male chauvinist.

Working as a cook at a trading post wasn't the way she'd envisioned ending her visit to the past. But then, she hadn't expected to fall in love either.

* * *

"What do you mean, she's gone?" Sloan roared.

Slim seemed to melt back into the wall of the tack room. "She and Painted Elk rode out three days ago."

He'd thought Rebecca was just avoiding him. No one had mentioned that she'd left the ranch. Run off, dammit! Sloan started to throw up his hands in exasperation, but the pain stopped him. Instead, he paced the confines of the small room, ready to punch his knuckles through the wood. "Why didn't anyone tell me?"

"Well, you were laid up. She'd been takin' care of you that first night an' day, stayin' with you, an' we jus' figured it wasn't any of our business if you two had a spat."

"So she just abruptly leaves, and no one thinks that's odd?"

"Hell, boss, ya didn't tell me to keep her here. An' besides, she tol' Claudia she was leavin'."

"Jesus Christ," Sloan swore, wiping a hand through his hair. "No one has any idea where she went?"

"Painted Elk's about the only one who'd know, and he ain't back yet."

"Damn." Sloan pointed a finger at Slim. "Let me know as soon as he gets back. I mean the very minute he arrives."

"Sure, Boss." Slim frowned at him, still looking about as comfortable as if he were trapped in a cage with a mountain lion.

Sloan stormed out of the tack room, wincing at the pounding of his feet on the packed earth. Each step caused a painful vibration of pain in his ribs and up through his jaw.

Unfortunately, each step didn't bring him closer to locating Rebecca.

She'd been in his thoughts almost constantly since that night they'd argued, but he'd had no idea how to approach her. Her story of time travel was preposterous. Her evidence was insubstantial. Still, there had been something compelling and honest in her eyes. He couldn't shake the feeling that he was the crazy one for not believing.

Instead of giving credence to her story, he'd focused on the betrayal of trust. She'd known how he felt about the Radburns. Despite all his warnings that he didn't discuss Leda or his past, Rebecca had pursued the answers anyway. She'd defied his orders and forged ahead with her own agenda.

For a long time he'd doubted her, believing her to be a spy or a lunatic. Now he thought perhaps she was the bravest person he'd ever known.

He kept thinking of the first day she'd ridden off on her own. Now he felt the same sense of panic he'd experienced then. He hadn't wanted to admit it then, but he couldn't imagine life without her. He'd finally admitted it several nights ago, before they'd made love in her bed. But then he'd lost his faith in her, and in the future.

He had to find her. He finally believed, but was it too late?

* * *

Near dusk, Rebecca finished her duties and went around back to tend to Squirt. There was no barn here, or corral, and she felt negligent for leaving the mare hobbled most of the day.

"Hey, Squirt, how are you?" She rubbed the mare's forehead and gave her some slices of carrot she'd put aside before making the stew.

A nice, steady breeze blew through the cottonwood trees, rustling the leaves. Inside the trading post, the men were smoking and talking. Their voices drifted out the open windows. Usually, they played cards after dinner, and shared a little liquor. But they weren't big drinkers, and she didn't feel too unsafe out here alone with them.

She just felt lonely.

Squirt raised her head and pointed her ears forward. She nickered softly and stamped her hoof.

Riding toward the trading post were five Indians.

Rebecca dropped the lead rope she was about to attach to her mare's halter and ran toward the post. Indians! Were they the ones who had killed that man—what was his name? Muley something. Her heart raced as visions of torture and death ran through her head. She propelled herself around the doorframe and came to a halt in the middle of the room.

"Indians are coming!"

The big, middle-aged men rose from their chairs, grumbling beneath their breath as they reached for their rifles. *Hurry!* Rebecca wanted to shout. *They're coming!*

The men formed a line in front of the trading post and looked east, where the Indians approached at a slow trot. Dressed in woven shirts and pants that were enhanced by beaded vests and necklaces, they didn't look aggressive. Rebecca watched from just inside the doorway, wondering if she hadn't overreacted. Maybe these weren't the hostile Indians who attacked settlers.

The traders relaxed their grips on the rifles as the Indians rode up. Exchanging greetings, soon they all appeared to be old friends. She couldn't overhear their conversation, but they seemed to be sharing news. She exhaled a breath, tried to relax her tense muscles, and slipped out the back.

Squirt was in the same spot, grazing under the cottonwoods. Rebecca slipped off the hobbles and hooked a lead rope to the mare's halter. Leading her away from the trading post, she angled toward the Wind River.

It was a terrible feeling to be afraid of a group of people because of their skin color or ethnicity, but that was exactly what she'd experienced since the first week, when she'd learned of the Indian attack nearby. She didn't like what living in the past was doing to her. She was beginning to feel like a victim, but she didn't know the rules well enough to change her own behavior. If she approached the Indians with an offer of food or coffee, for example, would they be offended, surprised, or might they misunderstand her action?

She reminded herself that she wouldn't be

around long enough to worry about adapting to the past.

She reached the sandy river bank, where wild grasses grew tall at the water's edge. Squirt helped herself to a drink while Rebecca slipped off her tennis shoes, picked up her skirts, and waded into the shallow water.

Again she was assailed by a sense of loneliness. At the moment, and perhaps during the rest of her time here, her only friend was a runty little mare who had a good heart but not much personality. Rebecca recognized that her situation had changed a great deal in the last few weeks. When she'd first arrived in the past she'd missed her new job and apartment, her friends and family. Now she missed Sloan and his ranch. His house had begun to feel like home. And yet it wasn't. She didn't belong here.

She wondered how the bitterroot plants were faring. Maybe Claudia would water the flowers Rebecca had planted beside the house. Perhaps Painted Elk would come to visit her again, if she decided not to ride to the ranch. At the moment, she wasn't sure what the best course of action would be. If only she knew how Sloan really felt. His own fears spoke louder than his dreams; of that she was certain.

Sloan was sitting at his desk, staring into the rapidly darkening dusk and sipping his third bourbon, when Painted Elk walked into the room.

"Where is she?"

Painted Elk sat in Sloan's big chair. His banty legs didn't touch the floor. "She is safe."

"I want her back. You had no right to take her away."

"You did not believe her. She did not wish to stay."

"Dammit, I don't care! She shouldn't have run off."

"Your heart is closed."

"Where is she?" Sloan roared. He slammed the glass of bourbon onto the desk, splashing some on the wood.

"Why do you wish to find her?"

"I . . . I need to talk to her."

"You have talked too much, and not said what needs to be said."

Sloan felt the fight go out of him. Painted Elk was right. Sloan knew he'd listened to what she'd said but had discounted anything that didn't fit what he wanted to believe. She'd pushed him to think about things he'd buried deep, but had always dug their way back into his life. Things he couldn't avoid any longer.

"I'm ready to listen with my heart," he said.

Painted Elk pushed himself out of the chair. He looked old, Sloan thought, and tired. "Then I will tell you where she is in the morning. You must rest and gain your strength to fight for the woman."

"She's not in any danger, is she?" Sloan rose from the desk chair. He knew how afraid Rebecca had been of many everyday occurrences. She wasn't prepared to be on her own.

"No, she is safe. Your fight is with something more powerful than a man or beast."

"What?"

"It is time for you to fight your past."

Sloan nodded. "Rebecca told me the same thing, but I didn't want to try. I'm not sure how to win this battle."

"You will know."

I hope you're right, Sloan answered silently as Painted Elk walked out of the room. Rebecca needed him, and he needed her.

The door creaked open on sprung hinges, scraping against the dusty wooden floor of the house. Nudging it wider with the butt of his rifle, Sloan led his men into the seemingly deserted dwelling.

"Clark, Jones, Baker, take the upstairs. Carstairs, Hughes, to the left," Sloan whispered, his eyes searching the gray doom of the interior.

"Yes, sir," the soldiers answered, almost in unison.

He watched as his men silently fanned out through the house. An odor of decay and neglect permeated the rooms as he walked to the right of the central hall. There was nothing left of the grandeur that was apparent in carved casements over the tall, narrow windows, and in plaster detailing near the ceiling. Cobwebs hung from the corners and draped to the fireplace. One window pane sported several holes, from muskets or rifles, and another had broken, jagged glass.

Like so many other Southern homes, this one

329

was deserted, picked clean by fleeing slaves or army deserters.

He walked through the parlor, his feet leaving their mark in the dust on the floor. No one had been here in many months. And why should they? It was September and hotter than blazes; almost all the people who had lived near Atlanta had long ago relocated farther north or deeper south, under General Sherman's orders.

What had probably been a study or office adjoined the parlor. Ceiling-high bookshelves stood empty, draped by cobwebs. Up high, a bird had built a nest of twigs and shredded paper.

A massive desk stood broken in the corner, as though a giant ax had fallen on it. It had obviously been too large to carry off, so the scavengers had simply destroyed it. Sloan trailed his finger over the dusty surface, exposing the fine red sheen of cherry beneath the filth.

"What a waste," he whispered to himself.

Several books remained in the corner, stacked neatly, as though someone were going to pick them up and read more later. He walked closer. The odor of death was stronger in this room; perhaps an animal had died there.

Overhead, he heard the boots of his men as they conducted a similar search. The floorboards creaked, as though they hadn't been walked upon for many years. Bending, Sloan picked up the first book.

"The Courtship of Miles Standish," he read. Longfellow's epic of the Puritan story, Sloan knew the tale well from his studies. He placed

the book to one side as he hunkered down on the floor, ready to read the titles of the rest of the books in the stack. Apparently, the former owner of the library was well read.

He wasn't sure what made him look around. Perhaps there had been a small noise, or his eye had been attracted by the play of light on the desk. He tensed, instantly aware that something was wrong. With small, unobtrusive movements, he scanned the room for life.

Where the split top rested on the floor and formed a *V* with the pedestal, he saw what looked to be a tiny shoe. He used his rifle to nudge the shoe, but it barely moved. He rose from his position on the floor and walked slowly to the desk.

He didn't want to do this. All his instincts told him to run from the room. Although he had never fought on the front lines, he'd seen his share and more of death and destruction. A supply officer's job was to scour the countryside for provisions between the arrival of the trains from the north. He reconnoitered farmhouses and mansions, ordered the slaughter of cattle, confiscated horses, and did whatever was necessary to keep Sherman's army fed and housed.

Whatever was necessary . . . Somehow he didn't think this tiny shoe peeking out from a broken desk fit that description.

He leaned his rifle against the wall. With trembling hands, he grasped the edge of the desk and shoved, toppling the broken furniture backward onto the floor.

Dust rose, momentarily obscuring his vision,

then lazily floated back to the ground. He stared, arms at his side, at the shoe. At the tiny leg, withered and dried. At the dress, lace edged and dirty. At the little hand that even in death grasped a favorite book.

The mummified remains of a child, hiding beneath her father's desk, another victim of the war . . .

Sloan woke with a scream on his lips, the echoes reverberating in his head. It was a dream. It was only a dream.

He sat up in bed and grasped his hair, hands over his ears, his eyes pressed tightly shut. Breathing heavily, he tried to block the image from his mind, but it wouldn't budge. The sightless eyes of the girl stared into his soul.

Would he ever forget her? Would he ever stop hating himself for taking part in a war that killed women and children as readily as soldiers?

He shuddered, wishing Rebecca were beside him. She would banish the pictures he couldn't forget, with her softness and warmth. She was so alive. He needed her now, but all that stretched beside him was the blackness of night and the whisper of the wind.

Just after dawn, Sloan went to Painted Elk's teepee. Before he could call out the old man emerged, bent over as he exited the small opening. He straightened slowly, as though his joints and muscles protested the new day.

"I will tell you where she is, but you must ride alone," Painted Elk said.

Sloan nodded. "I'm ready to go. But are you well?"

"I have ridden too long these last days. You must take care, Sloan Travers. I am an old man and cannot ride in your tracks."

"I'll try not to need rescuing again," he said with a slight smile. "Did I thank you when you came after me? I don't remember much."

"There is no need for thanks between friends. You saved me from death once, and now we are bound together. I will be here to see your woman return."

"Return to the ranch, or return to her own time?"

Painted Elk didn't reply at once. "Cherish your time together; she must face her own fate."

Sloan shook his head. He didn't want to hear riddles; he wanted facts. Painted Elk would not tell everything he knew. Or perhaps he knew nothing of the details of Rebecca's journey.

"Tell me where she is and I'll bring her home."

"She is at the trader's post on the Wind River."

"She's living with those men?"

"They will not harm her."

"You have more faith in them than I do."

Painted Elk gave a very dry chuckle. "I have more *faith* than you do. Now go and find your woman."

Sloan rode out on Buck. His back still hurt and his ribs ached, but his heart felt lighter than it had in days. Soon Rebecca would be his again.

All he had to do was bare his soul.

Chapter Eighteen

Sloan galloped into the yard of the trading post. With each mile he had traveled closer to Rebecca, Sloan had felt his anticipation grow, until he'd pushed his horse and his mending body to the limit. Now all he could think of was Rebecca.

He dismounted as Buck still pranced, then strode into the low-ceilinged room. "I've come for Rebecca."

"Hey, Sloan," Harvey greeted him. "You haven't been around lately."

"I've been busy. Where's Rebecca?"

"She's a danged good cook," one of the men said, digging into a plate of bacon and fried potatoes.

Sloan held his temper in check. He was in no condition to fight four men today just because he was impatient.

"Pull up a chair, Sloan," Harvey offered. "There's coffee if you've a mind to—"

"I've a mind to get Rebecca and take her home," he gritted out.

"Well, now, we'd hate to see her go. It's been nice having a woman around," the man eating the plate of food said.

Sloan reached him in two strides and grabbed the front of his shirt, lifting him from the chair. "How nice?" he asked, barely able to restrain himself from beating the man senseless.

"Calm down," Harvey said. "Brewster didn't mean anything. Fact is, we're fond of her like a daughter."

"Yeah," another man chimed in, "a daughter who can cook."

Harvey gave a weak laugh. Sloan glowered at the man he was holding and began to release him. Just as the man slid downward into his chair, Sloan sensed another presence. He whirled to face another challenger.

Rebecca stood in the doorway, backlit by the morning sun. The basket she had held dropped to the packed dirt floor. "Sloan," she whispered.

"It's time to go home," he said, turning all his attention to her. Even in silhouette, she was the most beautiful sight he'd ever seen.

"The bitterroot has died?" she asked in a strangled voice.

"No! No," he continued, walking toward her. "It's time to go to my home. Back to the ranch." He reached out and gently grasped her upper arms. "It's time to talk about the past . . . and the future."

She reached out and embraced him, burying her head against his chest. "Oh, Sloan, yes. Yes, let's go home."

His arms enveloped her, holding her tight as he fought the tears that rose to his eyes. She was safe. He had one more chance to tell her about the things he'd done and seen, about his dreams . . . and his nightmares.

He heard her sniff. She wiped her eyes and cheeks, pulling back slightly to look up at him. "I wasn't sure what I was going to do. I think maybe I would have ridden after you if you hadn't come."

"I didn't know you were gone for two or three days. Then Painted Elk came back. He only told me where you were this morning."

"You didn't waste any time," she said, smiling.

"I don't have any time to waste."

Her smile faded. She held him tight again, her short nails digging into the raw skin on his back. "You're right. We don't have time to waste. Let's go home."

He saddled Squirt while she threw together her few pieces of clothing. She'd taken only the three skirts and blouses, leaving behind the unworn, plaid-skirted dress at the ranch. She'd thought perhaps he might be able to take it back for credit. Now she would wear it proudly, for him.

Sloan was leading her mare to the front of the trading post as she said good-bye to the men. "I hope you can find someone else to cook," she said.

"Ah, we'll get by. We knew you weren't going to stay long."

She tilted her head. "How did you know?"

"Painted Elk told us. Said Sloan would be after you in a wink."

"Oh, he did, did he?" She wondered if the old medicine man had set all of them up.

"I'll get your money. Two bits a day; that was the deal."

"Never mind about the money. I don't need it anyway."

They looked at her as though she were crazy. *Join the club,* she said to herself, but she no longer felt any bitterness toward those who'd doubted her. In the end, Sloan had come to believe, and that was all that mattered.

"Good-bye, Harvey. Good-bye, guys."

" 'Bye, Miss Rebecca. You take care of yourself."

"I will."

She walked toward her mare but paused to wave to the men. Suddenly she realized that she'd never see them again. They'd been nice; male chauvinists, to be sure, but nice.

Sloan put his hands on her waist and whispered, "If I hadn't ridden Buck almost into the ground, we'd ride double and I'd hold you all the way back to the ranch."

A thrill of pure pleasure rippled through her. "Some other time I'd like to ride with you on a horse."

"Then I promise we'll do it."

If we have time, she added silently. She put on a smile for Sloan. He was opening up to her. She could see it in his eyes, in the open way he communicated with her. She'd do nothing to dissuade him, or remind him how few days they might have together.

Besides, she didn't want to think of the negatives. She wanted to love him for however many days they had left.

He helped her into the saddle, then mounted Buck.

"I'm not sure I can keep up with that monster of yours, but we'll try," she said cheerfully.

"Believe me, we won't run off and leave you."

With a final wave to the men, who stood in a line in front of the trading post, waving back awkwardly, she and Sloan rode south toward the ranch.

He pushed the pace, but not too much. Rebecca knew he wanted to get her home . . . to bed, to be more accurate. That was fine with her. They'd communicated well between the sheets, and just thinking about making love made her wish for a speedier mode of transportation than a horse. Like maybe a dragster, or a jet, or the Concorde.

She giggled at the thought. Sloan looked at her and laughed. He held out his hand and she took it. They rode like that for a long time, until the terrain and the differing strides of the horses made them pull apart. But even then, she felt one with him. Something magical had happened.

They handed the horses to Slim, not even apologizing for their sweaty condition. Rebecca felt Sloan pull away slightly, now that they were back at the ranch, but she attributed it to his natural reserve, not to any second thoughts about their relationship. She didn't try to hold hands with him as they walked toward the house, but she did smile at him and caught his answering wink.

"Hello, Claudia," Rebecca called out as they passed the older woman, feeding her chickens behind the house.

"Well, I'll be. You did come back."

Rebecca laughed. "Sloan insisted."

She proceeded him up the steps to the back door, holding in check her impulse to run into the house. She walked to the center of the kitchen. "I've been spending a lot of time cooking. I think I'll pass on fixing dinner tonight."

"Good," he said, walking up behind her and cupping her breasts, "because I have a better idea."

He stroked her through the thin cotton of her blouse and the stretchy fabric of her bra, until her head rolled back onto his shoulder and she moaned.

"You like that."

"I love it. But someone could walk in here, and then your reputation would be shot all to hell."

"Still cussing," he observed, kissing the side of her neck.

"If you don't stop that, I'm going to have my way with you on this kitchen table. Then what would Claudia say?"

"We wouldn't want to shock Claudia," Sloan replied, tracing the lace-edged collar of her blouse.

Rebecca felt her knees go weak at the same time Sloan spun her around.

"So I'm going to take you upstairs." He swung her into his arms.

Rebecca gasped and clung to him. Suddenly she thought of his poor, battered body. All those scratches and scrapes. The bruised ribs and tender flesh. "Sloan, no! You might hurt yourself. You're injured."

"Nothing is hurting much at the moment except a part of me below my waist. And I think you'll be able to make me feel better real soon."

"Are you sure you're okay?" she asked as he negotiated the steps.

"I will be as soon as I get you in bed."

She tightened her arms around his neck. "Then I'll kiss you all over and make it better."

He moaned and pushed open the door to her bedroom. "I want you in here, where it's fresh and clean and smells like you."

A surge of love welled up as she realized his room reminded him of sickness and nightmares, blood and pain. She'd do her best to wipe those away from his mind and his heart.

"Love me, Sloan," she whispered as they sank to the bed.

He didn't answer her, but took her lips in a kiss that made all rational thought flee. She gave herself completely, in the bright sunlight of the Wyoming afternoon, until she felt the healing power of love push away all her doubts and fears.

She fell asleep beside Sloan, feeling as though she'd finally come home.

Rebecca awoke to a dusky room. She stretched, rolling toward Sloan's solid weight on the soft feather mattress. Smiling, she snuggled against his side. He'd brought her home, gone against his basic nature and carried her upstairs in the middle of the afternoon to make sweet love to her.

In the midst of her romantic thoughts, her stomach growled, reminding her that she'd missed lunch and, probably, dinner. Unless Claudia had taken pity on them and left something on the stove. Rebecca hoped so; she'd told Sloan the truth when she'd said she had cooked enough lately.

"Did that unladylike rumble come from you?" Sloan said sleepily, rolling toward her.

"Guilty as charged." She kissed his shoulder, and then his chest. "I'm starving."

"Why do I feel like I'm about to be dinner if I don't come up with something more substantial?"

"Umm, nothing could be more substantial than you."

"Is that a compliment?"

"Absolutely. But I think I'd rather have some real food at the moment." She ran a hand through his chest hair and over his flat nipple. "You'll do just fine as dessert."

Sloan chuckled, then groaned. "If you don't

quit that, we'll never make it downstairs."

"Okay," she said, but she didn't stop exploring the hard contours and taut skin of his upper body.

With a heave, he sat up in bed. "Let's see if we can find some clothes. Then we'll rustle up something to eat."

Downstairs, Rebecca sliced ham while Sloan retrieved some biscuits from the bread box. Claudia had left some easy-to-assemble food. Rebecca found some early radishes, peas, and tender lettuce leaves in Claudia's garden. It was almost dark when she assembled a simple salad with a vinegar dressing.

"Let's eat on the porch," she suggested. The night was beautiful.

They took their supper outside. Overhead, the sky was streaked with purple and indigo, with only a pink glow remaining above the mountains. Rebecca settled on the bench, as Sloan went back into the house.

He returned with the silver candelabra from the dining room table. "My mother sent this as a gift for my new home."

"It's beautiful. And very romantic. Thank you."

He lit the candles. Fortunately, the breeze was almost nonexistent, so the flames glowed brightly in the twilight.

Rebecca knew that they needed to talk, and somehow, beneath the wide-open skies, she felt they would be able to say the things they'd held back for so long. Sometimes talking was easier in the darkness.

"I remember when I was a little girl and shared a room with my sister Sara. At night, after our parents put us to bed and turned out the lights, we'd stay awake and talk. Even though we were six years apart in age, we always found something to talk about."

"I have a sister too. She's married and lives in Philadelphia with her husband and four children. My mother dotes on them."

"I think she's awfully fond of you too."

"She's never given up hope that I'll return home someday."

"And will you?"

"I . . . I doubt it. I think that when I first came out west I was running away. But now I love it here. I know the weather can be brutal, and there aren't many people yet, but someday the land will produce more cattle and even large farms."

"Yes, but even in my day Wyoming is home to only about 450,000 people. There are more people living in many large cities than in Wyoming, Montana, South Dakota, North Dakota, and probably some other states I've forgotten. And farming never did take off too well, because of all the problems with irrigation."

"So Wyoming is a state."

"Yes, though I'm not sure when that happened."

"A few years ago there was talk of dividing it up and giving the southern part to Colorado."

"That doesn't happen. As a matter of fact, one particular area around Jackson is considered quite the place to live, or at least have a vacation home, if you're a celebrity."

At Sloan's baffled look, she continued. "Celebrities are a big thing in my time. Most of them are movie stars or sports figures or politicians. Sometimes they're just people who have been hanging around the rich and famous for a long time. Anyway, regular people are just fascinated with celebrities."

"They worship them?"

"No." Rebecca laughed. "Well, not exactly. It's kind of hard to explain. I'm not sure you have anything comparable in your day. Maybe a famous stage actress or actor, only on a much larger scale."

"I'm not sure what some of those words mean, like movie stars and sports figures, but I doubt you have time to explain everything to me."

"I don't want to spend all my time talking about other people." She reached over and held his hand. "I want to talk about us."

He nodded. "You need to know about the war. I've thought about what you said, about veterans of the war who couldn't forget what had happened."

"Post-traumatic stress syndrome. It's been called by many names, like shell-shocked in World War One, but whatever you call it, the symptoms are the same. And you can be helped."

"What can make a man forget what he's seen and done?" Sloan asked with a trace of bitterness. "In the daytime I can stay busy and not think about those days. But at night I remember . . . and I dream."

"I know you do. And you'll always remember. You can't make those memories go away, at least not forever. You are a combination of all your experiences, and when your experiences are suppressed, or pushed away from your conscious thoughts, you can become what we call dysfunctional in other areas."

"It sounds as though you're saying that there's no hope."

"But there is. The secret is understanding why you're thinking about whatever happened in the war. Do you know?"

He shook his head. "No one would want to remember seeing the numbers of dead and wounded, or the faces of the civilians who lost their homes. Or the children . . ."

"Do you feel as though you were responsible for their suffering?"

"Yes!" She felt the sudden tension in his hand as he clasped her fingers. "That was my job—to confiscate their homes, their food, their animals. I was a supply officer, and Sherman was fanatical about keeping his troops supplied."

"I've heard that. He marched across Georgia, didn't he? The march to the sea, I think it's called."

"He marched out of Atlanta and destroyed Georgia so it couldn't be used by the Confederates."

"And you were there?"

"I was there, looting and burning along with the rest of the army."

"You were doing your job, ordered by your

commander. Do you remember the conversation we had before, about the bombs that were dropped on Japan? Terrible things happen during wartime and sometimes we have to choose the lesser of two evils."

"Rebecca, you don't know what it was like."

"Then tell me. I know you have nightmares. They could be the key to understanding your feelings."

"You don't want to know," he said softly.

"I want to help you. Normally, I would never say that to someone I . . . someone I cared about. But there's no other counselor I can refer you to. I know I'm too close to you to treat you, but I don't have a choice." She paused, stroking the back of his hand. "Tell me," she ordered quietly.

He looked into the darkness. Pain etched his face in harsh planes and angles; the candles cast shadows under his eyes and made his cheeks appear more hollow. She waited patiently, hoping he'd decide to share his fears.

"There was one house we came across, just outside Atlanta. At one time I'm sure it was a beautiful plantation home, but by the time we arrived it was ransacked and deserted.

"I was investigating one side of the first floor while my men searched the rest of the house. It wasn't uncommon to find deserters living in these old mansions. I was looking through the library when I found . . ."

He stopped speaking. She saw his Adam's apple bob as he swallowed.

"I saw the body of a little girl. She was all dried

346

up, like an old apple that had been left in the barrel. She was dressed in this lacy dress, and she was curled up like a baby underneath her father's desk."

"Oh, Sloan, that must have been horrible."

"It was sad. So damned sad. There was a book in her hand. I thought it was a favorite, like maybe she'd curled up beneath the desk to read a book, but it wasn't."

"What was it?"

"A diary."

Rebecca watched him take another deep breath and battle the memories.

"The book fell from her hand when I moved her body. The pages opened, and I saw her handwriting. I didn't want to know . . . but I had to know. Can you understand?"

"Yes."

"While my men dug graves for her and her parents, who we found upstairs in a bedroom, I read the diary of that little girl. It was so . . . so horribly sad."

"Is that what you remember?"

"I remember everything," he said fiercely. "I remember her sightless eyes, her brittle bones, and her paper-thin skin. And I remember the words she wrote, every day, until she curled up beneath that desk and died."

"Sloan . . ."

"She had such a simple life. All she wanted was to go visit her cousins, to play with their new kittens. She wanted a new dress for the summer, and her mother promised her one. She wrote about helping her mother sew the lace and buttons." Sloan's voice broke and he looked away.

Rebecca sat beside him, tears forming in her eyes. He loved children. She'd seen evidence of it all along. Because of this little girl, or perhaps before? Yet he was separated from all of them—his nieces and nephews, his own son, and even the memories of this little girl.

"I read the whole diary in that dusty study where she'd died. When the graves were ready I went upstairs to see if I could find any of the favorite things she'd mentioned, like a doll or the lacy gloves her father had brought back from Charleston for her. But everything was gone. All of her belongings had been looted.

"We buried her beside her parents in back of the house. I kept her diary, though. It was all there was left of her. If I'd buried it with her, it would be like she'd never lived. Everyone who had loved her was gone."

He broke off. Rebecca saw the unshed tears in his eyes through the sheen of moisture in her own. She clutched his hand harder, unable to find words to say what was in her heart.

"I think I went a little mad that September in Georgia."

"I think anyone who had a heart would have died a little themselves. How could you not? But Sloan, you were wrong about one thing: Not everyone who loved her was gone. You were there. You read her words and understood."

"I wasn't there when she needed me."

"No, and there was no way you could have

been. She was one little girl, a victim of a terrible war where hundreds of thousands of people died. Do you know that even in my time there have never been more Americans killed in a war than in the Civil War? And believe me, we've found hundreds of new ways to kill people efficiently. But you didn't do anything to hurt that little girl."

"I took part in that war. I volunteered for a commission."

"You thought you were fighting to keep the union together. Answer this: Do you think we should have let the Southern states secede from the union? Do you think they would have survived without any industry and with the economic burden of slavery?"

"No. I think they would have collapsed, or maybe even have been taken over by a foreign country."

"And that would have been an even greater threat to the United States."

"Yes."

"Knowing what you know now, can you think of any other way to save the union?"

"No," he whispered. "They believed in their way of life, in the rights of their states. They wanted to fight."

"So there was nothing that could have been done, by you or anyone else. You followed your convictions and tried to help your country."

"But the war was too high a price to pay!"

"War is always too high a price to pay."

He stared silently into the night for long moments. A breeze wound across the land, fluttering the candles and making dancing shadows on the porch. Still, Rebecca sat, holding his hand, until he turned back to look at her.

"You must think I'm a weak man, to be so—"

"Don't you ever say such a thing! I think you're a kind person who feels very deeply. That's why you hurt so much. You're not weak; not when you can cry for a child who died senselessly. The weakest person is one who cares for no one except himself."

"I thought I should be able to control my feelings. Other men didn't have nightmares. They didn't frighten their wives or families."

"How do you know? Do you think they'd be any more willing to talk about their problems than you were? No, those who felt deeply about the war hide their pain."

"You're saying that there are many men who feel the way I do?"

She smiled at him. "Many other men, and women too, go through the stress of living with traumatic experiences—war, famine, natural disasters. Do you think you can forgive yourself for something that wasn't your fault, and acknowledge that the war was terrible? Do everything in your power to stop another war from happening, but don't blame yourself for this one. You didn't cause this war."

She squeezed his hand, watching his eyes as he comprehended the words she'd just spoken. "To answer your question, I must admit that no other man I've ever met is quite like you."

She leaned toward him, caressing his strong

jaw with her free hand. "I love you, Sloan."

His gaze darted over her face as though he were memorizing her features. She saw longing and something more in his eyes. But he didn't say "I love you" in return. Seconds ticked by. Oh, how she wanted him to admit the depth of his feelings.

He remained silent. *Perhaps in time,* she thought. If they had the time.

He closed his eyes and kissed her, sweetly, tenderly, until her lips parted and their tongues mated. She wished she could really heal him with a kiss. But perhaps she had started the healing process with her words.

Chapter Nineteen

The next day was the Fourth of July, the centennial celebration of America's independence, yet no one at the ranch had planned for the holiday. Rebecca wondered if there were any festivities scheduled in Lander. Probably, but that might mean seeing Leda and Vincent Radburn again, and Rebecca knew that Sloan wouldn't allow his beating to go unpunished. She didn't suggest going to town for the holiday, and neither did he.

While Sloan worked on the ranch, Rebecca stripped the sheets from Sloan's bed, opened the drapes, and aired the room. His was a larger, more comfortable mattress, and she intended to sleep there tonight, and every night, while she was here.

After lunch she filled a pitcher with water and walked to the side of the house. She should have checked the plants yesterday, but she'd been so happy to see Sloan, so caught up in his passion, that she hadn't given the bitterroots a second thought.

Sinking to her knees beside the flowers, she examined the shriveled remains of those already bloomed. Only one more bud remained; when it bloomed and faded she'd go to her destiny in her own time.

Frowning, she soaked the ground with water, wishing she knew a way to prolong the life of these plants. But there was nothing she could do, not if Painted Elk was correct. She wasn't sure why or how her stay in the past was tied to the blooming of this specific type of plant, but even Sloan had said they lived only for a certain period of time.

With a heavy heart, she walked to the medicine man's teepee. "Painted Elk?"

There was no answer. She opened the flap just a bit and peeked inside. The fire was cold and the teepee empty. He had obviously gone on one of his trips, but she had no idea where, or when he would return. She hoped it was soon; she needed to ask him how she was tied to the blooming of the bitterroot.

If there was a way to undo the mystical connection, she needed him to perform whatever ceremony was necessary to keep her together with Sloan. She'd always respected Native American beliefs, although she didn't understand them; few non-Indians did. However, being personally involved in something this strange made her view their beliefs and abilities in a whole new light.

Painted Elk was a wise man, but he was also a man who knew more than he possibly could from observation alone. If he'd been performing in a night club or magic act, she'd be suspicious, but living on the prairie in Wyoming she couldn't doubt his abilities. What reason could he have for exaggerating?

She walked back to the barn and checked on her mare. Squirt nickered softly, looking for a treat, but Rebecca had forgotten to bring anything. She supposed she was still distracted by her predicament.

"Next time, girl." She patted the mare's soft muzzle.

Sloan rode in as she wandered out of the barn. A spark flared in his eyes and he smiled when he saw her. *He looks like a man in love,* she thought. Even though he'd never said the words, she knew he cared. In time . . . but they might not have time.

"You're home early," she said as he pulled Buck to a halt.

He leaned down from the saddle and kissed her quickly. Her lips still tingled when he sat up and adjusted his hat. "I had a reason to get home early."

"Oh," she said innocently. "And what was that?"

He dismounted, grabbed her around the waist, and brought her up against his hard, hot body. "You," he said with a growl. Holding her tight with one arm, he kissed her thoroughly, until she went limp against him and grasped his shoulders.

He broke away finally, but only after Buck snorted and butted them both with his head.

"I think your horse is trying to tell you something," Rebecca said shakily.

"Let me put him up, and then I can give you my undivided attention."

"In that case, I'll help."

Rebecca filled Buck's water bucket as Sloan unsaddled the horse. She measured out a scoop of oats while he rubbed down the buckskin. "Do you know what I wish?" she said as they were finishing.

"What?"

"I wish you had a bathroom with a shower. I'd love to take a shower with you right now."

"A shower?"

"Warm water comes from an overhead pipe. It's like standing outside when it rains, except it's indoors and the water is warm."

"I've seen a rain bath. That must be similar."

"Yes, I'm sure it is."

"And you'd like to take one of those showers with me?"

She ran her hands over his chest, loving the feel of his muscles. "It's very sensual."

"I could have one built for you."

Her smile faded. *I won't be here that long,* she wanted to say. But there was no reason to bring up the inevitable, not when Sloan was in such a good mood. "That's okay. I can think of other things we can do together."

"Let's go to the creek," he suggested.

"It's broad daylight? Anyone could see us there."

"Then we'll wait until later."

"I have a better idea."

She took him by the hand and led him to the house. Once inside the kitchen, she filled a large pan with water and put it over the burner. "We can take a bath together."

"Together?"

"Yes."

Within fifteen minutes, Sloan had filled the enameled tub in the bathroom off the kitchen.

"Go in and take off your clothes," she ordered, "and I'll be there in a minute."

"You've gotten to be a very bossy woman," Sloan grumbled, but he was smiling.

"Just go. The water's getting cold."

Sloan stepped into the bathroom and closed the door. He'd never thought of taking a bath with a woman, but now that Rebecca had suggested it, he thought it was a wonderful idea. Just the thought of holding her warm, slick body against him made him hard.

He eased into the water. The cuts on his back made him wince, but then the pain eased. In fact, the water felt good against his sore spots. He lay his head against the back of the tub and closed his eyes. Warmth swirled around him, and he felt himself growing sleepy. He probably should have opened the small window high on the wall.

His eyes opened with a snap. Rebecca closed

the door and leaned against it. "You aren't falling asleep on me, are you?"

"Never," he said. Just the sound of her voice made him want to pull her into the tub on top of him. Rebecca liked to be on top when they made love.

He watched as she unbuttoned her blouse. The edges parted to reveal her single undergarment. He shifted in the tub and placed a washcloth over his lap. "What do you call that . . . ?" He pointed to the lacy fabric covering her breasts.

"A bra."

She smiled and reached around back to unbutton her skirt. Her breasts thrust forward, straining against the thin fabric of her bra. In moments the skirt dropped to the floor.

She wore nothing but the undergarment that matched the fabric of her bra. It was also tight and lacy, and he could see the triangle of dark golden hair beneath it. He'd never taken the time to watch her undress before, never noticed the sensual appeal of what she wore beneath her clothes.

He should have paid more attention; Rebecca was definitely worth watching.

She let the blouse slip down her arms.

"Come here," he said.

She walked to the edge of the tub. Sloan reached out and hooked a finger in the top of her undergarment. "And what is this called?"

"Panties," she replied, looking down at him with languorous green eyes.

He reached higher and ran the back of his fin-

357

ger across one tight nipple. "How do you take this off?"

She reached to the front, but he pushed her hands away. "Tell me."

"Grasp it here and twist," she said breathlessly.

The tiny fastener felt awkward in his big, callused hands, but he finally got it open. Her breasts pushed free, filling his hands.

She moaned with pleasure.

He hooked his fingers on either side of the panties and pulled them down, watching her face instead of the skin he revealed. She blushed—or was that a flush of sexual pleasure? Dragging his gaze away from her face, he skimmed her body. She was beautiful, with firm, full breasts, a small waist, and that intriguing triangle of golden curls against her pale skin.

She kicked out of the panties and stood still as he stroked her hips. "Come here," he said softly.

She stepped into the tub, holding his hands for support. "Don't make me wait for you."

She settled her knees on either side of his hips and sank immediately on his arousal. He couldn't stop the moan of pleasure, or the way he arched into her, holding her close with his hands on her bottom.

"I wanted to make it last."

"I wanted you now." She rotated her hips, drawing him deeper. She held on to the tub, on either side of his shoulders, and closed her eyes. With breathless moans, she increased the pace.

He lost the ability to speak, or even to think,

as she clenched around him. With a cry, he erupted within her.

The world went blank as he floated in the bliss of pleasure. Distantly, he felt the water lap around him, the blessed weight of Rebecca on his chest, the humid warmth of the air. But he couldn't move, or speak, for several long moments.

"That was . . . you were wonderful."

"Umm."

"You made me crazy for a few minutes. Did you . . . ?"

"Umm hmm." She stirred slightly, shifting on his chest.

Sloan smiled. He'd never felt more content. He could stay like this forever, with just the sound of their breathing in the silence of the small room.

"You're going to get all wrinkled," she finally said.

"I don't mind."

Rebecca stirred, then twisted around. He opened his legs and she settled her back against him. After a few moments she said, "There's something important we haven't talked about."

He didn't want to talk about anything except building a future together. But first they had to defy the destiny Painted Elk had predicted. He remained silent.

"Sloan?" She twisted around to look at him.

"What?"

"We need to talk about Leda . . . and Robert."

He shifted in the water, sitting up a little more.

"There's nothing to talk about. She's in the past, and I can't do anything about my son."

"Don't you pull away from me, Sloan Travers. I won't have it." She grasped his forearms, folded his arms across her chest, and settled back against him once again. "And we do have to talk about Leda. She's the reason you were so angry, and it was your hatred of her that made your anger come into the future and try to kill me."

"I didn't try to kill you."

"Not personally, but you hated her so much that you sought revenge on her descendants—namely, me."

"I didn't know that you'd be harmed. I only wanted them to suffer."

"I understand. But I think that you have to resolve your feelings for her. If you don't, when . . . if I go back to my own time, I'll be dead."

"We're going to find a way to keep you here. I won't let you go."

"And what if we can't find a way? What if the bitterroot dies and I go back, only to find that Jordan has indeed strangled me to death? Are you willing to take that kind of chance with my life?"

"Are you so willing to leave me?"

She turned in his arms, looking him in the eye. "If I have a choice, I'll never leave you. But I can't be sure. I can't even find Painted Elk to ask him about it."

Sloan held her tight, afraid to let her go. His life had been an empty shell before Rebecca. He'd thought he was condemned to loneliness until the last few days. He didn't want to ruin what they shared, but neither did he want to endanger Rebecca's life on the chance she couldn't stay with him.

"Painted Elk will be back. He's probably in the mountains."

"I may not have much time. Have you seen the bitterroot blooms?"

"Yes." He'd gone out early that morning to check the plants, and when he'd seen the withered blossoms a little part of him had died. He didn't want to believe that her stay was tied to the bitterroot, but he wasn't willing to wager her life on his doubts.

"Sloan, I'm afraid," she said faintly.

He held her tight, then pushed his way up from the cool water, bringing her with him. Stepping out of the tub, he reached for a towel and wrapped it around her, rubbing her arms and back. She leaned toward him, and he felt her vulnerability and fear.

"It will be all right," he said softly.

After fastening a towel around his waist he wrapped her up and carried her upstairs.

She clung to Sloan's neck as he set her on his mattress. He was still refusing to talk about Leda, and time was running out. As he pulled away to stand beside the bed, Rebecca felt a sense of panic that not even their shared passion could override. She didn't want to leave Sloan, but she was afraid to go back to her own time; afraid to face death, or life without him.

Perhaps she was the one who needed a therapist.

"Rebecca, you're right. We should talk about Leda."

Her head snapped up. She gazed into Sloan's blue eyes, unsure what had caused his change of heart.

"Why?"

He looked confused. "Because you've been asking me for weeks."

"No. I mean, what made you change your mind?"

He framed her face with his large, callused hands. "I finally realized that I care more for you than I hate her."

She reached out and held him around the waist. "Thank you."

Sloan sat beside her on the bed. "I told you that Leda and I had been childhood friends. When I went to the university we had an understanding that we'd become engaged after I obtained a degree. I had just asked her father for her hand when the war became a demand I couldn't ignore.

"In the north we assumed that we'd defeat the rebels within weeks. We had the industry, the railroads, and the money to launch aggressive campaigns. But months passed, and then a year, and we were still fighting. I thought I could make a difference."

"What did Leda think of your call to duty?"

"She didn't want me to go. She couldn't see the need of it."

"I can understand her view. I wouldn't have wanted you to go either."

Sloan nodded. "But she accepted my decision. I thought I'd be home in months, as if I would make that much of a difference," he said harshly, as though he mocked himself. He ran his hand over the white sheet.

"You did what you thought was best."

"I should have listened to Leda, to my parents. I made no difference in that damned war."

"You don't know that. And you did make a difference . . . to the memory of that little girl. You honored her, Sloan, by reading her words and remembering."

He looked up from creasing the sheet between his fingers. "I hadn't thought of that. I suppose all I focused on was how the war had changed me."

"There's nothing wrong with thinking of yourself, especially after seeing such devastation. But now it's time to see the good, no matter how small."

"You're right."

"Tell me what happened when you came home from the war."

"Leda went ahead with the engagement. She thought everything would be as it was before, but . . ."

"But you didn't feel the same," she finished for him.

"I'd wake up screaming. I couldn't stand to be around people. My parents became alarmed. I

363

couldn't stop thinking about what we'd done to the south."

"You didn't talk to Leda about it, did you?"

"No. What could I say that she'd understand? Finally I decided to leave Philadelphia. I broke the engagement, told her to find someone else. I headed west on the train, all the way to Laramie. Then I outfitted myself and kept on, until I got to South Pass."

"The mines."

"Yes. And you know the story from there."

"Did you write to Leda?"

"Not for a long time. After a few years I thought maybe I was better. I decided to look into the land my grandfather had seen, and when I found out that it was available I thought maybe I could build a new life there."

"So then you wrote to her?"

"Yes. I asked her if she would still consider becoming my wife. I built this house. My mother helped me with the furnishings. She expected me to come home for the engagement and wedding, but I couldn't. Somehow, I felt free of the war out here."

"That makes sense. There was nothing here to remind you of your old life."

"Until Leda came."

"Did that trigger your nightmares?"

"Perhaps. I only know that when she arrived I started having the same kinds of problems I had had after the war. I tried to keep them from her, but I believe she knew something was wrong."

"What did she do?"

"She thought that if she could make life just as it had been before the war, I'd forget what had happened. She tried hard, I have to admit, but the more she talked about the past, the more I felt . . . I don't know how to explain."

"You probably had cold sweats, a sense of panic, maybe the urge to run away."

Sloan nodded. "That about sums it up. I guess you really do know this counseling business."

"I think so," she said. She knew Sloan found it difficult to talk about his past, and his problems, but she also realized that he was making a giant effort to communicate honestly with her. She not only loved him, she was proud of him as well.

"So, she lived here at the ranch. Didn't that cause raised eyebrows among your neighbors? I mean, they assumed I was a floozy for staying with you."

"Leda traveled west with a widowed aunt, so she was chaperoned."

"Not all the time," Rebecca added, then wished she could have bitten her tongue. She had no right to be flippant about Sloan's former fiancée, and the fact that they'd made love at least once.

"I didn't force myself on her, if that's what you're thinking."

"I wasn't. As a matter of fact, I would assume that she came to you. She loved you, and you were in pain. She must have thought that she could make everything all right by showing you that she loved you."

"I didn't want it to be that way. I felt as if she'd sacrificed herself."

"I understand; really I do. But Leda was doing the only thing she could to make you into the man she'd known all her life."

"I wasn't the man I was before, no matter what she thought."

"She didn't understand, Sloan. I do, because I've been trained to know the symptoms and causes of PTSS. There was no way Leda could have imagined what had happened to you, and how you felt."

"I suppose," he said reluctantly.

"I'm sure Leda blames herself for not being able to help you."

"That's ridiculous. She didn't cause any of my problems."

"Yes, we know that, rationally. But in her heart she probably feels that her love should have healed you." Rebecca shrugged. "That's the way many people think: parents, siblings, husbands, wives. They want to believe that love can conquer all."

"And you don't believe that?"

"No, I don't. I think love is very powerful, and that knowing you are loved is crucial to good mental health. But I know that sometimes we experience events, or have problems, for which we need professional help—someone who isn't personally involved. That's one reason that falling in love with you was so difficult for me. I knew you needed the detached evaluation and treatment that a counselor could provide, but I was also a woman in love, a woman who wanted her man to be healed."

"I didn't know . . . I never realized. . . ."

"I just want you to understand that I love you and I want to help you. Maybe sometimes I won't be perfectly objective."

"Rebecca, I don't understand what you're worried about. You've already gotten me to talk more than any other person I've ever known."

"I know, but your happiness—and maybe my life—are at stake."

"What can I do to prove I'm not the same man I was when you first came?"

She took a deep breath. "Meet with Leda . . . and your son."

He closed his eyes, and at first it seemed as though he was going to shake his head and say no. Then his tightly compressed lips eased, and the wrinkles between his eyebrows relaxed.

"I'll have someone contact her tomorrow. But I can't say that she'll agree."

"I think she will, if she can. Her husband seems to keep a tight rein on her."

"He's a bastard."

"Well, I'm not sure she can get away from him."

"In two days there's going to be a meeting in town with the editor of the *Wyoming Tribune*. He's visiting the area. Radburn will be busy posturing for a grant to promote immigration."

"So you think Leda will be able to get away?"

"We'll see."

Rebecca leaned over, resting her head against Sloan's chest. *Two days*. They'd have that long, surely. The bitterroot had one bloom left.

"Rebecca?"

"Yes?" She felt the tickle of his breath on her hair.

"Tell me what you know about Robert, about who he marries, and his children. Tell me about my son."

Tears filled her eyes, but she blinked them away. With a smile, she tried to remember everything she'd learned at the family reunion, everything that was contained on that single sheet of paper that told the false history of the Radburn clan.

Chapter Twenty

The day and night passed much too quickly for Rebecca, who alternated between the heights of bliss and the depths of despair. She gained a new understanding of and sympathy for her manic-depressive patients, she thought as she fluffed the pillows behind her and leaned back against the headboard of Sloan's bed.

When she and Sloan were together they shared a passion she had never imagined before. He had only to look at her and she wanted him fiercely. And not just sexually. She wanted *him*, forever and always—not just for a few hours or a day.

"It's arranged," Sloan said, walking into the bedroom and interrupting her melancholy thoughts. He sat on the bed and she took his hand.

"What time?"

"I suggested midafternoon. That will give me time to stage a bit of a diversion."

"Why? What do you have planned?"

"I'm going to move part of my herd to higher pasture, up in the hills where we rode that day."

"Is that normal?"

"Yes. We take advantage of the high pasture in summer, and the plains and valleys in winter. After Leda passes by on the road I'll send the herd over to hide her passage."

She felt a bit of unease. Suddenly she remembered the beating Sloan had received, and this meeting took on sinister connotations. "I thought Vincent would be busy in town. Do you think that's necessary?"

"You can't be too careful when dealing with him," Sloan replied, rubbing the backs of her knuckles with his fingers. "I don't want Leda or the boy hurt because of this."

"I don't either," Rebecca said, grasping his hand, "nor do I want you hurt again."

"I'll be ready for him this time. I won't be surprised again. It's Leda and the boy who have to live with him. If he knews they went behind his back, there's no telling what he'd do."

"I doubt he'll ever know. I'm sure Leda will never tell him."

"I'm going to do my best to keep you safe too," Sloan said. "Painted Elk returned last night. I've already talked to him this morning. He's promised to have a sweat lodge ceremony, just like he did before you arrived."

"So you think he brought me into the past?"

Certainly something had triggered this journey, but she'd assumed it was Sloan's anger. She believed Painted Elk knew much beyond the realm of reality, but to think he was involved in getting her into the past was a different matter.

"I'm not sure what I think. All I know is that I told him I wanted revenge, not on Leda or Robert, but on Vincent Radburn's descendants. I was angry. Later I changed my will to leave everything to Robert, with a public announcement that he was my son and heir. By the time he inherited this ranch, I'd planned for it to be the most successful one around, maybe in the whole territory. That's the kind of revenge I put into action."

"You wanted everyone to know Vincent had lied about Robert?"

"Yes!"

"Sloan, didn't you see how much that could hurt Robert? You publicly brand him a bastard, say his parents are liars, and leave him a ranch he may or may not know how to manage. If he's never really known you, he won't appreciate what you've done. This is a no-win situation for everyone."

Sloan pushed himself off the bed and walked to the window. As he stared out across the landscape, Rebecca watched him flex his shoulders and roll his neck.

"I'm sorry, Sloan, but that's the way I see it. Maybe I shouldn't have said—"

"No, you're right." He turned away from the window. She could barely see his features in the morning light. "I was thinking of myself. I was so angry. . . ."

"That's normal. You had a lot of pain inside."

"I don't feel that way any longer." He slid beside her on the bed, wrapping his arms around her and pulling her to his chest. "You've driven away my demons and given me a reason to live. You've given me joy and hope, something I never expected to find again."

"I'm glad," she whispered. "I love you, Sloan."

He rested his head against her hair. She felt his breath on her scalp and waited for him to say the words she wanted so much to hear.

"I want to be with you always," he finally said. "We'll find a way—or Painted Elk will. I'm not letting you go. After this afternoon my past will be just that—the past."

Rebecca hugged him back, resting her cheek against the smooth, clean cotton of his shirt. "Perhaps Robert can be a part of your life too. Maybe Leda will allow that much."

"I don't expect miracles. Radburn would never permit her or 'his son' to see me. But maybe she can tell the boy, when he's older, about me. And maybe, after today, she won't be afraid or embarrassed to admit that she cared for me once."

"I don't think she ever felt that. She was just frightened."

"For a reason. I never knew what I might do."

"I have faith in you."

"I know you do."

"Sloan, if I do have to go back—"

"No! Don't talk about it."

"I must. If Painted Elk can't change my destiny, I want you to know that I'll live. I won't be strangled because of your anger and thirst for revenge. I'll live, and every day I'll still love you and think of you."

"Rebecca, don't—"

"I have to say this. If I go back to my time, I'll pray that I take a part of you back with me. I'll pray that I have your child."

"Rebecca." He whispered the word with pain, with hunger, as he held her tight.

She clung to his strength. Although he'd never said the words she longed to hear, she knew he loved her. Someday he would tell her. He'd been through so much; she couldn't blame him for not baring his soul. But he would. Someday, if they were lucky enough to stay together.

"What do you want to do until it's time to go?" he asked, rubbing circles on her back.

"I want to make love with the man I love. Then I want to walk around the house, the buildings, the barn. I want to see everything one last time, just in case."

"Painted Elk will find a way."

"I hope so. Lord, I hope so," she said, tilting her face up for his kiss. The sheet fell away as he pushed her into the mattress.

After they'd gotten dressed and Rebecca had grabbed a quick breakfast of strong coffee and cold biscuits, she walked outside. Sloan had offered to come with her, but she wanted to be alone for a few moments. Despite his optimism, she felt destiny nipping at her heels.

She walked through Claudia's garden, relishing the smells of herbs and growing vegetables. Bees buzzed around the blooms of pole beans, staked up and reaching toward the sun. The lacy tops of carrots drooped like tiny willow trees in the hot sun.

Rebecca paused near the garden, looking around her. The smokehouse, with its gray weathered boards and tightly fitted door, stood about fifteen feet away. To the side of it, Claudia's small house perched, calico curtains fluttering in the breeze. Between the smokehouse and the cottage, back another ten yards, sat the outhouse. Rebecca smiled as she remembered how appalled she'd been that Sloan didn't have indoor plumbing. Of course, that was when she thought he lived in 1996. Now, she'd gotten used to the little house, although she still searched for lurking bugs and couldn't imagine what she'd do in the wintertime.

If she was still here this winter, she reminded herself.

She walked toward the barn. To one side the corral provided room for the horses used daily by the hands. Sloan had explained that each man needed several mounts. She didn't know the horses, or the men, for that matter. They kept to themselves in their own bunkhouse, and Rebecca guessed that Sloan had told them to leave her alone.

If she couldn't stay, she wanted to remember everything. The smells of horse manure, sweat, and hay; the sweet smoke of meat curing; the sound of Claudia singing off key when she thought no one else could hear. All this and more, from a special time that she'd never expected to know. The land might look familiar, the wind might feel the same, and the mountains still jutted toward heaven. But this time, this ranch, was a piece of history that could never be duplicated.

When she couldn't delay any longer she walked to the side of the house where she'd planted the flowers. With halting steps she neared the rock garden.

She felt a burst of panic. At first she couldn't find the bitterroot bloom. But no, it was there, nestled between the red rocks, the edges of the petals brown and the pink color fading. She placed her hand over her mouth to stifle a cry.

The last bitterroot was almost dead. Her time of reckoning had come.

A steady breeze blew down from the mountains, but the day was hot and dry. Sloan turned around and looked at Rebecca, who rode her mare slightly behind Buck. Puffs of dust rose with the horses' hooves but settled down quickly among the tufts of grass. She hung back, as though she was reluctant to follow.

She'd wanted him to do this, yet now that the time was here she seemed hesitant. Did she doubt his true feelings?

"Rebecca, come ride beside me."

She nudged Squirt forward. "What is it?"

"I wondered if something was bothering you."

She looked around. "Where are we headed?"

"Not far. About the only landmark around here is the stand of cottonwood trees near Sweetwater Creek."

Rebecca pulled the mare to a halt. "Not there."

"Yes. Why?"

"Didn't I tell you?"

"Tell me what?" Her face had paled; she looked stricken. He pulled Buck around to face the mare. "Rebecca, what's wrong?"

"The stand of cottonwoods. That's where I was picnicking with Jordan. That's where I was strangled."

"I didn't know."

She looked down at her hands, folded across the saddle. "I suppose it doesn't matter. I was just surprised."

"If it bothers you that much, I can go to Leda alone and change the location."

"No. You've got this all planned. I'm sure it's just a coincidence."

"Rebecca—"

"Don't worry. I'm fine."

She put her heels to her mare and trotted forward. Sloan shook his head, not sure what to do, even though she'd dismissed her own worries. Perhaps he should find Leda, talk to her somewhere else.

He clicked to Buck and they took off after Rebecca. When he pulled abreast with her, she turned to him and smiled.

"It's okay. I was just being superstitious."

"If you're sure . . ."

"I am. I just wish Painted Elk were here to tell me that he'd reversed the 'spell' or whatever it was that brought me here."

The medicine man was still deep into his chants and ceremonial acts in the sweat lodge he'd built behind the teepee. "I'm here, and I'm telling you I won't let you go."

Rebecca smiled, but her eyes were troubled.

"All I'm going to do is talk to Leda and see my son. Then we'll go back to the ranch. Everything will be fine. You'll see."

"I know. I'm just a little nervous."

He was too. The bitterroot bloom had faded to brown around the edges. Today it would close up and never open to another dawn. By tonight the bitterroot blooms would be dead.

They rode in silence to the stand of cottonwoods, near a bend in the creek that formed a small overflow pool when the water ran high. Sloan had always liked the area; he would have built his house here if the land around it had been more protected. But in winter, storms swept across these rolling hills, with nothing to break their eastward march. In spring the stream could flood. He certainly appreciated the beauty of this higher stretch of land; however, the location he'd chosen for his house and outbuildings was much more practical.

He pulled Buck to a halt in the shade of the swaying branches, dismounted, and tied him to a low limb. Rebecca rode up, her expression sober, as though she was trying not to show any emotion. He knew, though, that inside she must be feeling a great deal of trepidation about coming to a spot where she'd suffered the trauma of strangulation. He could vividly recall the deep bruises on her neck and the fear in her eyes when she'd first arrived.

"How are you feeling?" he asked, placing his hands around her waist and helping her off the mare.

"I'm okay. It's just kind of strange to be here . . . especially today."

"What I have to say to Leda won't take too long. We'll be back to the ranch this afternoon; then we can see Painted Elk and everything will be fine."

She smiled at him, but again he saw mixed emotions in her eyes. She led her mare to another branch and tied the reins. "Do you think she'll be here soon?"

"I hope so." He scanned the hillside, not seeing a buggy or a rider approaching. "Let's just relax. I believe she'll come."

He sat with his back against one of the largest trees and motioned for Rebecca to lean against him, resting between his legs. She settled in, but he felt the tension in her body.

"Relax," he said softly, kneading his fingers into the tight muscles. He moved the neckline of the blouse off her shoulders somewhat so he could gain better access to her tension.

She leaned her head back against his chest. "Umm, that feels good."

He felt her relax. The day was warm, their

sleep had been brief, and soon he felt himself slipping into the arms of sleep. He folded Rebecca into his embrace and closed his eyes.

He hadn't really slept; a noise jerked him awake. He blinked, then focused down the hill. A buggy approached, and he could see Leda handling the reins of the single horse as it struggled up the incline.

"She's here," he whispered to Rebecca.

"I know."

Rebecca used his bent knees to push herself up. She dusted the grass and dirt off her skirt—the denim one she always used for riding.

Sloan rose also, swatting the leaves and grass from his bottom. Leda drew the horse to a halt some yards away but made no effort to climb down from the seat.

He walked over, hoping her mind would be more open than his had been. As he watched her closed expression, he realized what Rebecca had been dealing with in him: the desire to cling to old beliefs, to be defensive to any challenge.

He stopped a few feet away from the buggy. "Hello, Leda."

"Sloan," she said, nodding her head.

His eyes shifted to the little boy sitting beside her on the seat. Dressed in white short pants and a tailored jacket, Robert regarded the world around him with a frown on his chubby face.

"He does look like me," Sloan said finally, feeling a sense of awe as he gazed at his son. His son; the boy he'd never be allowed to claim.

Robert's eyes were a clear blue, his eyebrows

slashing across his wrinkled forehead before turning down at the corners. His little chin had a tiny indentation. Sloan assumed that when Robert grew older, his face would reveal a stubborn streak that he could trace back to his real father.

Sloan smiled. The boy studied him, then smiled back. Two dimples appeared in his cheeks. Sloan felt a surge of love so powerful, he could have dropped to his knees, or shouted with joy. He had the urge to lift Robert from the seat, hold him close, and tell him that he loved him.

But he couldn't do that. Leda wouldn't allow it, and the boy wouldn't remember. "Thank you for coming," he said to her. "I know this wasn't easy."

"This seemed the best way . . . since you were so insistent that we had something to discuss."

Leda looked at Rebecca. "Good afternoon, Miss Hartford."

"Hello. I'm so glad you came. But please, call me Rebecca."

Sloan glanced at Rebecca. She looked at Leda with gratitude and what might be a bit of awe. Of course, she was looking at her own great-great-grandmother as a young woman. That alone was cause for wonder.

"Don't you feel that we have some unfinished business between us?" Sloan asked.

"What happened can't be changed. I don't think that throwing my indiscretion in my face will serve any purpose."

"That's what you think this meeting is about?"

Sloan asked incredulously. All this time she'd blamed herself?

"You're obviously angry with me. I've known that since the day I left your house."

"Yes, I was angry. And hurt. I never blamed you for . . . for the events that led to Robert's conception. I blamed you for leaving me and marrying another man, and for taking my son away from me."

"I thought it was for the best. I didn't have many choices," she said softly, looking at the boy. She placed an arm around him and hugged him to her side. "Robert needed a father."

"And you needed a husband. You didn't think I'd be suitable for either." Sloan tried to keep the pain out of his voice but knew he was only partially successful.

Leda's chin came up. "I did what I thought was best."

Sloan expelled a breath. "I probably wasn't a suitable father or husband back then. I didn't know it at the time, but Rebecca has made me understand."

Leda looked stunned that he'd made the confession.

Rebecca stepped forward. "Why don't you get down and sit in the shade? It's much more comfortable under the trees."

Leda seemed torn, but then she picked up Robert. She couldn't step down from the seat, even with assistance, holding an almost two year old. Sloan watched her dilemma before reaching out his arms in the direction of his son.

She handed Robert to him. Sloan hadn't held a small child in a long time, but this seemed so natural and right. Robert settled against him, looking up at Sloan's face, and said something unintelligible before reaching for his hair.

Sloan smiled and hugged his son tighter. His wishes had come true; he held his own flesh and blood, he had the love of a good woman, and he was putting the past behind him. Again, he felt the urge to shout for joy, but instead, he touched Robert's soft, brown, wavy hair and smooth baby skin. With a grin, he carried Robert into the shade.

Rebecca walked beside Leda toward the trees. Her heart overflowed with love as she watched Sloan carry his son. She'd been so afraid, but her fears seemed to have been unnecessary. And the end product—the meeting of father and son, and the reunion with Leda—all seemed worth whatever reservations Rebecca had felt.

They reached the shade of the cottonwoods. Robert wiggled to get down, and Leda indicated that he could.

"I'll watch him. I know the two of you have a lot to talk about," Rebecca offered.

Leda looked as though she wasn't accustomed to giving her son into the care of virtual strangers, but she finally nodded. "Please don't go far."

Robert sat down on his bottom and ran his short fingers through the grass.

"Leda, there is something I didn't tell you before."

"What is it?"

Rebecca pulled the locket from her blouse. "Does this look familiar?"

"No, not at all."

Rebecca opened the clasp. "How about these photos?"

Leda leaned close to gaze at the likenesses of herself and her husband. Her face paled, her mouth forming a startled *o*. "Where did you get these?"

"They were given to me at a family reunion, many years from now."

"But those are the photographs that were taken in Lander by that traveling photographer. He was in town the day I saw the two of you at Grant's store. I haven't received the finished ones yet, but that's my dress, and Vincent's suit. How did you get these?"

Rebecca heard the panic in Leda's voice, but she could do little to alleviate her fears. "Do you remember before when I mentioned that we might be related? You denied it—"

"We aren't related! I've never seen you before."

"I know you haven't, but as incredible as this seems, we are related. I just wanted to let you know."

"But I have a small family. I've never met you, or heard your name."

"I know. Just trust me. I have something for you, but I don't want you to read it until later, when you're alone." Rebecca reached in the pocket of her skirt and handed a white envelope to Leda. "I've written this out from the original, which was also given to me at the family reunion."

"What is it?" She turned the envelope over in her hand.

"Please, just wait until later. I think you'll understand. Before, when we talked the first time, I wasn't sure why I was here. All I knew was that my visit was tied in some way to Sloan and to you. Now I understand. And I wanted you to understand too."

Rebecca reached out and gave Leda a quick hug. The other woman was startled, probably too surprised to say a word. Rebecca smiled, knowing she might be seeing Leda for the last time. Then she walked to Robert and hunkered down beside him, examining with him the fascinating green grass.

When she looked back over her shoulder Leda was placing the envelope in her own skirt and turning her attention to Sloan. Rebecca was glad. She'd done what she'd intended, letting Leda know their connection to each other. She couldn't go on with her life—either in 1996 or 1876—without making that effort.

Robert levered himself to his feet, his chubby legs pumping as he ran across the level grassy area beneath the trees. Not far away was a white butterfly, flitting among the tiny blossoms of some wild plant. Robert gurgled his delight and chased the insect.

Rebecca had to laugh at his antics. He was such a sweet, well-adjusted little boy. She was glad, because Vincent's bad temper could have seeped into Robert's young mind. Or Vincent could have hated Robert because he was Sloan's son, and had nothing but contempt for the child. That didn't seem to be happening. Apparently Leda was a good mother, providing a nurturing environment for her son.

Rebecca looked toward Sloan and Leda, who still stood talking some fifty feet away. She hadn't realized that she and Robert had ventured that far. But it was a beautiful day, breezy and sunny, and Sloan had much to explain to Leda.

In an instant Robert's attention was diverted from the butterfly to an antelope, bounding across the hill as if the hounds of hell were chasing it. He squealed and ran after the graceful animal, which was rapidly making its way up the foothills. There was no way they could get within a hundred yards of a wild antelope, but Robert didn't know that.

Rebecca felt the ground tremble and rumble as she walked quickly after Robert. She swooped him up into her arms, standing still and feeling the vibrations coming from the earth. What was going on? Earthquakes were rare, but they did occur. Thankfully, they weren't in a place where falling rocks could be a problem. Just to be safe, however, she started walking back toward Sloan and Leda.

The rumbling grew louder. This was no earthquake! Rebecca couldn't tell where the sound was coming from, but she began to run toward Sloan. She saw him leave the shade of the cottonwoods, trying to quiet the horses as he made his way toward her.

Leda ran toward her also, holding out her arms to Robert. He squealed and tried to get away from Rebecca's grasp. The combination of running and holding a squirming child was too much for her, and Rebecca fell to the ground, twisting so that she absorbed the impact.

The breath whooshed out of her for a moment. She felt Robert toddle away, heard his cry of alarm. And above that she heard Sloan call to her; from a distance she heard the shouts of other men.

Gaining her breath, twisting around, she looked over the hill to the north. A herd of cattle, running wildly, spread out.

"Stampede!" someone yelled; she didn't know who.

She pushed herself to her feet, running toward Robert, who was almost to his mother. Out of the corner of her eye she saw Sloan reach into the saddle holster and pull out his rifle.

Riders circled around to the sides of the cattle, guiding their direction—right toward Robert, Leda, and Rebecca. She screamed, then heard a rifle shot. Darting her attention back to Sloan, she saw that he stood nearby, firing into the air, screaming as he tried to turn the cattle.

The front wave broke, turning down the hill. Rebecca could see the whites of the animals' frightened eyes as they ran away from the gunshots, despite the efforts of the men to keep them coming straight toward her.

Suddenly another shot rang out, coming from the direction of the men. Her head jerked up and she scanned the riders.

Alone, holding his nervous horse in check, Vincent Radburn leveled his revolver at Sloan and fired.

Chapter Twenty-one

"No!" Rebecca screamed the word. For just an instant she felt frozen in place. Then she began to run just as Sloan jerked backward, a hand fanned out across his chest.

"No, oh God, no." She ran to where he'd fallen, hearing the shouts of men in the background, the cries of Robert, the sobs of Leda. Then Rebecca reached Sloan, dropping to her knees in the tall grass where he lay.

"Sloan?" She gently cradled his head, staring in horror at the crimson stain that kept spreading over the front of his shirt.

"The bastard finally got me," he whispered, almost in awe.

"No!" She tore off the hem of her skirt and used the calico fabric to staunch the flow of blood. "I won't let him win. I won't let you—"

She broke off, unable to say the word. Not now, God. Not when he'd just gotten his life together.

"Is the boy safe?" Sloan asked weakly.

Rebecca glanced over her shoulder. "Leda has him. And Slim and the rest of your men have surrounded Radburn."

"That's not going to do me much good," he said with the kind of resignation she'd never heard from Sloan before.

"We'll get a doctor. I'll keep applying pressure. You'll be fine."

He reached up and grasped her wrist. "I'm not going to make it, Rebecca."

"Yes you will! I won't let you go. Sloan, I love you so much."

"I know." He coughed, grimacing at the movement. "Just let me say this before . . ." He paused, closing his eyes for a moment. "I never expected to find someone like you. A miracle sent you to me. We didn't have a lifetime together, but Rebecca, it was more than I ever dreamed, more than I probably deserved."

She wiped the tears from her eyes. "Sloan, don't leave me. We have to fight this."

"I can't win this battle." He tried to smile, but he was obviously in pain. Her heart broke as she watched him.

"Go back to your own time, Rebecca," he whispered. "If God is willing, I'll find you again someday. If there's a way, my soul will follow yours for all eternity."

She leaned down and kissed his lips, his cheek.

Tears splashed on his face and she wiped them away, gazing deeply into his eyes. He tried to say something, but the words wouldn't form. With her own vision blurred she watched the light go out of his eyes, felt the breath leave his body, and knew that he was gone.

She held him close, crying openly, wanting to force life back into his broken body. But only silence greeted her. He was gone.

She felt a hand on her shoulder and turned, startled. Painted Elk stood behind her.

"Can't you do something? Please, I can't lose him. I love him so much."

Painted Elk remained silent.

Leda walked up to her, her eyes filled with tears. "I'm so sorry," she said, hugging Robert close.

"Why?" Rebecca cried out. "Why now, when he had everything to live for?"

There was no answer. Rebecca looked around at the faces of Leda and Painted Elk, but all she saw was sorrow. Rebecca turned back to Sloan, closing his eyes, knowing that, at last, he no longer suffered. She stared at his face, needing to memorize his features, just as she would remember his smiles, his passion, and his goodness for all the days of her life.

"It is time," was all the medicine man said. He reached into a leather pouch at his waist and pulled out a handful of some powdery substance. Rebecca watched as he raised his hand, letting the substance blow in the breeze, scattering across the land.

"The bitterroot," he said, "food of my people. Nourish the souls of Rebecca and Sloan."

Her vision blurred even more; she could no longer see Sloan's face. She tried to call out, but no sound came. A sensation like spinning inundated her body, and she felt herself stand. She could see the scene as though she were rising above the ground.

Sloan lay still as death, Painted Elk and Leda standing above him, but Rebecca could no longer see herself in the picture. Then the white light came, bleaching everything until there were no images, no sensations, no feeling except her breaking heart.

Rebecca awoke slowly, lying on her back in some outdoor setting. Overhead she saw blue sky and bare limbs swaying in a cool breeze. Something was wrong, but she couldn't remember just what. She took a quick physical inventory; no bones were broken, and she didn't seem to be injured. However she felt as though her heart had been ripped out and trampled.

Trampled. That was it! The stampede, the danger to herself and to Robert. Sloan firing his rifle, then Vincent Radburn firing at Sloan.

The blood. Oh, God, there had been so much blood on his chest, soaking his shirt. She'd tried to stop the flow but couldn't. The ruffle she'd torn off her skirt had been red with it. And his eyes—his beautiful blue eyes—had lost all life and fire as she watched, and he'd died in her arms.

She blinked back more tears. How could she

go on without him? Only the thought that she might be carrying his child made her want to live. Otherwise, she wanted to just roll over and die, perhaps to see Sloan again in some benevolent afterlife.

But she was alive; the tree limbs were bare, with only the buds of leaves to come, and she knew she was back in April of 1996. And she was alive. She raised a hand to her neck and rubbed, feeling no swelling or pain from the bruises.

Which meant that she hadn't been strangled. Jordan hadn't killed her after their picnic. Raising her head, she looked down at her clothes, seeing only the denim skirt and white peasant blouse. She looked at both hands, but there was no blood, nothing to show she'd held the man she loved in her arms as he lay dying. She glanced to the left, seeing the quilt pattern of the blanket they'd used for their picnic. The box of chicken and the trash from the meal sat at the edge of the blanket. Her heartbeat accelerating, she glanced to her right.

At first she thought she was hallucinating. Was Sloan dead and lying with her on this quilt? She rolled to her side, raising herself on an elbow to stare at the man beside her, his head turned slightly away in a half profile. His shirt wasn't covered with blood and his chest rose and fell in sleep. Sun-bleached brown hair fell over his forehead.

"Sloan?" she whispered.

He smiled in his sleep and turned toward her, coming awake slowly. She held her breath, afraid o hope, afraid of what he might say or do. He looked like Sloan, but then, he didn't. Was her mind playing tricks on her?

Then he opened his eyes and focused on her face. His smile widened, showing straight white teeth.

"Hello," he said softly.

"Sloan?"

"What? You've forgotten my name so soon?"

"I don't understand."

"We must have fallen asleep after that big lunch. Not the most romantic gesture on my part."

"I wasn't sleeping."

"No? I thought you were." He rolled toward her, lying on his side. "I had the most fascinating dream."

"About what?"

"You and me," he said, bringing her hand to his lips and kissing the backs of her knuckles.

"And what were we doing?" she asked, feeling suddenly breathless.

"I suppose I was more influenced by the family reunion than I thought, because we were back in the past, at the time when our ancestors first moved out here."

"On the ranch?"

"Yes. And it was summer—"

"And Painted Elk? Was he there?"

"I don't remember," he said, clearly confused. "I remember you and me, and it seemed as though you saved me . . . from myself, I think. And . . ."

"And what?"

"And I fell in love with you."

She didn't care at the moment whether he was Sloan or Jordan; she only knew that something magical had happened. With a sob, she threw herself at him, wrapping her arms tightly around his neck and holding on for dear life.

"Rebecca, you're going to strangle me," he said, laughing.

She laughed back, gazing into his blue eyes, seeing the truth that perhaps he didn't realize. "No one is getting strangled here today."

"I'm happy to hear that. I have a better idea."

He kissed her then, with lips that claimed and coaxed, and she returned his passion. This wasn't the man who had kissed her before on this same picnic blanket. This was the man she'd fallen in love with 120 years ago, the man who had defied time to be with her again. She melted against him, reveling in the escalating beat of his heart, drinking in his special fragrance.

If God is willing, I'll find you again someday. God had been willing, and Sloan was with her now, in spirit, in the body of his great-great-grandson. The past had been changed, and this man, this warrior from a modern age, was her destiny.

Finally they broke apart, breathing hard. "You can't know how I feel at this moment. You probably wouldn't believe me if I told you," she confessed. "But I know I was there with you, back in the past, and I know it wasn't just a dream."

"I'm not a believer in things I can't see or hear,

394

but I have the strangest feeling, as though we've been together always." He smoothed back a strand of hair from her face, looking deeply into her eyes. "You're the woman I've been waiting for all my life. And you'll probably think I'm crazy, but I've got to say this. I've fallen in love with you, Rebecca."

"I love you too. More than you'll ever know."

They kissed again, and when they broke apart Rebecca rested her head on Jordan's broad chest and looked around. The cottonwoods still swayed in the wind, the blue sky overhead stretched forever, but there was something very different about this special place.

Pushing herself up, she looked around in wonder. Blooming all across the hill were bitterroot plants, their pink blossoms reaching toward the sun, as numerous as the grains of powder that Painted Elk had sprinkled across the landscape.

Jordan sat beside her, confusion and amusement on his face. "What is it?"

Rebecca laughed, feeling her heart swell with hope and life. She turned back to Jordan, placing a hand on his lean, dear cheek. "Destiny," she whispered.

Author's Note

For purposes of this story, I described Lander as it was in the mid- to late 1880s. In the mid-1870s, the town was changing from Camp Brown, a military outpost for the protection of the Wind River Reservation, into Lander, a center for pioneer families who moved into Fremont County after the Shoshone cessation of 1872. Also, the cottonwood grove where Jordan and Rebecca picnic is fictitious. Other historical and geographical details are accurate, to the best of my knowledge. For more information on the area, visit or contact the Pioneer Museum in Lander, Wyoming.

MIRIAM RAFTERY

Taylor James's wrinkled Shar-Pei, Apollo, is always getting into trouble. But the young beauty never expects her mischievous puppy to lead her on the romantic adventure of a lifetime—from a dusty old Victorian attic to the strong arms of Nathaniel Stuart and his turn-of-the-century charm. One minute Taylor and Apollo are in modern-day San Francisco, and the next thing Taylor knows, a shift in the earth's crust, a wrinkle in time, and the lovely historian finds herself facing the terror of California's most infamous earthquake—and a love so monumental it threatens to shake the foundations of her world.

_52084-2 $4.99 US/$6.99 CAN

Dorchester Publishing Co., Inc.
65 Commerce Road
Stamford, CT 06902

Please add $1.75 for shipping and handling for the first book and $.50 for each book thereafter. NY, NYC, PA and CT residents, please add appropriate sales tax. No cash, stamps, or C.O.D.s. All orders shipped within 6 weeks via postal service book rate. Canadian orders require $2.00 extra postage and must be paid in U.S. dollars through a U.S. banking facility.

Name_____
Address_____
City _____ State _____ Zip_____
I have enclosed $_____in payment for the checked book(s).
Payment <u>must</u> accompany all orders.☐ Please send a free catalog.

PASSION'S TIMELESS HOUR

TIMESWEPT

VIVIAN KNIGHT-JENKINS

Bestselling Author Of *The Outlaw Heart*

Propelled by a freak accident from the killing fields of Vietnam to a Civil War battlefield, army nurse Rebecca Ann Warren discovers long-buried desires in the arms of Confederate leader Alexander Random. But when Alex begins to suspect she may be a Yankee spy, the only way Rebecca can prove her innocence is to convince him of the impossible...that she is from another time, another place.

_52079-6 $4.99 US/$6.99 CAN